Oh Gad!

A NOVEL

Dear Reader:

I am pleased to introduce award-winning author Joanne C. Hillhouse and her debut full-length novel, a literary project based in her native Antigua.

Oh Gad! is an expression heard in coal pot making and the fragility of the craft parallels the persona of the novel's protagonist, Nikki. She leaves her home and sister, Jazz, in New York, where she was raised by her father, Professor Baltimore, to return to her birthplace after her mother, Mama Vi, passes. In Antigua, she soon encounters a colorful cast of characters and faces the challenges of reconnecting with siblings; romance and employment.

Sit back, relax and indulge in this novel with authentic dialogue and dialect, and one that will offer a refreshing insight into island culture. The brilliant cover captures the intensity of the plot and beauty of the Caribbean, while *Oh Gad!* shows that there also can be flaws in "paradise."

As always, thanks for the support shown to the Strebor Books family. We appreciate the love. For more information on our titles, please visit www.zanestore.com and you can find me on my personal website: www.eroticanoir.com. You can also join my online social network at www.planetzane.org.

Blessings,

Zane

Zane
Publisher
Strebor Books
www.simonsays.com/streborbooks

ZANE PRESENTS

Oh Gad!

JOANNE C. HILLHOUSE

STREBOR BOOKS

NEW YORK LONDON TORONTO SYDNEY

SBI

Strebor Books
P.O. Box 6505
Largo, MD 20792
http://www.streborbooks.com

ISBN 978-1-59309-391-4
ISBN 978-1-4516-4524-8 (e-book)
LCCN 2011938322

First Strebor Books trade paperback edition April 2012

Cover design: www.mariondesigns.com
Cover photograph: © Keith Saunders/Marion Designs

10 9 8 7 6 5 4 3 2 1

Manufactured in the United States of America

For information regarding special discounts for bulk purchases, please contact Simon & Schuster Special Sales at 1-866-506-1949 or business@simonandschuster.com

The Simon & Schuster Speakers Bureau can bring authors to your live event. For more information or to book an event, contact the Simon & Schuster Speakers Bureau at 1-866-248-3049 or visit our website at www.simonspeakers.com.

*This book is dedicated to the memory of Tanty and Mama,
my grandmothers; and to Antigua,
where, as we say, my navel string is buried.*

ACKNOWLEDGEMENTS

Thanks to my God and my Family; among whom I single out my mom, who gave up her pepperpot recipe, and dad, rock solid support. The Hillhouse clan (especially Hyacinth) because their generations-old involvement in coal pot making surely inspired the book's main motif, the beautiful and breakable clay (coal) pots. My sister—who I'm sure I asked to print something at some point—my always there in a pinch big brother, and their families, especially my nieces and nephews who continue to steal pieces of my heart and raise up mi pressure.

My friends…

Alstyne, who was this book's cheerleader and midwife in more ways than one;

Carole, for giving me the space to work on this book (especially during a productive week in Montserrat);

Gisele, who didn't edit this one as she did my earlier books, but who did weigh in early on with a perspective that challenged me;

Althea, for taking the time to read the manuscript and for her helpful and detailed review (and here it would be remiss not to mention author Christine Lincoln for taking the time to give me feedback as well, on a portion of the manuscript earlier in the process);

Mali and Noval, without whom I would never have known of the real slave dungeon that inspired the fictional one in my book;

and all the others in a very tight circle whom I count as friends.

I have to give credit to…

The expanding list of writers who inspire me;

My summer at Breadloaf, and especially my workshop leader Ursula Hegi, for fresh insights on the writing process and the fresh burst of energy that pushed me to tackle the final draft of the manuscript in the months thereafter;

Joy Lawrence's *The Way We Talk and Other Antiguan Folkways*, a useful guide for some of the proverbs used;

The Museum of Antigua and Barbuda for the research I was able to do there into Antiguan place names, the history of the Sea View Farm pottery culture (via writings by Desmond Nicholson and Selvyn Walter, especially);

Eric Jerome Dickey, whom I met through the Antigua and Barbuda International Literary Festival, for helping me to make a key connection;

My agent, Sara Camilli, the connection, who never wavered in her commitment to find a home for my manuscript;

Strebor, and its parent company, Atria, and its parent company, Simon & Schuster, for taking a chance on this book;

Booksellers like my Wadadli Youth Pen Prize (http://www.wadadlipen.wordpress.com) patron and partner, the Best of Books, and others;

The teachers, students, and readers in general who've championed my earlier books (*The Boy from Willow Bend* and *Dancing Nude in the Moonlight*);

Every critique that helped this book to grow, even if it came with a rejection attached;

The *Oh Gad!* characters who hung around long enough for me to get it right;

and

To all, named and unnamed, who inspire and believe in me. Bless.

"Plantin' Sucker follow de Root."

—Antiguan Proverb

CHAPTER ONE

"Mama dead."

Nikki didn't know how long the phone had been ringing before she heard it. With it, other sounds filtered in. The rusty refrigerator hummed and dripped in the corner. The dusty desk fan whirred; blowing warm, stale air at her. Foxy Brown's "Big Bad Mama" trumpeted, tinny, through her computer's tiny speakers. The footsteps of one of the upstairs tenants provided the drum beat. The chorus was the cacophony of cars and chatter just outside the basement apartment of the ancient Harlem brownstone, one of the few not yet swept up in the gentrification wave.

This was work these days for Professor Winston Baltimore's youngest daughter: Girl Friday in the office of a less-than-profitable, non-profit organization, duties ranging from fundraising to tenant complaints. It would be reaching to call her basement abode an office; just her, the "classic" rotary phone, an ancient computer, a dented file cabinet, a square discoloration on the floor where a stove used to be, a fridge with suspect cooling abilities, and a faint but persistent smell. Some days, taking in the bleak scene, Nikki felt there just might be such a thing as taking rebellion too far. At some point she had to grow up, right? Figure out where she fit? What she wanted? Problem was she didn't have a clue. She didn't lie to herself about that. If you'd delude yourself, you'd delude anyone. She'd heard a beauty pageant contestant say that once, along with her desire for world peace and the alleviation of poverty. Nikki had scoffed, but at least those perfectly coiffed, lipsticked and sequinned girls had a compass and a clue. She felt as frozen as this building in which she was now sleepwalking through—the latest in a parade of so-so, bottom-barrel jobs.

Today, eyes locked on the computer screen, she felt frozen by indecision.

That was when the phone rang.

Nikki picked it up to the surprise of Audrey's voice, out of place in this place. As out of place as if Antigua, all 108 square miles of it, had been lifted wholesale from the Caribbean Sea and squeezed into Marcus Garvey Park. As usual—if there was a "usual" between them—Nikki tiptoed gingerly. "Audrey?" was all she could think to say. And the gruff voice offered up its blistering truth.

"Mama dead."

Nikki felt the burn of it, swallowed. It was a precursor to speaking, but the words turned to ashes and vapour before making it out. She'd never been able to talk to Audrey, didn't know what to say to her now. They were sisters, Nikki and Audrey, though Nikki tended to think of Audrey as Mama Vi's daughter, as if neither her mother nor sister had anything to do with her. In truth, they didn't. Mama Vi and her many offspring were as far from Nikki's life as New York from Antigua: if the 1,700-plus miles separating the two were multiplied by 1,700 times 1,700.

Nikki had visited Antigua only a handful of summers growing up, and these days, never called. The favour was almost as uniformly returned. But there was that "almost," and here was Audrey, sounding eerily like Mama Vi.

"Mama dead."

She gave the report bluntly, and Nikki felt the sounds retreat again, and the physical world with them. Even the e-ticket website she'd zoned on blurred. Then, there was Mama Vi, clear as day: coal-black face, long body, busy hands. Mama Vi, an unseasonal chill, then nothing. Nothing but the echo of Audrey's voice.

"Mama dead."

"When's the funeral?" Nikki asked to fill the silence, hearing how distant and machine-like she sounded, knowing Audrey must be hearing it, too. She stared at nothing, as she took in the details.

The booked and paid travel itinerary on her computer slipped in and out of focus. It was her boyfriend Terry's *mea culpa* for an affair he would never actually admit. But Terry and everything else retreated in the face of this one certainty.

"Mama dead."

She hung up from Audrey, and had dialed Jazz's number before even deciding to do so.

"Jazz," she greeted brightly. "You up for a trip to Antigua?"

Jazz—Jasmine, by birth—was also Nikki's sister. She was no relation of Mama Vi's; she came instead from Professor Baltimore's loins. She was his eldest and Nikki's one true friend.

"Antigua?" Jazz asked after a stunned pause. Stunned, Nikki knew, because much as she'd been born there, she'd evinced no great affection for this "home" she barely knew; certainly not in the eleven or so years she and Jazz had crossed over from half-sisterhood to friendship.

"Yeah, all the beaches, sunshine, soca, and rum punch you can stand," was Nikki's falsely sunny comeback.

Another pause from Jazz, then, "Not that it isn't tempting, but I'm not exactly budgeted for it."

Under Jazz's voice were the *click-clack-clack* of her keyboard and the hum of office activity.

"Tickets are paid for," Nikki replied. "Terry's I-didn't-sleep-with-my-firm's-newest-associate-but-here's-my-apology-gift-anyway."

"Uh-huh." Jazz's voice was slower now, and the clickety-clacking stopped. "Nikki, what's going on?"

"Audrey, my mother's eldest, just called," Nikki replied. "Mama Vi's dead."

It was as blunt as Audrey's announcement had been. "I'm changing the reservations to Antigua," Nikki continued breezily. "It should even work out to be less. So, come with?"

After a too long pause, Jazz asked, in the soothing tone she reserved for the frightened kids she worked with, "How're you doing?"

"God, Jazz, don't give me 'The Voice,'" Nikki replied, head thrown back, saggy chair precariously tipped. "I'm fine. I mean, we weren't close or anything. I've been in New York since I was three, remember? I wasn't even sure it made sense for me to go, you know. But there it was...e-ticket on the computer screen, Audrey on the phone. I decided to take it as a sign."

"You don't believe in signs," Jazz reminded her.

"Okay, fine. But why waste the tickets?"

"Nikki."

"What?!"

"Don't do that," Jazz chided, as only Jazz could.

"Do what?" Nikki shot back, false cheer beaten back by her irritation.

Jazz was not intimidated. "Don't bury your feelings, like you always do."

"I don't always do anything."

"Stamp your feet all you want," Jazz fired back. "It's me, remember?"

"Whatever. You comin' or what?" Nikki definitely wasn't up for a session on Jazz's "couch."

But as ever, Jazz was persistent. "Nikki, your relationship of four years is on the rocks..." Jazz began.

"Over," Nikki interjected.

"Fine. 'Over,'" Jazz conceded, and Nikki easily pictured the sarcastic air-quotes. "Your mom just died. Whatever time and distance there was, don't tell me you're not feeling anything. I know you too well."

That's the thing, Nikki acknowledged, as the fire went out of her irritation. Jazz did know her too well. Somehow, inexplicably, considering her birth had effectively ended the marriage of Professor Baltimore and Jazz's mom, Bernadine, Jazz was the one who knew her better than anyone. Not that there was a crowd of anyones.

Nikki sighed. "Okay, I won't. But I can't talk about it. Okay?"

"Yet," Jazz countered.

"Bitch," Nikki grumbled, without heat. "Fine. Yet."

"Okay," Jazz agreed, satisfied. "When do we leave?"

So it was that within a blink they were hovering over a sea so blue it seemed like something a heavy-handed preschooler might have crayoned, before carelessly adding rich, uneven spots of green. Nikki couldn't deny the Caribbean, spread out below her seemed like effortless perfection, like the paradise it claimed to be.

On landing at V.C. Bird International Airport, she immediately felt the Antigua heat rush up to greet her like an old, barely remembered, but overenthusiastic friend.

As ever, everything about her birthplace conspired to anchor her in the here and now: the pinkish-peach airport terminal, the crowd of arrivals already on a pre-Carnival high, the Burning Flames soca music blaring through the public address system, the elaborate gold-and-green, peacock-feathered Carnival costume at the entrance beneath the signs bidding visitors: *"Bienvenu, bienvenido, willkommen, welcome!"*

The long lines, brusque immigration officers, bustling red caps ramming their way with precariously piled carts through the chaos, and sour-faced customs officers ransacking carefully packed luggage were not as welcoming.

By the time she and Jazz had negotiated a taxi and were bumpily navigating the route to their beachside resort, Nikki was fighting back a single but insistent pain throbbing in her right temple. She closed her eyes against the barely remembered Technicolor scenery blurring by and against Jazz's eyes, which were by turns, darting about excitedly and skating with worry in her direction.

Her sister didn't speak the question in her eyes though. Soon enough they were in their hotel room—second floor, beachside, along Antigua's northwest coast, complete with fruit basket—mangoes, oranges, bananas. Nikki was grateful for the air-conditioning, the chilled and waiting bottled water, and the painkillers lifted from the medicine cabinet in the bathroom. She pulled back the hibiscus-patterned bedspread and crashed.

When she woke, the room was mostly dark, and, eyes adjusting, she looked up to see the thick drapes, also hibiscus-patterned, were drawn. She could hear the sea beyond though, and followed Jazz's trail to the balcony and fading sunlight.

"Not bad," greeted Jazz, sipping some kind of pink drink, another hibiscus sticking out of it. "Especially for what we paid."

The resort tickets had been kind to their credit cards. "Times rough, plus is the off-season," their chatty taxi driver had explained, without prompting. "Not much tourist." When Jazz had commented on the crowd at the airport, he'd replied, "Mostly people coming home for Carnival; they goin' be staying with family."

Nikki sat across from Jazz, also facing the beach and the infinite blue beyond that. Inevitably, Jazz angled her head to look at her properly. Nikki stared resolutely ahead.

"Feelin' better," Jazz quizzed gently.

"I'm okay," Nikki lied.

Coming back to Antigua always twisted her up, mostly because, like New York, it didn't feel like home. Nowhere did. But while in New York she could lose herself in that alien feeling; here everything was so uncomfortably close, everyone so *familiar*. The disorientation wasn't helped by the vague sense of knowing coiled inside her; Antigua was a place she didn't quite remember, but hadn't really forgotten.

Jazz seemed to take her at her word though, and went back to sipping and regarding the scene before them—hopeful vendors laden with gaudy scarves and T-shirts, a handful of baking tourists catching the last of the day's rays, a child playing 'catch-me-if-you-can' with the surf.

They sat like that until the colours signaling sunset exploded in the sky—red, orange, yellow, other unnameable hues; they sat until the sun was gone and only the faint afterglow remained. The tourists retreated, the vendors packed it up, and the child was pulled away screaming his protest. Nikki, fuzzy and detached like she'd taken one too many pills, which she probably had, was having difficulty feeling the world again.

"Thanks for coming," she said to Jazz, after a time.

"And where else would I be?" her sister responded.

Nikki shrugged. "Well, a funeral isn't anybody's idea of a party, you know."

Jazz eyed her in that probing way she had; she seemed to want to say something—probably something about not disassociating, about feeling your feelings. Going away—disassociating, or whatever fancy word Jazz wanted to put on it—was what Nikki knew best. It's what got her through Professor Baltimore's punishing daily tutorials in how to wash the island off of her. "Where's your brain?" he'd snapped more than once as she stood before his creaky leather chair. "You're not putting in the effort." That because she'd failed to satisfactorily complete a set project, or read one of his weighty assigned volumes, or "speak properly," as he shouldered the burden of "making something" out of her. She imagined herself as baker's dough, his words digging into her roughly, shaping her. When Jazz touched her, pulling her out of herself, she swore she could feel where it pressed against phantom bruises and she let the pain pull her back, back to this too-pretty-to-be-true place that she'd never really trusted. Give her the grey, littered, colourlessness of her dad's Bronx neighbourhood any day; it made a strange kind of sense that this place never had. "Don't worry about all that," Jazz was saying, and Nikki wondered if Jazz had done her psychic thing. But when she continued, it was to say "You don't have to entertain me. I'm family, remember?"

It was true. Jazz was family in a way Professor Baltimore never tried to be, to either of them. And she could hold on to that; it would do. As ever, she was mystified at how it came to be in the first place, but leave it to Jazz. The strong bond they'd forged was mostly her doing, from that first meeting following Professor Munroe's political science lecture. "You're Nikissa, right?" the stranger with the weird and familiar hazel-to-amber-hued eyes and a braid so long it brushed the top of her bottom, had said to her. The girl was her twin in almost every way, including the stray strands of hair tickling her face. While Jazz was a full year and change older, Nikki's fast track through high school had landed them in the same place at the same time. They did a lot of catching up during that first meeting; Jazz latched on as though she never planned to let go. They chatted about everything from majors—Nikki's was sociology, Jazz's psychology and social work—to living arrangements; Nikki was still taking the train in from the Bronx; Jazz had remarkably found a low-rent city squat. They even chatted about Professor Munroe. "Sexy, don't you think? He's from Jamaica, you know, your neck of the woods, right," Jazz said.

Mostly Jazz chatted and Nikki stared. Jazz was like an alternate reality version of herself; she was a reality where they grew them shorter and more effusive. She was fascinated, and clearly so was Jazz, maybe for all the reasons they should have hated each other. Jazz, after all, was the offspring of Professor Winston Baltimore's one legitimate union. She, Nikki, was the product of the unlikely—and adulterous—coming together of a West Indian-American intellectual snob and a rural Antiguan coal pot maker. Knowing the Professor, she didn't understand how that was even possible. But there it was. Nikki knew herself to be the cause of the rift that still existed between her father and Jazz's mother. Growing up with him, she'd never met Jazz. But somehow when those twin "pussy" eyes connected in a packed lecture hall, they'd known each other.

Both had Professor Baltimore's so-called good hair, his eyes, his long narrow features, and his full lips. The only things Nikki had from her mother, Mama Vi, were her considerable height and darker colouring. Jazz was shorter and ochre-coloured, kind of like the muddy used to make coal pots by Nikki's family in Sea View Farm, Antigua. Nikki's mother had been tall and long-limbed, like pictures she'd seen of the Maasai. It was a combination that made Nikki awkward and self-conscious as a child and early teen.

Though she hadn't known her mother very well, sitting with Jazz on their hotel balcony, once again on Antiguan soil, Nikki felt a familiar ache. The absence of her mother was the single constant in her life. Now that the navel string well and truly severed, Nikki's heart began to crack, slowly, like a poorly built coal pot left too long in the heat.

CHAPTER TWO

Nikki didn't go to the funeral home. Didn't know where it was, or what use she'd be. She didn't want to see her mother laid out and lifeless. She taxied instead to the family compound on the Sea View Farm main road.

She hadn't called. They were always there, working the muddy.

As a child, it had fascinated Nikki to watch her mother, seated under the huge date palm tree in the open yard, take the brown lumps of clay and build up, up and up like a child fashioning a sandcastle. In the end, those piles of mud would be a coal pot for cooking; jars for keeping water cool, trays, pots; vases. candleholders. These would be set in the cool inside the adjoining galvanized shed, and later baked on a kiln, a large lit trash bed packed with the shaped clay, then overlaid with grass. The flame raged, but somehow, never got out of control. By Saturday, the finished pots and such would be taken to market. That practise had already started to peter out by the end of Nikki's last Antiguan summer, even as the trade to hotels and tourists picked up. Most Antiguans over time grew to enjoy the convenience of a stove over a coal pot. Who wanted to coax heat from coals, fanning at a coal pot arch, when they could turn a knob and go about their business? It had been a dead industry fifteen years ago; even then, Mama Vi, was one of the village's few remaining commercial potters, still applying the craft the way it had been handed down—no potter's wheel, just hands and instinct. It had seemed to Nikki time had moved on and left her there.

Not much had changed, at least on the surface of things.

The dented, askew, metal sign announcing "Mama Vi, Coal Pot Maker" was still there, and the big date palm in the yard, the galvanized shed, the old violet wooden house with its always-chipping paint. Even without proper directions it wasn't hard to find, the only business that wasn't a dry goods store or house front outlet for cell phone top ups on the main road of the village known as Sea View Farm, where there wasn't much to be seen in the way of farming and no sea view to speak of.

"Audrey," Nikki called out, knocking on the door, then circling the yard. She found instead Christobelle, called Belle, in the little galvanized shack behind the palm tree, amidst clay wares in various stages of completion. Belle, Nikki's other sister, was alone in the shack, desolately working a mound of muddy, tears unashamedly streaming down her face. It was a pretty face, dark, moon-shaped with guileless eyes, framed by the same simple single plaits Mama Vi had worn. She started, then jumped up and grinned when Nikki and Jazz entered.

"Nikki, Nikki, Nikki," she chanted with the unrestrained glee of a child, though she was many decades from that. Nikki surrendered to her eager embrace.

"Hi, Belle," she said. "Where is everyone?"

Belle shrugged. "Sis gone town. She tell me stay here. Mama gone."

Belle was half of a twin. Like her womb-mate, Christopher, called Columbus, Belle was slow. Nearing fifty, Columbus and Belle had still been largely dependent on Mama Vi, a task, Nikki guessed, that would now fall to Audrey, or Sis, as Belle called her.

Belle and Columbus weren't useless. Belle was as good at fashioning pots as Audrey. Columbus' thing was gardening; he'd tended the vegetable patch at the edge of the family dwelling as long as Nikki could remember. In most ways though, they were like children, and maybe that's why Nikki had always felt comfortable with Belle in spite of the twenty-year age gap. She didn't do grown folks' stuff like pay bills, shop for food, or give orders. Though she had a son, Toney "Tones" Toussaint, it was Audrey he called "Mammy" and Audrey who had raised him. Belle was the sweet spirit with the ready smile and huge hugs. Nikki remembered the lumpiness of her and the baby powder smell. She also remembered that not even the bravest or most malicious dared call Belle or Columbus "retard" where Mama Vi could hear. "Just move you retarded self," she remembered Audrey saying once, and like a hurricane, Mama Vi lit into her, everyone else in the yard just hunkering down and waiting it out. Nikki had never thought of Audrey as Mama Vi's daughter in the way she was before that day; she might have been ten at the time, and Audrey about thirty. Yet Audrey sat in sullen silence, suffering the tongue-lashing of her life, never once giving Mama Vi an excuse to come after her with the fists clenched at her sides. Mama Vi was the alpha and Columbus and Belle were under her protection; that much had been clear.

As for what made them the way they were? Nobody knew or bothered to find out.

"Belle, honey, this is my sister, Jasmine," Nikki said now, attempting an introduction, even as Belle—muddy hands and all—patted her face affectionately.

"Sister?" Belle questioned, puzzled, hand stilling. "Me ah you sister." She'd laid claim to Nikki years ago, and the long gaps between visits, this last thirteen-year gap, seemed to make no difference.

"Yes," Nikki agreed. "But Jazz is my sister, too. She's my sister on my father's side, just like you're my sister on Mama Vi's side. Jazz lives in New York, too, with me."

"New Yark?"

"Yes, New York, where I live."

Belle seemed to accept that, favouring Jazz with one of her famous hugs before returning to the muddy, bottom resting on a crocus bag on the ground. Nikki and Jazz sat across from her on the weathered wooden bench, the only seat available in the cluttered shed.

"Where is everybody?" Nikki asked again.

"Sis gone town," Belle again intoned. "She tell me stay here. Mama gone."

"I know, Belle," Nikki said, feeling her own eyes burn, as fresh tears reappeared in her sister's eyes. "Where are the boys?"

"The boys" was Nikki's collective name for Mama Vi's sons, with whom she had only a vague acquaintanceship. Alfonso, called Fanso, was the youngest of the lot and the only one with whom she had an actual relationship. Fanso and Tones, Belle's boy, had been Nikki's playmates during her childhood visits to Antigua. She'd always felt a kinship with Fanso. Maybe it had to do with the fact that he'd seemed as out of sync with the rhythm of the yard as she'd felt. Everyone told him what to do; Audrey was forever beating or chastising him for some wrongdoing, perceived or real. Whatever the reason, there was affection and a thin thread of communication between Fanso and Nikki still.

"Sis gone town," Belle began again. "She tell me..."

"She's at the funeral home?" Nikki asked, if only to stop the flow of words.

Belle nodded. "She gone, Straffie…she tell me stay here. Mama gone." The mantra was like a calming lullaby she sang to herself, even as her tears once again fell freely.

"And Chris?" Nikki prompted gently.

"Columbus out in he garden," Belle continued in a sing-song. "Lars gone work, Ben-up gone work. Nobody know where Deacon be."

Ben-up, Nikki remembered now, was so called because of his lame hand, and Deacon had earned his moniker due to his brief foray into street preaching. He was heavily into the bottle now she recalled Fanso saying in one of his emails, and was prone to lengthy absences. He'd turn up in time for the funeral, she supposed. Apart from Nikki, who'd never really belonged there, and Fanso, who'd never really fit, none of Mama Vi's children had wandered far from this Sea View Farm homestead. Fanso, who had years ago gotten the opportunity—on a tourism industry scholarship—to study in Bermuda and later in Paris, worked as a sous chef at one of the island's hotels. He lived near town.

By the time Audrey returned, it was past lunchtime, and Columbus had come up from his garden. Nikki was checking the cupboards in the small kitchen to see what she could fix for lunch when a shadow filled the open doorway, and she looked up to see her eldest sister standing there.

Nikki had always been intimidated by Audrey, and felt a tightening in her belly, even now.

The older woman was tall like Mama Vi, but also thick. She had a man's square, broad-shouldered build, an image that wasn't softened by the fact that she wore worn jeans, thick boots, and shapeless button-down shirts almost all the time. She also wore the disapproving look Nikki remembered well.

"You reach," was Audrey's only greeting to Nikki, who shook

off a sense of déjà vu at this. Her mother had greeted her in exactly the same way when, as a child, she'd returned to Antigua for the first time.

"I was just going to fix them some lunch," Nikki replied awkwardly.

"Yeah, well, no need for that," Audrey said, moving into the kitchen to take over.

Nikki stepped out of the way and went to join the others at the scuffed wooden

table, one on each side.

"This is my sister, Jasmine," Nikki said into the void.

Audrey continued working silently.

"How are things…with, uh, the…uh, funeral plan…can I do anything to help?" Nikki said, sounding halting, uncertain and distant, even to her own ears. She cleared her throat, stated more assertively, "How can I help?"

When Audrey didn't even turn to look at her, she knew she'd still got it wrong. "I can manage," was all her sister said, like she'd offered money, which maybe is how her stumbling offer had come across. But then what else did she have to give to people she barely knew? Not that she had much of that either, given her chequered career. In the end Nikki wasn't sure what she'd have done if Audrey had said yes to the offer of money or anything else. She felt so inadequate, and suspected, Audrey knew just how inadequate she actually was. It was what she always saw in her sister's disapproving eyes in any case, even as a child… especially then.

By contrast, Audrey moved capably around Mama Vi's kitchen—stove to cupboard to sink—no more than two paces in either direction. She filled up the space as if it were her own, which Nikki supposed it now was.

Nikki remembered how when they were kids, Fanso and Tones for sport would pull and fold their eyelids so the insides were out—raw, red, and exposed. And they'd laugh as she cringed from the ugliness of it. Her eyes felt like that now—raw, red, exposed—but still no tears. It was a relief and a worry. Nikki blinked rapidly, blaming the funny feeling on the scent of onions, lime, hot sauce and sardines suffocating in the small kitchen-dining area.

A pressure on her foot under the table, Jazz's foot on hers, helped centre her. She smiled in Jazz's general direction, but didn't meet her eyes, while Belle, happy to have her little sister back, filled the room with her bright chatter. And somehow, Nikki made it through the rest of the awkward lunch, tasting nothing, before happily escaping to the cocoon of the hotel room.

Terry, the boyfriend whose make-up tickets she and Jazz had used, called that night. He was livid.

"This is how you're going to deal with things, by running away?" he demanded.

He didn't shout, rarely did. It was more a hardening of tone. It made her think of granite, unyielding, something off of which things bounced.

"What things? I thought you said it was all in my head?" Nikki lobbed at the solid stone nonetheless. "And I'm not running." *Liar*, a little internal voice that sounded suspiciously like Jazz piped up. Behind her, she heard Jazz slip quietly into the bathroom to give her some privacy.

She wondered where he was, home balcony or office, both with Lordly views of the New York City skyscrapered skyline. There was no sound apart from his voice, a sure sign he was perched high above. A familiar resentment settled in her; she grabbed on to it, a counterweight to her guilt. She knew she hadn't been fair to him, though she admitted to herself she sure as hell didn't know the etiquette for this situation. Still, she should have at least told him about Mama Vi. But she'd avoided dealing with him—period, and here they were. He was saying something... "That's your *modus operandi*, running from anything real..."

Nikki cut in with a sigh. "Terry, what do you want?"

There was an answering sigh through the phone. "I want you to come home," Terry said, with less heat. And this was the thing she'd learned about him, the quality that held her; the granite had give, in places, though those places were well-camouflaged.

"Home," Nikki echoed, the word mocking her. "Where is that?" she wondered as much to herself as him.

She could picture his eyes hardening at this, the little, almost amused, twist of his mouth. She heard the huff of breath that ended in what sounded like a laugh but really wasn't.

"Our apartment, our life," he said in a clipped tone. She almost reminded him of his increasingly-less-idle talk of unloading the apartment and reinvesting in a more upmarket co-op. She could've blown the lid off the lie that it was about location, since they both knew the spacious high-rise was a gift in a city where quality real estate was rare, and costly. She could've hit him, as he was hitting her, with the truth; it was truly about acceptance, about confirming the success of his self-transformation. After all, his backyard might have been Projectsville, USA and hers Povertyville, Antigua, but she recognized another ashy-footed alien when she saw one. She could've thrown that at him and all his pretensions.

"*Your* apartment," she said instead. "And as for *our* life, let's not forget that your lies brought us here."

"Not your coldness? Not your frigidity? Not your uptight, closed-off bullshit?" Terry demanded, gloves coming off.

That was rich, she thought, coming from the Granite King himself.

"Well," she mocked, "sounds like you're well rid of me."

He huffed, but when he spoke again, there was a desperate quality to his voice that nearly undid her. "Come on, Nikki, wake up. Fight for us. Fight for this."

She felt like a fraud then, and was eager to just end things before they were rolling about in the muck of emotions they were both ill-equipped to deal with.

"Terry," Nikki said, before ending the call, "I wouldn't even know what I was fighting for." She hung up and unplugged the phone.

When Jazz emerged from the bathroom, ocean-scented steam following her, Nikki was still there, sitting at the edge of the bed, the TV flashing chaos somewhere in the world still on mute; the disconnected phone cord was at her feet. Jazz sat next to her, as warm as Nikki was cold, and slipped an arm around her waist. "It's going to be okay, you know," Jazz said. "It may not feel that way now. But it will, in time."

"I want to believe," Nikki joked hoarsely, borrowing a line from one of her favourite TV shows, a show about aliens and conspiracies and an outsider hero. She felt Jazz's chastisement without it needing to be said.

"Stop pushing your feelings away." Rewind, Play, Rewind, Play, Rewind. Nikki sighed, her head slipping to Jazz's shoulder. And on cue, her sister intoned, "Nikki, come now, you have to let yourself feel."

But that was the problem, not feeling, but feeling everything and not knowing what to do with it; in the end, packing it away at the back of things for safekeeping until she forgot it was there, like people did things they never used.

"Talk to me," Jazz said. "Let it go."

And she did, sort of, because talking to Jazz, as much as she could anyone, was inevitable. Nikki couldn't even remember really how they'd gotten from that first spontaneous meeting, to tentative joking about Professor Baltimore, to sharing space, to occupying space in each other's lives. Nikki didn't bother to wonder about it anymore, though she once had, afraid of it.

"I feel like if I start, I won't be able to stop," she confessed blearily. But it wasn't the whole truth. True, "letting it go" was not written into her DNA—both Mama Vi and Professor Baltimore had seen to that—but it was also true she was so cut off from herself, so unsure of herself, she didn't even really know what she was mourning. Only that she was.

Jazz rubbed her arm; it felt like sandpaper against her skin.

"What did Terry say?" Jazz ventured. And Nikki coughed or laughed or cried; she wasn't sure which.

"Terry." She sighed. "I'm not sure anymore if he was simply convenient and safe, if we loved each other, or if we just fit. I feel angry and betrayed about what he did, but I also feel this immense sense of relief. And before you start, I'm deeply aware of what that says about me, us. Four years is a lot of wasted time if there was nothing there."

Jazz offered nothing at this, and if she was surprised at the coldness suggested by the sentiment, it didn't show.

Nikki continued, without prompting. "And Mama, I never knew her." The words an indictment not of the mother who sent her youngest away, but of the daughter who never tried to find her way back; the daughter who'd tucked away Christmas and birthday cards with bad script, never bothering to reply; the daughter who'd stopped visiting as soon as she had a choice in the matter. Nikki felt, for the second time that evening, like a fraud; whoever thought Terry and her mom would have had anything in common. Well, they both had this—the ability to pull this truth from her; her relationship with both of them had been a lie.

"What kind of person does that make me?" she wondered out loud. But Jazz, of course, didn't have the answer, and Nikki never felt more alone than she did right then, and she knew alone well. They were good friends; they had been since she came to know herself within the organized chaos of New York housed with a man who never stopped being a stranger. She remembered him as a big, bushy bear of a man who never hugged, in fact barely touched her, whose every conversation was filled with lessons and verbal lacerations. A man who told her he was her father, but never taught her what family was.

Tears threatened. And she knew if she gave them leave, it would be like opening a Pandora's box of self-pity and grief and confusion. Then she'd be truly lost. A noise like a generator starting up, that coughing grind, tore out of her, causing her to snap her mouth shut. She kept the sound in, but the trembling that spiraled out from her belly put up more of a struggle, and she shook with the effort of it. Jazz's arm tightened around her, and for a time, Nikki allowed herself to lean into it and let her sister take the weight of her.

CHAPTER THREE

Nikki didn't remember leaving the little, chipped, violet, wooden house on the Sea View Farm main road. But she remembered clearly the first summer she came back. She was six, and her father was off to England on some fellowship or other.

A flight attendant kept an eye on her on the plane, and one of her brothers got a friend from his current job site to bring him to the airport to collect her. Both were dusty and smelled of sweat; neither spoke to her or each other the entire drive, though they were squeezed together into the front cab of a pick-up. On arrival, he drove off with the friend back to work, and Nikki stepped into a crowded yard, hands gripping her child-sized suitcase, all eyes on her but no one coming forward. The boys, Fanso and Tones, were there, eyeing her curiously as they sat picking stones out of the wet mud. They were the only males there; she'd later learn that coal pot making was considered women's work. A fleshy girl-woman, Belle, smiled shyly, and another, more solidly built, Audrey, eyed her stormily, not pausing in her work of fashioning what looked like a huge vase. Finally, a tall woman, as stately as the date palm under which they were huddled, stepped into Nikki's light, and she felt like she was in the shade of a huge tree. The woman wore a loose dress that had lost its colour, and twin plaits peaked from beneath her wrapped head. The woman stood tall over her. And for the first time she remembered, Nikki looked up into her mother's face, backlit against the sun.

"You reach," Mama Vi said gruffly. She wasn't a soft woman, given to endearments, Nikki would learn. A hard life and the burden of raising seven children with no reliable support had seen to that. Still, when her rough hand took one of Nikki's and led her into the violet house, the painfully shy girl felt a little more at ease.

She changed into a top with orange and black horizontal stripes and buttons along the collar bone, and went back outside to hang about on the periphery of their loud conversation. Fanso caught her eye and winked, a second before Audrey barked at him to mind his work. Picking stones and other debris from the wet mud and pounding the muddy to make it malleable, Nikki would soon learn, was Fanso's "work" before and after school and on summer breaks—that and collecting the clay needed for the family business. She would accompany him and Tones many times over the course of that long summer to collect muddy from the clay deposits to the west of the village—clay and trash, bits of *cassi* and other dry wood for baking the pots. He'd run his errands using a donkey box slung over his pet donkey, Beast, whose gentle nature belied the moniker. She was never allowed to accompany them on those days when they led Beast off for the trek to far-flung villages like Willikies and Barnes Hill to sell the coal pots and other items. She would huddle next to Mama Vi or Belle under the date palm tree until such time as the boys returned; the two of them now riding the considerably lightened donkey.

Nikki's second clear memory was of trying to ride Beast, or rather of being placed on the beast's bony back, by Fanso. She remembered screaming at the top of her lungs to be let down.

She remembered vividly Audrey exclaiming scornfully, "But she fooly bad. Anybody carry on so fu ride donkey?"

"She jus' 'fraid," Fanso defended.

And never needing much of an excuse to light into him, Audrey did just that. "Boy, anybody ah chat to you. You always ah put yourself inna big people business."

Fanso wisely did not point out that Nikki, being afraid of riding the admittedly gentle Beast, was hardly "big people business."

To Nikki, it seemed like Audrey was always angry, with Fanso most often absorbing her verbal and physical barbs.

Nikki's next memory was of Audrey standing over Fanso in the open yard, a hastily grabbed stick in her hand as he shied away. "Boy, you hear me say come ya to me," she raged, about what Nikki couldn't remember now. Nikki remembered though, watching from where she'd hid behind Belle's skirt as Fanso looked around the yard, eyes lingering on Mama Vi, a silent plea for aid that never came. She remembered Audrey's hand coming down, the red flowing from the cut on Fanso's brow; Belle shrieking as she grabbed him away from Audrey and sopped at the cut with the hem of her dress; Audrey *chuupsing* before she stomped into the small house. Mama Vi's hands never slowed over the huge flower pot she was making.

These were Nikki's earliest memories of Antigua, and perhaps best explained her uneasy relationship with home. Still, Fanso, too, was home, and with him things were never quite as hard.

The memories and the image of the scar on his brow came to Nikki now as she chatted with him over the phone line.

"I been wondering when you goin' get 'round to calling me," he chastised. "Audrey tell me you were in Farm yesterday."

"Yes," Nikki admitted.

"So when I goin' see you?" he asked gently.

Nikki had visited Fanso's house once before. She and Terry had taken a cruise nearly two years earlier, and the ship had docked for a few hours in Antigua. Fanso was the only one she had contacted. Terry had spent most of the day on an island tour. Nikki had hidden out on the ship's deck. From there, she had a bird's-eye view of the yellow-tangerine-green-blue-pink double-decker buildings, and an orderly garden of upscale duty-free shops right along the dock. Beyond that, less orderly, was the older, multitextured city of colonial-type wooden buildings and ultra-modern high-rises. She could even see the dreadlocked steel pan player in the canary yellow T-shirt and the bare-chested limbo dancer moving elastically to the beat in the clearing between the shops, though she couldn't hear the music. When that perspective lost its appeal, there were the weathered yet colourful wooden fish boats emblazoned with names like *Lady Vida* and *Stop-a-Gap* further along the shoreline. If she squinted, she could even make out the market just beyond that: vendors hawking everything from freshly gutted raw fish to Antigua Black pineapple, to the purple *antroba* or eggplant, to the pale-green christophene, to pumpkins cut to expose their rich orange centre, to fat mangoes the colour of sunset. Maybe she just imagined she could see and smell them, hear the chaos of sound, drawing on sense-memory from one of Mama Vi's rare visits to the city, the prodigal daughter hanging on to her skirt.

Finally, Nikki had given in to the urge to look her brother up. When Terry had returned—buzzing about the loping bus ride through country villages—it had been to a dressed and ready-to-go Nikki.

Fanso's house was a two-bedroom, single-story concrete structure in Upper Gambles, a modest building for the area. Just up the road from him, he related, taxis routinely paused so that tourists could snap images of the home of Antigua's biggest cricket star, Viv Richards. With gated properties set back from the main road hidden by thick shrubs and yellow-budded neem and flame-coloured flamboyant trees, and policed by eager dogs, it was pretty far from the shoulder-to-shoulder Sea View Farm environment of his childhood. So were his wife—Caucasian, French—and his pair of biracial sons. He was the same Fanso though, as warm as ever, and his *hand* as sweet as Nikki remembered. He cooked for them: steamed fish and fungi, a yellow ball of turned cornmeal and okra that really shouldn't taste as good as it did.

It wasn't the food's fault that after they launched back out to sea later that night Nikki felt queasy and claustrophobic. She was anxious to escape the ship by the time they docked in Puerto Rico. She convinced Terry to cut the trip short and hop a flight back to the U.S.

The Caribbean cruise had been his romantic idea, in any case. A *Northern Exposure* fan, Nikki had voted for Alaska.

"You coulda stayed with me, you know," Fanso was saying now.

"I...I have my sister Jazz with me," Nikki replied, taken off-guard. "I couldn't impose."

"Nikki, come on, family is not no imposition," Fanso replied. "Besides, it good to be with your people, times like these."

She didn't fill up the opening with the request he clearly hoped for, and imposition might have been the excuse, but it wasn't the reason. He knew it, too. Even so, he let it go. "So," he said instead, "when I goin' see you?"

"Well, Jazz and I are going to pick up a rental and spend the day touring," Nikki replied. "I thought we could stop by in the evening on the way back to the hotel."

"Sounds good," he agreed.

"Okay," she said, but hesitated. "Fanso, how're you doing? I saw Belle yesterday. I've never seen her so sad. I..."

"I holding up okay," Fanso said quietly. "It was no surprise, really. Mama been sick a while now."

And with that comment, fresh shame ate at Nikki. She'd known her mother wasn't doing well. The cancer diagnosis had come months earlier, and the disease was well advanced by that time.

Fanso ended the silence on the line. "I have to go," he said. "I'm going to be late for work."

"Yes, of course. I'll see you later," Nikki replied, ending the call.

By the time she and Jazz pulled up at Fanso's lavender and white house that evening, both were drained, having taken turns driving around the island, guided by a confusing little map—confusing mostly because so many of the streets didn't seem to have actual names. They even had a little adventure when the rental cut out up at Shirley Heights Lookout, a hilltop liming spot and former naval fortification overlooking the white sails of the many yachts in Nelson's Dockyard below. While tourists imbibed rum punch and danced badly to the music of the Halcyon Steel Orchestra, Nikki and Jazz wondered how they were going to get the clunker all the way back to town. They got a jump from one of the tour operators, and kept their fingers crossed all the way to Fanso's house.

Fanso hadn't changed much. Beneath the bare, shiny head, long neck, and narrow features lived, still, the boy who was always up to and up for anything. His slender body held the same restless energy and his lips quirked, as ever, on the verge of a smile. He was still dressed in his work clothes, a white chef's jacket and black pants. He hugged both Nikki and Jazz warmly, his handsome dark brown face and the paler gash on his brow splitting at his broad smile.

"Oh, baby sister, baby sister, it's good to see you," he exclaimed. His wife, Antoinette, small-bodied and pale complexioned, with white blonde hair, looked on. Nikki didn't know her well in spite of the fact that she and Fanso had been married over ten years now. She was dressed in a tank and cut-off jeans, hardly seeming that much older than her boys. She was the French teacher at the Catholic school the boys attended.

"…Twenett is tutoring from home now, too," Fanso told her as he stood over the grill on the back patio, preparing a simple dinner of barbecued pork steaks and vegetable kebabs, baby onions and carrots, skinned red potatoes, and zucchini. "I keep telling her she should open up her own school," he continued. "I not for this business of working for people your whole life. Look at me. I can't go much further in the hotel; people that look like me don't make it to executive chef in this industry for purpose, black country or not. Next step is to come off that road and do my own thing. Is just the money. But not long now."

Fanso was perhaps the most talkative of Nikki's siblings, Belle aside. Despite Audrey's best efforts to beat his spirit out of him as a child, it had proved to be distinctly irrepressible.

Sitting on his back patio, citronella sweetening the air and keeping the mosquitoes at bay, Nikki could almost pretend it was just a regular summer evening in paradise; that she wasn't in Antigua to bury her mother.

"So how you liking Antigua, Jazz?" Fanso asked.

"Well, it's nothing like Daddy said," Jazz blurted, before colouring a little.

"Why? What he say?"

Jazz shrugged. "You know, stupid stuff…"

"What?"

"Nothing," Nikki piped up.

Fanso paused, studied her for a minute, then shrugged. "Well, it's not paradise. I'll grant you that. But, as a man who lived at least two other places in my life, I have to say I don't know where is. It have it problems, yes, but where don't?"

"Well, what I've seen of it is lovely," Jazz said.

"Yeah," Nikki teased. "'Oh look at the cows, look at the goats!'"

Jazz shrugged, unembarrassed. "What can I say, I'm a tourist?"

"Tourist wha tourist, you're family," Fanso insisted and Jazz smiled. Nikki figured she ought to have known these two would get along.

After dinner, Fanso, Jazz and Nikki drove in their rental to Tones' home, a white wooden lean-to in a Lower Gambles yard filled with car skeletons and bikes.

Tones lifted Nikki off her feet in greeting, then proceeded to give Jazz some of the same treatment.

His wife was a Jamaican named Carlene, a woman, Fanso had told her, of whom Audrey did not approve. That, she figured, probably explained why Tones had wandered so far from home. Carlene seemed nice enough to Nikki, bringing out a bucket of icy water and a few Wadadli beers as Tones worked, examining the rental for its stalling problems.

A young boy, Judah, still in diapers and nothing else, hung on to Carlene's skirt. Another baby swelled her belly.

They talked late into the night, sitting on the cement blocks that constituted Tones' front steps and sipping beer, as they reminisced about childhood adventures with Carlene throwing in some of her own "back ah yard" talk. They even laughed— Tones and Fanso—about beatings they'd received, battling to one-up each other, as though it was some sacred rite of passage.

Nikki shook her head, tuning out their words in favour of the rhythm of their voices; the way they tumbled over each other as the boys had when they'd been young, during play wrestling matches and all-out fights.

Behind her eyes, images played like the faded film of a Hollywood classic, invoking that same sense of nostalgia. Fanso and Tones climbing trees, flying kites, catching insects either to keep as pets or kill for sport. Fanso and Tones playing two-man cricket with a drink box for their wicket while Nikki watched for traffic. Fanso and Tones performing stunts they'd seen at the makeshift movie house across the way in Parham town. Fanso and Tones, and her, "Miss Socie," dragged along for the adventure; there was always one to be had. The boys teased her, even now, about her "Socie" ways, and she didn't cry as she often had as a child.

CHAPTER FOUR

*T*he church sat on a rising a little way from the village. It was one of those old stone buildings that lured tourists and other shutterbugs.

Today, death songs wafted down its aisles—"Rock of Ages," "Amazing Grace"—as old women fanned, babies cried, and children shifted restlessly.

The church sat maybe two hundred. Today, they were spilling out of the doors as the entire village, it seemed, came to pay its last respects. It was a bit of a surprise to Nikki, who'd often seen her mother at odds with this or that member of the village, especially when it came to politics. She was Blue, most of the village was Red; simple as that. Rumour went it was politics that had split Mama Vi and her husband, a cane cutter and rabid government supporter, with only the bit of backsliding that resulted in Fanso punctuating their estrangement.

Nikki had witnessed, as a child, the cold war her mother waged with the neighbour across the street. There was no stoning or shouting in the streets, no gathering crowds. It was a battle of words dropped here, picked up there, and hurled gently back. It was voices raised in song, and the right Bible quotation used just so.

"The sun shall not smite me by day, nor the moon by night; My Lord shall preserve me from all evil."

"Hmm, without love in my heart, I am as a sounding brass, or a tinkling cymbal."

"I will fear no evil or malice, 'cause God nar wear pyjamas."

"It shall be better for the devil self on the day of salvation than for the likes of *memelippe neaga* and evildoers."

They were often quite liberal with the translation, each claiming God as her personal warrior.

Not that her mother was a religious woman. No one, in her seventy-plus years, had or would ever accuse Mama Vi of being virtuous. But as they declared in testimonials to the capacity crowd, she wasn't a woman to be trifled with; she'd worked hard all her life to keep her family going, and she had a strong spirit.

It hardly seemed possible to Nikki that the vital, imposing woman she'd known, and yet not known, could be the same body lying so still in the coffin in front of the altar. Granted, she hadn't been able to look for very long, but the glance was enough to reveal the faint smile and the fire engine-red, synthetic suit. Nikki had rarely seen her mother smile. It hardly seemed right to leave her with a forced smile forever. As for the suit, well, it was the kind of thing that Mama Vi would only be caught dead in. Nikki wondered if Audrey was making some kind of point. Surely, if Nikki knew this about Mama Vi, Audrey did. Apart from the wrongness of the colour, that it was the colour of the political party Mama Vi abhorred, Nikki had only ever seen her mother in bleached, worn, cottony clothing. It didn't seem right, but she'd been kept out of it, and stayed out of it.

These distractions preoccupying her, Nikki didn't feel the wave of melancholy hit until later, as they walked down the sloping hill to the church graveyard. Belle's damp hand was clasped in hers on one side, Jazz kept sentry on the other side; both were subdued. The ground was muddied by the recent unexpected showers, making it slow-going, even as the dragging funeral songs pulled at Nikki's spirit.

The grave diggers grunted as the thick mud made them work for their money. It seemed too much suddenly to have to stand there through the long process of covering the casket, hearing the squishy sounds as the mud was lifted and the thuds as thick clumps hit the wood. The smell was getting to her, too. The funeral party stood in the shadow of a neem tree, the yellow buds of which were in full bloom, the smell of which was making her nauseous.

Fanso and Mama Vi's other boys took up shovels and started helping; the standing and watching maybe becoming too much for them, too. With the extra hands, it was soon over, and the trek back up the hill began. Thankfully, they finished it before Nikki brought back up the coffee and toast she'd had for breakfast many hours earlier.

The mourning over, it was time for the party. For that, people descended on the Hughes' family yard. The men stood around in groups drinking. The older women, Mama Vi's contemporaries, sat in the few available chairs, nibbling sandwiches and chicken wings. The younger women, Audrey and even Belle among them, served. The much younger women posed and flirted with the boys, who were swaggering in sagging pants and loose shirts that swallowed their lanky frames; the children ran through the crowd, working off the stress of having to sit still for hours. Deacon, drunk as ever, teased the even younger ones with *Jumbie* stories, which they slurped up like soft ice cream.

It hardly seemed possible to Nikki that they'd just buried her mother, that something so vital had gone from this place.

"You're the one from the States," a woman's voice, rough like gravel, said close to her ear, startling her.

Jazz was off somewhere, and Nikki had been sitting at the edge of everything, trying to hold herself together. She did not want conversation. But the woman was persistent.

"Nikki, right?"

"Yes," she said shortly.

"Nikki Baltimore," the woman agreed. "Winston child."

That caught her attention. "You know my father?" she asked, turning fully to the woman now. What greeted her was a sixty-ish-looking face framed by a startling burgundy wig. With a face to put to it, Nikki remembered that voice now. It was the pianist from the church. Her rough contralto had led the choir as her fingers abused the piano keys. It was curious to hear her father's name mentioned on the island. Most days, she completely forgot that he, too, was from Antigua.

"Not really," the woman admitted. "He wasn't from this side of the island. Plus, he gone long, long time. Don't have no people left here that I know of. But I remember when he came through the village, taking pictures and stories about life before time. Most of them didn't understand half of what he was talking 'bout. But I'm an educated woman, one of the first from the village to go to high school. Antigua Girls High School. *Mel Est Bonum, Sic Est Doctrina.* 'Honey is sweet, so is learning.' That was our school motto. Still is. I used to teach music there. Then I was working from the ministry, running the music programme in all the schools. But I'm retired now. Not too long, as a matter of fact. I play in the church, and I give lessons from home. I direct both the youth and adult choir up at the church."

Nikki wasn't sure why she needed to know all of this; it was like the woman was providing her résumé. "So, you were interviewed by my father when he was here?" Nikki asked, trying to get her back on track.

"Not directly, no. Winston Baltimore only had time for Mama Vi back then." The woman sniffed, still offended by an insult more than three decades old.

Before Nikki could press her further, however, she plunged on. "I'm Marisol," she said. "Marisol Adams. People call me Ms. Mary. Never Ms. Adams. Personally, I always preferred Marisol. Such a different-sounding name, you know."

Again Nikki opened her mouth, and again Marisol revved up. "My grandfather gave it to me," she explained. "Picked it up during his days working over in one of those Spanish places: Cuba, Dominican Republic, Panama. He didn't talk about it much, though Lord knows, I tried many times before he died to get him to document it. Such a vital part of our history; a lot of us went over there back then, you know. Cutting cane and such. A lot of their people coming back now, though truth be told, some o' them that coming can't rightly claim any people here. That's just the passport."

The woman sniffed at this, her disdain for this latter breed clear. Nikki waited, realizing that Marisol was a woman who liked to tell a tale, and take her time about it. "My grandmother hated the name," Marisol continued after a time. Nikki was only half-present by this time. Marisol chuckled. "Probably thought it belonged to some woman he'd picked up over there. She was always good to me though. Played in the church before me; she taught me to play. She'd learned from one of them old white nuns at the Catholic convent."

Marisol interrupted her conversation with herself to peer at Nikki. "You remember me?"

Nikki shook her head.

"Well, your mother and I didn't exactly move in the same circles," she continued. Another sniff. "He spent a lot of time here.

Your father. Stood out because, you know, in those days, people from overseas used to have a look about them."

Nikki waited, hungrily this time, for Marisol to continue. In her own time, she did. "Don't know what it was, but even in jeans and T-shirts, they had a kind of sophistication about them," she mused, "and your daddy wasn't a jeans and T-shirt man."

She continued. "He would sit down right next to Mama Vi in the yard here on an upturned cheese tin fascinated by the pottery-making thing, asking her a million questions, taking pictures. People said they would see her laughing. Mama Vi, laughing! People laughed at the whole thing, really. What was so fascinating about muddy? It was just part of life. You make your wares, you pack them on the donkey box and take them village to village, to market come Saturday time. People had been doing it for generations, since slavery days. But in a sense, your father was ahead of his time, because now, with so few holding to the traditional style of pottery making, it become heritage." The last word was delivered with her now familiar, scornful sniff.

"Back then though," she continued, "people couldn't make head nor tails of it. From what I understand, the research was for his doctoral thesis. He left near the end of summer. Some months later, you came."

Marisol shook her head, still mystified all these years later. "People were surprised," she said. "Thought Mama Vi was done with that."

Marisol's tale had ensnared Nikki in spite of herself. She struggled with the image of her father sitting in this yard; her mind couldn't hold on to or make sense of it.

"So, you're a big girl now," Marisol rattled on, looking almost like a proud mother herself. "You married yet? Any children?"

Nikki shook her head, wishing once again to be left alone.

"I live further out, at the edge of the village, near the big Jehovah Witness place," Marisol continued, oblivious. "You should stop by some time. We could talk more."

Nikki nodded absently, grateful for Jazz's return at that moment. The sight of the food in her sister's hand made her stomach restless, but she greedily sucked on the offered beer bottle.

The woman did a double-take. Nikki and Jasmine looked enough alike for people to assume they were twins, only Nikki's superior height and the difference in their colouring really marking the difference.

"This is my sister Jasmine," Nikki introduced when the silence verged on becoming awkward. "Jazz, this is…"

"Marisol. Marisol Adams," the gravel voice filled in. "I was just telling…"

Nikki zoned out, preoccupied with the image of her parents' unlikely courtship in this same yard.

"…I have a picture…"

"What did you say," Nikki interrupted, refocusing.

"I said I have a picture of your parents together from back then," Marisol repeated. "Well, not an actual picture, but I guess you could say I'm kind of an unofficial village archivist. I clip stories of anything having to do with our little community here, a rare enough occurrence as it is."

"Where'd you say you lived?" Nikki asked.

Marisol smiled. "Just near the front of the village, after the Jehovah Witness place; it's a yellow cottage with lots of flowers and fruit trees."

The picture turned out to be just a standalone, Nikki discovered later that week. "Antiguan Doctoral Candidate Explores Village Life" the headline read. And true enough, there was her mother, sitting under the palm tree, glaring suspiciously at the camera; her shirt-jacketed father sitting nearby on an upturned can, sporting those square, black framed glasses he still favoured. Her mother looked to her as she always looked, what she remembered of her, but her father seemed so young, hair even wilder then.

She and Jazz had tea with Marisol in her dainty little sitting room complete with delicate doilies, dainty figurines, and in spite of her lush garden, fake fruit and plastic flowers. A somewhat scuffed-looking piano took up a sizable portion of the space in the room.

Nikki had to admit it wasn't a bad way to pass the late afternoon. And as it happened, Marisol wasn't the only interesting acquaintance encountered at her mother's funeral.

CHAPTER FIVE

*S*he'd observed him observing her for much of the late afternoon to early evening. He approached during a rare moment when Marisol wasn't holding her hostage. She had a moment to panic and wonder where Jazz, her buffer against such intrusions, had wandered off to before he was on her, taking up more space than a man had right to.

He wore a navy suit with a pale greyish-blue silk tie and paler still blue shirt in the warm evening. While she couldn't fault his taste, it was something else—in addition to the enormity of him, not fat but tall, a man with heft and presence—that made him stand out from the others in the dirt yard around him. The other men had long ago chucked their cheap, ill-fitting jackets, which ranged from trendily colourful to dark and dour, and rolled up their sleeves. He though was as unwrinkled as if the day had not even begun. There was no sign he'd sat in a too-narrow, hard-bottomed and straight-backed pew, stood too long at a squishy grave site, grieved or sweated.

He reminded her a little of Terry; he was always so cool in a hot suit on a warm day. As was the case with Terry, this man's suit was clearly custom made and of very high quality. It sat comfortably on his broad shoulders, and neither swallowed nor cinched as it ran the considerable length of him. There was a respectable pocket square the same hue as the tie, silver buckle, tie pin and cuff links. Everything about him bespoke a sort of practiced affluence. She imagined that, like Terry, he was a man who'd pulled himself up from nothing, and slipped in with the boardroom crowd, whatever passed for that here in Antigua, as if he'd always belonged. She used to imagine if she chipped away Terry's practiced cool, she'd find not a man, but a scared boy inside; or maybe she just longed for a twin to the little girl hiding inside of her. Misery loves company and all that. She suspected however, that Terry's chiselled exterior was so set there was nothing of the boy growing up in a hard knocks existence left, not enough to understand all the insecurities that lived inside her. She looked the part; that's what had attracted him to her in the first place, she supposed, when he'd plucked her from the crowd at one of those here-today-gone-tomorrow New York City clubs. She wasn't much for the club scene, but sometimes things—and people—are meant to converge; and there she was, there he was, clearly not a regular either and they danced up to each other. The rest, as they say, was history.

Now, in Mama Vi's backyard, here was this one dancing up to her. He moved with big, certain steps, but it was a dance none-theless, no way of missing the interest in his eyes. Nikki realized she was frowning by the time he came to an expectant stop. She forced another smile, one of many pained smiles that day.

"Nikissa Baltimore," he greeted too loudly. "My condolences on the passing of your mother. She was a fine woman."

Nikki frowned at the use of her full name. It reeked of over-familiarity. No one called her that, not even her father who'd raised her, or her mother who'd named her.

She stared at him. He couldn't have been one of the boys Fanso and Tones knocked around with when they were kids; he had at least fifteen years on her by her estimation.

He pressed on, his smile that of a smarmy salesman peddling something you neither needed nor wanted, or a politician. "It's been a while," he said. "But I grew up right here in this village. Remember you coming home for summers, a time or two anyway. Hensen J. Stephens; I'm the parliamentary representative for the area."

Nikki found she was more confused than ever at this bit of news. Her mother's opposition to the dynasty that had ruled this country long before political independence—ruled it still— was legendary.

He laughed outright at her expression. "Don't look so shocked, Nikissa..." he began.

"Nikki," she cut him off.

He blinked at the tartness of her tone, but the smile didn't slip. "Nikki," he said, offering a slight nod. "And, please, call me Hensen."

She couldn't help but smile at that. "If I have occasion to call you, I will."

His laughter became brassier, trombone-like in pitch. This, for the first time, marked him as one of the village and made him fit finally with the people eating and drinking, chatting and laughing as twilight settled around them. This laughter was real, open and rich. It recalled rare instances of her mother laughing—tied head thrown back, body rocking with unexpected and unaccustomed glee, dress riding up, and the muddy between her parted legs briefly forgotten.

Memory? Or invention?

Nikki had no way of knowing.

Tears sprang to her eyes.

The concern on Hensen's face was immediate. "You okay," he asked gently.

"My mother is dead," she responded quietly, desolately.

They were suspended: Jazz, nearby and suddenly eyeing her worriedly; Hensen J. Stephens at a loss for words. Incongruously, that tickled Nikki...a politician, one that exuded confidence as surely as he did his assertively spicy and faintly leather-scented cologne, at a loss for words. When she started laughing, that same backyard belly laugh, a timbre of laughter she didn't know she had in her, Hensen and Jazz wore matching expressions of worry. She must look all kinds of crazy: she was teary-eyed and laughing, unravelled like the wisps of untamed hair brushing her wet cheeks. She couldn't bring herself to care. She wondered if this was what crazy felt like as the weird trembling she'd been feeling since coming here stirred in her again. It was a weird thing—like being inside an earthquake as it rumbled outwards towards the surface where things would fall over and come apart. That image struck her funny somehow, and soon she was laughing harder, more people turning at the sound, and her caring even less. She laughed until tears flowed stronger. People, even Jazz, kept their distance as though afraid her craziness would infect them. The only real thing was Hensen's hand suddenly on hers. It was solid, and weirdly quieted her. She hiccupped a breath, and another. Two breakdowns in as many weeks. Nikki felt like she was making up for lost time. She was present enough now to feel embarrassed, and to feel the awkwardness of this man she barely knew grounding her with a half-touch. A part of her wanted to lean into the bulk of him and lose herself for a while, but she shook off the feeling, the last of crazy's beckoning. She retracted her hand reluctantly, hiccupped another breath, declared, "I need a drink," before turning toward the makeshift bar under the palm tree where Mama Vi once held court. "A Heineken, please," she told the boy manning the bar, as sound stirred up around her again.

He called her at the hotel.

"How did you know where I was?" Nikki demanded, peeved, and not a little embarrassed by her earlier behaviour.

"Small country," he replied. "Any information can be had, if you know who to ask."

His smug assertion irked her even more, and it snuck out with her next words. "So, what do you want?"

"Well, I don't know what your plans are, but I would like the opportunity to get together with you before you leave," he said, unruffled by her snappy tone. "Perhaps you'll consider being my guest at the calypso show. I have access to the Viv Richards Pavilion. We could meet for drinks before."

The calypso show was the only major show left of the Carnival season, a season of pageants and parades that slipped by in a blur for Nikki. She'd gone with Jazz to some of the shows, sometimes with Tones and Carlene, Fanso and, once or twice, Antoinette. Not much of it had registered, however, and Nikki had only made the effort to ensure Jazz got a bit of fun out of the trip.

"Sorry, I have plans with my sister," she said now.

"Bring her along," Hensen suggested.

"No thanks; I think I'll pass."

"Why?" he pushed.

Irritation knee-jerked out of her. Didn't anybody ever tell this wannabe-slick-politician no?

"You may not like the answer," Nikki informed him, attitude filling the spaces between the words.

"I'm a big boy, I can take it," he assured her. She couldn't help but smile again at how unperturbed he seemed by her temper. And he was a big boy, no doubt about that. He continued, "Besides, I didn't get where I am by being afraid of a little straight talk."

Nikki laughed a little at this. "I can't speak for where you are, but I've rarely heard of a politician who liked straight talk."

"Call me an anomaly then," he lobbed back, unfazed, "because I can't stomach much else."

She laughed more genuinely now, liking him in spite of herself. "Look, I don't mean to be rude," Nikki said, all traces of attitude gone, "and I say this knowing that I've already been very, very rude. But I don't know you; I honestly don't remember you at all. I am here with my sister and my mother just died, and I'm not looking for company or whatever you're after."

The line was silent for a long time. She hadn't thought it was possible, but she seemed to have well and truly stumped him, or maybe hurt his feelings. His subdued tone, when finally he spoke seemed to confirm that.

"Well, can't get no straighter than that," Hensen said. "Maybe another time then. Once again, my condolences."

On that note, they ended the call.

"Let me give it to you straight," Fanso explained. "Round this time o' year nothing 'tall more important than calypso. Not politics. Not *picknee*. Not church. That thing you breathin', that's calypso. And we don't make joke when it come to our air; after all, is life." The scene at the Antigua Recreation Grounds—the sardine-tight crowd, the grounds seemingly filled with every last body in Antigua, the fierce discussions in between bouts, the intense expressions during the onstage theatre—seemed to bear him out.

"Looka muddy," someone shouted out in response to a perfectly landed lyrical barb.

"She go do for he, nuh worry," a fan of the singing artiste's rival piped up, promising retaliation.

Onstage, the male singer was dressed, Nikki assumed, like his rival—complete with fake breasts, micro mini, wig, makeup and heels, an acceptable cross-dresser in a notoriously homophobic culture. He sashayed exaggeratedly from one end of the stage to the next, shouting into the microphone. The crowd hooted and the "discussion" being bellowed in Nikki's right ear got even louder. It reminded Nikki of something Fanso had said about the relationship between politics and calypso: "is like dropping water in hot oil. Look out!" She edged a little away from the combatants, which wasn't very far in the tight space, hot in spite of the fact that they were in an open-air stadium.

The energy, she had to admit, was infectious, and even Jazz, who was as out of her element as Nikki, seemed to be enjoying herself. But then Jazz had a way of enjoying herself anywhere, a natural fit in ways Nikki had never been.

The crowd sang along with the onstage singer, even as he upped his antics to include one-legged gyrations, teetering dangerously on his narrow heels. Remarkably, he didn't fall, and as he turned to go, bottom rolling, someone remarked loudly, "He batty look nice though." The crowd roared long after his exit.

As the band broke ahead of the second round of singing, Nikki made a bar run; that's where she ran into Hensen J. Stephens. He was squeezed, like her, amidst the crowd of people clamouring for the unhurried bartender's attention. When their shoulders touched, she smelled the leather and spice of him and turned, just as he turned to her. He smiled as if their earlier conversation had not happened. Perhaps it was a combination of drink and the night and the fact that she was a little impressed with his irrepressibility, but Nikki found herself smiling back.

"Thought you were in the VIP," she said by way of greeting.

"Nah, that was just to impress you," he replied, eyes twinkling. "I like to move with my people."

Nikki's eyes widened. "Impress me?" She said this even as the bodies behind them got impatient with their lack of movement and Nikki found herself pushed into the bulk she'd mused about earlier. She righted herself quickly, and with a little manoeuvring by Hensen found herself out of the thick of it.

"Welcome to Antigua, eh," he said wryly. His face was shiny with sweat and he looked ruffled; Nikki found she liked this look on him. She wondered if her hair was behaving, but in this humidity, doubted it.

"How you enjoying the show?" he asked.

She grinned, nothing else to call it really. "It's an experience."

He laughed. "It is that. What you drinking?"

"A bottle of Cavalier for my group actually," she replied. "We have a cooler with ice but the beer's run out." Both Fanso and Jazz had offered to come with her but she'd assured them she could carry the single bottle of rum herself.

"Just Cavalier, no Coke to go with it?" Hensen asked. Nikki wasn't sure. At her hesitation, he squeezed her shoulder and said, "Wait here," before diving back into the crowd at the bar.

She was still feeling the pressure of that casual squeeze when he returned with both the Cavalier and a couple cans of Coke in a plastic bag in one hand, and his own drink of what looked like a vodka and orange juice in the other.

"How much?" she asked, and he frowned at her.

She smiled. "Well, thank you. I better go, I have people waiting."

"Yes, I remember," he said, bobbing his head. "Your sister, right?"

She blushed at that. "Look, I know I was kinda rude to you earlier…"

"Kinda rude?" he teased, and she blushed some more. But when she attempted to speak again, to apologize, he waved it off.

"Grief is a funny thing," he said. "I can't hold you responsible for any of that. I still hope we can get together for lunch before you leave though. You leaving right after the season?"

They met for drinks the evening after Last Lap, the colourful parade and street after-party that marked the end of the season. There was a strange feel to the city, what Fanso described as "the quiet after the hurricane." To Nikki, it felt like the city, the whole island, was catching its breath. That's what Jazz was doing back at the hotel, fighting off a mild case of the flu, likely from the dousing—of rainwater, beer, rum and God knows what else they'd received between J'ouvert and Last Lap. Their meeting place was Somewhere Else, a cozy, garden restaurant in the heart of the city. A popular song of the season, Claudette Peters and Da Bhann's "Somet'ings Got A Hold on Me" was playing and Nikki felt herself rocking a bit to the irresistible rhythm as she sipped her Wadadli.

Hensen smiled. "You look good," he said. "Look like you relax little bit, allow yourself to have a good time."

Nikki shrugged, her head dipping a little, though she couldn't shake the smile.

"It's Carnival," Hensen assured her. "It have that effect on people. Come Carnival time, you can't hold on to nothing, not even grief. Is like the song say…" He sang the bit in a nice baritone and Nikki hummed along. He smiled encouragingly. "That's it." She picked up the tune. Why not? She got most of the words wrong but it didn't matter one bit as they sang together, feeling the music to the last note. Another high-tempo soca tune kicked in. Hensen leaned back. "Is a nice buzz, ent? I tell you, if we could bottle it, we'd be rich."

"But that's what you sell, isn't it; why people rush here? A good time?" Nikki replied.

He looked at her, like he was reading her. "You got it," he said. "You got it."

She couldn't help feeling like there was much more to those three words. But there was something more pressing on her mind.

"Do you really remember me from when we were kids?" Nikki asked.

"Well," he replied, sipping his Screwdriver drink. "You were a kid. I was just outta school, working at the Antigua Commercial Bank, bleary-eyed from counting money and looking for a way out. You had come back from *away*. Even if I didn't have America-shaped stars in my eyes, I woulda noticed you. In a small village, ripples stand out. Even when they're quiet, bewildered-looking ripples."

"Bewildered-looking," Nikki bristled.

He teased, "Skin and bones, eyes like a deer in a hunter's sight; there was nothing of Mama Vi or any of the Hughes clan about you, nothin' 'tall. Looked like if somebody pinched you little too hard, you were going to just crumple up."

"Thanks," Nikki said sarcastically.

His teasing continued, unabated, "When I saw you at the funeral, though, hmn! I couldn't believe it was the same little girl."

"What, I don't look 'bewildered' anymore." she sniped.

"Sure," he was unapologetic, "you seem a little 'bewildered,' appropriate to the circumstances, wouldn't you say?"

She wanted to knock the smirk off his face. "But," he continued, leering openly now, "you also grew into yourself nice. Looked at you and said, 'That girl have potential.' Then I came over and you shot me down. Which I have to tell you, only made me more determined."

She shook her head. "Men."

He threw out his arms. "Guilty."

His grin was at once impish and smug, annoying and endearing. And while she sat at a loss for words, he settled back, signaled the waitress. "You want anything?" he asked.

For this whatever-this-is to end, she thought reflexively. That wasn't quite true though. Sure, he irritated her, but he also intrigued her. It was an unsettling feeling, a feeling that marinated through the ordering of a fresh round of drinks and hot wings for him.

"So," Hensen asked, when they were alone again. "What kind of work you doing up North?"

And just like that, real life was back in her face: her dusty basement office, and Terry. "Some fundraising and marketing, some property management," Nikki embellished.

Hensen was studying her again, and just when she was about to call him on it, he asked, "You headin' back right away?"

She shrugged. "Life goes on, right?"

He seemed satisfied with whatever he was reading from her, but didn't speak more on it until the wings and drinks arrived. Unaccountably hungry all of a sudden, she nipped a leg or two from the overflowing basket and soon they were both shiny lipped and sticky fingered.

"So," he said, around a mouthful of chicken, "how married are you to your situation there?"

She almost asked what situation, but, of course, he couldn't know about Terry or her job or any of it.

"You have the look," he continued, "of someone on a fence, wondering which way to jump."

More perceptive than she thought; it bothered Nikki that she was that transparent. All seriousness now, Hensen ploughed on,

"No offense intended. I mean, we all been there. It's natural. For me, that time was just before the last elections, when my elders and others started pressing me to come home and make my contribution. Labour's old guard was on its last legs; fresh blood was needed. I decided to let them take some of mine."

Nikki found herself asking, quietly, "What decided it for you?"

A gleam in his eye, Hensen opened his mouth, and it was her turn to cut him off. "And if you say they made you an offer you couldn't refuse," Nikki interjected, "I may be forced to send you to sleep with the fishes."

Hensen laughed, heartily, and Nikki with him. When he answered though, the imp was gone, as was the smug bastard, and the polished politician.

"I followed my heart," he said.

"Now see," Nikki quipped. "I didn't know politicians had those."

"Well, they wouldn't let me into the cabinet room until I'd signed it away, of course," he lobbed back.

That tickled her; self-deprecating was a good look on him.

Several drinks and many laughs later, he made his pitch.

CHAPTER SIX

"Tourism Development Consultant with Special Responsibility for Communications," Jazz said, as she dumped clothes into her suitcase the night before her scheduled departure. "What is that? Is that even a real position?"

They'd been over this many times already, and Nikki was tired of having to explain a decision she didn't quite understand. She couldn't just chalk it up to Hensen J. Stephens' charisma. Sure, he'd hooked her, but she'd wanted to be hooked.

"Not only is it a real position, it's a good move for me; the best damn prospect I've ever had," she responded. "Tourism is the biggest industry here, so it's kind of a big deal."

"And he's offering it to you because of your vast experience in the field, I suppose," Jazz argued. "Nikki, this doesn't make any sense."

"What does make sense?" Nikki rebutted. "Rushing back to a dead-end job, when I could have a real power position that I could potentially turn into a full-fledged consultancy?"

"In the Caribbean?" Jazz ranted. Nikki had never seen her so worked up. "Do you even know the first thing about the Caribbean, much less tourism? Come on, Nikki, this is Antigua. When have you ever, ever expressed any interest, any interest at all in returning to Antigua?"

Nikki sat heavily on the bed. "That's just the thing, Jazz. I haven't felt much of a yearning for anything," she said. "But when Hensen opened this door, I could see the possibilities. I mean, what have I been doing since college? Just rolling along. Maybe it's time I held on to something solid."

"Solid? 'Tourism Development Consultant with Special Responsibility for Communications'?" Jazz was incredulous.

"Yes," Nikki insisted firmly. "Look at it this way; it's undefined."

"It's undefined, all right," Jazz scoffed.

"I can make it my own," Nikki continued.

"You know, a bit of career angst, especially at our age, is perfectly normal," Jazz ventured. "You ride it out, it passes. You don't chuck everything."

"This isn't career angst," Nikki stressed.

"Well, what is it, Nikki? 'Cause I gotta tell you, I'm not getting it," Jazz said, frustration evident in her voice.

"Well, get this," Nikki shot back, tone hardening. She did not want to be talked out of this and if anyone could talk her around, it was Jazz. "I want to do this. I am doing this. It's done."

At that, the wind seemed to go out of Jazz's sails. She sighed.

"And this isn't about Terry?"

Nikki offered no denial.

"Oh, come on, Nikks," Jazz sighed, hands thrown up, body falling back exhaustedly onto the bed. "He's just a man. He breaks down, you trade him in, get an upgrade. Or, you find a way to get a few more miles out of him. You don't chuck your whole life."

Nikki huffed, "Will you stop saying that? Nobody's chucking anything. I'm embracing an opportunity. This is not about Terry or hurt pride or career angst."

Jazz raised a skeptical brow.

"Okay," Nikki conceded. "Not just about that."

She sighed heavily, struggled to explain the unsettledness of her thirty years. Found she couldn't. In the end, she borrowed a reference. "I'm on a fence," she said inadequately. "This is the way I choose to jump."

"A fence," Jazz said, with a roll of her eyes.

Nikki kept stubbornly quiet. Jazz regarded her for a long moment, and in the end, seemed to accept they'd both said all they could. "Well, I just hope you know what you're doing," she grumbled.

I don't, Nikki thought, but didn't say. She kind of figured Jazz knew anyway.

"And who am I supposed to call in the middle of the night to dish with, huh?" Jazz asked.

"Well, Hensen assures me that free utilities, including overseas telephone service, is a perk of the job," Nikki informed her.

"I'll tell you what," Jazz said, going for light but not quite making it, "I'd give anything to be a fly on the wall when you tell Professor Winston Baltimore about this one."

"Hmm. You just need to make sure Terry doesn't kick all my stuff to the curb before I get it in storage," Nikki shot back. She'd climb the mountain that was the Professor when she came to it.

"You sure you know what you doing," Fanso said over beers that night on his back patio. They'd just enjoyed Jazz's lip-smacking seafood lasagne farewell dinner and were lounging, full and lethargic, contemplating the stars. They were plentiful that night, every night.

"We've been down that road," Jazz reported.

Nikki regarded her sister with a little smile. Jazz still wasn't behind the idea, but she'd given up fighting it. Nikki was happy for small mercies.

"Hmm. I don't trust politicians," Fanso said. "You shouldn't either."

"I think I could be good at this," Nikki said, hearing the earnestness in her voice and wondering whom she was trying to convince. "It feels new and exciting and, I don't know, meaningful."

"I not saying no," Fanso said, palms up. "I just…"

"…don't trust politicians," Nikki finished with him. "I get it."

Well, she didn't either, but figured what did she have to lose?

It was the coward's way, she knew, but Nikki emailed instead of calling or waiting to speak directly to Professor Baltimore. One of his teaching assistants would print it out for him, and he'd dissect it as though it was a paper to be graded. But at least she wouldn't have to sit across from him while he did so. Even so, she laboured more than an hour in the hotel's Internet café over the exact wording.

"…*an interesting opportunity has opened up here for me,*" she wrote. "*I've opted to pursue it. I'll be working with the government, as a consultant. It eclipses anything I've done before, or am doing now. So, it seems foolish to pass it up. I'll be returning shortly to get my affairs in order, prepare for the move. I had to stay on a bit longer to meet with the Prime Minister and Cabinet, work out contract details, and sign on the dotted line. Yes, it's a government position, but fairly independent. We can talk more, if you wish, when I return.*" The End.

"This is all happening a bit more quickly than I expected," she confessed to Fanso and Tones and their significant others one evening, sitting on Fanso's patio.

"Well, Antigua dis," Tones said, as though that explained everything.

At her quizzical look, he clarified, "Things move as slow or as fast as the people with the power want them to."

"You find place yet to live," Carlene wanted to know.

"No," Nikki responded. "Haven't been looking really."

"There are a few empty houses behind the school, not far from here," Antoinette volunteered.

"A house?" Nikki exclaimed. "I'm not sure I want anything so permanent." That earned her an unreadable look from Fanso. But, house. It just sounded so settled, even a rental.

"Cheaper to rent than most apartments," Tones said, "and, for sure, cheaper than that hotel."

Nikki didn't respond to Tones' comment, nor did she meet Fanso's eyes.

"So, you sure 'bout this?" Tones asked as they drove along All Saints Road to Sea View Farm. They were in one of his cars, a blue Ford Fiesta with a powerful engine that roared as they sped along the highway. Tones hugged the road's curves and dips with a velocity that had Nikki gripping the sides of her seat. He looked across at her, and she fought the urge to tell him to keep his eyes on the road.

"Antigua different to New York, you know. You sure you ready?"

She could tell he was teasing but still the question unnerved her. "Sure as I can be," she said.

Tones' eyes swept her stiff posture. "Relax yourself, man," he said. "Everything good."

Nikki smiled and did allow herself to be soothed, though he'd likely misread the source of her tension; or maybe she had. "Everything good"…that had always been Tones' philosophy. He didn't let anything bother him, and he seemed happy enough.

"Everything good," Nikki repeated, and Tones smiled across at her. "Couldn't be better."

They were on their way to Sea View Farm; it was her last visit before returning to New York, her last chance to tell the family of her decision. Tones had offered to drive her, said he was due to pay "Mammy and Belle" a visit anyway. Nikki decided to pay a visit to her own mother first. Tones dropped her off at the stone church on the hill. She told him she'd walk the short distance to the house. She had a difficult time finding her mother's grave. Even after such a short time, the grass had grown in in thick patches. With no headstone to mark it, it was the still-ripe neem that guided her to it.

It was weird being there, alone, with so many dead people. Nikki wasn't terribly religious or spiritual. A lifetime with her eternally skeptical father had seen to that. Still, there was a mood about the place. It was quiet, except for the whistling wind, and heavy with the sadness left behind by people like her.

She stayed for a good long while; part of her wanting to admit her insecurities about her crazy decision, here, where no one could judge her for it, or seize it as an opening to talk her out of it. But why should talk be any easier between her and her mother now than it had ever been? Truth was, she had never tried to know her mother, and if Mama Vi was still here, still alive, there would have just been more silence between them. If her mother was here, really here, Nikki wouldn't be here. So, who was she fooling? She wouldn't have come back to Antigua, she wouldn't have met Hensen J. Stephens, wouldn't have been seduced. "But here I am," she whispered.

Nikki found the family—Tones, Audrey and Belle—in the little shack behind the palm tree. Tones was sitting close to his biological mother, while engaged in conversation with the mother who had claimed him as her own. They were both so focused on him, they barely noticed her entrance. Belle patted the bench on the other side of her, however, and Nikki gladly sat.

At a bit of lull in the conversation, Nikki blurted, "So, did Tones tell you my news?" This was directed at Audrey.

"News, wha news?" Belle asked.

"I'm moving to Antigua."

She waited, through Belle's hug and excited babbling, but Audrey offered nothing in response.

"So, what do you think?" Nikki asked finally.

"Think? What there for me to think?" Audrey said dismissively.

"Mammy…" Tones began.

"What? Wha me supposed to do?" Audrey demanded, voice rising. "Jump up and down? Me nah fooly like Belle, know, fu get all excited because she now remember she have people; people she never pay nuh mind 'til now. Besides, she go learn soon enough na fu mix up with dem politician an' dem. Hensen J. Stephens just the same like all the rest. But she just swell up enough in she own importance fu feel flattered at all de courting and all de bullshit. And is we supposed to be unsophisticated."

This was punctuated by a *chuups* and her back as she exited the shed. Belle was wide-eyed. Tones frowned. "No bother wid mammy," he said. "She na mean nothin' by half ah what she say."

Nikki was sure just the opposite was true; Audrey meant every word. However, Tones wasn't the one she needed to be arguing with. She got up, and Belle grabbed at her. Nikki favoured her sister with a gentle, reassuring touch before leaving. Confronting Audrey was the last thing she wanted to do, but, after that outburst, if she was, in fact, moving to Antigua, it now seemed inevitable.

Nikki found Audrey in the kitchen, doing nothing in particular, but doing it with terse, angry movements. She stood in the doorway, as if needing an escape route.

"Audrey, what did I ever do to you? Why do you hate me?"

It was a weak opening, as openings went, but the best she could come up with. It was enough.

Nikki recoiled as Audrey uncoiled, spittle flying every which way. "Hate you? Girl, I don't waste time thinking 'bout you. Comin' 'round here like some queen. Thought Mammy had sense 'til she start sniffing after that 'professor' and allow him to blow her mind with his big talk. Better than everyone, that one; raise you the same way. Sendin' you back here when he wanted to be rid of you, with your little uptight ways, and your 'I don't eat this, don't do that' ways. She treating you like some queen because you was his, and smadee laka he bother fu gi she the time of day. Just gi me a break."

Audrey was breathing heavily, her body tensed, like she'd been fighting, when her words finally stopped.

Nikki's chest was heaving, too, and she felt that weird quaking in her belly again. She felt like Audrey had taken a belt or tamarind whip to her; she felt shredded.

"That's a mouthful," she said, not understanding the Antiguan dialect word for word but getting the gist. "Considering you don't have time to waste thinking about me."

Her voice sounded broken; to her ears, weak. Audrey didn't even acknowledge it, turning away from her again, and Nikki found herself pushing against the silence.

"So the accident of my birth is my sin?"

More silence.

"Well, you know what, Audrey?" Nikki said. "I'm tired of this, whatever this is, between us. You hate me? Fine. But I can't change the past…that Mama Vi sent me away, that was her choice…that maybe I don't belong here. Well, if that's what it is, that's what it is. But, I'm choosing to come back now, and that's still not good enough for you. Well then, to hell with it. I'm not asking your permission anyway."

More silence.

"I'll stay out of your life from now on, unless you invite me in," Nikki continued. "I'll still come visit Belle, when I get back. But I won't impose my presence on you any longer. With Mama Vi dead, we can all stop pretending."

She stopped talking and the silence that followed was like another presence in the room, imposing and solid.

Nikki huffed out a breath. "The other thing I did want to talk to you about, apart from me leaving, was Mama's grave." Audrey's shoulders twitched, but still no words. Nikki huffed again. "I want to get her a headstone. I want to make arrangements for that before I leave." The shoulders tensed. Nikki felt something like satisfaction at that. She asked, hearing the vinegary sweetness in her voice, "Can you recommend anyone?"

Audrey's hand landed with a hard clap on the counter, and Nikki jumped. Audrey turned on her, and she took an instinctive step back, almost tumbling out the open doorway. Her oldest sister was looking at her like she wanted to grab onto her and wrestle her to the ground. When Audrey spoke, her voice was incredulous, "But what a fresh, forward picknee! What a likkle, nuff, edge up, better-than-smadee picknee! Ah wha de ras me ah hear ya tall! Lord, you see me crosses! You see me crosses, Lord! Wha me do for Mammy not good enough for you, New Yark?"

Nikki stepped in to her; they were breast to breast. "She's not just your mother!" she shouted. "She's my mother, too. If I want to get my mother a damned headstone, I will."

"Your mother? When last you talk to she? When she was dying, how often you visit she? Call she? Say, 'Dog, how you feeling?' to she? How much night you sit up with she while she moan and groan? Eh, wha de hell you know 'bout she? Look, gyal, you better back offa me, if you know what good for you."

"Move me," Nikki challenged, feeling so alive with emotion, she didn't know what to do with herself. The quaking, tamped down until now, pushed its way to the surface until it felt like the kitchen was moving. She wanted Audrey to touch her, wanted to hit her, wanted to push all this rage and pain and confusion into her, move her off her feet with it. She almost screamed when Audrey turned away from her with nothing more than the long *chuups* she felt the last comment deserved.

Nikki swiped at angry, hurt, frustrated tears, thinking "more damned tears," knowing this was weakness in Audrey's eyes. "She's the only mother I had," Nikki said, more quietly, raggedly. "She didn't belong to you. She's the only mother I had, and I never had her. She's my mother. She doesn't belong to you. If I want to buy her a fucking headstone, I will. If I want to move back to Antigua, I will."

"So, who stopping you?" Audrey demanded, back still turned, and walked out.

Nikki was too wired to return to the shed, to be calm and gentle as she'd need to be with Belle. She walked out of the kitchen and up the road, not sure how she'd get back to her hotel, not really caring. Before clearing the village, she heard the roar. Tones pulled alongside her. They drove back to town in silence.

CHAPTER SEVEN

Nikki sat over breakfast, with her father on his small balcony, playing with her food while he picked at her decision.

Behind them, faintly and scratchily, Ella sang what might have been "Mack the Knife"; before them, the street was quiet. Soon, it would be busy with folks returning from the church at the top of the street. She remembered sitting here on Sundays just like these, an assigned book in her lap, watching the neighbour her father never spoke with tinker with his car in the driveway, watching the girl she never played with ride up and down the sidewalk on her pink roller skates. She sat there now, suffering his judgment. It was their ritual, as surely as this Sunday breakfast was her father's. It was the only discernable bit of the island still in him—saltfish, antroba, and bread with hot cocoa on Sundays. The elements, including the Antigua-made bread and the Dominica-grown cocoa, were easily procurable from his favourite West Indian shop over in Brooklyn. Her father's downstairs tenant and part-time housekeeper, an Indo-Guyanese woman, worked all the way over in Brooklyn. *Why not just live over there*, Nikki often wondered; it was a hell of a commute. But it meant she could easily pick up his Sunday groceries at the "Comforts of Home" when she did her own weekend shopping.

He used the bread now to sop at the gravy before shoving the whole soggy mess into his mouth. Then, he began picking at his teeth with his pinky, as he always did, while Nikki looked at her own food, her stomach turning over. Her father's food manoeuvres did nothing to still his tongue. For all his talk of etiquette— "you have no etiquette," he used to shout at her, at every slip—he thought nothing of talking around the partially chewed food in his mouth.

"...granted, it's got more meat to it than the jobs you've been playing at, wasting your life," he said. "On the surface of it, it seems as flimsy as any of those, sure. Finding ways to sell sun, sea water, and sand to pampered white people isn't exactly a higher calling. But it is an opportunity to have a hand in policymaking for a country, as much as Antigua can be called a country—a highly debatable point, mind you. Still, I give you six months before you come haring back to civilization."

He was slurping his cocoa now, a sound Nikki had become intimately familiar with over many Sundays like this. She turned her eyes to the street, as little distraction as it offered. This movement of her eyes aside, Nikki was still, her limbs burning and her insides shaking with the effort. As she had since childhood, she wanted to run away from him and his razor-sharp tongue. She'd never been able to build suitable armour against it, much less fight back.

Somewhere in her head, another conversation was taking place, one where the little girl had grown tough, not afraid, under his steady rebukes and disdain; one where that girl, a woman now, easily showed him the face of his hypocrisy. "Antigua made you," that woman said to him calmly. "If it's as meaningless as you insist, then so are you." But in this fantasy, as Nikki feared would be the case in life when he didn't respond, the child broke through, increasingly agitated, "So are you, Daddy; so are you; so are you!"

"Are you listening to me?" he called, and the inner conversation once again became inner.

"Antigua's not like you remember it," Nikki said dully.

Her father scoffed.

"Seriously," she said, with more energy. "Sure, things move at a different pace, but who says that's a bad thing? Are things so great here?"

Her father, done with his food, studied her. She remained still, and tried to hold his gaze.

"Well," he said, after a time. "It's your life; you should know."

Her eyes once again on the street, not really seeing it, Nikki decided to take that as the blessing she'd long ago told herself she didn't need.

Enduring her father's verdict on another of her life's turns wasn't the only bit of unfinished business Nikki had in New York. There was still Terry to be faced; they hadn't spoken since the long distance argument they'd had before Mama Vi's funeral.

When Nikki told Terry of her decision, he thought she was just punishing him for a sin he would not admit. So he admitted it, finally. As she had already known, that didn't change anything. Then, as she packed up the last of her things in the shared apartment, he speculated maybe she just needed time, time to get it out of her system. He said as much. That closed a door for her, though a part of her mind argued that she wasn't being fair. How was he to know this was important to her, when she hadn't?

"So much for not running," Terry accused tiredly. Nikki didn't answer, just continued packing.

Her life packed up—some of it in storage, some with Jazz, some in the cargo bay of the Caribbean Airlines flight taking her back into the sun—Nikki's insides shivered. She had plenty of time to think on the lengthy and circuitous flight, first from JFK to the somehow cold and impersonal Piarco in Trinidad. Then, after transferring to a smaller LIAT flight, hopping to St. Lucia and finally Antigua—touching north, south, and eastern Caribbean in a single trip. The flight, the several flights, left Nikki feeling wrung out and tired, or maybe that was just her whirlwind thoughts. The entire trip she hardly saw the seemingly limitless aquamarine waters laid out below her; she hardly heard the pepper pot of tongues that marked these islands, for all their closeness and likeness, as distinctive. She didn't taste the bland food so particular to airlines of any class anywhere in the world. She was too preoccupied with second-guessing her decision; the voice in her head alternated between Jazz's voice giving her "the Voice," the dry timbre of her father's judgment, and Terry's lofty tones. Nikki's stomach bottomed out with every dip of the plane, and the churning wreaking havoc with her insides didn't settle when the plane did.

She worried that she'd made the biggest mistake of her life, several at once, but knew there was no looking back.

"Come see me ah one ting,
come lib wid me ah one 'nodder."
—ANTIGUAN PROVERB

CHAPTER EIGHT

Her nights were a blitz of dreams from which she often woke up tired. Sometimes she awoke in motion, her feet running, her arms thrashing. Some nights, sleep didn't come at all. Some nights, her father sat in his favourite aged leather chair, quietly berating her. Some nights, she sat on the cream bedspread in Terry's cream-on-cream apartment while he stood over her, calling her a coward. Some nights, Audrey talked at her in Mama Vi's small kitchen, while somewhere Belle laughed. Some nights, it was Jazz giving her "the Voice." Some nights, the better nights, she dreamt of her mother's hands, big and graceful, deeply bronzed and leathery as they worked the clay. Some nights, companion to this image, would be her father, quietly reviewing papers in his office, legs laid across the edge of his desk, the old leather chair teetering, the nicked brown pipe— more of a prop than anything else—hanging from his mouth unlit. Some nights, Nikki's mind, in its dream state, adjusted the picture; it placed the Professor in Mama Vi's world or vice versa. He would be attired in his uniform of shirt jack, khakis, and loafers, hair ever-wild, glasses perched on his ample nose. Her mother would sport her usual faded, ill-fitting dress, the one with the faded violet flowers.

In these dreams, they sat together, laughing and talking with ease she'd never seen either possess. These dreams both puzzled and soothed her.

Nikki struggled to fit in the ample space allocated for her at the Tourism Ministry where all the public service clichés came out to play—from burnt-out and belligerent employees to antiquated processes and the fine art of looking busy while doing nothing. As the minister had personally recruited her, there were stage whispers of "political prostitute."

"Anybody can come ya an' be big shot 'long as dem have foreign accent," she overheard the tourism director complain, the now familiar *chuups* putting the exclamation point on her disdain. Hard not to hear when the voice was pitched to flow through the slightly open door of Nikki's office.

"Anybody can yank," the director's faceless co-conspirator chipped in. "Don't mean dem have anything sensible to say." Nikki got up and closed the door fully, not soon enough to miss the malicious laughter as the pair wandered off.

Nikki had to admit the director, technically her superior, and certainly superior in attitude, got to her with her forked tongue, savage glares, and a too-put-together look that confused expensive with stylish. The woman was right. It was a hell of an upgrade; she had gone from a Harlem basement to the top floor of one of the more prestigious buildings at the edge of St. John's City. Hensen's office, in fact, had a glass wall which opened to St. John's City, sloping away from it. Meanwhile, Nikki's office balcony opened to a colourful water lily pond and the playfield beyond. If she happened to be there late or on weekends, she'd sit outside and watch the shapely young men in sweats and T-shirts, shorts and vests as they chased after a little red ball and ran the length of the cricket pitch. She still didn't understand the game Fanso and Tones had played with drink boxes and coconut boughs in the street as children, but she liked watching. These cricket fantasies were as far as her sex life went these days, despite

whatever soap operas the gossipmongers used to occupy themselves. One of her conditions to herself: if she was going to give
this job a real go, she had to let go of this flirtation between her
and Hensen. It would've just been a rebound, in any case, and
that wasn't fair to him. He seemed to accept this unspoken contract, being all business as he oriented her to her new work place.
Maybe he'd heard the rumours, too. Certainly he couldn't have
missed the news leaked to the media about the perceived "perks"
of her job. It was the talk of the town as one particularly rabid
radio host went through document after document about her
high salary, phone, travel and wardrobe allowances, government
vehicle, and housing allowance. It was more than she'd ever
gotten at any of her dead-end jobs before; true, but she was
working to earn it. For the first time she could remember, she
was fired up about what she was doing, not that that mattered to
any of them. "Make them talk," Hensen told her repeatedly, dismissively, unruffled by the political grief. Truth be told though,
most of the venom was spat in her direction; something, maybe,
to do with her being an outsider, or with Hensen being a man,
or something. Didn't matter, fact was they hated her and made
her adjustment hell. If it hadn't been for Hensen, she might have
given up.

"Wouldn't be surprised if he is the one leaking stuff to the
press," Fanso speculated.

"To what end?" Nikki asked, never having considered this.

Fanso shrugged. "To make sure people know who to blame
when everything go to shit."

Nikki's mouth twisted involuntarily. "Thanks for the vote of
confidence."

Fanso threw up his hands. "Hey, I have every confidence in
you. Politicians, now that's another story."

Nikki's office was the second biggest in the building, in a space previously occupied, she soon learned, by the tourism director.

"You kicked her out of her office?" Nikki demanded, not believing his nerve. "No wonder she hates me."

"She hates everybody." Hensen shrugged, unconcerned.

Perhaps it was this physical proximity, coupled with the fact that he felt like her only ally, that made honouring her pact with herself particularly challenging, though she did; just. Hensen made it difficult when he was being so nice, personally shepherding her around for introductions over leisurely lunches at hotel after hotel, touring remote tourism heritage sites with her, ordering her steamed vegetables and roast chicken from the Hong Kong Palace or ital from the Rasta Shop or roti from Roti King when she was working late. She told herself it wasn't the other unfinished business between them. As for the evening chats on his balcony, that too was mostly business.

Hensen lived in the Lightfoot area, just outside of Sea View Farm, and had a pen where he kept various domestic animals, and some not so domestic.

"My daddy was a livestock farmer," he explained. "I guess I still have it in me."

Hensen lived alone. He and his wife were broken up, he said. "In America, that would have been the end of my political ambitions, eh," he joked. "Here, people talk about a politician personal life, sure, but when it come right down to it, they will vote as they always have. We're not a bunch of hypocrites like them boys up in Washington, giving a man a public thrashing over private business. Meanwhile, half of them have their own skeletons and a good portion have their hand deep, deep in the pockets of the lobbyists. You can't tell me nothing 'bout America, nuh. Remember, I used to live there."

They were sitting on the patio that doubled as the roof of his peach-and-white, castle-styled home. From there, almost the centre of the island, the view of the lights all around—the plentiful city lights in the distance, the spottier village lighting—was magnificent.

Nikki sipped her white wine. "So, in politics, there are no good guys, eh?" she mused.

"Now see, if I say 'yes, you looking at one,' I sound just as pretentious as the ones I'm criticising."

"True."

He shrugged.

"Nikki, you're a big girl," he replied casually. "You know how it go. Truth is, I'm from this community. I used to play in these pastures, used to take my father's cattle through the bush from All Saints to Bottom Village, or Clark's Hill, as it's called these days." He managed to make the "Clark's Hill" sound snooty, never mind that he now lived in a castle. In that moment, Nikki got a hint of his platform persona, the guy he was on the campaign trail. "There's nothing to be gained," he continued, "for me politically or personally in bad playing these people. I love this community. But I'm not gonna pretend I don't like to live well. I do. I've had enough of sucking salt in my youth. I don't need to walk barefoot to prove my moral character. My record speaks for itself. This is one of the fastest-developing residential areas on the island. That's not by accident."

He shrugged. "It's also true that politics is all about compromises, and when push come to shove, it's about party solidarity. So, some decisions might not sit well with everybody, but this ain't no fairytale. I'm not happy with everything or everybody in my party, but I can do more inside than outside, criticising. As for the personal, when I came home, my wife decided life in

Antigua wasn't for her. Her people come from the Caribbean, Trinidad, but she grow up in the States like you; decide her parents didn't go North for her to turn back South. She say in life, you have to move forward, not backward, and far as she concerned, Antigua and the rest of these islands backward. But look around you; ent you livin' better here than you ever did there?"

Nikki wanted to ask him what he knew about how she'd been living, but was distracted and intrigued by the whole "my wife" thing. She regarded him for a long minute. "How long have you been apart?" she asked finally.

"Since just a few months after the election," he replied, easily enough.

"I'm sorry," she said.

But Hensen only shrugged at that.

She looked across and up at him; he stared out at the lights and sipped his vodka and orange juice.

CHAPTER NINE

*N*ikki's ex, Terry, called her office. She'd lied about not having a home phone as yet—no phone, no cell, things moved slowly on a small island. She was getting good at lying to him. He was getting good at pretending he didn't know a lie when he heard one. Every time he called, the excuse of work kept the conversations brief and specific: he'd found a stray piece of jewelry, underwear, lock of hair, did she want it, and by the way was her tantrum over yet?

Then, he started threatening—Nikki couldn't think how else to see it—to come visit for the Christmas holidays. Nikki tried to discourage him, but he was Terry; persistence was his first name. It was what made him a good lawyer; he didn't like to lose. That's how she saw it as she knew both of them must know by now that they had never been the love of each other's lives. She did anyway; and it didn't hurt to admit that, not like it should. That said, something, she figured.

She got serious about organizing her new world, accepting that a visit from him was inevitable.

Carlene, her nephew Tones' common-law wife, helped a lot. Currently on maternity leave from her government job as school watchman, she had the time. "Not like me can run down criminal with dem kinda big belly ya," she joked. "Though true say most ah de gov'ment watchman dem do just wha de job say an' nothing more. 'Mi did see 'im tek up the TV, nuh sar, but me no pay fi catch, just watch.'"

She proved a lively, talkative—if irreverent—companion as she helped Nikki clean, move furniture, and hang curtains in her new, modest green-and-beige wooden cottage, rented with an option to buy at Elizabeth's Estate. It was part of a colonial era sugar plantation, built unto the old stone foundation of one of the outbuildings from the main house. The end of the wrap-around porch overlooked a pond even more beautiful than the one below her office balcony, pink lilies lying placidly on the surface of the water. The owner, a white woman with whiter hair and sun-dried skin, had warned her to stay out of the water; more people she said had drowned in ponds like these, for not realizing the depth of them, than had drowned in the sea.

Carlene's verdict on the place: "Me na know wha mek you waan' lib all de way behin' God back so in dem pile a bush bush. You nah hear 'bout de man dem wha bruk out ah 1735 prison jus' today? Me hear say one ah dem ah rapist, so you can go 'long. Mek me tap 'round people." Tones' other half had an opinion on everything Nikki quickly discovered.

"The sweetness must did real good fi bring dis Terry all de way from New Yark to Antigua fi run you dung," she said, cracking herself up.

Nikki reflected on "The Sweetness." Truth be told, it had never been particularly sweet for her. Terry knew it, too, hence, his still hurtful reference to her "coldness, her frigidity, her uptight closed-off bullshit." Maybe that's what caused him to stray. Maybe the other woman had been abandoned and sensual in a way Nikki was not. Maybe she was everything Nikki was not.

Carlene was oblivious to the dark direction of her thoughts.

"...Tones now," the Jamaican continued, "he got the sweetness, hm hm hm! I woulda married him just for that. And is not just the size of the wood, mind you. Though me nar complain, him penis powerful. But him know how fi use it, too, and let's face it, that ah de important part. Oh Gad, it get me hot just thinking 'bout him." She fanned exaggeratedly.

"Carlene!" Nikki chastised, scandalized.

"What? Girl, I's a married woman; is not like I talking 'bout giving him bun. The man make me feel good. How much married ooman can say that? Is so he adventurous. I think we done do it everywhere; pon table top, pon beach, in car, one time even during Carnival Last Lap right up 'gainst..."

"Carlene!"

"What?!" The hugely pregnant young woman was laughing now, tickled by Nikki's blushes. "So he flexible..."

Nikki turned on her heel, and exited the room, leaving Carlene rolling noisily on her new couch.

"...what, the kitchen too hot?" her niece-in-law roared. "Your Terry needed to give you some good loving. Is that! You'd still be in New York all now."

After that, Nikki couldn't talk to Tones without picturing his "powerful penis," and him and Carlene rolling around on her pristine ivory couch. Carlene smirked, reading her face, easing up as close to Tones as her big belly would allow.

The baby came a week before Christmas, the same day Terry arrived from New York. It was late afternoon. Nikki was making the near-silent journey from the airport with Terry when Tones, at Carlene's request, called her on her cell.

She made a beeline for Adelin Clinic.

Tones paced the hallway.

"How's she doing?" Nikki demanded. "Why aren't you in there?"

Tones looked at her askance. "Who me? Me nar go in dey."

"It's your child; what do you mean you're not going in?" she demanded. "Somebody ought to be in there with her."

"The doctor and nurse and dem in dey," Tones replied, resuming his pacing.

Abandoning Terry to the silent hallway with Tones, a pacing stranger, Nikki managed to talk the medical staff into letting her scrub up and go in to hold the hand of her new, often infuriating, friend. Carlene was sweating and huffing, face twisted in pain, legs high and wide as the medical team hovered. Nikki stood next to her head and tried to smile encouragingly as she took her hand. Largely, it was Carlene who, in between contractions, consoled her, like the old pro she was. Nikki often found herself wishing she was in the waiting area pacing with Tones. But then Terry was out there, too, and she had to admit that she would gratefully avoid dealing with him as long as she could. She did have the presence of mind to feel guilty about the less-than-welcoming welcome to which he was being treated, though a part of her blamed him as well for forcing this visit on her.

Soon, even Terry was forgotten as Carlene suffered through the rest of the birthing process, no longer having words of reassurance for her shell-shocked in-law. Carlene's blood pressure got dangerously high, and the medical team couldn't quite mask their worry. Nikki found herself yelling at Carlene. Carlene responded to the bullying, pushing another son, wailing and screaming, into the world. She didn't even get a good look at him before she shut her eyes and slipped into much needed rest. Nikki was the first to hold him after the nurse. He was tiny, and cried like the world had done him some great injustice.

When she emerged to tell Tones the news, Nikki found him still pacing, and Terry sitting tall and stoic on one of the cushioned seats in the waiting area as though no time had passed. Tones whooped, and Fanso, who'd joined the party at some point, hugged him, and Terry sat stiffly. Nikki avoided his eyes.

"Where's Judah?" she asked when Tones quieted, finally noticing the absence of Carlene and Tones' other son.

"He with the neighbour," Tones said distractedly, pulling out a joint to celebrate the birth of his latest. Fanso dragged him outside, into the shadows, leaving Nikki and Terry alone.

He was angry; his silence on the drive to the house said as much. Nikki's own resentment blossomed anew in the face of his silent reproach. She showed him around her own white-on-white living space perfunctorily, before installing him in her newly made-up guest room.

"This passive-aggressive shit is so tired," he said the next morning, sipping coffee.

Nikki was dressed for work, red to make herself feel strong, and had just placed a telephone order for flowers to be delivered to the clinic. A cloud of snow-on-the-mountain, which Carlene had once remarked was her favourite, set against a large red-petalled poinsettia, always plentiful around this time of year.

"What?" Nikki said, turning to Terry where he sat on a stool at the kitchen island, after returning the phone to its cradle on the wall.

"You don't want me here," he responded tightly, eyes holding hers. "So you go out of your way to make me feel like an inconvenience. It's childish."

Nikki broke his gaze. The kitchen was small enough that she felt trapped. She moved out into the living area, across to the couch, double-checking the contents of her wallet as though some frisky poltergeist might have gone through it in the five minutes since she'd packed.

"Terry, I told and told you it didn't make sense for you to

come," she responded through these motions. "That was very direct. You came. I did not go out of my way to time Carlene's delivery to your arrival."

Terry came to her, standing in front of her, and again the room, even with its open layout, felt too small. "Who is this woman," he demanded, voice quiet but strained, "that you dump me for her, leave me to fend for myself among strangers?"

Nikki pushed around him. "She's family, that's who she is," she replied, as she did so.

"Family?" He scoffed. "These people, who for the four years I've known you, you barely managed to speak of and have never visited? Oh, well, except for the cruise; let's not forget the cruise. I was there, Nikki. I saw how, after tolerating one of them for a couple of hours one night, you couldn't run back to the city fast enough. This isn't about family. This is classic Nikki, running from any real emotion, because she never learned how to deal with it. You used me to buffer you from them then, and you're putting them between us now. "

That pissed her off, and she turned back to him, moving into his space. "Spare me the character examination," she said. "I may be fucked up, but at least I'm honest with myself."

"What's that supposed to mean?"

"Nothing. Just look, I'm getting to know my family. If everything you've said about me is true, then that's gotta be a good thing, right?" Except, it wasn't true. Fanso and Tones aside, she'd pretty much avoided her family since returning. But Terry didn't need to know that.

"Good for you," Terry replied heatedly. "Never mind me. Just sit me down in a corner like forgotten luggage while you hare off to…"

"Oh please, don't act like I dropped you off at East Bus Station and told you to find your own way home," Nikki interrupted, temper rising as well. "You're just spoiled. If it isn't about you all the time, you want no part of it. Well, newsflash, I have a life here."

"One that clearly has no place for me. I mean, it's not like you invited me to be a part of it, is it? You accuse me of being spoiled, but you're the one who ran; you never gave me the choice."

"And you're the one who cheated?"

He actually rolled his eyes at that. "Like that's what this is about."

Nikki didn't answer.

"You know what I think," Terry said. "I think you wanted out of our relationship. You never gave yourself fully to it, not in the bedroom, not anywhere. You never let me in. I told myself it had to do with your upbringing and what a cold, critical shit your father was. That you would warm up. But in four years, you never did. You say you want love in your life, but you don't make space for it. How did you get like this?"

And he looked at her, shaking his head, like she was something alien.

That stung. "You know, this is bullshit," Nikki cocked and fired. "Blame me if it's easier. But you're the one who cheated."

"And you're the one who ran away rather than deal with it," Terry shot back with heat.

But then all the wind seemed to go out of his sails. He turned, took a deep breath, then another.

"Maybe I did it to get a reaction, any kind of reaction, out of you," he said finally, quietly.

Nikki didn't want quiet; her temper was still up. She laughed at him. "Is that your latest line? Infidelity as a test of loyalty?"

He looked shocked and lost, giving her that *"who are you?!"*

look again. When finally he spoke, his tone and words were alien to her...alien, coming from him anyway. "Fuck you, Nikki," he spat.

Just like that, the fight went out of her. She knew he was right in his assessment of her, at least in part. There were times she felt like there was something broken in her, something that wouldn't allow her full access to her feelings or anyone full access to her.

"Why did you come here, Terry? Why are we doing this?" she asked.

"Because I love you," he said, sounding as tired as she felt. "And you won't fight for us. Dammit, Nikki, stop being your father's daughter for once in your repressed life. It's like you were waiting for an excuse to cut me loose. Like you never cared for me at all."

Nikki didn't rush to defend against any of this. Not that Terry gave her room. Uncharacteristically, he couldn't seem to stop the runaway train that his tongue had become.

"Did you care for me? Love me?"

His voice sounded so lost, not like him at all.

Nikki didn't answer, didn't know the answer. Truth was, he was right; it shouldn't have been this easy to just walk away.

"Did you?" he demanded, angry again.

"I don't know," she said. Honesty, finally...honesty she immediately regretted. He looked more vulnerable than she'd ever seen him. He would have hated her, she knew, if he knew how broken he looked, that she was witness to this. She felt like she was seeing him for the first time, getting a glimpse finally of the boy she'd always suspected was in there. She felt no sense of triumph though, for breaking through; wished she could wrap his sense of self back around him and they could go back to lying to each other. They both stood there sucking up each other's air.

He was the first to speak.

"I'll find a hotel," he said, "and get my reservations changed as soon as possible. There's no point, really, is there…"

And like that, he was gone from the room.

CHAPTER TEN

*N*ikki heard him from the deserted waiting area of the small clinic, still crying at the cruelty of being born into the world, his anguished wails a beacon guiding her to the room.

Carlene's face was turned toward the window. Her breathing was heavy, as though each breath caused untold pain. She didn't seem to know anyone was there. How she could sleep through the racket the baby was making, however, Nikki had no idea. Who knew something so tiny could make so much noise?

Nikki took a moment to look at the baby as he wiggled and cried. His face was ugly in its intensity, and his uncompromising neediness made her weak. Perhaps Tones had had the right idea all along—that it was best for anyone not directly involved in the birthing process to stay out of the labour room.

"He look just like 'im father, don't," Carlene's voice, coming from the bed, asked tiredly, startling her.

To Nikki, he didn't look like much of anything; hair plastered to his sweaty forehead, face wrinkled.

"Yeah," she mumbled.

"Bring 'im here," Carlene said, with a chuckle. "Eat like him father, too. De way him ah carry on you would think say nobody nar feed 'im. With him leeching off me, mi sure mek haste lose the weight."

Nikki's limbs resisted the order while Carlene watched her expectantly. When Carlene's look changed to curiosity, a weird echo of Terry's alien look, Nikki forced herself to move. She picked up the squirming baby gingerly, stepping across to the bed, laying him in the curve of his mother's arm, her movements at once hurried and excruciatingly careful. Carlene was still visibly uncomfortable, but she soon had him suckling from her breast.

"Him sweet bad," the proud mother said, stroking her newborn's hair. "Tones say we goin' call him David. You know say David ah one of him heroes the way 'im stand up to Goliath with just the little *caterpuller*. His second name goin' be Amberchelle. That was mi grandpappy name. Tones hate it, but mi tell 'im say this one is at least half mine and he got to name the last one, so. He just laugh and say, 'Okay, okay. Go 'long. But we go call him David.'"

"How are you feeling?" Nikki asked.

"Been better. But..."

"Did you get the flowers?"

"Yeah, see dem there."

Nikki glanced across, and indeed, there they were, near the window, toward where Carlene's face had been angled when Nikki came in. "Nobody never buy me nuh flowers before," the new mother said, pleased, "and you remember say 'snow-on-the-mountain' is mi favourite."

Nikki was surprised at this revelation, but indeed, the rest of the room was bare of anything but medical implements and the hospital-issued crib. "Yes, I remembered," she said. Being around the talkative Jamaican had resulted in lots of Carlene-trivia junked into Nikki's head. Remembering hadn't been a hardship, and getting the flowers had seemed the natural thing to do. It now seemed monumental, as monumental as Carlene asking for her, as monumental as Nikki being the one there to support her through the labour.

"I didn't know it would be so rough," Nikki said. "Was the first one like that?"

"Mhmm," Carlene said, smiling at her baby, now blessedly quiet though no longer suckling. "Well, maybe not just as. Still, wasn't easy. But de memory na linger."

"I don't know about that. I won't forget that experience for a while," Nikki said.

Carlene laughed softly, retucking her breast and shifting the baby. He had closed his eyes and seemed to be sleeping, having exhausted himself on crying and feeding, like he'd been the one doing hard labour for hours. Nikki stared, realizing this was another new experience, never having been up close with a new-born before, never having been the first to hold one, the one to witness him tear his way into the world. Between that and her throwdown with Terry, she felt tired and...alien.

"I can't believe you knowingly put yourself through that again," she mused. She hadn't meant to say it out loud, and her eyes flashed quickly to Carlene's face. But the plump, bread-brown face that dimpled sweetly when Carlene smiled, showed that no offense had been taken.

Carlene only shrugged. "Me would go through anything fi bring Tones picknee dem in the world. Mi love him plenty, you hear. How mi grow up...seeing the things Mammy went through... struggling back ah yard...mi never think say mi coulda love no man so. Seem like man was the cause ah every suffering woman go through in the world. But me love that man bad, you hear. When the doctor tell me last time, don't have no more, try get me fi tie up mi tube dem, Tones wouldn't go for that. True say, he want one daughter bad. Mi wan' gee 'im that."

Her voice was a little sad as though blaming herself for failing.

"What? They've advised you against having more," Nikki demanded, horrified.

"Two time now. Dem come again last night. Tones tell dem straight how it go. Dem say, 'She could die.' Same thing dem chat say last time. Ent we pay all dem money come private clinic fi mek sure everyting straight. Dem too lacking in faith. Ent mi still dey ya?"

"Carlene, don't you think you ought to listen to the doctor?"

Carlene sucked her teeth. "Please. Nikki, look pon dis sweet sweet face. If me did listen to dem before, him wouldn't dey ya. Tones' daughter in de palm ah God hand jus' ah wait fi come in the world. Me suppose to deny her that? Deny him that?"

Nikki didn't know what to say to this. "Besides," Carlene continued, "even if me agree, Tones wouldn't. And is he is mi man, mi husband."

"It's your body," Nikki said forcefully. Carlene's attitude and language, she could barely translate, much less understand.

Carlene gave her a look. "Come on, Nikki, you know ah na so it go. Is him have to agree, not me."

As Nikki opened her mouth to speak again, Carlene finished, "Anyway, it don't matter. Wha natural, natural. Be fruitful and multiply, so God say. And like me say, me love Tones, even more than me love dem picknee, and me love dem bad. He want a daughter, and is me goin' give it to him, not nuh matey out dey."

Nikki had no comeback, and watching mother and child, she felt a wave of melancholy. She might think Carlene's rationale was foolish, but a part of her envied the depth of feeling voiced unashamedly by the younger woman. Carlene loved Tones with everything that was in her. Nikki wondered what that felt like. Everything about her relationship with Terry had been about what she should have felt, rather than what she did. Even now, this pain at the pain she'd caused him felt secondhand, like it belonged to someone else and had been passed on to her. She didn't know this love, this love that ate away even at one's sense of self-preservation. She felt inadequate watching Carlene snuggle the baby. Was Terry right? Was she a husked-out thing? Did this hollowness have to do with how she was raised?

Nikki sighed.

"Wha happen?" Carlene asked, hearing the heaviness of it.

But Nikki didn't have the words for all she was feeling; it was unlikely that she would have shared them, even if she had. Carlene wasn't Jazz after all, and even Jazz might be too far away for this level of sharing.

"Is Terry? Tones tell me say him come with you to the hospital straight from the plane, but now you ya but no sign ah him," Carlene pressed. "Wha happen?"

"Terry's…gone," Nikki replied reluctantly. "No, it's not Terry. It's nothing."

"Is something," Carlene insisted.

Nikki didn't deny it, but she offered nothing further; and the baby stirred, eyes still closed but face puckering up for another round of crying, effectively distracting Carlene again.

Before Nikki left, maybe an hour later, just after Tones returned to the clinic with Judah in tow this time, they asked her to be the baby's godmother.

"Hey, you earn it," Tones said, like he was giving her a prize. Nikki tried not to feel ungrateful, and dredged up a smile.

"Plus," Carlene piped up, "we want you come up with a third name fi him."

"I mean me," Nikki complained that evening, to Jazz, over the phone. "Jazz, you know I don't have a maternal bone in my body.

When I look at him, all I can see is how much she suffered to bring him into the world."

"Well, that's why they call it labour, I suppose," Jazz said, sounding distracted. "It's hard work."

"Joke all you want, but they need a name soon, and I'm blanking."

"Well, Tones is Rasta, right?"

"I don't know if I'd exactly call him Rasta."

"Well, you know what I mean," Jazz said. "His hair's locked, and he's into all that Reggae stuff. You could name him Bob, or better yet Marley."

"Marley," Nikki responded. "That sounds like a girl's name. I don't think Tones would go for that. Besides, he's more of a Peter Tosh fan."

"Didn't they ask you to provide a name of your choosing?" Jazz shot back.

"Still."

"Okay, what's wrong with Bob? Or, better yet, Peter," Jazz suggested.

"*Wha white man name dat you wan' gi mi picknee?*" Nikki said, doing her best imitation of Tones.

"Hey, not bad," Jazz commented, and the sisters laughed at Nikki's mangling of the Antiguan accent.

"Hmmm," Jazz seemed to speaking to someone else.

"What?" Nikki asked.

"How about Imani?" Jazz suggested. "It means faith in Swahili. They should dig that."

"Now, how the hell would you know that? I doubt you could even find Africa on the map." Nikki was incredulous.

"I'm not ignorant, you know."

"Never said you were, sister. I just know that you don't have an

Afrocentric bone in your body," Nikki replied. "Wait, it's that new guy, isn't it? Is he there? Are you living together now?"

"No, we're not living together, but we are together," Jazz shushed. "And yeah, he suggested Imani. What? It's a good name."

"No, it's good, it's good," Nikki said. "Didn't realize you guys were at the sleeping-over stage though. You're keeping me in the dark."

"We're not…we're…oh, shut up," Jazz said.

Nikki smiled. "Well, looka here, looka here, look who's all blushy and not sharing her feelings," she teased.

"Shut up," Jazz slapped back, a smile in her voice.

"What's his name again, something Italian, right?" Nikki tried to remember.

"Giovanni," Jazz supplied.

Nikki laughed.

"What?"

"Nothing, nothing. I'm not hating, not hating at all," Nikki said, still chuckling. "So, he the real deal?"

And Jazz sputtered, sounding hopeful and uncertain at the same time, "Maybe, yes, I think so." She'd been whispering ever since Giovanni had entered their conversation, and Nikki pictured him, an unformed shadow, within touching distance, maybe trying not to listen, on the bed in Jazz's bedroom. She decided to let Jazz off the hook.

"I hear you," she said. "But be sure to send me his stats. Gotta make sure he's good enough for my sister. Too many shades o' shady out there."

Jazz didn't answer right away, and it took Nikki a minute to read the silence, to realize she had led them firmly into the territory of significant others, toward the conversation she'd been avoiding since Terry's aborted visit.

"Look, Jazz, there's nothing to talk about," she said, pre-empting Jazz's efforts to get her to talk about how she was feeling. "Terry and I are over. It's probably been over for a long time, maybe even before it started; and don't worry, I'm not crying into my pillow or anything."

Jazz was in full "Voice" mode. "Maybe that's what has me worried."

"Well, don't. I'm fine. Fine. Fine. Fine." She hummed the Whitney Houston song of the same name, hoping Jazz would play along. They both shared a passion for the pop diva. But Jazz was never so easily distracted.

"Nikki," she chided.

Nikki sighed. "Okay," she admitted. "I'm not fine. But I will be."

She didn't have more to offer than that. "I guess I'll have to settle for that," Jazz said after a while. "But I'm just a call away if you need to talk."

Nikki smiled. "Yeah, talk to you soon."

"Bye," Jazz said.

Wide awake now, Nikki popped in and just as quickly popped out her Whitney Houston's *My Love is Your Love* CD. She wasn't in the mood for sappy love songs; they only made her think of the things she'd lost, or the things she didn't dare reach for. She flipped on the TV to the opening strains of *The Jeffersons'* "Moving on Up." Late-night TV it was then, she decided, settling for another long night of too little sleep.

CHAPTER ELEVEN

"What you doing Old Year's Night?" Hensen asked in that lull between Christmas and New Year's, sitting against the edge of her desk. His blue-and-sunflower-yellow tie was loose, his blue shirt unbuttoned at the neck; he'd given up all pretense of staying late for any other reason than to keep her company. She took a moment to breathe him in, his vintage cologne and underlying musk, his sharp eyes, sharper jaw line, the nose almost too big for his face, smoker's lips though he didn't smoke, the bigness of him.

"What did you have in mind?" she asked, hearing the huskiness in her own voice. They stared at each other.

"Party, Paradise View," he said, eyes still locked with hers, lips curling upwards. "Biggest on the island. Good opportunity to meet all the players, or just play."

The rippling in Nikki's stomach pulsed downward this time.

All the heavyweights were there. There was the Prime Minister, taller even than Hensen; he was bigger, too—ample stomach preceding him. A girl, as red as a Valentine's night, with a Rapunzel-like weave, hung on his arm. There was his deputy, bald spot sweating, arms flying every which way and hips grinding obscenely; another lady of the night, all but disappearing into his bulk. It seemed to Nikki more a conquest than a dance.

"Can't hold his liquor." Hensen smirked. They were all there—
the cabinet ministers, their top allies, even some Opposition
parliamentarians. They were all jacketless with their sleeves
rolled up like they were getting down to serious work. Their eyes
glittered at the shapely, colourful, tightly wrapped packages
waiting to be opened and played with. For her part, Nikki had
splurged on a black dress from Calvin K., very *Breakfast at
Tiffany's*, with upswept hair to match. But these girls made her
feel downright schoolmarmish. *Where are their wives?* she wondered, marveling at the politicians' open profiling with girls a
quarter of their age. She knew they had wives. She'd met some
of them; professional, age-appropriate women, women who didn't
look like they were playing dress-up in mommy's heels and
hooker-glam wear.

"In church," Hensen quipped. "The circus is more fun, eh."

He introduced her to the ringmaster, Kendrick Cameron, top
local businessman and old Antigua Grammar School chum of his.
Cam, as he was called, was red-faced and portly, and, Hensen
said, wielded a lot of influence due to the depth of his pockets.
Except for the unlit cigar clamped between his lips like a prop,
he reminded Nikki of a Norman Rockwell impression of Santa
Claus, a younger and slightly more sunburned, russet-haired
version, eyes blue-green like faded sea glass. His wife, Nikki
noted, seemed nothing like Mrs. Claus; she was svelte and tall,
and her preternaturally youthful face, though beautiful, had a
frozen quality—a brown-skinned Nicole Kidman. She flitted like
a bee seeking nectar, giving the impression of being everywhere
at once, the sour-lime pucker of her lips transmitting disapproval.
Cam, ruddy and boisterous, sloshing a dark liquid that was likely
rum and Coke, the go-to drink in Antigua, seemed her direct
opposite. Nikki couldn't picture them together, but Hensen said
they were—happily so.

Hensen explained that Cam was of Scottish descent, a throw-back to the time when Scots were plentiful on the island; controlled so much of the business in the area now known as Market Street that it had been called Scot's Row. "Now is mostly people like Ben there—the Syrians an' dem," he said, pointing to the country's deputy minister, "that run Market Street." The way he said it, and not for the first time, Nikki sensed a thinly veiled contempt that wasn't there when he spoke of Cam. Cam, he said, was one of them, never mind his complexion. Cam had inherited a one-pump gas station-cum-car parts business-cum-car dealership when his father, a Scot, died suddenly of respiratory failure just after his son graduated from law school.

Hensen described Cam's mother, Rabina, who was a mix of Scottish, African and Portuguese, as a formidable woman. "When it come to business, Cam kinda like her," Hensen said. "His father was kinda softy softy, always sickly."

In his wife, Raisa, Cam had found his mother's equal, Hensen said. "Boys always marry their mothers, right?" He chuckled. Rabina had put up a fuss, of course, despite her own mixed heritage, when Cam had opted to marry brown-skinned, local girl, Raisa Pilgrim. "It was marrying down, the way she saw it," Hensen explained, without seeming offended, in spite of his own dark complexion. The proverbial meeting of the rock and the hard place had resulted in Cam eventually having his way, marrying Raisa. That he could get his own way with Rabina, Hensen said, was telling in itself "…because she wasn't ah easy woman."

With Cam at the helm, Cameron's Automobile Dealership and Service Centre became the flagship of a local juggernaut that touched on every sector—insurance, banking, imports, manufacturing, wholesale, retail, real estate, construction, pharmaceuticals and much, much more. Cam even had a hand in medical laboratory services, vacation planning and tours, aviation, and jewelry design and retail, thanks respectively to Donella (legally Rabina II), Isobel, Aeden, and Bridget—Cam's children, who, Hensen said, he often complained needed to "...go find real work to do." Hensen suspected, however, he was secretly proud they were all entrepreneurs in their own right—albeit in fields he didn't begin to understand. Cam often joked, Hensen said, that he had yet to sire his business heir.

But then, Cam was miles from being ready to surrender the reins, Hensen mused, so that was just as well. Kendrick Cameron was the classic big fish in a small pond, and arguably, Hensen said, the most powerful man on the island. He could easily have been among the most hated, but he had charisma, easily making friends of his enemies, at least on the surface. If he channeled money under the table to one political party, while openly funding the other, well, that was just hedging your bets, right? "And in politics that's what matter right, if you can pretend to get along," Hensen mused, "a long, occasionally joyful marriage of convenience."

Nikki was used to, by now, his mocking contempt of his own profession. It hadn't killed his passion though. She liked that. He was always tightly focused on the goal, and she filed away the crib notes on Cam, knowing that Hensen wasn't telling her all this to hear himself talk.

Eventually, everyone found their way to Cam; when it was Nikki's turn, he greeted her with the same big, boisterous energy and warmth he greeted the boys he'd knocked around with on the St. John's cricket grounds.

"You have a lovely home, Mr. Cameron," Nikki said.

Hensen, who'd been close all night, had wandered off to refresh their drinks, leaving her alone with the compelling bear of a man.

"This? I don't have a thing to do with this," Cam boomed.

"This is all Raisa, my wife. Is she control my life. I just come here to rest my head at nighttime. I just cough up the dollars. Had a certain blue-eyed businessman was after the same spot, too; pulling it out from under him just made the deal a little sweeter. Enough of our lands done sell off willy nilly to dem foreign robber barons, thanks to the short-sighted, grabby-grabby politician an' dem."

If any of the politicians within spitting distance heard him, they didn't let on; not that he seemed to care. And the fact that he was himself, white and blue-eyed, held no irony. He threw an arm over her shoulders, like they were buddies, steered her towards the balcony rail; the other arm, the one with the drink, sweeping the landscape like he had created it. Nikki took in the impressive drop below where they stood, the lights, natural and man-made, in the distance, and further still, the play of lights on the sea water. Nikki recognized they were way above the hotel where she and Jazz had stayed, looking out over the same indigo-coloured water.

"Nice spot, ent?" Cam said, not waiting for an answer. "Best view on the island. Nice, nice view. It cost a good change, but worth it, nuh?"

"It's a very lovely view," Nikki agreed, not sure what to make of him.

Then another hand was there, at the small of her back, shifting her, and a fresh drink slipped into her hand as the old friends, Hensen and Cam, chatted. The night was cool, the hand at her back warm, and soon one too many drinks was bringing down Nikki's walls. It wasn't often she drank like this, but it had been a tense and unsettling few months. Nikki figured she'd earned it, and it felt good to relax.

Soon, she was on the dance floor, calypso tunes blasting. There were other dance partners, a blur of them really, but each time, she was soon back in Hensen's embrace as though he was waiting to reclaim her. Calypso music was the kind of music that invited touching, *back to back*, *belly to belly*, as the song went, so that felt natural enough. Well, with him it felt natural. Better than that, it felt good. Maybe it was the drink, her long drought, or the slow dance they'd been doing in this direction these past months, but Nikki found herself remarkably open to the possibilities, eager even to drink this new wine, become intoxicated by it.

At midnight, fireworks exploded across the sky from all directions, including Cam's backyard; then people danced on into the wee hours.

Afterwards, Hensen took her home and she invited him in. Sex with him felt like a good long draught of chilled coconut water on a blistering day.

"Look, it don't have to be complicated," Hensen said. They were sitting the following evening on the back patio of her cottage, overlooking the water lily pond at the bottom of the slightly sloping yard. It had been the pond that had attracted her to the property; the novelty of having her own backyard pond. The property owner, while she'd warned about the depth of the pond, had neglected to mention the mosquitoes. Still, the lit citronellas doubled as a good mood-setter, if one was looking for that kind of thing. Nikki wasn't sure what she was looking for; she had to admit her body felt more alive than it had—ever. She felt anchored by the pleasant achiness of it, the memories they evoked; she was happy the alcohol had loosened her up without greying out the experience. Still, she fought it.

"I don't make it a practice to get involved with people I'm working with," she told Hensen.

"I had a good time, didn't you?" Hensen asked, easing closer to her. Her body leaned in in response.

"Yes," she said, admitting to herself that it had been the best sex she'd ever had— ever. "Though I was pretty high." And it had been a while.

"Well, maybe we should try it again, sober," Hensen suggested, straight-faced.

"Hensen," Nikki groaned. "This is a bad idea."

"You think too much," he said lightly. "We're just two people. Two big people. Taking a little joy in each other. No harm in that. It don't have to be more complicated than that."

"But it is…"

"It don't have to be."

He kissed her lightly on the lips, pulled back, looked at her, saw no resistance, leaned in again. She kissed him. She liked his lips. They were full but firm, as firm as his hands tilting her head just so, and his tongue battling hers for dominance. She liked the way he nipped almost painfully at her nipples, her skin, her lips. She liked that he seemed to understand a woman's body; the things it needed but couldn't ask for, and that her alcohol buzz had intensified every touch, including the strange battle of wills that made the victory and the taking that much sweeter.

The truth was, she wanted more of him. It had been so long, and she had felt so free, like he was unlocking a secret part of her, a part that yearned to hand over the reins to someone else. As determined and confident there as he was anywhere, he took them firmly and guided her to her own pleasure. It felt good. She was curious to see if it had all been illusion.

Nikki found out that Hensen was just as skilled sober.

"Girl, relax and enjoy it," Jazz coached. "The man's right; you think too much." Nikki's eyebrows shot to her hairline and her mouth hung open.

"Okay, who is this and what has Giovanni done with my sister?" she wanted to know. "This is his doing, isn't it?" She'd been hesitant to tell Jazz, anticipating her sister would've steered her towards examining her feelings for Terry, Hensen, her father, maybe even the midwife that birthed her. In the end, she had to tell Jazz because it didn't quite feel real until she did. But she was bemused by the laughter now flowing through the phone line.

Jazz laughed. "What can I say...Hensen's cute for an old guy, and big; big all over, I bet."

"He's not old; he's like forty-five or something," Nikki rebutted, deliberately ignoring the rest of her sister's comment.

"And you're thirty; that's like a different generation."

"Thirty-one this year."

"Still."

"Wait, are you trying to convince me or unconvince me?"

"Nikk, I wouldn't think you'd need convincing. If he gives good love, give it back."

CHAPTER TWELVE

Nikki was sure everyone knew about their affair, could smell Hensen on her, and read the sub-text of his frequent invitations to join him in his office to discuss this or that. But she couldn't seem to stop herself, had never known herself capable of addiction like this. Finally, something felt good, and she didn't know how to turn away from it. It didn't help that Hensen was as determined in this as he was in everything else, and her usual voice of reason, Jazz, was caught up in her own love affair.

It made it hard to say no to him, to say no to herself, even if it was an invitation to a midday delight in lieu of lunch on the squeaky leather couch in his office. She worried about the open vertical blinds and the glass wall, though they were too high up for it to matter. She worried that the *squeak squeak squeak* rhythm travelled, even over the surround sound blasting of Observer Radio's "Voice of the People." And who could make love to the rambling of the radio pundits? Well, apparently Hensen could, and he was skilled enough that soon it became white noise to her, too; no contest for the music rippling through her, one leg thrown over the back of the couch, the other flopping about over his shoulder. Most unusual, as she peaked, was the absence of shame at this image of her writhing beneath him as he played her like a steel pan, and she tinkled and rumbled and crescendoed; she didn't recognize who that person was, had never before heard her sing in such dulcet tones. It was surreal.

Surreal, too, was afterwards, wandering in the afterglow, while he easily picked up on their work; at times, lecturing her on Cam, or prepping her for the Barbuda meeting.

His voice dipped in and out. "He born here," he was saying. "His father…his father father… his family marry…no outsider… PM's current blue-eyed boy…de Syrian an' dem…native son inside out." She knew the bullet points.

"You listening," he said, snapping his fingers, leaning forward, vaguely irritated. Nikki tried to focus. "This is important," Hensen picked up. "Cam know what his currency is, and we know what his weakness is. And that's how we goin' sell it to him; let him know Lewis interested in the same property. He cyan stan' to lose, especially not to that 'interloper.'"

Nikki ingested it, with difficulty, like it was fungi, slimy with okra.

Cam was not the main thing on her mind, far from it. Hensen was reseated at his desk, Barbuda maps and other papers spread across it, looking as unruffled as ever. Nikki, having cleaned up in his private bathroom, sat at the very edge of his leather couch, where they'd, only moments before, been occupied with business other than Cameron.

"Wait 'til you see Barbuda," Hensen continued, Nikki marveling at the rapidity with which he was able to switch gears. "There's nowhere else like it in the world. Natural, quiet, some good eco-tourism spots like the caves and the bird sanctuary. We don't want to lose that, but at the same time, it could do with some building up. You get an investor like Cam—who surprisingly don't have no substantial tourism investment to speak of— you can make things happen. But Barbudans are a different breed to Antiguans; if they not behind a project, they will shut it down. No two ways about it. With force, if they have to. They forever at loggerheads with central government. They determined, and determined their land mustn't end up in foreign hands."

Nikki watched Hensen's hand, which absently caressed his prized gold pen with the embossing of the Antigua flag, as he talked; her nipples and nether regions tingled at the sense-memory.

"And that's why Cam is so ideal for this," he continued. "He's no foreigner. Nothing he take out or put in going nowhere but right here. The land will have to be leased, which Cam won't like. You can't buy land outright in Barbuda, not even if you Antiguan, though is Antigua sister island. But this is a good fit for him; we just have to make him see it."

"And the people," Nikki said, finally catching up. "They'd have to buy into it, too."

Hensen flicked his wrist dismissively, like the people at the calypso show at Carnival chorusing "gone a gwassa." No need to worry about that, he said, they'd buy in; Cam was the trump card, he said. "He's one of us, trust me." This last was said in that other voice; the one he used on the leather couch and in his huge custom-made teak bed. Nikki's instinctive reaction to it was, to her horror, starting to border on Pavlovian.

They traveled to Barbuda—Nikki, Hensen, and Cam—in a red chopper labeled *Cameron's Charter Helicopters*; Cam's son, Aeden, at the controls. The boy was clearly a bit of a rebel. He was casually dressed in a purple-and-pink tie-dyed tee, a tattoo peeping out from beneath the tattered collar, green cargo pants—more tattoos around his ankles. Handmade sandals clung to delicate-looking feet and wannabe, reddish-brown locks curled over his shoulders, not really laying right. His freckled face was a browner version of his father's. Nikki didn't know what to make of him.

He was as quiet as his father was talkative; the old chums, Cam and Hensen, shouting back and forth at each other on the flight to Barbuda. Nikki was feeling a bit rough by the time they landed, but had to admit that Barbuda was well worth it, from the pink sand, to the neighbourliness of the people, to the red-chested male frigates preening at the bird sanctuary.

"You know, in all my years, I never been over to Barbuda," Cam confessed as they drove along the badly potholed dirt road, past the mountains of sand—products of the booming sand mining industry.

"Really?" Nikki was surprised at this.

"No. Never been," Cam replied good-naturedly.

"Most Antiguans haven't," Hensen piped up. "They have this perception the island backward. Plus, it's not the easiest place to get to, if you don't like traveling on those little planes or by sea."

"Well, I guess that's part of its charm," Nikki said, in spite of the number the flight over had done on her stomach. "It's not the kind of place you'd want swamped with thousands of cruise ship passengers like St. John's."

"No," Hensen agreed. "What Barbuda needs is a carefully managed stream of adventure or eco-tourists."

When they landed back at the helipad in Antigua, Cameron turned to Hensen.

"Put some figures together for me nuh, ole boy; let's see what we talking 'bout," Cam said. "But I'd want to own, not lease."

"Cam…" Hensen began. "You know the rules regarding Barbuda."

"Rules? Ole boy, you know I live to break the rules." Cam laughed.

"Cam…" Hensen began, before a heavy hand came down on his shoulder. Hensen was taller than Cam, and Cam had to angle up to paw his shoulder, but somehow he seemed like the bigger man, the one with the power, to Nikki, in that moment.

"Don't be so negative, ole boy. Just draw up something, then le we talk, eh," Cameron said, before striding off.

"Well," Hensen said, rubbing his shoulder idly. "Looks like we have some work to do."

"And by we, you mean me," Nikki said wryly.

"Well, that's why we pay you the big bucks," he replied.

CHAPTER THIRTEEN

*D*avid Amberchelle Imani Toussaint was christened in the same church on the hill in Sea View Farm village where his great-grandmother had been buried. Despite her promises, it was Nikki's first time seeing her second favourite sister, Belle, since her return to the island months earlier. Belle, in a yellow frilly dress, a style better suited to a child, hugged her warmly, beaming, clearly holding no grudge.

No words were exchanged between Nikki and Audrey.

Nikki took her seat with the other godparent, Tones' car racing sponsor. She'd met him briefly at one of the pre-baptism sessions the church insisted on.

The ceremony was well-attended. The baby cried at the dribbling of the water on his forehead. The proud mother shushed him before slipping on the white gown that symbolized his spirit had been washed clean as snow, and removing the red ribbon she'd tied around his wrist, since birth, to guard him from evil.

Her feelings about Carlene notwithstanding, Audrey went all out for the christening party for Tones' second son, and it seemed as though all the church made a beeline for her backyard. Johnny cakes, saltfish, chop-up, fried plantain, and ginger beer were being served up by Fanso, the chef for all family events. The music was pumped loud but it was Kirk Franklin, Brother Emmanuel, Andre Crouch, Gospel Gems, Gospel in Motion,

Tammy Faye Bakker, Mary Mary, Yolanda Adams, The Winans, Shirley Caesar, and the like, in deference to the Sabbath. But, as the day cooled, someone opened the first bottle of beer and switched the music over to Burning Flames. By the time the dancing started, Man-man, as his father called him, having taken a liking to the name Imani, was resting in one of the rooms in the family house.

Nikki spent most of the party making up for lost time with Belle, while Hensen mingled as only politicians could.

They didn't cut the cake until evening, after Man-man woke from his nap, and fed at his mother's breast, his mother unashamedly smearing some of the icing on the nipple for him to lick.

When the people finally started wandering off, a little less steady on their feet, wrapped plates piled high, Nikki started to help with the clean-up.

"So, is like that now," Audrey's voice barked at her back, startling her.

They were out on the curb, by the garbage skip. Nikki had just dumped one bag, and when she turned, she found Audrey behind her, carrying another.

"What?"

"The boy Stephens, what he hanging 'round here for?" Audrey demanded. "Is you he sniffing 'round? Is that you come back here for?"

"What?"

"You hear me."

"I hear you," Nikki agreed. "But I can't believe what I'm hearing."

Audrey was unmoved, waited as though it was her right to interrogate Nikki about her private affairs; this, in spite of the long silence between them, the blow-up that preceded it, the long silence before that.

"Is this the first time Hensen's come into this yard?" Nikki demanded. "What are you playing at?"

"Play? Girl, I'm a big woman, I don't play. And one thing I know I don't play at, as you put it, is no politician can ever say they use me as no finger towel."

Nikki was speechless.

Audrey dumped the garbage bag in the skip, turned to walk away.

She paused, turned back. "Is not you make big fuss 'bout head-stone for Mammy, say you goin' fix her up?" she pecked. "What happen? You done move on already? Is just like I thought, just like usual. Outta sight, outta mind."

Last word in, she walked away.

Nikki stood beside the skip, blinking back tears, raging in her mind, determined to get her anger and hurt under control before showing her face back at the house, assuming she went back to the house. Except there didn't seem to be much choice about that; her pocketbook was there, plus, she had enough guilt about how she'd blown off Belle before. Also, she'd driven to the christening in Hensen's SUV, and he was still in the yard.

It was Fanso, bearing yet another garbage bag, who found her standing outside.

"Wha happen?" he asked.

Nikki shook her head, her throat tight.

"Wha happen, Nikki? You okay?"

"Who the hell does she think she is?" she demanded finally.

Fanso sighed, not needing to ask who "she" was.

"Nikki, you take everything to heart too much," Fanso counseled. "Most of the time is best to just shake off what Audrey say."

She only stared at him, and he sighed again. "Look, the thing with Audrey, you just have to accept is so she stay and leave it."

"I don't know if I can do that," Nikki said.

"Well, I don't know what to tell you, Nikki, 'cause she not goin' change," Fanso said. He sounded a little irritated with her, and Nikki felt her eyes prickle even more at this. They were victims together where Audrey was concerned; that's how she saw it anyway. What business did he have defending Audrey? But she didn't ask him these things, just hunched in on herself even more, wanting this moment, this day, to be over. Fanso sighed, pulled her into a hug, and she didn't resist. "Don't let her get to you," he said.

They stood like that, hugging at the side of the road in the evening light, oblivious to the strange looks this earned them from passers-by.

"What she say?" Fanso asked, after a while.

"It doesn't matter," Nikki said, drawing back, drawing into herself again.

Fanso eased back, held her at arm's length, looked into her eyes. "That's right, it don't," he said.

Nikki went back into the yard with him, his arm casually over her shoulder. She said her goodbyes, then asked Hensen to take her home.

CHAPTER FOURTEEN

"So, hear nuh, I think I making the girl this time," Carlene said, and Nikki paused, the speared banana from her fruit salad halfway to her mouth. She was working at home on revisions to the Barbuda proposal. It was an option she'd been exploiting more and more lately. It helped her reset the boundaries. She told herself it had nothing to do with Audrey. For his part, Hensen offered little protest, but was due to stop by later as had become the pattern. Nikki hoped to be done with the proposal by then. She and Carlene, who had stayed on as her helper, were on a lunch break; the baby was fast asleep in the bedroom.

"What did you say?" Nikki asked now.

"You hear me."

"What are you saying?"

"You fooly or what? Me pregnant," Carlene spelled out, laughing.

"How can you be pregnant?" Nikki asked. "Mani is only, what?"

"Four month, next month."

Nikki stared at the beaming young woman like she'd lost her mind.

"Why are you doing this to yourself?" she blurted. "You just had a baby. One baby more, from what you've told me, than you should have had."

Carlene's eyes widened, then, as the silence stretched, she peered at Nikki oddly; rather, like Nikki was an oddity.

"What you have 'gainst picknee?" she asked finally.

"What? What? I don't have anything against babies."

"Eh-heh," Carlene tossed back, still wearing that odd expression. "What you be now, 'bout thirty? No picknee, no talk of picknee. That nuh normal. An' don't think say mi na notice how you never wan' hold Man-man, virtually pretend like him don't exist. Now you acting like I doin' something unnatural when is the most natural thing in the world."

Nikki should've been used to Carlene's frank talk by now, but still that assessment hurt and ruffled her. Part of her felt she should leave well enough alone. But straight talk deserved straight talk.

"Carlene, the doctors said you could die if you went back again," Nikki said baldly.

Carlene shrugged. "So? Dem say that before."

"So, what, you want to keep testing until you prove them right?" asked Nikki, incredulous.

"Nikki, just say, 'Congratulations, Carlene.' It nar kill you. The rest of it not none of your business."

And it wasn't. Except she was finding it difficult figuring out where to draw the line, once you allowed yourself to get drawn in. Besides, this was what Jazz always did for her; she would call her on her bad decisions, challenge her to examine them more carefully. She thought what Carlene was doing was dangerous; wasn't she allowed to say so?

"Carlene," she tried again, but her niece-in-law interrupted her with, "You know what, you just vex 'cause you want picknee and nuh hab none, is that." Her usually pleasant face was twisted in anger.

Nikki felt like she'd been slapped, felt the sting and burn of it. It was instinctive; she slapped back. "Well, I just hope Tones loves you half as much as you love him," she said. "Because what you're allowing him to do to you is abuse. You're just too blind to see that."

Carlene laughed. "Well, then the two ah we mussa two blind mice, because seem to me somebody need fi pick the yampie out dem own yeye."

"Meaning what?"

"Meaning mi na tell you nutten 'bout the married man you dey carry on wid, but you feel say you can chat to me 'bout me an' mi husban', mi husban', not no part-time lover, making picknee," Carlene said, her voice a disturbing parody of its usual teasing lilt. Nikki's heart hammered.

"What are you talking about?" she asked, not recognizing the small voice coming out of her.

Carlene sneered. "What? Big city chick like you what have the answer for everybody life, na know say she ah de keep-ooman like de Antiguan-dem does say?"

Keep-woman. Outside woman. Mistress. Adulterer. These words chased each other in Nikki's head.

"Hensen is divorced," she said finally. Weakly.

"Heh," Carlene huffed, "All me know ah he might lib ya, an' she lib dey ah foreign, but no divorce paper never sign, and him trip-dem overseas not all business all the time. But is Big Apple you come from, right? You done hip to all that already, right?"

Each word felt like a gut punch, leaving Nikki winded and speechless. She turned mechanically back to the kitchen island, picked up her fruit bowl, dumped the rest of her lunch into the garbage, then turned to return to her home office. At least, that's where she thought she was headed. She wasn't quite sure of anything at the moment.

Hensen admitted the lie when confronted. "My wife don't have nothing to do with us," he argued reasonably. "Besides, I never lied to you. You made assumptions. Anyway, nothing here secret; if you really wanted to know the deal, all you had to do was pay attention." There was no hint of remorse, and Nikki wondered how she could ever have been fooled by him. He had an answer for that, too. "You were so desperate when I found you, I could smell it on you," he said. "It's like I been saying, this is the best opportunity you've ever had in your life."

When had he said that? she wondered. Surely, she would've remembered that. But then, how could she trust her memory when she'd completely forgotten herself?

The argument, in the end, was swift and one-sided; the only regrets were the ones she carried. *So much for that*, she thought, as she measured this Hensen against the one she thought she'd known all along. Turns out they weren't that different.

Hensen, it turned out, lived two lives. True, his wife had tired of small island life, as he'd said. But they had not tired of each other; or perhaps it was their interests were a lot more intertwined than earlier admitted, making divorce an unprofitable prospect. Or maybe it was they still loved each other. Like so many of the local politicians, with both a wife and a woman or more on the side, his wife didn't seem to mind her husband's other life. It wasn't a politician thing, perhaps; maybe not even an Antiguan or a Caribbean thing, but here was where Nikki lived now, and it was hard to think in broader terms than that. It was hard not to feel like a little girl who didn't fit, who didn't get it: a "big city chick" and a fool.

Nikki drove long hours late at night along the same streets, feeling closed in. That was the problem with living on 108 square miles; after a while, the scenery, even in the dark where shadows shifted from night to night, started to look the same, and there was nowhere new to escape to.

Sleep allowed her to dodge her thoughts for a time. It wasn't restful sleep, but, at least, it wasn't the wearying chase of her dream-filled early days on the island. In fact, there were no dreams at all, simply a sense of restlessness and only skirting the surface of sleep.

"I tell you 'bout them politician," Fanso said sympathetically. She hadn't brought it up with him, of course, but then in Antigua, she didn't need to.

"Besides, blood will out like they say," Fanso continued.

"Meaning what?" Nikki asked.

"Well, you know they say he an' the Prime Minister spring from the same sucker, an' you know how *he* love woman," Fanso said.

"Who says?" Nikki wondered. This was news to her.

"Everybody," her brother replied. "Where you been living?"

Where she'd been living the past few weeks was a reality of increased boldness from co-workers and casual vindictiveness from Hensen, like shutting her out of negotiations with Cam and taking credit for her work on the Barbuda project. Fanso had anticipated this as well. "Better to leave on your own steam than have them stamp up on you," he advised. "I know how they can be."

After a while, something, perhaps his lack of surprise, clued her in. She asked, "Did you know about us? Me and Hensen?"

He shrugged. "Figured."

Nikki took a breath.

"And you knew he was still married?"

Fanso shrugged again. "Everybody know that."

Nikki didn't know how many more licks her body could take; she was still feeling tender from her encounters with Carlene and Hensen, and it hurt more when it came from unexpected places. "Not everybody," she said. "Not me."

Fanso couldn't have missed the betrayed look she was giving him then, but he didn't comment on it, and Nikki found she couldn't let him off the hook. "Why didn't you say something to me?" she demanded.

"Nikki, you're a big girl. I figured you knew what you were doing," Fanso replied with another of his shrugs.

Carlene was still a presence in her life. She had shown up, baby in hand, the week after their fight, ready to go to work, as though nothing had passed between them. Nikki could only stare.

Carlene had favoured her with a challenging smile. "What, friend an' friend can't talk straight to one another? Besides, far as mi know, nobody never fire me; so mi still hab work fi do."

Nikki let her get on with it. After all, it needed to be done.

She complained to Jazz, though, on the nights when even the pretend sleep didn't come, and driving the streets proved more torture than relief. Her sister, miles away, listened as only best girlfriends do despite the late hour.

"I don't understand them," Nikki griped. "On the one hand, they're up in all parts of your life with their opinions. But at the same time, they just look the other way, you know, like when your so-called man is knuckling you."

"Knuckling?" Jazz asked.

"Yeah, stepping out," Nikki explained.

It hit her then that the island lingo was weaving its way into her speech. Didn't make her any less of an outsider, the one without the inside information. Moving to Antigua, Nikki realized now, hadn't just been about a job, or about Terry, or even Mama Vi's death. She'd wanted to touch something, be connected to something. It was a feeling, Jazz aside, she'd never known. One she imagined she was feeling when Hensen touched her just so, or Carlene teased her, or Fanso cooked for her; a feeling that now felt like it had all been an illusion.

"Are things any better at work?" Jazz wondered.

"About the same," Nikki admitted. "I'm furniture, essentially."

"Hey, that's my sister you're talking about," Jazz said.

"Well, your sister is a damn fool," Nikki flipped back.

"Well, you know, don't be too hard on yourself; you're not the first fool for love in the world," Jazz said, not unkindly.

"Love," Nikki responded. "It wasn't love. Massive amounts of lust, but not love."

Jazz hesitated. "Okay, but..."

"I'm not hiding from my feelings, Jazz," Nikki said soberly. "I didn't love Hensen. I was sniffing after his pheromones like a bitch in heat, but he didn't have my heart. Okay?"

"Okay."

Nikki continued, "I just feel like a fool, that's all. Letting him anywhere near me was only one of several stupid moves on my part. And the job I moved here for, well, feels like it was part of the package, and now, whatever I imagined coming here was supposed to do for me, is gone. I don't know."

Admitting she'd screwed up was one thing; admitting she was well and truly lost, even to Jazz, cost her.

"So, why don't you come home?" Jazz asked. "It hasn't been quite a year; you can get back on track."

"What track? I was nowhere near the track and you know it," Nikki said.

"Come home anyway," Jazz coaxed.

"Home," Nikki echoed. Terry had said that to her. She hadn't known where home was then either. It had never been New York, not really. She didn't say that, though.

"After packing up my life," she said instead. "After boldly jumping off the fence? I don't think so."

"No one's keeping score," Jazz lobbed back.

"I am, okay?" Nikki stressed. "I am."

Jazz sighed, but let that line of argument give up the ghost.

CHAPTER FIFTEEN

*N*ikki trudged up to the church graveyard. Without a headstone, it should've been impossible to find Mama Vi's grave site; just another lump of soil amidst other lumps. But the neem tree, budding again, was the foul perfume that led her to the spot.

She hadn't specifically decided to seek out her mother, to keep coming back to her resting place. It was as much to distract her from her life as her renewed visits to Belle. She'd got into her government-issued car one evening after work, and feeling like she'd driven every road she possibly could, on a whim, took the road home. Technically, that's what that violet house in Sea View Farm was. It was, at any rate, the beginning of all things Nikki. It didn't feel like home, but maybe some part of her remembered it, or maybe there were no more roads to drive.

Belle was happy to see her as always; Audrey, taciturn as ever. Soon, Nikki started leaving work earlier and earlier, quit going in on weekends; there was nothing there for her anyway. She spent virtually all of her spare time in Sea View Farm, visiting with her mom, then visiting with Belle. One was quiet, the other chatty and spirited. She might still drive afterwards, but sometimes she was able to go home and go to sleep. For those nights, maybe, she kept coming back.

She'd even grown used to the smell of the neem.

As time stretched, so did Nikki's visits. She bought a straw mat from the Blind School in town, kept it in the trunk of her car for just this purpose. Nikki would sit on her mat, back resting against the neem. She'd sit there, stirring eventually when evening gave way to night, drive the car farther into the village, then sit well into the night with Belle on the front porch. She didn't say much, didn't need to; neither her mother nor Belle required it of her.

Audrey hadn't said anything beyond the very basic courtesies to her since the christening party, though Nikki was sure she was more than up to speed on the latest turn her life had taken. It was old news now anyway; even her co-workers had lost interest. Besides, Audrey had probably known all along, like everybody else, that Nikki had been playing herself for a fool. Maybe that's what she'd been trying to tell her, which made her the only one who did try to warn her. Still, Nikki couldn't bring herself to see it as a kindness.

"How you doing, doo doo?" a gravelly voice said, startling her.

Nikki searched for the name, then remembered, her mom's funeral. "Ms. Adams," she said. She stood, dusting her bottom reflexively though the mat, effectively shielded her from grass and dirt.

"Marisol, remember," the woman corrected. "How Mammy today?"

"Mammy?" Nikki asked, bewildered.

"Yes, your mother," the woman replied.

"I don't understand."

"She feeling good today?"

Nikki wondered if the woman was crazy, noting that they were alone in the cemetery. Marisol caught her look, laughed heartily, held out a hand. "Come, I have something to show you."

"I came across it the other day," Marisol said, after pouring Nikki some chilled sour sop drink, milky and sweet.

They were in a small breakfast nook just off the kitchen, clearly a recent addition to Marisol's home. It felt new. It had the feel of an enclosed veranda, and an orangey-yellow glow, thanks to the natural light of late afternoon, and the floral cushions—there were lots of sunflower cushions. Marisol stood in the middle of this bright room, looking around, arms akimbo. "Now, where did I put it? Oh yes!" She clapped her hands at this, like a delighted child, and exited the room.

"I had completely forgotten this," she said, returning to the nook with a battered, hardcover Bible of indeterminate colour.

"So many things over the years, you know," she mused. "Anyway, what must have happened; your father must have donated some of his pictures to the museum. A few years ago, they put on this exhibition on village life. Imagine! These pictures were all up in people bedgrass. It had people moving house; you know, like they used to on the back of a big truck; people sitting down to dinner in some squeeze-up space; people riding donkey; people washing clothes in the old-time iron bath; two woman out in the middle of the street cussing; everything everything." The burgundy wig, so contrary to the rest of her with her sensible shoes and long skirt, bounced as Marisol shook her head. "When I was in school, art was something else altogether."

Marisol "hmph'd" her disapproval before sitting next to Nikki and gently pulling a folded, somewhat faded, news page from the Bible. She spread the single, creased page out on the wicker and glass table in front of Nikki. It was a mini-pictorial on the museum exhibition; it wasn't hard to pick out her mother's face. It was the largest image on the page, and in close-up. Mama Vi's lips were parted as though frozen mid-speech, and her eyes were old.

Nikki found she could not look away from the faded image, the creases lining her mother's face, her old eyes, her head tie with the single-plaits peeking out. She found herself wondering what Mama Vi and the Professor had been talking about in that moment. How did he talk to her to get her to talk to him? What had made her able to relate to him? Had he seemed glamorous to her, perhaps? Or removed? Safe? Someone she could use as most people used a priest in his confessional or a psychiatrist? Did his alien status loosen her tongue, free her, as the life she'd been dealt couldn't? For, even in the midst of the pain, trapped in that moment, Mama Vi seemed so free. Free to indulge her pain. Nikki was evidence that whatever connection Winston Baltimore and Mama Vi had forged also had freed her mother to indulge her passion, if not her love.

"May I keep this?" Nikki asked. She hadn't intended to ask, but there it was. She couldn't take her eyes off this image of her mother. Couldn't bring herself to let go of it. Marisol hesitated, clearly hating to part with it as well.

"I don't have any pictures of my mother," Nikki explained, the words coming unbidden. "Sometimes, it's hard to remember the details of her face. I remember the colour of her skin. Like mine. The shape of her face shadowed against the sun. That she was tall. Like me. How imposing she seemed, bigger than my father, bigger than everything. She was tall and hard, and...and... there."

The words flowed like run-off rushing down the hill to the sea after heavy rain, murky and unstoppable.

Nikki stared at the picture as she spoke of "The way my hand felt in hers the first time I came back to Antigua...the feel of her hands in my hair...plaiting...tying a ribbon...powdering skin."

She was crying quietly, bewilderedly, but crying, and Marisol patted her, gently, reassuringly. She seemed neither surprised nor embarrassed by the tears. Nikki was chalking it up to life's recent hard knocks. But who knew what Marisol read from her tears. "Keep it," the older woman said. "Keep the picture." Nikki felt grateful warmth spread through her. She remembered how she'd wanted to be rid of Marisol at her mom's funeral, and at this un-expected kindness, felt ashamed. "Thank you," she said gratefully, and Marisol patted her some more, fed her sour sop drink, and listened.

It was the first of many conversations between them; one-sided affairs with Marisol carrying the weight of the dialogue. Nikki didn't seek it out. Marisol took to the habit of waiting for her up at the church while she visited with her mother, inviting her down afterwards for a sip of whatever fruit juice was on ice. During one of these visits, squeezed in between her time with Mama Vi and Belle, Nikki learned of a guy in the village who custom-made headstones. She mentioned, in passing, her desire to have a head-stone done for her mother. She didn't mention how Audrey had called her out on having been so easily distracted from the project. Since then, it had niggled at her, but she hadn't actually done anything about it, not unlike her derailed professional life.

Marisol had recommended Edwin highly. Nikki found him sitting on his front step, one leg chopped off at the knee. Leaning heavily on a makeshift wooden crutch, he took her around to his cluttered back yard where there were slabs and lion heads in various stages of readiness.

"So, what you want on the stone?" Edwin asked.

She didn't know.

She worked out a price with him and promised to return. Marisol suggested, "As a face is reflected in water, so is a person reflected by his heart."

"Plenty words," was Eddie's only comment on that, gap-toothed and serious.

Marisol insisted it was perfect. She pointed it out to Nikki in the Bible, Proverbs 27:19, as she explained, "I was just remembering what you said, you know, 'bout how her face won't come in clean, how it wavy wavy while her hands solid, you can see them, grasp them. So, that's what you should heng on to. Mama Vi didn't live in a world where you leave your heart out for dew and blight. Her hands did all the talking for her. That was the window to her; never mind all that nonsense 'bout the eyes being the window to the soul. Everything she felt, she spoke with her hands. The heart is what matters, and, child, you knew her heart; just remember her hands."

Nikki wasn't sure she followed the logic, but she appreciated the effort. "Too bad there isn't one about hands," she said.

"Oh, there is, Jeremiah 18:6, 'Behold as the clay is in the potter's hand, so are you in my hand,'" Marisol intoned from memory. Nikki was flabbergasted; she hadn't been raised in a religious household, but she doubted everyone who had, knew the Bible inside out. Marisol misinterpreted the reason for her surprised look. "Oh, the Bible have something on everything," she said with a delightedly infectious and girlish giggle. "It's not the book of life for nothing. But Proverbs 27:19 is the one, trust me." So, inexplicably, Nikki did.

She asked Edwin to inscribe the words found at Proverbs 27:19: *As a face is reflected in water, so is a person reflected by his heart.* "And a pair of hands, if possible," she added.

"Anything possible," he replied, insulted. "Is Edwin you talking to, nuh."

So, Mama Vi got her headstone, against which Nikki leaned, seated on her straw mat when she went to visit; Audrey, who'd surely seen it, offered no comment. The bit of newsprint, meanwhile, Nikki now carried tucked into the crease of her planner.

CHAPTER SIXTEEN

"So, guess what?" Jazz asked, joy masked by a strange tentativeness.

"What?"

"Well, I... how're you doin', you okay?" Jazz replied.

"Girl, I'm okay. I told you," Nikki said. It was a lie and yet not. Work sucked, and she wore her shame like a character out of a Nathaniel Hawthorne novel, and in this strange universe, listening to Marisol pound away at her piano while sipping oversweetened guava juice, was a weird kind of comfort. If she counted being able to avoid Audrey while visiting with Belle, which she did, she was doing okay. "Small comforts," Nikki murmured, settling into her pillow.

"Huh?" Jazz inquired.

"Nothing, nothing; what's up? What's up?"

Jazz's response, when it came, was clearly worried. "You don't sound like yourself."

Who's that? Nikki almost asked. Instead, she let out an odd bubble of sound somewhere between a sigh and a giggle. She could go through an entire day and think she was doing okay, and all it took was Jazz picking at the lies she told herself, and she wanted to blurt everything she hadn't been aware she was feeling.

"Nikki, I'm worried about you," Jazz said.

That makes two of us, Nikki thought.

"Jazz," she said, letting her annoyance bleed through. "What's up?"

Jazz was silent for a long time.

Nikki blew out an exasperated breath. "Jazz, can we please not do the couch tonight? We've gone in circles over all this so much, I'm dizzy with it. It'll all work itself out, or it won't. Next subject."

"You sound so bitter," Jazz said.

"Maybe I am," Nikki acknowledged.

Jazz had no comeback.

"Jazz," Nikki sighed. "Just tell me why you called."

"What, I can't call my sister?" Jazz asked, her voice off-key.

Usually, you don't, Nikki thought. Mostly, it was Nikki who called. Sometimes she resented her own neediness and the increasing distraction of Giovanni in her sister's life. But she didn't say any of that; waited instead for Jazz to speak. Jazz's stalling meant it was big, and Nikki's stomach was doing a sort of tumble and roll in anticipation.

"Okay," Jazz said finally, "I do have news, but I'm not sure if it'll cheer you up, or just make things worse."

"Only one way to tell," Nikki said tightly.

"Well, I was thinking of coming to Antigua this summer."

Her first instinct was that Jazz was coming to check up on her, and she had mixed feelings about that. She was a grown-up, after all, but it would be good to see each other face to face again, touch, stay up all night, feel her damn feelings.

"For Carnival?" Nikki asked.

"No, after; like late summer."

"Well, you're welcome anytime; you know that," Nikki said. "But you really don't have to check up on me." *Liar*, said the internal voice which sounded every day less like her sister and more like her mother, or more like her memory of her mother's voice. Maybe it was her voice.

"I'm not checking up on you." It was Jazz's turn to be exasperated. "I'm getting married."

The way she bit off what else might have followed told Nikki that Jazz was as startled by the abrupt announcement as she was. So much for beating around the bush.

"You're what?"

"Well, I didn't plan on blurting it out like that, but, yeah, that's my news: Gi and I are gettin' ready to jump the broom…in a manner of speaking."

Silence, and silence and silence: Jazz waiting for Nikki's reaction; Nikki, too, for that matter, then an eruption of sound, and somewhere dogs covered their ears in agony.

At the end of all the hurrah, Nikki had learned of Jazz and Giovanni's plans to marry and honeymoon at Sandals Antigua. She'd learned, too, that she was to be maiden of honour, and that a small wedding party, consisting of Giovanni's parents and best friend-slash-best man, Jazz's mother, and "the professor," would be coming to Antigua. Before she had a moment to panic about that, she'd been recruited to make the bookings, somewhere not too far from Sandals. "But not too close either," Jazz joked.

"Jazz, I am so happy for you," Nikki said. She was; kind of happy-sad like sunshine through rain. "The devil and him wife ah fight," Carlene had said once, describing this effect, and Nikki could certainly agree, because they were going all out in her stomach.

"Yeah?" Jazz asked, maybe hearing that mixed-upness in her voice. Jazz was downright psychic when it came to her.

"What do you mean, 'yeah'? Of course, yeah," Nikki responded. Sunshine it was.

She asked to speak with Giovanni. If he had been asleep, surely the babble of voices and shrieks had woken him by now. Unless, of course, he slept like the dead, a state of grace she'd envy him. He was the kind of Zen character you either loved or hated, she'd found. She'd never met him, of course, but they had spoken— briefly, awkwardly—a time or two over the phone.

"Hey, Sis," his Barry White baritone greeted. He had a voice that made her think of teddy bears; from the pictures Jazz had emailed, he was all bronzed, lean muscle and angles.

"Well, aren't you two sumthin'?" Nikki greeted back.

"Yeah, I've been thinking about it for a while," he said, sounding shy; shy and happy. "Think maybe I took her by surprise."

"No he didn't," Jazz piped up, in the background. Both Nikki and Giovanni laughed.

"Well, I'm happy for you; congrats," Nikki said. He said thanks and was about to ring off when she said, "But listen here, treat her right."

"The best," he said with all the promise in his voice that true love brings. Then Jazz was back on the line chatting about this plan and that; Nikki catching only about a third of it.

Two things of significance happened to Nikki before Jazz's return to Antigua. First, Fanso called.

"So, you still not talking to me?" he teased.

When Nikki couldn't find words right away, he sighed. "Look, Nikks, I'm sorry. The last thing I wanted was for you to get hurt," he said. "But I mean, everybody know everything in Antigua; didn't see how you could not know 'bout Hensen. I figured you knew what you were up to. I mean, you're a big woman."

She felt like a little kid, a chastised kid at that, like it was her fault for not dipping into every pot of gossip. According to gossip, she'd slept her way into her job, and she wasn't thrilled with herself for proving everyone right on that one.

Fanso was still talking, "…like that song go, 'all man ah dog,' even me."

She really wished he'd shut up, but she couldn't find her voice to tell him so.

"Sister, sister," Fanso crooned. "You precious to me, you know that. That not goin' ever change, even if you never talk to me again. It didn't change all them years, all them time you pull 'way from us. It not goin' change now. Been so ever since you walk in the yard that first time, looking scared scared. You precious to me. Like I just wan' put my arm an' dem round you, protect you."

"You didn't though," she challenged in a small voice. She hated how needy it sounded.

"Want me beat him up for you," teased Fanso, easing the awkwardness. "All I need is a dark corner and a two-by-four."

That broke her. She laughed. Truth was she wanted Fanso in her life; he was the only person in Mama Vi's family who made sense to her, made the terrain make sense.

"Hold that thought," Nikki was able to tease back.

"So," Fanso said, on a relieved breath. "How goes it, and when I goin' see you on my back patio again? Must be all skin and bones by now, and there wasn't much of you to start with."

She laughed again, as Fanso made it easy for them. Despite his own hard-knocks upbringing, Nikki realized this had always been his role.

"Seriously," he said. "Saturday."

"Okay," she agreed.

"Listen, I have something I want you to take to look at when you come," Fanso said.

"What's that?" Nikki asked, clearing her throat, finding talking easier now.

"A draft of a business plan Twenett and I knock up," he said. "I applying for a loan through this small business scheme the government cook up for election. I figure if they givin' it 'way, I might as well take it. Don't get me wrong, I not for sale, but that's for me to know. I want do my own thing, though, and this goin' open the way."

"Not sure how much help I can be," Nikki admitted. "But sure, I'll look at it."

"Okay, see you Saturday then," he said.

"Saturday," she agreed.

The second big development before Jazz's big day was Nikki's new job. She got a call from Kendrick Cameron—the man himself, not an assistant. Next thing she knew, she and Cam were sitting in a private booth at a dimly lit Chinese restaurant, Shanghai Palace, Hong Kong, or some other suitably generic name in a country where, inexplicably, Asian eateries were a dime a dozen. Cam settled his bulk against the red pleather as he asked, twirling a still-plastic-wrapped cigar between thick fingers, "So, what are your plans?"

"Plans?"

"Well, I'm assuming you wan' get back to work," he said, with knowing eyes.

His voice was uncharacteristically low, even with the lunch-hour rush being over. Except for the ancient Asian woman, with the kabuki-like makeup and what looked like chopsticks sticking out of her elaborate black-as-coal bun, holding court at the cash register, they had the place to themselves. Still, Cam spoke like they were in a confessional.

"If you ready to work, I have some work for you," he said. "I like that proposal you put together on the Barbuda project." He saw her surprise. "Come now, I look retarded to you. I know who did the work, and it was good work."

Nikki felt herself warm to the compliment like a dog unused to a kind touch. She was able to hold her tongue, though, wait to see where he was going.

"I already tell Hensen I passing on the Barbuda project," Cam continued, and that shocked her. Sure, it had been quite some time with no project announcement, but she'd figured that was the pace of politics. She felt a small measure of satisfaction as she imagined Hensen's reaction to that.

It was to be his big election project. "Jobs guarantee votes," he'd said. Plus, Cam was his old grammar school chum. Must explain why he'd been more bullish than usual at the office…when he was around the office, that is. He'd been gone a lot. "Up north," the gossipmongers stage whispered, "to visit his wife."

Nikki moved beyond the vague curiosity that brought her here to nosh on sweet and sour chicken with Cam to genuine interest.

"This close to the election, that Barbuda thing likely to be a hot potato," Cam was saying. "Make somebody else take on that headache. For my money, I looking elsewhere. I done tell Hensen I'm willing to pour some money into a development at Blackman's Ridge. I wan' you put it together for me."

Nikki scoffed. It wasn't likely she'd get that assignment. How to explain that to Cameron, though, without discussing why she was persona non grata in the office? "Not likely," was all she said.

"Because…"

"Well, I'm not my own boss, am I?"

"Do you want to be?" he asked.

She felt like they were on two different roads. "What do you mean?"

"I'm not asking you to work for the Ministry of Tourism on this," he said. "I'm asking you to work for me."

Nikki almost laughed out loud. Whoever said in America, you can be anything, clearly had never heard of Antigua where a tumbleweed like herself could land plum positions without even applying.

"What you say?" Cam continued. "We can call you a consultant. All you northerners like that word, eh?"

Cam laughed; Nikki didn't.

The sound ran its course, the laughter lingering afterwards in his eyes. "I'm just saying," he said finally, "you don't strike me as a woman who like to be idle, and God know, the way ole boy have his foot on your neck, you don't even have room to twitch. I figure you itchin' to get out from under."

Nikki's face burned, but she remained silent. She was interested; they both knew that. If nothing else, it'd be the perfect "fuck you" to all the jerks at Tourism enjoying her fall from grace, and to the king of the castle himself. Nobody, not even her father, could say she'd failed then.

Cam sipped his Cavalier and Coke casually. They were playing poker, but Nikki lacked a major card.

"I still have a year and change left on my contract with your 'Ole Boy,'" she said.

"Leave that to me," Cameron said.

She smiled cynically. "And what would I owe you for that?"

Cam laughed, his big Santa Claus face flushed, eyes dancing, and then took a deep drink of his rum and Coke, draining the glass.

"Call it a bonus." He chuckled.

Nikki kept her own counsel on this one, talking only to her mother, sotto voice, about it. To Mama Vi, she admitted her fear of trusting her own instincts; after all, they'd failed her in the

not-too-distant past. She admitted she didn't trust Cameron further than he could be thrown by someone much stronger than
her. But she acknowledged as well that going to work at Tourism
daily was making her heartsick, and she craved the little spark
of...something...that Cameron's offer ignited in her. Mama Vi
offered neither comfort nor advice, of course, but Nikki had known
before Cameron slammed the hundred-dollar bill on the counter
before the implacable Chinese matron, what her instincts were
telling her.

CHAPTER SEVENTEEN

*N*ikki gained her second client before even signing the contract with her first. It came when, after reviewing Fanso's plan, she'd suggested some alterations, and offered to rework it for him. "Okay, well, while you at it, put a consultancy fee in there," he said.

"Fanso, I'm not asking you for money; come on," Nikki replied.

"I know you're not," he said. "But this is business, right? Well. Hey, they giving 'way the money. Why shouldn't a cut of it go to you for your services? After all, you help me get the capital."

"I haven't yet," she reminded him.

He grinned. "I'm not worried."

Meanwhile, client number one, Cam, took her by helicopter to Blackman's Ridge, landing on a roughly groomed table at the summit, which seemed a bit out of place amidst the old ruins and wild plants. He showed her the old sugar mill and other ruins on the site, the green valley it looked out onto, a valley which stretched for miles, curving up in the distance, into other hills. He spoke of his plans to create an escape for high-end tourists. "Money people," he called them, as if he wasn't one of them.

"We could even bring some of them in by helicopter for a little extra," he said. "They have a sort of panoramic view of everything, and look, they even in walking distance of the beach. Plus, the chopper service could take them on tours; drop them off wherever they want."

Cam painted in broad sweeps; the details hardly seeming to matter. He slapped his son on the shoulder and joked, "Give this one a chance to build up himself."

The son was, as Nikki remembered from the Barbuda trip, silent. His only reaction was to drop his shoulder, effectively slipping from his father's grip. But Cam didn't seem to notice or care.

"This even better than the Barbuda idea, eh," he continued, still in good humour. "No botheration Barbudans. Nothing to get bothered 'bout. Closer to everything. All the amenities, but still with a sense of being away from everything. And it's not your typical beach resort, though it's within easy access of the beach. I want it to be a getaway, a spa, if you will. You know how them European and American money people always having some kind of breakdown, especially the famous ones. Don't know what hard living is, but they 'suffering from exhaustion.' Well, we have to position ourself to take their money. What you say?"

Nikki liked the place, she had to admit, and could see the possibilities. "Aeden here know the place well, so anything you want to know, just ask him," Cam offered.

She glanced at the son, who still seemed to be off in another world. She tried to guess his exact age but found she couldn't. Twentysomething, maybe. Today he had on baggy, knee-length pants, an old-time shirt jack like her dad might wear, worn leather sandals, some kind of wooden necklace thing, and a broad-rimmed maroon hat, like she'd seen on cricketers, over his pseudo-dreads.

Aeden dressed like a kid, Nikki decided, indifferent to matching

and style, caught up in the colours or some other obscure something. She wondered if he wasn't a little bit mentally challenged.

From the son, she glanced up to the blue sky, with its spatter-
ing of thin clouds, and back down to the lush valley—where all
manner of fruit trees and vegetable beds were laid out before her.
She had to admit it was a little bit of heaven.

"Who owns the land?" she asked.

"Well, that's the best part," Cam said. "Government. Some of
it, down in the valley, lease to farmers, but for the most part, it
just sitting there doing nothing, waiting for somebody with deep
pockets to do something with it."

Nikki chuckled at his casual assessment that this land, which was
single-handedly lighting up her day, was sitting doing nothing.
She marveled at how casually Cam joked about his own wealth,
his seemingly cavalier approach to business. His crudeness was
weirdly off-putting and attractive, at once.

"It feels wrong and right at the same time," Nikki told her
mother later that day, though she had to admit it felt more right
than wrong. Besides, she was tired of being in limbo. It was time
to take a chance.

"Cockroach no hab no right inna Fowl House."
—Antiguan Proverb

CHAPTER EIGHTEEN

*J*azz looked different. That was Nikki's first thought as her sister stepped from the plane. She was watching from the observation deck at V.C. Bird International.

It wasn't the hair, which fanned out around her face much as it always had, despite Jazz's best attempts to tame it into a long braid. She hadn't gained or lost any weight; nothing noticeable anyway. But it was her look; she seemed light, and happy and in love. Jazz glowed.

She was walking with a tall, broad-shouldered, dark-skinned man. Several hundred shades lighter and they'd have been Barbie and Ken; so perfectly matched did they seem.

And they were oblivious to all around them; none of that travel weariness, despite two hours in-transit in Puerto Rico.

Nikki and Jazz hugged eagerly when Jazz finally stepped out of the arrival area. And when Jazz was done with her, Nikki was swept up into another pair of arms. It felt comfortable. Nikki felt like she'd known Giovanni for years; she really couldn't find any fault with him, though a part of her still wanted to. The look Jazz wore told Nikki, more than the diamond ring she flashed, that this was for keeps.

"I'm so happy for you," she said, and not without irony added, "Welcome to paradise."

She took them to Sandals, saying she had strict orders to bring them to Fanso's for dinner that night.

At Fanso's, they were joined by Tones and his brood, including Carlene, now noticeably pregnant. "Forever pregnant," Nikki had taken to calling her in her mind. Carlene might have found it offensive had she known, but then again, she might have laughed. Either way, it helped lighten the situation from Nikki's perspective, and as far as she was concerned, whatever worked.

"You longing to taste my hand, nuh?" Fanso greeted Jazz, sweeping her up into a hug.

"Don't get jealous," he told Giovanni when he finally returned her to the ground, "See mine here." At that, he pulled Antoinette close, and she favoured them with a shy smile.

The mood was festive, the drinks—Cavalier and Coke and Wadadli—flowed, the pot of seasoned rice was bottomless, and the CD player spun tunes by soca artists Nikki was finally beginning to tell apart, from "Faluma" by Barbados' Square One to Trinidad's Machel Montano's "Jumbie" to Antigua's Noel Browne's "Never Miss a Fete." After dinner, the children camped out in front of the TV, playing video games, while the adults hung out on the patio.

Tones invited Jazz and Giovanni to come see him race cars at the John I. IV and V Grounds. "I can't get this one to set foot inside the grounds," he said of Nikki.

"Not my cup of tea," she concurred.

"Is a nice experience, though," Carlene piped up. "Plenty people, and plenty excitement fi de children dem. Is like Carnival."

Roll it, per the fading strains of Alison Hinds' instructions, in spite of her lack of a waistline; she immediately closed her eyes and threw herself back into the music. Tones smirked and got up to join her; win'ing up behind her, he stretched his arms around her middle.

"Speaking of Carnival, how was it?" Jazz interjected, smiling at memories of her one and only Carnival.

"Don't get me started on that," Fanso said.

"Oooh, Lord, here we go again," Tones said dramatically. "Fanso, let it go. The calypso show done." In his arms, Carlene leaned back and laughed, and Nikki noted how happy they looked, how right they seemed, like Giovanni and Jazz, snuggled into each other on one of the patio chairs. As if reading Nikki's thoughts, Carlene turned to Tones, just then, conversation already forgotten, singing, along with Destra's "Bonnie and Clyde." Around her, the ole talk continued as Fanso asserted, "But dem tief!" and launched into his usual tirade on the calypso judging.

The Professor arrived with an entourage—a former teaching assistant he'd never admitted to having a relationship with, and her toddler, Marcus, who sported the characteristic Baltimore eyes and hair. Nikki and Jazz exchanged looks. The sisters knew vaguely of this chapter in their father's life but weren't aware of an actual ongoing relationship. The presence of the boy and his mother was a surprise.

Bernadine, Jazz's mother, was livid.

"He has a lot of goddamn nerve," she fumed, as she brought her luggage into her room at the Inn, located just up the road from Sandals. Nikki and Jazz trailed with more luggage. "'This is Lorene and Marcus.' Fool thinks he's nineteen, thinks he's still some kind of stud. As if he ever was. I took pity on his island ass when I gave him the time of day, and look at my thanks. Bringing his ashy, bastard offspring around me like…"

"Mom," Jazz snapped, and Bernadine caught herself. Her eyes flicked to Nikki, who was fixated on a lone sugar ant crawling up the wall.

"Well," Bernadine finished, defiant, "it ain't right, is all I'm sayin'."

"It's over, remember." Jazz sighed. "Current topic, my wedding."

"Well, I hope you let that Gi-Gi know what for…" her mother went on.

Jazz sighed, and Nikki, bored with the ant, stepped outside for some fresh air, Jazz's and Bernadine's voices fading behind her.

Looking over the balcony rail, she caught sight of her father settling into a poolside chair, while Marcus, who should've been tired from the flight, ran the pool's perimeter.

The boy, though shoeless, was still dressed in the jeans and Wolverine T-shirt he'd arrived in.

"Not too close," the Professor called out, his voice sounding simultaneously tired and indulgent. He'd never sounded like that with her. Nikki stepped back, not wanting to be seen.

"It's weird seeing him like this," she remarked to Jazz. "He's so different, like the sharp edges have gone dull or something."

It was the night before the wedding, and the sisters were having a bachelorette party for two on Jazz and Giovanni's beachside balcony. Giovanni's best man had taken him out for his bachelor night, with Tones as their guide to Antigua's pleasure spots. "Just looking, no touching," Jazz had teased before they'd left, even as Giovanni leaned in to the kiss she'd offered.

Jazz and Nikki had opted to stay in, and Jazz had put a kibosh on any notions of hiring a stripper. Not that Nikki had any idea where to get one in Antigua; after all, they didn't do anything so bold as advertise in the Yellow Pages. Besides, she was enjoying this alone time, just catching up. The table between the sisters was littered with bottles, shot glasses, limes, and cherries.

Jazz shrugged. "So maybe he's being a father to one of his three kids. One for three; the Knicks don't even have that kind of game."

Nikki nodded at this. "Still," she added, "I have to say, I'm a little bit jealous. Get that. Of a one-year-old, or is it two? Three? How old is he anyway?"

Jazz shrugged again. "Ask the Professor. He's certainly not about to volunteer any information to his daughters."

"Heaven forbid," Nikki agreed. It was familiar territory, bonding over derision of the father they'd never shared.

"I was always jealous of you, you know," Jazz confessed after a time, and a few more drinks.

Nikki was stumped, and wondered if she'd already had too much to drink.

"Jealous of me?" she asked.

"Ooh, yes," Jazz declared, a bit too loudly, clearly over her limit as well.

"Why?"

"You had him, I didn't," Jazz said. "They split; no more Daddy. I was no older than that boy is now when he checked out of my life. I know you said he wasn't much of a dad, but you had him. I got to hear all the time from my mother what a cold prick he was."

Nikki considered this. "He was a cold prick," she mused. "And I never had him. Never did. I was just a project to him, that's all; and a disappointing one at that." It hurt to say it even now.

"Yeah, but you had him," Jazz insisted, with the kind of intensity and honesty liquid courage brings.

Silence descended, as each chased her thoughts as much as one could through a haze of alcohol. Jazz's feelings were a surprise to Nikki. Jazz was the bright-sider in their relationship, the no-baggage holder. But clearly Nikki wasn't the only one with mommy or daddy issues. It stirred a weird discomfort in her. She kind of counted on Jazz having it together, and yeah, it kind of bugged her, the insinuation she had it better for having had the Professor, especially coming from Jazz, who knew her insecurities better than anyone. Nikki didn't know what to do with any of these feelings, so she took another drink, encouraged Jazz to do the same, as they toasted to "tomorrow" and her "wedding day" and "her honeymoon" and "life happily ever after." Somehow that last hope lifted them from the maudlin to the happy phase of drunkenness and they embraced it. They sang Whitney's "How Will I Know" to "My Love is Your Love," until hotel security came to quiet them down. This amused them, no end. "Busted," they chorused, laughing even more loudly, before passing out, wrapped up in each other on the room's obnoxiously bright bedspread.

They made the wedding on time, if a bit hung over. Well, Nikki felt hung over; Jazz looked radiant in a simple, white, cotton dress, with red hibiscus in her hair and love in her eyes. It was held on a rising in a white gazebo overrun with purple and red bougainvillea and backdropped by the Caribbean Sea. Wind nipped at stray strands of Jazz's hair, despite Nikki's ample gelling. She wore hardly any makeup, only a simple pinkish gloss. Her eyes shone like a cat's at night, never straying from her husband-to-be. And Nikki's heart swelled and contracted almost painfully at how beautiful, and in love, she looked. After the "I dos," hotel staff released yellow-winged butterflies that danced around the small party before becoming airborne. And when the couple kissed for the first time as Mr. and Mrs. Giovanni Levy, everyone misted up.

Fanso insisted on having them over after the nuptials for a proper wedding reception. They danced on his patio, well into the night. Nikki even glimpsed her father and Lorene, Marcus' mom, dancing when Fanso broke out the old jazz, soul, and calypso CDs. "Ain't Nothin' like the Real Thing," "You're All I Need To Get By," "Love's in Need of Love Today," "Try a Little

Tenderness," "Do Right Woman, Do Right Man," "Melda," of all things. "Just Because," "Smoke Gets in Your Eyes." "Shiny Eyes." "Unforgettable." He even spun some Ella, one of Nikki's favourites, "Someone to Watch Over Me."

Nikki felt a wave of sadness overwhelm her as she kissed her sister goodbye, finally, around midnight; she was happy for her, but unable to shake the feeling that she was also losing her. Her father distracted her from her thoughts with a puzzling request to meet him for a late breakfast. They'd hardly spoken since his arrival on the island, as much a product of his preoccupation with his ready-made family, as Nikki's efforts to avoid him.

At breakfast, near the inn's pool, he presented her with a small stack of black-and-white notebooks. The binding was coming apart, and the edges were curling up and yellowing, but that had little to do with why Nikki hesitated.

"Lorene found these when she was cleaning up my office, shortly after moving in," he said. Nikki didn't allow her shock at the news that he was already living with Lorene, a woman his daughters had only just met, to show. At least, she hoped it didn't. Perhaps more shocking was him letting anyone mess with the mess in his office. Sure, it looked like a hurricane had been through it, but he didn't like anyone picking up his debris, or hadn't in the past.

"It's the journals of my summer here in Antigua," he was saying. "My personal journals. I hadn't been here since I was a boy; I didn't have any family left here by that time."

"Why are you giving this to me?" Nikki interrupted.

"Don't worry," he said in what sounded to Nikki like a teasing tone, unfamiliar as that was. "It's nothing that will embarrass you, I don't think. Me, perhaps, but probably not. It's all in the past."

"Why are you giving this to me?" Nikki asked again.

He shrugged. "I see you back here and I have to ask myself why."

"And the answers are supposed to be in your old diaries?" Nikki scoffed.

Unperturbed, Professor Baltimore shrugged, and Nikki wanted to throw the fragile books at his smug face.

"Why did you send for me?" she asked, and it wasn't the question she'd intended to ask. Even the Professor seemed ruffled, for once. For a long time, the question lay on the table between them, untouched, like the books.

When he opened his mouth, her father's words were unexpected. "You have her eyes, you know. Not the colour, of course, but still her eyes," he said, "and the shape of her hands, though not so much the measure of them. Your hands are soft; hers had lived lifetimes."

Nikki felt her eyes burn, willed herself not to cry.

Her father chuckled, a sound as dry and thin as cobweb strands. "I was alone," he said, returning, she realized, to her question. "My divorce from Bernadine, or rather Bernadine's divorce from me, had just gone through. I told myself I could make something out of you. More than Violet could, at any rate, in that yard. Give you a real chance. That's what I told her, and she wasn't a sentimental woman; she saw the wisdom in it."

Nikki had affected, unwittingly, that rigid pose, the one she always used to survive conversations with her father. Part of her, a great part of her, believed that after raising so many children alone, Mama Vi simply hadn't wanted to do it again. This feeling battered, now, against her walls, and she became desperate to end this conversation before the walls were breached.

"In the end," her father said, "I think maybe I just wanted a piece of her, and maybe she wanted to give me that. Between us, words were difficult."

He pushed the books at Nikki gently. She started to speak again. "Why?"

"Because I think you need them," he snapped irritably. "I don't."

With that, he was on his feet, moving heavily toward the room he shared with Lorene and Marcus. Nikki was left with the aging books and that now familiar feeling of things shaking loose inside her.

CHAPTER NINETEEN

Winston Baltimore, Antigua Journal, First Entry

It was one of several possible research sites. There didn't seem to be anything special about it, at first. In fact, there were other, stronger prospects:

All Saints, because it was the meeting point of three parishes—St. John's, St. Peter's, St. Paul's—hence the name.

Liberta because it was one of the first free villages, beginning shortly after Emancipation in 1834.

Otto's, which, I've found, is full of history, including the execution of conspirators of a failed 1736 anti-slavery insurrection in Otto's Pasture.

Parham...once the center of activity, the town, before being eclipsed by St. John's in the 1700s.

The slave dungeon at Parson Maule's lends some appeal to the area of Seaton's, a coastal village and one-time port town like Parham.

But then, there's also a dungeon at Blackman's Valley. The etymology of the name remains obscure, but the land there is fertile and is used to good effect by farmers from neighboring villages. There was some appeal in focusing the study on this point of convergence.

...But it is Sea View Farm, ultimately, that compels, and, I've come to acknowledge, not for strictly anthropological reasons. Though as a cultural touchstone, it is a community worthy of note. This is a village, after all, that grew up around the unique cottage industry of pottery making in the post-emancipation era, the craft surviving, much intact to this day. There's the dynamic of the matriarchal nature of Caribbean *culture, and how the structures of slave society and now village life both perpetuate and reflect that. Of the villages considered, nowhere is this more evident to me than in Sea View Farm, where the women are the backbone of this cottage industry, and mothers and fathers of their households. And there are other sub-plots related to this tale...the link to Pre-Columbian Antigua, as, according to the lore, knowledge of the locations of clay deposits was handed down to the enslaved Africans by the Caribs...the links to home, as the enslaved, in turn, drew on skills brought from Africa in crafting something uniquely Creole. Here, too, are the seeds of entrepreneurship, as commercial enterprise bloomed in the face of the demand for household utensils due to the post-slavery rise of free villages. Sea View Farm and these remarkable women were at the center of it.*

I want to study the process, and the rhythms of their life, and how the past and present connect. Connect the dots.

Everybody said, "Check Mama Vi."

Vi...

She confirmed it for me; this village is where I need to be. I've always had a weakness for women, especially strong and complex women who, by dint of their personality, make me feel challenged. The kind of woman Bernadine had been in the beginning. Of course, it never lasts.

Weak and predictable, I may be, but the chase never fails to get my adrenaline going. But she was unimpressed by me; her eyes and cocked head holding a challenge...

Nikki asked Cam's son, Aeden, to take her into the Valley on foot.

"Do you know anything about a slave dungeon through here?" she asked as she waded behind him through the thick bush, which scratched at her legs. Shorts had been a bad idea.

"Tanty might," he said, his voice soft and rusty like something barely used, or perhaps worn from overuse. She doubted it was the latter, though, given the brevity of his answer. As for Tanty's identity, Nikki had to figure she'd discover that in due course. She continued along behind him, half wondering what she'd gotten herself into.

The bush thinned out and soon, they were in an area where neatly laid and irrigated beds of vegetation lay. A young woman in big black boots, jeans, a shirt, and hat worked alongside an old woman, probably in her eighties, who wore heavy boots and an old dress.

"Uptown, you come check your sparring?" the younger woman teased Aeden.

"No," he mumbled, colouring. Given his serenity around his dad, Nikki couldn't help being curious. Now wasn't the time, though, for idle wondering. She stepped up as he made the introductions. "This lady work for my father. Her name's Nikki. She wanted to see the place. Wanted to find out 'bout some dungeon or the other, too."

"What your daddy want with here?" the girl challenged, her voice suddenly hard.

"Sadie," the old woman said warningly.

"No, Tanty, is one thing for this one to come through here looking for Little John. Little John is a businessman and I not standing in the way of nobody making a living, even if is from selling weed. Man must live. But wha he and he father have scoping out the land through here?" Sadie responded, agitated.

Weed, Nikki thought, finally placing the slightly sweet, slightly tangy scent he wore as consistently as he did his oddball clothing. It had tickled her nose, familiar and yet foreign, ever since the Barbuda trip. *So*, she thought, *Cam's son is a pot head*. Still, his father, who gave off the air of knowing everything, and had certainly known of Aeden's visits to the Valley, seemed to have no qualms about him behind the controls of a helicopter.

"Relax yourself, girl," the old woman said. "Ent we have a lease?"

The girl was cynical. "Like that would stop them."

Ignoring her, the old woman turned to Nikki. "What you want with that dungeon?"

"I just read about it, and I was curious, I guess," Nikki responded.

The woman studied her for long minutes, sizing her up. Then she nodded. "Sadie will take you. My knees an' dem can't make it up that hillside."

The dungeon was hidden behind more bushes, built of stone and brick and tucked against the hillside. Had she not had a guide, Nikki knew she would never have found it; it being a small dark cave, with two or three steps leading up to the opening. She got a chill when she stepped in—stooped over, as she was not able to stand all the way—and saw the dots of light dancing across the stone face. The place felt alive.

"What happened here?" Nikki asked in a hushed voice.

Sadie shrugged. "Tanty is the best person to say."

"This was a plantation?" Nikki asked.

"Like everywhere else," Sadie said dryly.

"I saw the mill," Nikki said.

"Hm," Sadie said, "an' me see the helicopter. Didn't think much of it at first because Aeden does sometimes bring people in here, you know, for the view. Now, I real curious. What you all want with this place?"

"I'm not at liberty to say just yet," Nikki said.

Sadie's eyes hardened and she turned away. "I have to get back to work," she said.

Nikki followed her out.

When they reached the bottom, Aeden was nowhere in sight and Sadie returned to ploughing her row with sharp, angry movements. Nikki took the opportunity to talk to Tanty. The old woman readily shared stories handed down from her parents and grandparents about how the dungeon, like the one at Parson Maule's, the one Nikki had read about in her father's diary, had been one more place of torture for black people on the island.

"Bakkra would stick them in there as punishment," Tanty said. "I imagine it feel like being buried alive: all manner of insect, hardly any air, and just the darkness. When I was little, I was afraid to go there; thought ghost was in there. My Tanty, she said the spirit of them that dead there might still be lingering, but I was from their blood and they wouldn't do me no harm. She said we mus' respect it and remember. We mustn' play there. That wasn't no place for play. It was to stay so, so we could remember how neaga people suffer in dis country."

Nikki remembered how alive the place had felt to her, and felt that chill again, despite the sun's intense glare.

When Aeden returned, there was no question of where he'd been or with whom. The perfume he wore was stronger, his eyes drooped lazily, and a little smile danced around his lips. Nikki fixed him with a glare of her own. He merely turned and began the trek through the bush with a careless wave goodbye to Tanty and Sadie. Nikki followed him out.

CHAPTER TWENTY

The summons, when Nikki got home from her day trip with Aeden, came by way of a message on her voicemail.

"This is Audrey; give me a call."

Nikki didn't call back right away; wasn't sure she planned to, really.

The second call came from Fanso. "Audrey call you," he said, without preamble. Just as she opened her mouth to tell him he didn't need to act as Audrey's intermediary, he said, "You have to come to the hospital."

Her first thought was that Audrey was sick. But then, he said, "It's Tones."

Tones lingered in the intensive care unit for four days before he died. He'd suffered a severe head injury when his bike ran into a Mack truck on the All Saints Road. He lingered, comatose, but never woke up again.

Nikki kept vigil with a ragged-looking Fanso, and intermittently, the other Hughes boys. For Nikki, it was the first time seeing the boys since Mama Vi's funeral. Carlene was in another room at the hospital; her blood pressure having risen dangerously high at the news. Her children were being cared for by Fanso's wife, Antoinette.

Audrey came and went, Nikki or Fanso driving her back and forth, as she couldn't leave Belle or Columbus for long. Audrey had decided to keep them in the dark until they absolutely had to be told. Belle's sombre mood had Nikki believing, the times she went to collect Audrey, that Tones' mother wasn't at all fooled.

Audrey was stoic, held her body stiffly, saying nothing on their rides back and forth. Once she mumbled angrily, "Neva like dem damn bikes." But that was it.

Nikki found herself remembering speeding along the same highway to Sea View Farm in Tones' car; the engine so loud they had to shout to hear each other.

It was easier, she found, to be with Carlene, who drifted in and out of sleep and cried incessantly, even in her sleep, than it was to stand vigil over Tones, waiting for everything to stop.

Finally, it did.

She was the only one at the hospital at the time.

The Hughes brothers had mostly returned to work, and Fanso was on the road taking Audrey home, with plans to swing by his house to see his family, have a shower and change. Though Nikki had been expecting it, it still rocked her. She kept expecting Tones to open his eyes and fill the room, and their lives again, with that infectious smile and that infectious spirit.

She didn't cry until she got home that evening, after calling Fanso on his cell and having him turn around, after they'd made arrangements to have Tones taken to Straffie's Funeral Home, after she'd broken the news to Carlene and held her as she cried.

Audrey's stoicism had held. Fanso, though, had cried and cried without shame.

Nikki's own tears felt like fire on her cheeks; lava rumbling up from a disgruntled volcano.

Audrey insisted on burying Tones as quickly as possible; said it was the best thing for Belle. She barely gave the death notice time to run before the day of the funeral arrived.

Nikki missed it as she held Carlene's hand through another birthing. It was déjà vu, holding her sweaty hand as she laboured to force new life into the world, a world that had been horribly altered. The labour was exhausting, Carlene's spirit weak. But eventually she came, the girl Tones had always wanted. She lived only a couple of hours. Carlene held her lifeless body for as long as they would allow after that.

It seemed to Nikki too much all at once. Mama Vi. Tones. The longed-for baby girl. The only thing to come out of it, perhaps, was the final caving of the wall that had come up between her and Carlene. The younger woman leaned heavily on her and she found she didn't mind the weight.

Audrey refused to come to the memorial service for little Toni Winsome Toussaint, refused to bring Belle or Columbus, saying it was nonsense and she didn't want to upset or confuse them any more than they had been.

Carlene's wails filled the church as Marisol plunked out "In the Sweet By and By" and "Shall We Gather at The River?" And within the hour, Toni Toussaint was laid to rest in a coffin hardly bigger than a shoe box in the churchyard cemetery. There was no after-party as Nikki remembered for Mama Vi, as there surely had been for Tones; just a restless Carlene pacing Nikki's guest room well into early morning when Nikki finally slipped into sleep.

"Maybe she could stay at Farm," Fanso suggested several evenings later. He was perched on the rail of Nikki's back patio, having brought Judah and Imani to visit with their mom.

Nikki scoffed at his suggestion. "That's just what she needs. You know she and Audrey don't get along. Audrey didn't even come to the baby's funeral."

"I don't think Carlene noticed," Fanso said lightly.

His affability, usually his best quality, bugged Nikki on this hot and muggy night. Maybe it was the pile-up of confusing emotions; from the high of Jazz's wedding to the new job, to Tones' and Toni's deaths. Maybe it was just Fanso and his cut-Audrey-some-slack attitude. Whatever the reason, Nikki found she was prickly with irritation.

"She gets on my damned nerves," she said fiercely, causing Fanso's eyes to snap to hers, eyebrow arched at whatever he saw there. Nikki ranted on, "She did with Toni's funeral the very thing she does with everything, same thing she did with Mama Vi's funeral, with Tones' funeral. Just what Audrey wants, and everybody else, and whatever they need or want, be damned."

"She grieving, too, you know," Fanso said mildly.

"Coulda fooled me," Nikki said.

She was damned if she was going to pussyfoot around this. She was tired of everyone walking on eggshells around Audrey, like her feelings were the only ones that mattered. Carlene was the one who'd lost her husband and baby in a matter of days. It would do them all good to remember that.

"She is a fucking, controlling, know-all bitch," Nikki hissed.

"Baby sister," Fanso chided.

The familiar endearment couldn't cool Nikki's anger, not this time. She was outraged, righteously, she felt.

"Oh, like she doesn't walk around judging every fucking body," she continued, voice rising. "What makes her off-limits?"

Fanso breathed deeply as he walked over and gently, but firmly, closed the balcony door, sealing them out while apparently working on his state of calm. Ever the family diplomat, when finally he spoke, he didn't disappoint. "Look, Audrey's Audrey," he said, "but she loved Mama. She loved Tones."

"Yeah, she loved Tones so much he had to run away from her to live his own life; she loved Tones so much she couldn't spare an hour for his daughter's funeral," Nikki argued back.

"And wha you be? Her judge and jury?" Fanso said, his temper rising now, despite his breathing exercises. "So, she don't grieve the way you think she should; don't mean she don't grieve."

"I don't get you," Nikki retorted nastily. "She treated you like shit, yet you're always defending her. What are you, a masochist? She pulls this shit because all of you make stupid allowances for her, so she doesn't have to think about anybody else's feelings. You all are so…"

"So what?" Fanso cut it. "Stupid? Country? Small island?"

"I didn't say that."

"No, but you think it."

Nikki had no response to that.

Fanso sighed. "Look, Nikki, I don't blame you for keeping yourself to yourself all these years. First, you were little, shy, scared. Then you were big and we were hundreds o' miles away; outta sight, outta mind. Besides, time longer than rope, right? But then Mama died, and you realized that time is a joke. That's why you here. I get that. I don't judge you for that. But whatever problem me and Audrey have, is mi sister that, and yeah, she knocked me 'bout, plenty plenty, but she was real to me. You, I couldn't hold on to you. You were barely there, even when you were. I hated Audrey sometimes, but she was real."

Audrey was real, and she wasn't. It hurt to hear it, especially from Fanso, but Nikki supposed she'd asked for it. He wasn't done, though, and much as he said he didn't blame her, Nikki certainly felt put in her place.

"She show me her face, you show me your back," Fanso was saying. "But you know what? It don't matter. It don't matter!

Family is family. It wouldn't hurt you to throw off your touchiness once in a while and remember that. You too touches, jack, make every little thing wan issue."

His words felt like punches, and Nikki stood there too shocked to react. Then he glanced at the door and did his breathing thing again, and Nikki wondered what else was bottled up unsaid. When finally he moved, he attempted to throw an arm around her and she shrugged it off, dropping heavily onto the balcony bench. He sat beside her.

"Family is family," he said firmly.

In that, Nikki heard all kinds of unspoken expectations; that she should forgive Audrey every slight or harsh word, that she should overlook the hurts, that she should nurture a familial bond that had all but atrophied. She inched away from those expectations as surely as she inched away from him.

When Fanso spoke again, there was tiredness and affection in his voice.

"I remember, must've been your second summer here," he reminisced. "We were playing at the beach, a picnic. I remember it was a holiday. Plenty food, people fuh days, plenty everything, and we were just wild with excitement. I end that day getting my ass cut 'cause of you. I went to bed hating you that night. All 'cause of this stupid game Tones and I used to play, dunking each other to see how long the other could hold his breath. That summer we let you in on the game, held you under, pressing harder when you start to struggle like we did with each other. I wasn't trying to hurt you; it was something we did all the time. When we finally released you, you were carrying on so much, Audrey, Mama Vi, everybody come running. Mama lifted you up outta de water. Audrey grab Tones, and I come out the water just knowing I was goin' get it from somebody…"

And as he spoke, suddenly, Nikki remembered that day vividly, remembered the feeling of drowning, the fear that had consumed her as the boys' hands pushed at her. She remembered crying in Mama Vi's arms, and being wrapped in a big brown towel, and standing in the sand, sniveling, huddled in the warmth of that thick towel as Mama Vi beat Fanso; it was the only time Nikki'd ever seen her do that. She remembered, too, losing sense of whom she was crying for, Fanso or herself.

"...I resented you then," Fanso continued, "the princess who was more precious than gold. All the softness Mama Vi had for you, she didn't have for us, for me. I resented you for every lick I got from that tu'n stick. But you were my little sister, princess or not. Not loving you was not an option. And the welts were still on my skin when I come, trying to make up. Brought you some *fowl batty* from the vine down by the outhouse as I remember and is so you screw up you face."

They both chuckled at that.

"Family is family," Fanso continued, "And I know this 'bout Audrey, too. She might not ha' liked Tones' choice of Carlene, and, tell you the truth, it didn't really have nothing to do with Carlene. Nobody would ever have been good enough for Tones. Tones knew that, too; that's why he wasn't vex with her. But none of that matter, 'cause she would still take in Carlene if she need to. Because is family she be. Simple as that. You don't get to pick and throw 'way family like sour dumms."

That same night, Nikki lay on her bed, planner out. As had become the pattern, she gave in to the impulse to pull from the flap, the creased bit of newsprint. Time slowed as she studied her mother's face. Still unsettled from her fight with Fanso, she searched that face as if for clues' as if her mother's face, with its deep lines and eyes of deep knowing, would show her the way. It was a yearning, though sometimes muted, that she hadn't been able to shake since Audrey's "Mama dead" of what seemed a lifetime ago. At its strongest, that feeling was like a living force, her mother's presence, or rather the absence of it, shadowing her. At times, she couldn't help thinking this was the root of all her missteps, that she'd never had a mother to help her make sense of the world as mothers do for daughters. Maybe that accounted for Jazz's earthiness; that her mother had been there, a steadying force. But what did she know; maybe family was overrated as she'd always suspected. There was no doubting, life had been simpler, if far from happy, before she'd become entangled with this one, before emotional entanglements of any kind.

A dull thud somewhere in the house caused her thoughts to scatter. She got up to investigate, and found Carlene passed out in the bathroom, an emptied-out bottle of Ibuprofen from the medicine cabinet on the tile next to her.

Later still, Nikki entered Carlene's room at Holberton; it was a private room this time, not like the maternity ward with its beds laid out side by side, a cloth-thin mobile partition the only hope of discretion. Nikki was happy for that, at least. There wasn't much else that was happy about this situation, and she wouldn't be lying if she said she felt out of her depth. She'd come to hate this drab hospital, which politicians promised would soon be replaced by a spanking-new medical facility, and not for the reasons most Antiguans did. As she stood alone, having elected not to call others of the family at this late hour, Nikki felt something like hopelessness. She wanted Carlene to live, as much because she was tired of death, as because of the young woman herself. She noted how sallow Carlene seemed, and how tired, even in repose. She was fleshy still, though she hadn't eaten much that wasn't tubed into her these past weeks; her belly still had its pregnancy swell. But Nikki hadn't seen the dimples in a bit, nor the saucy smile, nor the eyes dancing with mischief; all as endearing as they could be infuriating. To Nikki, it seemed as though Carlene was fading away.

She willed her desire for Carlene to live at the figure lying on the bed. It was vanity. The doctor with the Cuban accent had already said that she would live. But Nikki feared that it wasn't Carlene's body that lacked the will, but her spirit, and she didn't know what to do to revive that.

CHAPTER TWENTY-ONE

Winston Baltimore, *Antigua Journal*, Eighth Entry

I had never been one of those boys who took things apart, simply for the joy of figuring out how to put them together again. When something breaks in my home, I call someone who knows how to repair it. My mind doesn't spin that way; it doesn't turn itself to that kind of thing.

I have no skill for art either; not for making it or appreciating it. Oh, I can bluff my way, to be sure, but I've always been a bit envious of those with an instinct for it. Application, not talent, has been the key in the lock of any doors I've managed to open for myself.

Sometimes, I feel like such a fraud. My opinion, if ever I've had one, is buried beneath sheets and sheets of research; that's my life, research. I have a lot of knowledge when it comes to art, when it comes to lots of things, I suppose, but I lack conviction. I lack a perspective. She forces me to admit these things, at least here, at least to myself.

She is everything I have never been: independent, artistic, curious, and opinionated. I mean, she's not literate or even widely knowledgeable; she's ignorant of life beyond this village—in a deep and meaningful sense. She doesn't even go to market every Saturday to sell her wares. Her oldest, Audrey, takes charge of that, coming back at the end of the day with the latest gossip from town. Usually about politics.

Violet is a very political being. There's a neighbour across the street from her with whom she pointedly does not speak, and who pointedly does not speak with her, all because of the red and the blue. The idea of *two viable parties is still a fairly new concept in Antigua, and Violet is among the defectors from the red to the blue. Rumour has it that that's what split her and her children's father for good. But she doesn't talk of him, nor do her children—many of whom are grown, or practically so—if they know what's good for them. There is no doubt as to who's in charge of the yard they all call home.*

So, no, she's not exactly a talker, but the bits and pieces I've been able to pick up, since the day she turned that gaze, full of so many unspoken things, in my direction rather than grab her coconut bough broom, as she no doubt wanted to do, and run me from her yard, have intrigued me. She intrigues me. She's one of the most remarkable women I've ever known, callused and muddied hands, head tie, worn dress and all..."

Cam wasn't worried about the possible land dispute. He seemed to think that money could sort everything out. Nikki knew different. No amount of money was going to move Tanty and Sadie. But there seemed no way to make Cam see that.

"Look, I won't be part of moving people forcibly off of their land," Nikki said. "I became a part of this project because..."

"Because you were at the end of your rope at Tourism and looking for a way out," Cam interjected. "I got you out."

"Classy," Nikki commented, earning an amused look in return. She sighed. "Look, you're a businessman, right? Presumably, you hired me for more than a few laughs at my expense; either that or you're a piss-poor businessman. So, if you did hire me because you think I have something to offer, let me offer it."

Cam's mouth twisted and there was a hard edge to the amusement in his eyes, but when he spoke, his voice was mild: "Knew you had spirit in you. I don't need no meek mouse working for me."

Nikki stopped herself from rolling her eyes at men and their little pissing contests. With a wave of his hand, he invited her to continue. She did: "We need to find a way to work with the people in the area," she said. "Those people are not going to be moved by money. We have to earn their support for the project, reassure them that their way of life will not be disrupted."

"But it must," he interjected. "Agriculture is in the past. Tourism is this country's present. Nobody wan' work in agriculture nowadays. Young people don't even want university education now. See how they scrambling for jobs at them Internet gaming places, 'cause the money good. Car, name brand, *gyal*; that's the currency they interested in. Nobody wan' bruk dem back no more. And nobody about to cry over a little bit of agriculture land."

"They'll fight you," Nikki insisted. "These people that I met, thanks to your son, I might add, will fight you."

"What? Them drug dealers?" Cam said. "Antigua well rid of them."

"No, not drug dealers. Hard-working people who've farmed that land for generations."

"Government done convert how much agriculture land already for development," he said. "Why should this be any different?"

"Well, do you want it to succeed?" Nikki asked.

Cam was silent.

"Listen," Nikki continued. "This doesn't have to be an either-or situation. I'm convinced of it. Let me adjust the planning to incorporate the area stakeholders. Win-win, that's what we're looking for, right?"

Cam accepted this, but said he wasn't about to lose money over sentiment. "You won't," Nikki assured him. So, he gave her the go-ahead, and with it, the monster headache of coming up with a plan that saved the people's land and the relics of their past while fulfilling his vision. Nikki wondered, not for the first time, what she'd gotten herself into.

"You can wait, if you want," Audrey said. "I sure they coming back soon. She don't stay out much. Guess she na take shame out she eye yet."

Nikki had stopped by the family house after another evening with her mother's grave and her father's words, only to find out that Carlene, Belle, and the boys had gone for a walk.

She bristled at Audrey's comment. "There's nothing for her to be ashamed of. She's been through a lot."

Audrey shrugged. "Life hard for everybody."

"And what, everybody's not rushing to kill themselves? Is that it?" Nikki demanded. "Must be great to be right about everything, to be so strong all the time."

Audrey shrugged again, as if agreeing that "yes, it was hard to be right all the time but what was she going to do; she was just born that way." Nikki found it infuriating.

Audrey raised the pot of cocoa at Nikki, a silent question. When Nikki shook her head, she poured some for herself in a can cup and sat at the table in the kitchen/dining area, across from her younger sister. She sipped with a little slurp that reminded Nikki of the Professor; who'd have thought those two would have anything in common?

"So, you working with that Kendrick Cameron now, I hear," Audrey said, after a time.

Nikki felt the other shoe drop. She'd been waiting for it, ever since the last time Audrey had accosted her about her life. She felt it hovering over them every time they were alone. She looked longingly at the back door, which hung open, letting in the night breeze.

"Yes," she said.

"You know he and the other one, Hensen, are high spar, right?" Audrey said.

"Hmm."

"Them tight," Audrey clarified.

Nikki shrugged.

"Don't trust your shadow," Audrey advised. And Nikki smiled.

"What so funny?" Audrey wondered.

"You, advising me?" Nikki shot back. "You almost sound like you care."

Audrey shrugged, saying dryly, "You're my sister."

Nikki did laugh, heartily, at that. When she was done, Audrey, stoic as ever, said, "That Blackman Valley project is trouble."

"How do you know about that?" Nikki asked, startled. The project was not yet public knowledge.

"Is Antigua this, news travel fast," Audrey said, "Bad news faster than good."

"My business is not your business," Nikki said, annoyed. "I can't discuss the project with you, in any case."

Audrey shrugged again. "I don't know nothing 'bout that type of business anyway. I been working in muddy all my life. But I know them type of people, them politicians and them money people. And sophisticated as you think you are, you just a child to them. Except, you nuff enough fu t'ink otherwise."

Nikki started to rise. Audrey's voice, sharper now, stopped her. "Yeah, you didn't wan' listen before, either," Audrey snapped. "One thing I know 'bout life, though: *picknee who na hear wha dem mooma say, drink pepper water, lime and salt.*"

"What?" Nikki demanded, puzzlement joining her ire.

"Who don't hear will feel," Audrey clarified.

"Audrey, you're no sage; you're just a bitter woman who loves to rub people's mistakes in their faces," Nikki snapped back, before escaping, finally, through the back door. She inhaled deeply of the night air, rich with scents, pleasant and unpleasant. Sour sop bush and flowering Dumms, Nunu Balsam and, faintly, someone's outside toilet. She lost herself in the scents and the night sounds, struggling to shake off her sister's warnings and judgment.

Belle's lively chatter, mingling with that of Carlene's kids, was a welcome distraction from her irritability. She turned to see the little troupe, including a silent Carlene, returning from their walk. Belle, carrying Imani, ran to her, and Nikki took the child and hugged her sister, glad to escape the doubts and confusion in her mind.

She sat outside for a long time after Belle and the boys had turned in with Carlene, just holding her hand. Nikki found she missed her laughter, and her chatter, and her busybody ways. But wherever she was, Carlene didn't seem ready to come back yet.

CHAPTER TWENTY-TWO

Winston Baltimore, Antigua Journal, Twentieth Entry
*"It's taken a long time for her to agree to let me take her picture,
record her words, write her into history.*

*"...but finally she's bent, like a coconut tree in a hurricane, to my
will; grudgingly..."*

"...Public meeting, Public meeting tonight at East Bus Station.
Issues of national importance to be discussed. All are invited. Do
not miss this important meeting..."

The jeep with its blaring bullhorn crept past Nikki as she
jogged home, sweaty and energized, just as colours began to paint
pictures on the morning sky. It was early yet, but as election
edged closer, the amplified, sometimes overlapping voices, had
become more frequent, time of day irrelevant.

Nikki wanted to get an early start today. She was driving to the
Valley with the architects and engineers selected for the project,
a mix of local and Canadian. She wanted them to get a feel for
the area before they huddled up. She also wanted to pay Sadie
and Tanty another visit. She'd been back a few times since her
initial visit, had tried to ease into the subject of Cam's plans for
the area. Sadie was resistant. Tanty was polite, even friendly, but
equally resistant. Nikki was convinced the project could work,

blending the project on the Ridge with the existing ruins and agrarian culture in the Valley, rather than conquering and destroying. The dungeon, roughly midway between Ridge and Valley, she felt, need not be affected at all. She felt they might need to lay underground utility wires and pipes and cut a road through the Valley, certainly for use during the construction phase, and likely beyond, but that was it. Selling the farmers on the road, and Cam on having the farmers within such close proximity of his exclusive guests, were problems her mind had not solved as yet.

"You all want some water?" Tanty offered Nikki and her team.

This or that member of the team caught Nikki's eye and at her subtle, she hoped, nod accepted the ice water being passed around in the can cup.

"Oh, Nikki," Tanty said, "I have some carrots for you. Is not from our plot; it is from Ms. Drew across the way." Tanty had gifted her with some form of vegetable—okras to pumpkin—every trip back, but usually from her own plot.

"Ms. Drew? Have we met?" Nikki asked, surprised.

"Oh, no, no, no. No offense, but Ms. Drew don't like your type, you know. Don't trust them. Kinda like Sadie," Tanty said, in a hushed tone, though they were a bit away from the others, by this point.

It wasn't meant unkindly; and Nikki knew it to be true. But then Tanty surprised her with a whispered, "But me, my spirit tek you."

Nikki got goose pimples at that, and bent towards the bag of carrots to mask the burst of emotion she couldn't quite put words to.

"I feel like I'm dancing with the devil," she confessed to her mother that evening. Her mother had taken Jazz's place, these past months, as confessor-confidante. With her sister still caught up in the early days of her marriage, Nikki felt less and less able to talk to her. They were still sisters, but on different paths. She didn't feel comfortable talking to anyone else, not about this, and she'd found such comfort these past months in sitting with her mother on the straw mat that had a permanent home in the trunk of the red and rugged secondhand—though still well-conditioned—jeep she'd gotten to replace her government-issued sedan.

"It's not that I don't think this can work," she continued. "I can see it in my head. But, well, I guess I don't entirely trust the players to fall in line, or maybe my ability to line them up." She pulled idly at the grass as she talked about Tanty's affirmation and how she worried about letting her down, about meeting Cam's and her own expectations, about Carlene.

"You find it help?" Carlene asked her that evening as they sat on the front porch of the family house. "Going up by your mammy grave all the time, talking to her?"

Nikki was a bit startled at this. And Carlene laughed, some of her old mischief peeking through. "Please, you don't learn yet, nothin' secret in Antigua? Besides, you right out in the open; you nah figure smadee does see you?"

Given that the cemetery was on the hillside away from everything, and facing away from the village; no, Nikki hadn't figured that.

She shrugged, caught somewhere between embarrassment, irritation, and encouragement by Carlene's spark of life. Carlene leaned in close. "Miss Know-All in there. She say how people talking 'bout it. Find it weird, you know. Say she don't know who you ah; try fool, don't piss on Mama Vi when she alive, now trying reclaim morning when afternoon done gone."

Nikki bristled at this, but Carlene's arm on hers calmed her. "Nah bother with her, yah. Me know what she say 'bout me, too. Me weak. Try kill meself. People have plenty to say 'bout that, too. You know what, though; them not inside me. Them not. Them nah inside me. Them nah know how it feel."

She started to cry then, soundlessly, and Nikki drew her in closer, the tears wetting her blouse.

"True say, me feel weak without him, yes. With Tones, me did have everything me want in life. Everyt'ing."

Ridiculously, Nikki thought then of the Whitney Houston melodrama "I Have Nothing," and a little bubble of inappropriate laughter snuck out. Carlene regarded her quizzically, "Wha so funny?" she wanted to know. "Laugh pon me?"

Nikki smiled gently. "No, not at all. I don't think you know how strong you are."

Carlene looked unconvinced. And Nikki offered, "You're stronger than me at any rate. I remember walking into your room after you gave birth to Mani; literally, my knees were weak. But you, you had a spirit that would not give up, and then boldly faced the next challenge."

Carlene sucked her teeth. "Please, make picknee?! That ah something woman do every day. Nothing special 'bout that."

"I disagree, Carlene; it's very special," Nikki said. "But, anyway, that's not the point I was making. What's the expression you use, 'blood inna you eye'?"

Carlene laughed at her mangling of her accent. "That's how I've always thought of you," Nikki said. "You have deep, deep red blood in your eyes. Maybe your spirit has gone to recharge itself, but I've seen that spirit. It's indomitable; nothing can stop it. That's not Tones; that's you."

Carlene didn't respond, but to Nikki, she seemed to be listening, and she decided to settle for that. They sat in silence for some time in the gloom of the night, uncaring of the people passing by now and again, giving them odd looks at their embrace. Carlene laughed after a while. "Ha! New rumour: 'You hear say de Jamaican one and de American turn lesbian?!' Looka story!"

Nikki laughed with her, and hugged her tighter, before they collapsed again into silence. "So," Carlene said after a bit. "You never answer my question?"

"Which question?"

"It help?"

Nikki thought about it for a bit. "Yeah, I guess it does," she acknowledged finally.

"Well, she can't chat back, that's fi sure." Carlene cackled. "Make it easier, don't?"

"I guess it does."

Then Carlene chuckled.

"What?" Nikki asked.

"Nothing," she said. "Jus' wonder what you goin' do the day she do answer back. New story! 'Me never know say that one from foreign can run so. She come down de hill, speed pass she car, pass bus stop everyting, run clean ah St. John's.'"

They giggled like schoolgirls over a secret joke.

CHAPTER TWENTY-THREE

Winston Baltimore, *Antigua Journal*, Twenty-First Entry
I don't know what loosened her tongue.

The sun was soft. It was late afternoon and she sat where she always sat, under the date palm tree. It was Saturday and everyone else had gone to market. To me, it felt like we were the only two people in the world.

'How far did you go in school?' I wondered.

'I didn't get much schoolin',' she responded, easily enough. 'Since me know m'self, is work. I been working all my life in muddy.'

'Didn't you ever want to do anything else?' I wondered.

A shrug from her in response, and a hawk and a long, arching spit. This was not a throwaway action. It was contempt, and it irritated me.

I pressed. 'Didn't you ever want to be anything else? Leave Antigua, even? Do something with your life?'

Her hands kept going, shaping the clay, even as she tilted her head at me, as we locked gazes. She might be uneducated, but she knew when someone was pushing her buttons. She wasn't stupid.

I knew this, as I knew that goading her was playing with fire; yet that's what I was doing. I found her life to be so frustratingly unexamined.

Her gaze stayed locked on mine, holding me, and her next words, though casual, had bite and bitterness. 'Dreaming ah for people like you,' she said.

My annoyance grew, as she'd no doubt intended.

'We are more than mere hewers of wood and drawers of water,' I said, sounding self-important, even to myself.

I wasn't surprised when she laughed, gaze steely.

Her reluctance to meet my eyes at our first meeting notwithstanding, she had a way of staring a person down. I'd seen her do it with more than one of her children since I'd been there; they'd always hopped to it, whatever it was. It worked with neighbours, too. With her non-verbal vocabulary being as evolved as it was, it was no wonder she didn't speak much.

She had words enough for me now, though.

'Smadee must draw the water, smadee must chop the wood,' she challenged. 'You think me 'fraid you an' your word an' dem, boy?'

Her eyes, an unremarkable dark brown, burned intensely, beautifully, fiercely, as she continued, 'For wan long time, that's all we were in dis country, dis black country. Work horse. Mule. Life na easy. Never easy. But me na have nuh time fu complain. Only people like you, with luxury, ha time fu complain and look dung pon people like me. I don't envy you nutten. Not yuh full head, nor yuh weak, soft hands.'

She hadn't raised her voice, but then she didn't need to; her words carried authority. I'd seen it often enough. Her eldest, Audrey, would be dispensing some of her seemingly random and often harsh discipline on the only one in the yard over whom she held any real power. Then, when Violet had enough, a look sometimes backed by a level, and leveling, verbal command, would freeze the scene, and Audrey would seem as much a child as the child cringing before her.

'Why do you let Audrey abuse your son, Fanso, as she does?' I asked, following my mind's abstract track.

She seemed confused by the change in topic.

'Abuse?' she asked, like it was a new word, one she didn't know the shape of.

I nodded, afraid to speak actually; I was surprised that I'd had the temerity to go there. But yes, it did bother me, the casual and open violence; frankly, not only in this yard, but everywhere I went on this island. It was only one of the patterns, I suppose, conditioned into them by slavery, but they have another explanation for it—spare the rod, spoil the child. Of course, what I witness with Audrey and Vi's youngest has less to do with the rod of discipline and more to do with the girl's frustrations with her own life. Surely, I'm not the only one to see this; but then I understand frustration well, understand burying it until it desperately claws its way out via another route.

'Ah boy he be, you know,' Violet said finally, speaking as one would to someone who was particularly slow. 'Life full o' knock 'bout. He ha fu tough.'

I, of course, bristled at being condescended to by this woman. 'And that's Audrey's job, why?' I demanded.

She would've been justified in telling me then that none of it was my business, but for whatever reason she does things, she merely shrugged, and said, 'He father na dey. Audrey young. Me na so young no more. Besides, going back wid his daddy, having him, was a mistake.'

'So you resent him?'

'No.'

'What then?'

Her body shifted, almost petulantly. 'He there; he coming up.'

'But do you love him?'

She looked baffled. Maybe she was. This is not a place of endearments but of blunt discipline and hard knocks, survival. I know this, and yet there I was, pushing, as though blaming her for the reality she'd been born into. Pushing her to, what, question her entire existence? To what end? Out of sorts in my marriage and life, I was projecting and I knew it, pushing my expectations onto her, an anthropologist's cardinal sin. Part of it, I suppose, had to do with the feeling she's stoked deep in my belly, the illogic of it. She's the exact opposite of everything I want for my life, and yet something in her calls to me. Her self-possession, her fire, her rootedness, her unconventional beauty, some other things I don't know how to name. I don't like that she has me tongue-tied.

'Me love all me children an' dem,' Vi said finally, still sounding confused. Listening back to the recording now, I can hear it, the confusion in her voice, just as I can hear the bullishness in mine.

'And hate their father?' I pushed.

'Me na t'ink 'bout he,' she replied.

I was amazed that she had given me as much as she had. Talking pottery and village life was one thing; this was something else and neither of us, it seemed, were ourselves. 'Nonsense,' I heard myself saying. 'You allow that boy to be treated the way he is because you can't stop thinking about his father.'

She fixed me with another hard glare. 'Wha you know 'bout any'ting?' she demanded.

I stilled, you know, like when one comes up on a rattlesnake.

'Look, boy,' Vi said, voice menacing, leaning forward, 'the way things be ah how dem be. That boy father don' even cross my thoughts. He far from dis village long time, ever since me run he laas time wid wan cutlass. The boy dey, he ah come up; no worse nor no better than any of mi picknee an' dem before him. An' furthermore, don't stir up ants nest if you can't stand get bite.'

The last was a clear warning; I took a breath and paid heed. Next subject. 'What was your childhood like?' I asked her. And her lips tightened, even as her face—her eyes—danced; a flash of this, a flash of that. That was what was so beautiful about her eyes, the life in them.

She spoke finally. It was only when I let my breath out that I realized I'd been holding it. It could've gone either way, really. I'd observed her enough. It was all I'd been doing for much of the summer. I knew what a wall she could be—old stone such as made up the old sugar mills and slave dungeons on the island. I still don't know why she spoke. The conversation to that point had been such a tight rope. I'd slipped in those tense moments, I think, from being an amusing diversion to being another insect, a nuisance. I worried that she'd close up, bar the entrance; that

I wouldn't get what I needed. And what I wanted. What I needed, in addition to her words and her attention, was her visage, as much for personal reasons as not, I supposed. But I wanted it in the right moment, wanted it to capture all she was when I saw her in my dreams. And yes, I do dream about her. She's the opposite of everything I want in this world, and yet the only thing I wanted in that moment. It didn't make any sense, but, speaking of the unexamined life, I'd ceased trying to make sense of it.

When she spoke again, it was of her mother. She was a thin small woman, not possessing her height at all, who raised eleven of them without any steady male support. That was a constant of life in the former slave societies of the "new" world, not only this little island in the Caribbean—the transient male, the stable female family head, generations of women, men with many families. A legacy of slavery, a twisted version of the polygamy practised in parts of Africa, a bastardized hybrid of the two. Whatever the origin, it certainly had its impact on village life where, as I'd confirmed, women proved to be the backbone of the home and the community. Everything about their attitudes, if not the realities of their lives and relationships, was a feminist affirmation. Not that they would ever think of themselves as feminists; but then they weren't big on self-definition so much as they were doing, just getting on with things. That might be the title of my thesis—just getting on with things.

'Times was hard then,' Violet said matter-of-factly. 'Mama bring us up hard, to make sure we have the mettle. Beat you like you name donkey so that when life fire, it blow an' dem is like mosquito bite.

'I remember one time, one of my older brother an' dem get fed up an' leave his job. He was a cane cutter. That's what all boy children did then, soon as they was old enough. Plenty gyal picknee, too. Cut cane. Man and woman work like slave in dem cane field. An' some o' dem manager was wicked wicked people who na know slavery done. Tell the truth,

plenty of us, neaga people, like we didn't know slavery done neither. Slave wages, slave living, and bound to show up for work same way, whether you want to or not. Magistrate and jail cart, and de prison bull whip one side; bakkra and de cat-o-nine de other side. Free paper mighta did come, but you still couldn't leave massa work undone. So, when Mama find him, my brother, catch-up with some woman; she drag he back. It was one or the other—jail cart or the sting ah bakkra justice. Wasn't no choice; not on hungry belly. Every little cent count dem time. So, Mama march he straight back, and the bakkra give him a thorough rassing wid de bull bud and put him back to work. Much as slavery done long time, so dem say, dem kind of things was still...still...just life. An' wasn' that long ago neither.'

'What happened to him?' I asked, captivated by this tale.

Her eyes were bleak when she answered: 'He turn bad john after dat, end up on the jail cart anyway.'

I took the picture.

She jerked, tossed on a wave of light, back into the here and now. And I reached out to soothe her. She seemed so much like a deer caught in the headlights then, vulnerable. My hand on hers, I lost track of who was comforting whom, fell into her pain..."

"Nikki Baltimore, I didn't realize you were still here; thought you'd given us up." It was the chorus of too many voices, assaulting her like cheap perfume. In this particular moment, it flowed from the lips of the Tourism Director General, who, like the other tourism department lackeys, knew very well she'd never left. After all, in Antigua, there were no secrets.

"Still here," Nikki responded tightly.

"Working with Cameron these days, I understand," the snippy woman said, contradicting herself.

Nikki slipped away from her, and then, noticing Hensen making a beeline for her, ducked back into the house and kept going, all the way out of the front door.

"Can't take no more?"

It was Cam's son, Aeden, sitting on the edge of the mermaid fountain that dominated the driveway at the front of his parents' house. He was openly inhaling a joint.

Nikki paused. "Guess not." She hadn't wanted to be there in the first place, but it was another Old Year's Night, another party, and Cam had insisted. The boy, Aeden, studied her; sweet-swelling smoke swirling around him. He seemed to come to a decision then, as they both waited for the others' next move. He offered a pull on the spliff in his hand. Nikki shook her head, but found herself joining him at the edge of the elaborate fountain, party dress, heels and all. It beat going back inside. Unfazed, he shrugged and took another pull.

Nikki sat, thinking of leaving, but not actually making a move. Aeden puffed. Water trickled from the stone mermaid's urn. It was strangely companionable.

Aeden startled her a little bit when he piped up brightly, "Hey, you wan' go for a ride?"

CHAPTER TWENTY-FOUR

Nikki and Aeden were atop Blackman's Ridge when the night flipped over to a new day, a new year.

He'd piloted them there in his chopper, landing soberly enough in the circle of lights in spite of the grass in his system. Still, as the cold hit her, Nikki found herself wondering if she'd finally lost her mind. Without much resistance, she'd let him talk her into driving to the helipad and then, into the helicopter to this place where there wasn't even a proper helipad; only a clearing hewed with cutlasses. Full moon or not, it was a miracle they were both in one piece, as far as she was concerned.

What the hell am I doing here with this loony tune? she wondered.

There was enough grass in Nikki's system, however, for her to find that thought amusing. Yes, she had indulged after confiscating what was left of his spliff when he'd taken the controls. She giggled, finding it difficult to stop, once started. He didn't ask what was so funny. She suspected he knew.

"This is the only way to see Antigua," he said, as they stared over the lip of the ridge into the blackness up close and the faraway lights.

"My father shouldn't be allowed to corrupt this place with his money," he said, tumbling to the ground much like a kid would in spite of his own party clothes, which were expensive she could tell, notwithstanding that they were the ultimate in mismatched grunge.

This prompted Nikki to ask, "So, what's up with you and this 'poor little rich kid' routine?"

"There's no routine," he said.

"Well, yeah, there is," Nikki insisted, joining him on the ground, careless of her party dress, an off-the-rack, iridescent number, courtesy of Rain Boutique. "If you hated your father's money so much, you wouldn't take it for your little toys, like that helicopter of yours."

"That's an investment," he said.

"Please, what are the terms of this investment? What kind of returns has he had?" she asked. "You're like this big kid. I swear, it always amazes me when people don't know how good they got it."

"Okay, pot," he said dismissively, sucking a fresh joint.

"What does that mean?" Nikki demanded, her back up now.

"What you doing here, sister?"

"I'm not your sister, freak."

"So, what you doing here?"

"Where? In Antigua? On this planet? Up on this stupid ridge with you?"

He shrugged. "Take your pick."

She was angry at him now, angry at herself, and wondering at the same time what it took to get him going; her jabs having bounced off with nary a flinch from him. She lurched up from the ground and paced to the edge of the ridge. "I don't know, to all of the above," she said. "Guess I'm as screwed up as you are. A pot, as you implied, calling the kettle black."

"Screw it," he said coaxingly. "Here, take another pull." It occurred to her that he maybe wanted to talk her back from the edge, but she gave in, falling back to the ground beside him. She lay back, losing herself in that feeling of smallness the night sky in the Caribbean inspired; the feeling that you were a part of something infinitely bigger than you, something at once magical and frightening. She refused the joint, though, remembering last Old Year's Night: too many drinks, too much dancing, and illicit and soul-stirring loving.

She realized, with a jolt, that she'd been in Antigua two Christmases already.

"Do you ever feel small, Aeden?" she wondered. "Like an ant. A worker ant carrying loads and loads of crap God knows where, oblivious to the big foot waiting to crush you."

"All the fucking time," he said. "Except I know the big foot there, and that there's nothing 'tall I can do 'bout that. So, know what I do?"

"What?" she wondered, turning her head to take in his profile, the grass brushing one of her cheeks; the wind, the other.

"I get high," he said, his giggles filling the air around them and drifting away on the breeze.

"So, did you hear the news?" Jazz asked. It was the first time they'd spoken in weeks.

"You're pregnant," Nikki half-joked. It wouldn't have surprised her. She knew it was what her sister wanted.

"I wish," Jazz lobbed back. "Daddy's gotten married."

Nikki felt the air rush out of her. "Getting married? Daddy?" she asked, incredulous. "It doesn't seem possible." She wasn't sure how she felt about this new development. She was kind of used to the Professor being single and, until recently, commitment phobic.

"Sister," Jazz said. "You're not listening."

"What?"

"I didn't say Daddy Dearest was getting married. I said he'd gotten married."

"What?"

"Yeah, a civil ceremony apparently, about two days ago. Unsentimental as ever. Apparently, he called to inform Mom, for whatever reason. She told me, practically foaming at the mouth as she did."

Nikki was sitting at the desk in her home office, which faced her backyard and pond, completely stunned. Unbelievable.

"Unbelievable," Jazz said, echoing her thoughts. "I know."

Then, she switched tracks. "How are things going with Fanso's restaurant?"

Nikki exhaled, still mentally stuck on the unreality of her father being married. "He opens next month," she said absently. In fact, as they spoke, she was reviewing the mock-up of the menu submitted by the graphic designer. It was Fanso's idea, really; it was a coal pot with a turn stick and a steaming pot of fungi on one side and a delicious and decorative plate with the fungi as the centerpiece on the opposite side. They'd taken the pictures earlier in the week. The tag line Fanso favoured was "Made in Antigua." Nikki wasn't sure but they were almost out of time, so "Made in Antigua" it was.

"So, give me the details. What's it called? Where? When, et cetera?" Jazz pressed, clearly excited and curious.

"Well, he's calling it Mama Vi's," Nikki said, "and he's commissioned Audrey to provide the candleholders and vases and stuff. He's a big designer all of a sudden; 'Antiguan classic,' he calls the look. The curtains and tablecloths are being made out of the Madras. Belle is doing that, with help from Carlene. It's been good for her. He brought in this artist named Artiste to do a mural stretching along all the walls. A village motif sort of thing, featuring the pottery making. A bit busy for my taste, but he insisted. He's going to serve up local dishes—pepper pot, fungi, season rice, doucana, potato dumpling, saltfish…"

"Stop, stop, my mouth's watering." Jazz laughed. "Wish I could be there, but give him my best."

"Will do," Nikki said.

"Must be chaotic right about now," Jazz said.

"It is," Nikki continued, "but it's got everyone going again you know since…"

She couldn't bring herself to say Tones' name, though. But Jazz got it. "Yeah," Jazz said.

Nikki steered them to steadier ground. "It's actually been fun getting everything going. I'm helping to plan the opening, helping out with admin, and marketing, and budgeting. Between this and Blackman's Ridge, I'm exercising all kinds of muscles I didn't know I had."

"That's good, I'm glad," Jazz said. And it made Nikki happy to have good news for a change.

"I mean, don't get me wrong, it's not all gravy," Nikki said. "Cam intimidates the hell out of me."

"Please," Jazz said.

"We make our formal pitch to Cabinet next week," Nikki said. "Which means I'll have to see Hensen, of course, and I don't expect him to give me a pass."

"Please," Jazz said again.

"He's vindictive," Nikki reminded her.

"And you'll be prepared," Jazz countered. "I'm not worried. Besides, if this Cam's as big a shit as you say, likely Hensen won't want to step too far over the line, even to play you."

"Your lips to God's ears," Nikki said.

"Wait, don't tell me you've found religion," Jazz teased.

"Praying for a miracle more like," Nikki said. "Although I have gone to church a time or two with Marisol."

"I can't get over how tight you two have become," Jazz said.

"We haven't become…" Nikki began, then, "well, she makes good fruit juice."

Jazz laughed heartily. "I thought you said it was too sweet."

Nikki shrugged, though Jazz couldn't see her. She couldn't find the words, though, to explain how the pattern of Marisol waiting for her and serving her fruit drink—even oversweetened—helped make her feel like she was part of the fabric of things. She changed the subject. "So, what's up with your mission to make me an aunt? Having too much fun working on it to stop?" she teased, and Jazz's laughter swelled.

The opening of Mama Vi's turned out to be a media event as was the case with most things this close to election, especially where government money was involved. Top local pannist Lacu Samuel caressed the steel pan like she was his lover, teasing everything from Stevie Wonder's "Lately" to Enrique Iglesias' "Bailamos" out of the one-time oil drum. People mingled, sampling mango-stuffed tarts fresh from the oven, the house special—Moonlight Samba—and lots of pretty-looking, dainty concoctions Nikki couldn't name and was too busy to taste. Swathed in a dramatic Sandra Barton original made up of the red, blue, black, white, and yellow of the national flag, she was playing hostess for the night. Fanso nervously hid out in the kitchen as much as he could get away with, and mumbled his greetings when his time came to speak. Carlene looked pretty and lively in her puffy-sleeved, ankle-brushing madras uniform, matching head tie, and frilly white apron. Antoinette was un-usually jazzy in a flapper-inspired, shimmery number; her white-blonde hair sheared into a Louise Brooks bob. Her boys were there, stiff in their matching suits, and uncomfortable in the crowd of grown-ups. Among those grown-ups was none other than Hensen J. Stephens; he was the Tourism Minister, after all. With election this close, Fanso said they couldn't resist taking credit for "the little penny ha'penny dem gi me." Audrey had echoed this—"All kind of politician and socie smadee come to dem kinda subben ya, dem dey ah na fu me kinda people"—making clear that she would not be attending. Fanso had insisted that she receive an invitation, though he predicted she wouldn't come.

It had irritated Nikki. This wasn't exactly her crowd, either, but wasn't Fanso the one that said "family is family"? She still wasn't getting the rules of that particular relationship.

After all, for family, she was busy playing another game of hide-and-seek with Hensen. The last time she'd seen him was at the Cabinet meeting that netted Cam government approval and subsidy for the Blackman's Ridge project. At that meeting, he'd been as much of a dick as he could get away with being, of course, but with Cam at her shoulder, that wasn't very much. It had felt a little like a victory; it didn't stop her from moving in the opposite direction every time she saw him at her brother's restaurant opening, however. The bubble of shame that rushed up like vomit every time she thought of her indiscretions with him had settled somewhat, but still, the less she saw of him, the better, and if she could avoid speaking with him altogether, it was even better.

They did end up side by side in the beaming photo in the lifestyle section of the paper under a caption: "Local Chef Cooks Up Something New at Mama Vi's." "Politicians always know how fu find the camera, boy." Fanso laughed. Nikki wasn't amused. You wouldn't know to look at the picture, though, all that had passed between her and Hensen. She was proud of herself for that, at least; sending up a silent prayer to God, Cam, Fanso, and whatever other fates had made it possible for her to land on her feet. She dumped the paper, and the entire Hensen chapter of her life, in the garbage, and didn't look back.

CHAPTER TWENTY-FIVE

Winston Baltimore, Antigua Journal, Twenty-Ninth Entry

After that first time, Violet and I found other stolen moments. We didn't talk much.

She did talk more in other times, talked of her art, for instance. 'It simple, is just in the knowing,' she'd say. 'See, we build a relationship wit the soil over the years. It know us, we know it.'

And I watched the muddy take shape under her capable hands. It was a coal pot. She always had to make one, she said, no matter what else she was making that day. It was the first thing she'd learned to do, she explained, and they were still quite popular, even with more and more people investing in kerosene burners and gas stoves. There were some things, she insisted, that didn't taste right unless cooked over a coal pot, like fungi (pron. foongee). This is turned corn meal and okra, fairly bland for my taste but quite popular here. The coal pot arch, she continued, was also the only proper place to roast peanuts. As for roast corn, you absolutely needed a coal pot for that. I could've done without roasted corn personally; it is hard as rocks and hell on the teeth. But everyone here seems to love it. Besides, roast corn is good for making Ashum; dry as dust, but sweet! Sweeter still when licked from a dry palm.

Vi's talk was punctuated by long silences always; times when she just went away or got lost in her task. '…Me ha fu set um fu dry,' she explained. 'But in de shady, not in the sun; 'cause it will crack. It fragile, see. One slip, foops, and that's that. That's why some people call it Oh Gad!' And *here was the side of her few saw, her funny re-enactment of a falling coal pot and a frantic exclamation of 'Oh Gad!' followed by that cackle of hers. She clapped gaily as she laughed, as though applauding her own humour. Then, a note of pride, 'of course, that hardly ever happen to me; me know wha me ah do. The knowing in the doing, see.' She said this like it was her mantra.*

I marvelled at how at peace she seemed, how relaxed her limbs, her face, everything. She wasn't as tightly coiled as she'd once been around me, as she was still around everyone else. Maybe she'd come to feel as deeply for me as I had for her; maybe she realized I was no threat.

Whatever the reason, I came to treasure those Saturdays with her and the weird distance we affected during the week when others were around.

It felt, feels, weird and unfamiliar, this reaching for more when more would likely upset the fragile whatever it was we'd found. Then it would crack crack crack like this thing they called the 'Oh Gad!'

Oh Gad!

What else would you say, really, if you couldn't hold on to things; a coal pot...your sense of yourself?

'The one part me na fancy ah de baking,' Violet confessed. I'd seen her and Audrey do this before, pile the pots, vases, yabbas, and what-ever else unto a heap of trash, collected by Fanso on that donkey cart of his, for burning. To me, it seemed dangerous business. But then life was dangerous business, wasn't it, leading you to unfamiliar places, uncom-fortable realizations, and inevitable partings.

...as I write this, I'm on the flight home, not yet sure how to label this chapter in my life."

Cabinet was torn, it turned out. "Half of them want to hold off on announcing anything 'til after the elections," Cam reported.

"They think it too hot. Some others, the PM included, think is just the shot in the arm they need. 'Jobs, jobs, jobs; that's what you sell to people come election time.'" This last was said in an ugly imitation of the country's leader, leaving little doubt as to Cam's feeling on the Government's pussy footing. Still, he didn't seem terribly upset, considering it was his project and dollars in jeopardy.

"What do you think?" Nikki asked him.

They were at the same restaurant where he'd first proposed his idea to Nikki, the ancient Asian woman still holding court at the cash register.

"Me," Cam replied. "Well, elections just a month away, give or take. Not much time either way. I say we sit on it, meantime continue courting the candidate for the area, from the other side. Quietly. We don't want to force them to have to take a public position now because it can only go one way against us. We just continue talking with them quiet-like. The way things stand now, I have a feeling the guy from the other side is the one we might have to be dealing with after this next election."

Nikki's surprise must have shown on her face.

"What?" Cam asked, with a smirk. "I'm a businessman, not a politician."

From where Nikki was sitting, it was hard to tell the difference; there didn't seem to be much loyalty in either.

Post-election, Nikki stood outside the school room, sweat drying on her skin, as the village people filed out and milled around in the school yard chatting.

"You ready?" Aeden called.

He'd come to the meeting with her, a friendship of sorts having developed between them, since Old Year's Night. She was driving, as she never let him pilot her unless he was at his helicopter's controls. His tone this night was deferential as he approached her, having peeled himself away from a group of rough-looking guys—one of whom Nikki could only guess was his dealer, Little John, if the smell coming from the shadows was any indication. They'd been outside the entire time, but likely had heard the commotion inside.

Relations with the community had not improved, even with a new administration in power. Some, like Sadie, had even begun to threaten protest action.

The Parliamentary representative for the area, formerly the opposition candidate, squeezed Nikki's elbow as he passed. "Give me a call tomorrow, nuh?" he said. She gave him a little nod, then turned towards her car, throwing a "let's go" over her shoulder to Aeden.

Both were quiet as they put distance between themselves and the country classroom and crowd of uncertain villagers. Nikki had no idea what he was thinking, and frankly didn't care. She was becoming a bit frustrated with the villagers who seemed only to throw up more obstacles as you cleared the previous ones. She gave them answers, they wanted more answers, and their elected representative was providing no leadership on the issue as far as she could see—content to let the uninformed and determined to stay-uninformed rabble set the tone. It was frustrating and she was getting nowhere, a fact she and, unfortunately, her boss were well aware of.

"Told you," Aeden said after a few miles of this contemplative silence, just as they crossed the bridge from rural to suburban Antigua.

Nikki wasn't in the mood for it. With his amused-at-everything snarky ways, there was more of Aeden's father in him than she'd realized initially. "Surprise, surprise, an 'I told you so' from the poor little rich kid rebel," she snarked back.

Nikki caught his shrug out of the corner of her eye, and rolled her eyes. What did she expect?

"It's a good compromise," she insisted. "They get to keep their land. All we need is to cut a road. They are not listening."

"Whatever," Aeden said, relaxing further into the passenger seat and closing his eyes.

"It's been how many months now?" Nikki griped to Fanso the following day. They were in the kitchen at Mama Vi's as he got ready for lunch. Nikki had dropped off Carlene, part of the wait staff, to help set up the eating area. "Two, three. I feel like I'm going in circles with these people."

"These people," Fanso, chopping spinach at lightning speed, said. "That kind of attitude not goin' help."

"Yeah, I get it, I'm the elite outsider," Nikki snapped.

"I'm not saying that," her brother sighed, "but honestly, Nikki, what you expect? The people an' dem worried 'bout losing their land to people who done have more than enough."

"I've tried to make it clear that that's not about to happen," she stressed. "I mean Cam is not some pirate. This is his home. And sure, he's not the most tactful or the warmest of men, but he's not the devil. Whatever he does to these people, he has to live with, too, and so he knows that he has to do them right."

"They have no reason to believe that," Fanso replied. "They been screwed too many times by government."

"We are not government," Nikki insisted.

"No, you guys are just the puppeteers."

When she glared, he shrugged, returned his attention to the task at hand. "Hey, is so they see it."

"That's not how it is," Nikki insisted. "I went to great lengths to strike this balance."

"Well, don't look to them for no medal," Fanso said, without looking up. "They want you to go away."

"And Hensen and his crew," Nikki continued, as though he hadn't spoken, "they were behind this project just before the elections. Now because they're on the outs, they're all doom and gloom. It's sickening."

"It's politics," Fanso said.

"It's bullshit," she said. "They could turn the tide with their support, but they're just muckrakers and liars, because they know there is no basis for what they're saying."

"Wow? Shady, insincere politicians! Didn't see that coming!"

"You're not helping," Nikki told him, a little tired of the suggestion that she was either naïve, obtuse, or plain ignorant.

At that point Carlene came in. "So, wha de special today, Boss?"

"Spinach rice, steamed vegetables, fried fish stuffed with green mango. Hibiscus drink."

"Mmm," Carlene said. "My stomach standing at attention." She grabbed some more utensils and headed out to the dining area. Both Nikki and Fanso watched her.

"She seems to be doing better," Fanso said, with a little smile.

"Yeah," Nikki said, "This job helped."

Fanso shrugged. "Well, I needed staff."

"Still, it was a good thing to give her a chance," Nikki said.

The compliment seemed to make Fanso uncomfortable and he soon changed the subject. "You staying for lunch?" he asked.

"Can't," Nikki said. "I have a meeting to get to."

En route, she had heard the news on her car radio. "Blackman's Ridge area farmers have threatened to take action against local businessman Kendrick Cameron, if he does not abandon plans to run a road through prime farm land towards what has been described by one protestor, as a 'hedonistic playground for the filthy rich'…"

Then Sadie's voice came on. "We not goin' take it so. Is human being we be, nuh. And we have as much right to live as them. How much more they want? Look how much they have; look how much we still breaking our back to get by, an' is bread they wan' take outta arwe mouth. They not satisfied and God go vex with dem; taking way people livelihood to build some, some hedonistic playground for the filthy rich who done have more than they share. Well, they goin' have to run through me, Sadie Philip, to get my land. You hear me good?"

"Hot air," Cam proclaimed.

"No, not hot air. I know this woman and I guarantee you, if she's mixed up in this protest action, they're not going away easily. She's been mumbling about it for a while. If she's gone public, she's dead serious," Nikki insisted.

The political representative for the area sitting next to her nodded sagely. To Nikki, with his red shiny head, he looked like nothing more than an apple bobbing in water.

They were like two kids in the principal's office seated side by side across from Cam over the stretch of his expansive but beaten up wooden desk, which took up half of the office space. Of course, that was no big feat as, despite his millions, Cam's office, was a modest earth-toned box of a room located just outside of town above the original family gas station. It was probably the same desk used by his mother when she was alive. The usual loud gas station talk spilled through the open window and Nikki wondered, not for the first time, how Cam got anything done there; sentiment aside, it was no wonder he held so many of his meetings in restaurants.

"So, what do we do?" Cam demanded.

"Well, we've had a lot of requests for interviews with you," Nikki began.

"You know I don't do that stuff," Cam said. "That's what I pay you for."

"No," Nikki said. "You pay me to plan, strategize, execute. That's what I'm doing. Right now, the people need to see that you're not a monster. They need to hear from your mouth that you have Antigua's best interest at heart."

"How much years me and my family here, they don't know that yet?" Cam boomed. "I more Antiguan than most of them."

"I know many who would argue passionately that the opposite is true," Nikki said.

"Please, what, because I'm not black, I'm not an Antiguan? Bullshit!"

Nikki only gave him a look; he knew well enough how some grassroots people perceived him. Arrogant he may be, but he was no fool.

Cam blinked. "So what you want?" he said, almost sullenly.

Nikki leaned forward. "Sincerity. That's what you've got to sell. You can't be cocky." She held up her hand as he opened his mouth to interrupt, and rushed on.

"You've got to be sure but earnest," she continued. "I'll set up a press conference. Then, we've got a meeting with the community. The media will be there. You have to be. After that, maybe tour the area, meet with some of the farmers, invite the media out, take some of them up to the Ridge in Aeden's chopper. Face time, face time, face time. You, your money and your influence are what have these people spooked. You've got to show them you're not the boogieman."

"Fine, set it up," Cam snapped.

CHAPTER TWENTY-SIX

"Yeah, he know how to massage people when he ready," Aeden said. "He just too boast to try most of the time."

They were hanging out on her back porch, and Nikki had remarked about how well his father's meet-and-greets with the community had been going. Aeden, looking at her through the locks hanging over his brow, smirked. "He worked you, didn't he?"

These were the moments, and they were often, that made Nikki wonder how she and Aeden came to be hanging out in the first place. The starting point, she supposed, had been that impulsive trip to Blackman's Ridge last New Year's Eve. The way he'd come to dog her steps since, made Nikki think he had no friends. Not that she was surprised, given his attitude and dress. Tonight, he was quite tame by his colourblind standards; threadbare jeans, a white Bob Marley T-shirt, and a red-and-black jumbie bead necklace, which he fingered like it was a rosary. Cam was no GQ model but he was always clean and ironed, and while Nikki hadn't had much interaction with his wife, Raisa, she couldn't imagine her with a hair out of place. Both projected laser-sharp focus and a certain ruthless intelligence. Aeden just didn't seem to fit with them. So maybe that's what they had in common, that they were both outsiders; maybe that's why she didn't mind having him around. Or maybe it was when she went to meet with community leaders and other groups, it made her feel more secure to have someone, even Aeden, who knew the lay of the land. She wouldn't have met Tanty if not for him, and she liked the old lady and felt she could be an ally through this tenuous Blackman's Ridge development project. Also, she liked taking helicopter rides with him up to the Ridge or even orbiting the island, escaping the prison of gravity and the occasional claustrophobia born of being on a tiny rock with water all around. Loopy as he seemed usually, that helicopter was like an extension of Aeden, and Nikki never felt anything but safe sitting beside him as he angled it this way and that. She'd orbited the Montserrat volcano with him as he took a honeymooning couple on a pleasure trip. They'd pointed and clicked, and she'd stared at the greyness spread over the communities in the volcano's path, and the way it contrasted with the almost defiant greenness in the still living communities beyond. She'd looked across and caught Aeden's eye just then and he'd smiled as if seeing it all as she did, though he'd seen it many times before. There was also their hop over to Nevis, his clients, an elderly pair of botany hobbyists, exploring the Botanical Gardens while she and Aeden headed to Sunshine's for a sip of its famous killer bees. There they passed the day, the sand between their feet, the sun warming them, and the killer bees giving them a buzz they had to walk the length of the beach to shake off before the journey back to Antigua. In moments like those, Nikki actually liked Aeden. But he was hard to take sometimes, swinging from snarky and intense, to casual and indifferent, at whim. He seemed to have no internal censor and she sometimes wanted to smack him; mostly though, she tried to take him in stride. He was pretty harmless most of the time.

"Don't be embarrassed," he teased now. "Daddy could work the devil himself. God, too, if he had a mind to."

"Nobody worked me, okay," Nikki bit off. So much for not letting him get to her.

Aeden threw up his arms in a mock-defensive gesture. "I'm just teasing, Ms. Chip-on-her-shoulder. Why you always trying to be such a hard ass, anyway?"

"I'm not trying to be anything," she shot back, definitely irritated now and not entirely sure why. Aeden was being no more or less himself than he usually was.

"Well, you sure na give me wan easy time," he said, amused.

"Aeden, you're the least of my worries," she tossed back, without thought. She reached for her glass, took a sip of the coconut water he'd been kind enough to pick up on his way over.

He leaned forward, lips tipped up. "Don't fool yourself," he teased, at least she thought it was a tease, "you been wondering about me since day one."

He had her there. But she played it off, with a hollow laugh, another sip, a head shake, and a "men, all ego, like I have time to wonder about your scraggly ass."

"You could do worse," Aeden replied.

"I could? How?" Nikki scoffed.

When he didn't respond, she realized she may have hurt his feelings. She sighed, rolled her eyes a little. "Aeden, come on, I'm not trying to hurt your feelings or anything, but, I mean…me and you? Oil and water. Or didn't the bickering give it away?"

When he still didn't reply, she conceded, "Okay, I like you. I do." He looked up. And she nodded. "Surprised the hell out of me, too," she continued. "I mean, you are scraggly…"

He actually smiled at that; and she continued, with a little relieved smile of her own.

"You float around like a displaced hippie…"

Hypocrite, her inner voice charged, reminding her of her own professional rootlessness over the years, but she ignored it.

"Then there's the eau de ganja you seem to bathe in."

He laughed outright at that.

"But, in spite of all, I like you," she finished.

"And I like you," he replied, voice lighter now. "In spite of your uptight bourgieness."

"Thanks," Nikki said sarcastically.

Aeden shrugged, and she continued, all seriousness now. "But, I can't string you along and pretend I see this going anywhere. For one thing, I'm not looking for anything, anyone."

"Because of that prick Hensen," he guessed.

Her eyes snapped to his. "Does everybody know about that?"

"Pretty much." This was said casually, with one of his patented shrugs.

Malicious intent or not, it caused an intense ripple to crash through her. It was so intense, in fact, that she physically braced herself, fingers gripping the edge of her seat. When it passed, what was left was fresh shame and disappointment that the memory of her dalliance with Hensen-fucking-J-Stephens still had such power over her. It didn't make sense. She'd been with Terry for years and walked away with barely a backward glance, and after mere months with Hensen, she was still putting herself back together months later, shame proving to be just as powerful a feeling as passion. She'd certainly felt both during and after her time with him. Maybe if she had to run into Terry, or hear about him constantly, it wouldn't have been that easy to move on either; certainly, it wouldn't have been if he'd played her for a fool and everybody knew it, except her.

Unaware of the direction of her thoughts, Aeden continued.

"Were you in love with him?" he asked.

Nikki smiled tightly. "Would you believe it was the best sex of my life?"

He looked over at her askance, searching for the mood of her statement.

"So, you've given up on love, is that it?" he prodded.

Nikki shrugged. "No, not given up, but, for now, it's not something I'm looking at."

"From what I hear, you don't so much go looking for it as it come looking for you," Aeden replied.

"Said the great philosopher," Nikki snarked.

Aeden didn't answer, just reached into his pocket for a joint and a light.

"Aeden," Nikki hissed. "You crazy? You can't do that here?"

"Why not?"

"Because I said so," she snapped, still irritated with him for stirring up things in her.

His eyebrows rose at that. "Are you serious? Because I said so?!"

"My porch," Nikki said, refusing to back down, "and with my luck, the police are hiding in the bushes."

He grumped some, wondering aloud if she was for real, but tucked away the paraphernalia. "Well," he asked, after all that, "you have any liquor?"

She raised a brow, never having seen him imbibe before. He shrugged. "Hey, you ha fuh give me something."

She looked at him. His body was slouched as it always was, but there was unfamiliar tension there. Nikki sighed, exasperated with both Aeden and herself, unwanted memories and unrequited affection. She really didn't want things to get complicated between them. "Aeden," she began. But he cut her off.

"Hey, no worries," he said, "is I set myself up with hope and all that."

"Hope isn't a bad thing," she offered, though she had her doubts.

"No," Aeden agreed, "but it unpredictable."

Much later, sucking on the last of her Wadadlis, Aeden said, "You wan' know how I know 'bout you and Hensen?"

"Actually, no," Nikki replied, her arms wrapped around herself against the dewy chill. "I don't think I do. I think actually that I want to go to sleep. You about done?"

"Chicken," Aeden teased, a lazy smile spreading across his face.

Nikki fixed him with a glare. "Aeden, I'm a big woman. That nonsense hasn't worked on me in years." She looked away. "Besides, I assume it's the usual street gossip. Isn't that how everything spreads here; where you can't throw out your piss without somebody smelling it?"

He got up, somewhat shakily. "Speaking of which…"

He wandered to her backyard where she soon heard a steady stream spraying, hitting the water of the lily pond at the edge of the yard. "Shit!" she exclaimed. "Aeden, I do have a bathroom, you know. I don't know what it is with you men. You're like animals. Up against a wall, up against a tree, like some dog peeing against a tire to mark its territory."

"It's nature's way." Aeden chuckled, as he returned to the porch and eased back into his seat.

"Whatever," Nikki sniffed. "That's gross. Now I've gotta smell your piss."

Aeden sniffed the air. "I don't smell anything."

She rolled her eyes and considered cracking one of the empty beer bottles littering the porch over his silly-looking, curly, dread-locked head. He laughed. "Hey, it's not my fault God wired us up with more convenient equipment. If you ask me, we're the better model. That's why I personally believe God is a man."

She looked at him. "You are crazy."

"Hey, crazy is just a state of mind." Then, tickled by his own turn of phrase, he laughed until he nearly toppled over.

"Anyway, serious serious thing now. I heard it outta Hensen mout' self," he said, killing any hope Nikki had that he'd been diverted from his earlier line of conversation. It didn't help that she was curious as to what exactly Hensen had said, masochistic though it was. She waited and Aeden didn't need further prompting.

"He was chatting to my father," he continued. "This was right about when Daddy was twisting his arm to release you from your contract. It was up at the house, and Hensen was so pissed he was raising his voice to Daddy. Something nobody 'tall do. Seems he had you right under his thumb where he wanted you. But both he and my father knew Daddy was goin' get his way. He always does. So anyway, he start spewing all this shit 'bout you, swear to God. 'She? You think she ah anybody? Because she come from away? She ah wan' nothing. It didn't take nothing for me to get her to lie down and spread out, anywhere and any way me want she. She was a stray cat in every sense of the word.'"

Maybe she made a sound. She didn't know. But Aeden stopped talking and looked at her. She was shaking, and her vision was blurry; his face getting larger and wavier around the edges as he came closer.

"Oh damn, Nikki, I'm sorry."

Nikki swallowed; she licked at the salt on her lips. "Well, we're even. I hurt you; now, you hurt me. And you're drunk, right, so it's not like I can hold it against you."

He tried to pull her into an awkward embrace; she resisted, slapping at his arms.

"It doesn't matter what Hensen J. Stephens or anyone says about me," she squeezed out.

"No it doesn't," Aeden agreed, trying to caress her hair. She jerked her head away.

"I know what I am. The people that matter know who I am." But she didn't believe that, not really.

"I do know."

She pushed him away. "You don't know shit."

He didn't know that Hensen wasn't lying. She had been wild with him, feeling a freedom previously unknown because, yes, he had known how to make her body sing. Bully for him and shame on her.

"You'd better go," she said.

"I'm sorry," Aeden said again.

She got up. He sighed, but stumbled to his feet.

"So, are we done?"

She shrugged. "Go sleep it off, Aeden."

He sighed. "I'm sorry."

"Good night, Aeden."

He left.

Nikki refused to feel guilty about shutting him out into the night, mostly drunk. Would serve him right to have to walk his ass all the way back to Paradise View.

She called later, much later, to make sure he'd got home. "Yes," he said. "I safe." She hung up abruptly before he had a chance to say anything else.

CHAPTER TWENTY-SEVEN

Winston Baltimore, Antigua Journal, Thirtieth Entry

Vi's youngest daughter, Belle, was raped. Apparently the culprit was a paramour of the elder girl, Audrey. Evidently, one evening, he found Belle alone, took her into the bushes and took her. She'd never said anything and the pregnancy had gone unnoticed. The girl, Belle, 'dropped' the baby a few evenings ago, right there at home. That's how Violet said it to me. "Dropped" the baby, "the picknee" actually; like she was livestock, a bitch dropping her pups. As she told it, still fuming about what had gone on right under her nose, she'd attempted to slap some answers out of the girl, but Belle only cried. It was the other one, Audrey, who finally confessed that she'd known all along about her sister's pregnancy. But then they shared a bed, how could she not know? I suppose the amazing thing was that she'd dared incur her mother's wrath by keeping the whole mess a secret; but then maybe she feared Vi would've made the girl drink some kind of bush to get rid of the baby—they have bush remedies for all kinds of things here. It seems that, although she lost the boy, she wanted to keep the baby. That one, I don't claim to understand her, and her sister's too simple, retarded really, to know better. I've never met the boy. He'd stopped coming around long, long before I first set foot in that yard.

Nikki was already in bed, cuddled up with Blackman's Ridge blueprints, when the phone rang. "Meet me at the crazy house,"

Audrey said abruptly, then hung up. Nikki stared at the now dead receiver and thought about hanging it up, and forgetting about it. Whatever it was, it sounded like more trouble; besides, she huffed as she got out of bed. Would it kill Audrey to not phrase everything like a command? Did she even know how?

When Nikki arrived, the waiting room of the country's lone mental home was empty save Audrey, sitting in one of the plastic chairs lined up in front of the reception desk. She was truly alone, as even the desk was unmanned. Nikki had taken a minute to twist her hair into a hasty roll and change into a pair of jeans and T-shirt. It was Audrey who looked like she'd been dragged out of bed. Nikki was struck most by the pink rollers, since she'd never seen Audrey's hair looking curled. Usually, it was corn-rowed until it frayed enough to require re-plaiting. But there she was in pink rollers, wearing a blue windbreaker over a knee-length cotton nightgown, jeans, and Timberlands. She sat unnaturally still, except for her hands, which pulled and twisted at each other, and though she looked up at Nikki's entrance, it was the younger sister who spoke first.

"What's the matter?" Nikki asked. Between trying to remember the location of the mental home, cursing Audrey in her mind, and imagining the worst, she'd worked herself into a state on the way over. Faced with a stricken-looking Audrey, though, she was stumped, and found herself instinctively offering comfort.

Also out of character was the way Audrey seemed to relax slightly at that. "I had to bring in Carlene," Audrey said.

"What? Why?"

Audrey launched into her tale. "She was good-good there with the children. All of a sudden, she start act crazy. The children start cry, Belle and Columbus getting upset. I ask her what stupidness she doing. 'I wan' die, I wan' die. I can't take this. I can't take this.' One set o' carrying on. Just so. I doin' my best for her, an' all of a sudden she just start attack me. I tell her well if she wan' kill sheself, kill sheself. But do it right next time. Next thing, she grab the big kitchen knife out the drawer. The children scream-ing now, Belle moving toward her, I had to grab for the knife before things get outta hand. Slice up my hand, too."

Nikki noticed, for the first time, the cloth bandage around Audrey's hand. But her mood had already shifted from concern to anger, and Audrey's cut hand wasn't the source of it.

"Why would you tell someone who had attempted suicide just a few months ago to go ahead and kill herself?" Nikki asked, in-credulous. "You know she's depressed. You know she lost her husband and her baby. Yet you're always making her feel like a failure."

"Me?" Audrey sounded genuinely shocked at this accusation, stirring Nikki's anger even more.

"Yes, you, Audrey," she insisted. "It's what you do. With every-body in this goddamn family. It's what you've been doing with Carlene. She's told me about all the things you say, like words don't mean nothing. But you peck, peck, peck, eventually the person's gonna bleed."

Nikki's eyes were drawn back to the bandage at that, white and tight with dried blood adding some colour. Audrey, meanwhile, was all hurt pride. "So, this is my fault?" she demanded. "I tell you, you do and you do and you do for people; do your best, and the good you do, the bad you get."

"Listen," a voice barked from the counter, causing both sisters' heads to snap in that direction. Neither had seen the white uni-formed, pink-sweatered nurse resume her station. The woman was middle-aged, stern-looking. "You all goin' have to keep it down," she said. "I can't have this nonsense here. Hear?"

The sisters fell silent.

"How's your hand?" Nikki asked, after a while.

Audrey's eyes flicked down, the hand twitched, she shrugged. "It's all right, just a scratch. Belle, wrap it up for me."

Nikki raised an eyebrow, amused at that, and at the little bow that finished off the tie. "So, she and Chris are okay then?"

"Yeah," Audrey replied, somewhat distantly. "Calm them down, leave the children with them, wasn't the best plan but couldn't do no better. After me get the knife, she settle down little bit, still talking crazy but not violent. But somebody, one of the nosy curtain twitchers, had done call police; them decide fu bring she in. Somebody had to come with her."

The fight had to have been louder and longer than Audrey's retelling suggested if the police had been called; but Nikki said nothing on this. She did note there was now no police around. In fact, she was just now truly registering, no other family members either.

"Did you call Fanso?" she asked. She didn't wonder about the others—Lars, Ben Up, Deacon—each of whom seemed to divide his time between squatting at the family homestead and squatting with one of his baby-mamas. From what she'd observed after Tones' accident, Fanso was, ironically, more likely to be called to Audrey's aid than any of the others. In fact, Audrey didn't seem to rely on them for much, least of all relief from her caretaker duties. Nikki had thought of it as a dominance thing, but had come to think that maybe it was just that Fanso was steadier. He was certainly Nikki's anchor in this family.

But when Audrey replied, it was to demand, sounding annoyed again. "For what? You're the one that she wrap up with."

It sounded almost like an accusation, but yet Audrey had called her, and it seemed, only her. She didn't quite know what to make of that.

"So, what're they gonna do with her?" Nikki asked, tipping the conversation toward the woman responsible for the unlikely circumstance of she and Audrey sitting shoulder to shoulder in the waiting room of a mental hospital.

"Carlene?" Audrey asked. "The police out of it, I think. They didn't ask me much nor write down nutten. Guess dem half-assed approach to dem work good for something. As for the hospital, no doctor was here when dem bring she in, so they sedate her; say the doctor go evaluate her in the morning. Take it from there."

The talk of police, doctors, sedation stirred Nikki's anger and uneasiness anew. "What's to become of her if she gets locked up, eh?" she wondered.

"Is me call police," Audrey hissed, immediately on the defensive.

"No, you're just the one who pushed her," Nikki said, "knowing fully well she was depressed."

No denial from the Audrey front, only an almost meek, "She was doing better."

"What? Because she was smiling and working again?" Nikki replied, exasperated. "Depression doesn't work like that. It's not always about what you show the world; it's about how you feel inside."

"And she's the only one that feel anything inside? Tones was my son!" Audrey finally snapped.

Nikki snapped back, "No, he wasn't. He was Belle's son."

Maybe she meant to be cruel; she wasn't exactly sure. She told herself she was being honest. After all, Audrey took pride in being honest with all of them. Maybe she was mad that Carlene was locked up in this place, because Audrey didn't know how to shut up about other people's lives. Maybe it was the still fresh words from her father's diary; her feeling, like him, that nobody, least of all Audrey, had looked out for the childlike Belle against someone who was essentially a sexual predator.

Didn't matter, she ended up with a face full of spitting and snarling Audrey. "He was my son! Ah me raise he! Me!"

Nikki tried to retreat, but Audrey simply followed leaning into her, boxing her in. "Ar you na t'ink me lose nutten," the older sister demanded, her voice furious. "Everybody have me laka some witch, ar you na t'ink me lose nutten? Why you t'ink me ha fu bury he quick? Bury Mama quick? 'Cause me ha fu make haste go on. Is me one Belle and Columbus have. When something hit her and she asking me for Tones like she don't remember he dead, and me ha fu go through the whole thing again, or tell her he comin' soon, you think it easy? You think it easy, eh?"

Her voice cracked, but she didn't cry. In fact, her eyes were fierce, matching the ferocity of her voice. And when Nikki glanced in the direction of the nurse, she saw her frozen in place, eyes alive with unspoken admonishments, mouth twisted in disapproval, but not daring to say anything or even twitch in their direction. Nikki, too, remained silent. And by degrees, Audrey pulled back, resettled into her own seat and, it seemed, into her skin. When she spoke again, her voice was quieter—emptier—"me dey, no matter what. No matter what. Me ha fu stand still and stand up to it."

She shook her head like a dog with a persistent tick. Her tone was fiercer, though still whisper soft, when she continued, "And for what; everything just get tek way in the end. The boy you raise as you own. The boyfriend you thought was your own, who prefer your retarded sister to you. Because she was pretty and you was just tuff. That's life for women from the mud, unless you like Belle and can pick and choose what you see."

Nikki knew then that Audrey must have been truly shaken by the experience; this was more of her than she usually allowed people to see. Nikki didn't want to feel sympathy for her. She was still pissed at her, still intimidated by her, still didn't understand her. But she heard something in Audrey's voice she'd never heard before, something lost and hurt and broken. Something so fractured it envied the ignorant bliss of Belle, who would never be more than she was, never mature into all she might have been. It was a startling insight and Nikki didn't know what to do with it, how to fit it into the frame. And when she looked across at Audrey, it was to see her mother's face as it was in the bit of newsprint tucked into the crease of her planner. She'd never thought of Audrey as resembling Mama Vi in face before. But there it was, the sharp peaks and valleys of Mama Vi's face, its lived-in quality, the deep pain behind the eyes. And like that, it came back to her: her fight with Fanso after Tones' and Toni's death; his accusation, in spite of his own abuse at Audrey's hands, that she, Nikki, had no right to judge Audrey. Sitting there, eyes locked on her sister's eyes, she understood well how ill-equipped she was to assess Audrey's life, her choices, her mistakes. Hell, she was still grappling with her own.

Audrey wasn't done. "Women from the mud, that's all we are," she said. "Mammy forget that when she was up under that man you call Daddy." Her head was tilted towards Nikki, eyes stormy with contempt. Was she seeing Professor Baltimore's face, Nikki wondered, or was that all for her? "Me remember the first time he step in the yard," Audrey continued, "acting like she was something special, fooling her with it. Fooling her with his fancy words and dem. Knew when they started in with each other, too, could see it on her, smell it on her. And ent he leave in the end? Ent he tek you in the end? An' much as she mourn you loss like you dead, ent she give you to him? Because what? He could give you more. After all, all she was able to give the rest of us was life in the muddy, like that was some kind of shame. Thought better of her than that."

Nikki wasn't sure what any of this had to do with Carlene, but was struck by the unlikely notion of her mother grieving her, of it paining her to give Nikki away. For some reason, not that she'd ever imagined it was easy, that mattered to her all these years later. Truthfully, she hadn't much thought about what it must have been like for her mother to give her up; rarely thought of her mother, before moving here, as more than a woman she didn't know; a tall woman shadowed against the sun.

Audrey was quiet now, out of words, or maybe embarrassed by the words she'd spoken. Nikki couldn't think what to say. "I don't call him Daddy," she offered. "I call him Professor Baltimore or just the Professor." It was an odd thing to say. But when Audrey turned to her again, contempt had been replaced by amusement. Then her lips twitched and Nikki's did, too, in response.

"The Professor," Audrey repeated. Nikki nodded.

"It fit him," the elder sister mused. And they laughed together, the first time Nikki could ever remember them doing that.

Behind the reception desk, the nurse in the pink sweater looked at them strangely, and they laughed harder.

Winston Baltimore, Antigua Journal, Thirty-First Entry

The one, Audrey, who had hidden this secret like pirate treasure, said she could look after the child, was eager to do so in fact, like it was all she'd ever hoped for in life. I told Violet they ought to report the boy to the police for rape. After all, the girl, though womanly in body, was a child, incapable of consent.

She looked at me like I was speaking a particularly foreign-foreign language; there was no understanding there.

Eventually, she got tired of me pressing the issue, and annoyed, I think, of the condemnation she heard in my voice; my tone becoming increasingly impatient. Finally, she snapped, "Boy, this not your business!"

Boy. She hadn't called me that since Before. Hadn't looked at me in that hard, dismissive way either in a while. I saw this aggression now for what it was, defense. But it was a reminder of all the ways we were different, all the reasons we wouldn't be more to each other than we had been. Whatever that was, and of that I was no more sure than I was of my future with Bernadine; that I wanted or deserved more from either of them.

"Boy, this not your business!"

She was right. Scornful and dismissive, but right.

"Boy, this not your business!"

Those were her last words to me, and the last we saw of each other.

Nikki peeked through the bars near the top of the door; she saw Carlene lying on a hard-looking cot in a stark room. Audrey was waiting for her in the car, and she wanted nothing more than to run from all of this.

CHAPTER TWENTY-EIGHT

The demonstrations were gaining momentum and regional media attention. Cam's media rounds, successful in the short term, had succeeded long term, only in splintering the protestors. Sadie's faction, though smaller, had grown ever more militant. It was all the talk on the radio, with the militant splinter camped out in the Valley, around the clock it seemed, to ensure that no trucks got through the new, roughly graded path to the project site.

Cam dug in his heels. Cabinet called a halt to operations to give things time to cool down. Cam blew hard like a Category 5 hurricane, and they trembled, but held steady. Nikki had the feeling that, like her, they had grown tired of the whole debacle, and they were certainly losing political mileage every day. Watching Cam practically baring his teeth and snarling, she was reminded of what Hensen had once said about him being competitive.

"Things are kind of quiet now," she told Jazz. "For a while there, it was really hot. Media, opposition politicians...Hensen and his gang, even vendors camped out, police at the ready. I've never seen anything like it."

"Sounds intense," Jazz agreed vaguely.

"But with nothing happening right now, thanks to the Cabinet veto, most of the protestors have retreated," Nikki continued.

"That's good," Jazz murmured.

"Well, not so good for me," Nikki admitted. "I'm essentially being paid right now for doing nothing, and don't think Cam doesn't let me know it."

"Hm," Jazz said, definitely sounding a million miles away.

"Earth to Jazz," Nikki said. "Something wrong?" That was like her default button lately; she'd learned, or re-learned, since coming to Antigua, no matter how bad shit was, it could always get worse.

Things were quiet now with the project, with the family. Carlene, now out of the mental hospital, was back at Nikki's, and her boys back at Fanso's. She didn't want them with Audrey, and Nikki didn't have the space. It was quiet, and Nikki wanted it to stay still for a while.

"No, something right, actually," Jazz assured her. "I'm pregnant."

She was amazed at her sister for sitting on such big news through her twenty-minute ramble about her job; it seemed the kind of thing you'd open a conversation with. She was a little bit exasperated with Jazz, a little sheepish at monopolizing the conversation. Mostly, though, she was ecstatic for her sister, and her neighbours; if she had any, would've known it, too, for the amount of screaming both sisters were doing.

"Oh, Jazz, Jazz, Jazz…"

"That's my name." Her sister laughed, and she sounded so happy Nikki could swim in it.

Her face hurt, she was grinning so much.

"I'm happy for you, Jazz." She breathed, when she found words again.

"Thank you," her sister said. "And you'd better start thinking of baby names, Goddie."

Nikki laughed. "Goddie? Really?"

"Who else would I ask?" Jazz asked.

Nikki grew all warm and goose-bumpy at that. With Jazz, she knew such a deep sense of belonging, she sometimes wondered what she was doing in Antigua while Jazz was miles away in New York. She was stubborn, that's all there was to it; Antigua had been one pothole after another.

"You're the only sister I got," Jazz reminded her. "You're it. Goddie."

Nikki wondered, not for the first time, when she'd become such a crybaby. But certain feelings were catching up with her. Like how isolated she'd felt from Jazz, more so since the wedding; how envious she'd felt of her since the wedding. After all, there was Jazz living the dream, not her dream, but a dream. And there was her world, lying broken on the pavement like Humpty Dumpty; all the king's horses, all the king's men, and all the Super Glue in the world unable to put it back together again. But in this moment, all she felt for her sister was joy, and it threatened to overwhelm her.

"Joy," she blurted. "That's my choice."

"Joy?" Jazz questioned.

"Yes, for the baby's name."

"But you don't even know whether it's a boy or a girl yet," Jazz teased.

"What, a boy can't be named Joy?"

"I don't know about 'a boy' but no boy of mine," was Jazz's comeback. "Girl, are you crazy? Do you want this boy to grow up traumatized?"

"So, you're hoping for a boy then?"

"Well, yeah, knock on wood," Jazz said. "Mostly, I want it to be in good health, with all its parts attached, but I know Gi would love a son."

"When do you find out?"

"Not for a few more weeks, if we choose," Jazz said. "I kind of prefer to be surprised, though, so we're still debating that."

"Okay, well, I'll give it some more thought," Nikki said.

"You do that," Jazz said.

"So, give me the details. When are you due and all that?"

"Late December. Of course, the downside is we probably won't make it for Carnival as planned," Jazz said. "I really wanted Gi to see it and all, but…"

"…priorities have shifted. I get it." Nikki wanted to bite her tongue at the wistful note in her voice. She missed Jazz.

There was silence on the line, then Jazz's, "You'll always be my favourite sister. That'll never change."

"I'm your *only* sister," Nikki reminded her.

"Well then, the bar isn't that high, is it?" Jazz teased. "Seriously, though Nikks, this doesn't change anything."

"Jazz, everything's already changed," Nikki said. "But that's life, change, and just as you get used to that, more change. But, no matter what, you're still always in my heart. And I'm happy for you, never mind how I sound. I miss you sometimes, miss being able to chat your ear off all night."

"Well, nothing's stopping you from doing that," Jazz argued.

"I know, I know." Though truth was, Nikki also knew they'd grown worlds apart.

"You're coming up for the birth, right?" Jazz asked. Nikki hesitated. "Come on, it'll be Christmas…'pleease come home, for Christmass…'" Jazz sang at full volume to the tune of "I'll be Home for Christmas."

"Okay okay, just stop the caterwauling, please. You're scaring the strays over in the next village."

Jazz laughed. "Okay," she said finally. "So, you think about those baby names, and remember my child has to live it down for the rest of its life."

"Don't tempt me," Nikki teased.

Carlene was back out to work, bolstered by antidepressants, and Nikki allowed herself to relax a bit.

They'd spoken about her latest episode.

"I wasn' really goin' do nothing," Carlene insisted. "Tell you the truth, me na really know what fly up in me. But she always talking, you know; always letting you know wha wrong wid you. An' after a time, it come like the cover blow off de pressure cooker or the tire explode or somethin'. Like you can't take it no more, tamping down you feelings to make peace, you know. And you snap."

"Carlene, I want you to go see a doctor, to talk," Nikki said. "I'll pay."

"Ah na de dollars, Nikki. Well, not just de dollars. I didn't belong in no crazy house," Carlene insisted. "And I certainly don't need no head doctor. You start do that and everybody think you crazy."

Nikki gave it to her straight; she was getting better at that. "And what do you think being in a mental institution does for your reputation?"

Carlene's eyes flashed with old fire. "She didn't have no cause to put me there. She's a old bitch, an' God go do for her. Watch, you see."

"She didn't put you there," Nikki reminded her. "The neighbours called the police after you started screaming and waving a knife around. The kids—Belle, Chris—were scared out of their minds, and as for Audrey, I've never seen her so spooked."

"What? You defending her now?" Carlene demanded. "She never like me. Never. Never think say me good enough for her precious son. Her son. What a joke, like she could ever hold man long enough, with her bitter self, fi mek picknee."

"Carlene!"

"What, I not saying nothing you don' believe yourself."

"Audrey is a human being. She has feelings like everyone else."

"Since when? An' since when she have you jigging to her song and dance. You have memory like fowl. Is this same human being treating you like dog shit. She like you 'bout as much as she like me. You self know how she say as she feel without care for people feeling. She done do it to you. She do it to me that night."

"I'm not saying she was right to say what she did."

"You know what, don't say nothing 'tall to me," Carlene said angrily. "Don't defend her to me. Me can't stomach that."

She stalked to her room, the door slamming loudly behind her. Nikki left it alone after that.

CHAPTER TWENTY-NINE

I'm in the best physical shape of my life," she told her mother. "I run every day. I think I almost need it now, which is kinda funny, because in New York, I hated running. It was Terry who introduced me to it, and he had to drag me outta bed each time."

Nikki smiled at that memory.

"Terry is very into perfection and control—his mind, his body, the whole deal. He's the kind of guy that will never go to flab, though he claims he was quite flabby as a teenager and no girls paid him any mind. Hard to believe that, and mysteriously, there are no pictures."

Nikki chuckled at this. Terry was vain. Still, it was the first time she'd thought of him with affection since their break-up, and that felt like progress.

"When I first came here," she continued, "I picked it up again. I was having difficulty sleeping, and it helped. At first, it was weird doing it alone, my feet hitting the pavement. And let me tell you, running on these roads ain't easy. But there you are. You and your falling feet. You and your hammering heart. You and your breaths. You and the quiet in your head." Nikki laughed at herself. But she'd become addicted to this babbling to her mom. Impossible in life, it had become like manna in death. Often it was internal, but sometimes, like now, it segued to real talk, with actual words and sound, usually without her knowledge. "When I'd get done, I'd feel almost high," she continued. "I used to hope that life could give that high. That, in time, you get a chance to touch the things that would make you feel happy, you know, like you belonged to something."

"You worry too much; must come from living in America so long," a voice said, and Nikki laughed at herself a little more.

It was another of her internal voices, this one tired of the whining. It was, at least she hoped it was, one of the voices all people had, voices which pulled at each other sometimes, having spirited arguments about this path or that. It so happened that this one was remarkably similar to her mother's voice, a voice she struggled to remember in less meditative moments.

"I barely remember my mother's voice," she said aloud.

"You know," a voice said, this one nearly startling her out of her skin, "people likely to think you crazy; you sit down up hear chatting to yourself like this."

She relaxed slightly, tense for other reasons. This voice was familiar, and real.

"They're used to me," she snapped. "And they know better than to interrupt, or eavesdrop. Plus, I suspect they have their own business to get on with."

Aeden sighed.

So did Nikki.

"What are you doing here, Aeden?" she demanded. "Please tell me this isn't some weird stalker trip. And how long have you been standing there anyway?"

He came closer, leaned against the neem.

"I was at the entrance to the village," he explained. "I saw you come in. I had just come outta Freemansville on my way from Seatons. A friend of mine had invited me out on his new boat."

"You have friends?" she asked, before she could stop herself. She was being only partly sarcastic, too.

Aeden peered down at her with annoyance and disappointment, and suddenly, she felt small. She stood up, dusted off. "So, you saw me and what?"

"Impulse," he said. "I decide to follow you in. Didn' wan' leave things between us the way they were. I miss you. An' you won't cut a brother some slack. Not even after my flowers and my little desperate plea for you to call me."

His bouquet of white, red, and yellow flowers had since dried on Nikki's kitchen island where she'd left them untended.

When she didn't reply, Aeden hovered even more, chewing on his plump bottom lip, shifting from leg to leg. "Look, I was driving by, saw you and thought I'd catch up," he rambled. "I was flashing you but, boy, when you ah drive you na look back 'tall. Or maybe you didn' recognize the car. It hard to miss…loud, black, muscle car, vintage. Is one from Daddy garage. Where I was goin' was too far to walk and didn't have no bus route, so. Or maybe you see the car and couldn't picture me in it, so didn't give it a second look. Wouldn' blame you. It suit me about as much as one of Daddy's jackets. An even if you knew it was me, can't exactly blame you for not paying me no mind when me ah de one screw up everyt'ing, right? Anyway, didn't know what I was goin' do or say…was surprised when I see you turn up here; thought you were goin' by your people…just follow an impulse is all…"

He finally ran out of words.

Nikki felt exposed. "So you've been watching me the whole time?" she accused.

"Not really, no," Aeden replied. "Oh God, jack! I know what I say wha-night-there was thoughtless, but I not that insensitive. I figured you were coming to visit your mother grave. That's private business. I stayed up at the church. Was chatting little bit with this woman, the pianist up there. She say she normally wait up there for you when she done rehearsing, which she do practically every day now that she on retirement; help take care of the church, too, she said. Boy, she can talk. Anyway, she say she normally wait for you 'til you come up. I wanted to catch you on the way up, I guess, so I started down the hill, saw your lips moving. I wasn't spying, I swear."

He held his palms up. "I didn't hear anything," he assured her.

She believed him. After all, the problem with Aeden wasn't his deceptiveness, but his careless blathering once he got going. He'd been straighter with her than any of the people she'd worked with at Tourism, and less complicated than the family she was still trying to make heads or tails of. But the shame that had never quite gone away, since her Hensen chapter, had resurfaced big-time that night on her porch. That was Aeden's doing. But, she sighed to herself, maybe not his fault.

The silence stretched between them.

"What can I do?" Aeden wondered out loud. He was wandering around now, circling the grave, almost so that she had to turn with him to keep him in her sights. She'd never seen him so agitated. "Me na have plenty friend, Nikki. But from the first time me see you, something 'bout you grab me. You was all suited up, hanging on every word that walking-cardboard cut-out, Hensen, was saying. You weren't my type at all. An' me coulda see you min into he. I was by the helicopter watching you come up, that day we went Barbuda, remember?"

Nikki nodded slightly, a little dizzy with all the spinning now.

He continued, "He said something to you, and you look up at him and smile and it was like, it was like the difference between starlight and...and...and lying under the stars at Blackman's Ridge."

She grabbed his arm to make him stop and he met her eyes, which were huge and kind of wild. He breathed and she found herself taking a breath, too, and, uncomfortable as it was, made herself hold his gaze. She wanted to run from him and this complication but found she also wanted to hear what he had to say, wanted to make things right between them. She couldn't even begin to look at why; what was, just was.

"Mi spirit tek you right then and there," Aeden said.

Spirit tek…there it was again, the first and last word on whether a person was in or out.

"… looking at you in yuh sharp-as-nails green pant suit, I know you wouldn't give a ragga youth like me the time of day."

She rarely wore that suit; it was stiff and itchy. But she liked the colour.

"It set off your eyes nice nice. Never see eyes like dem before. Kinda yellow and green at the same time. Me say to me'self this gyal na normal."

Nikki remembered thinking the same about him.

"An' though you were giving it 'way to him…"

She stiffened, and he caught it, quickly clarifying. "Your smile, I mean. It was all for him. Still, me tell meself, see that gyal dey, she more than meet the eye. I was curious. I wasn't even thinking 'bout no girlfriend thing. I just wanted to get to know you. I never ever wanted to do nothing to dim that smile. Because, Hensen wrong, you know you are something special. And is his loss if he don't know that."

Their eyes held.

She saw out of the corner of her eye, his hand, his right hand, coming towards her face, hesitating, then caressing her, cheek to chin, feather light. All kinds of uninvited things stirred in her at that.

"You know what?" Aeden continued. "I think he do know, and I think it eating him up."

His other hand came up until he was cupping her face, and she found herself leaning into that caress. Then he was leaning forward, and his lips were soft on hers, their touch a mere whisper.

"So, that boy," Marisol began later, as Nikki sipped the guava drink that had been offered, and nibbled on guava cheese. "He's not one of Kendrick Cameron's children?"

"Yes," Nikki replied cautiously, wondering how much Marisol had seen.

"Thought so," the older woman said. "He's the spit of his father."

Then Marisol jumped up with that little clap Nikki had come to find quite endearing.

"Oh, listen," she said. "I have something I want to play for you."

Nikki sighed internally, but smiled nonetheless, getting up to follow Marisol to the homey parlour. She grabbed some extra guava cheese for her saucer, figuring she'd need the fortitude.

Marisol opened her piano, played with it a bit, limbering her fingers. Nikki sat, drawing one of the crocheted cushions unto her lap. She recalled the parade of compositions Marisol had tested on her since the start of their friendship. Usually, they were church hymns or patriotic fare that sounded like church hymns, and not the Kirk Franklin variety either, but the kind people dosed through in stuffy old cathedrals. They moved one to dispassion, even as Marisol's heavy touch with the instrument she loved grated on the nerves.

Nikki listened. But, remarkably, Marisol's fingers were light on the keys, as light as Aeden's lips on hers.

The music leapfrogged, with abandon, and then slowed to a wistful sigh, deepening to pain that Nikki felt as an ache in her gut. And Marisol was mercifully silent, none of that humming or gravelly singing she never seemed to realize she was doing. That would have been distracting. The music spoke its own tale. Lyrics would have been superfluous.

"That was beautiful," Nikki said, unable to hide the surprise in her voice.

Marisol smiled. "Well, it's something different I wanted to try. Actually, it came to me and I went with it, working it out, working it out these past months."

"It's beautiful," Nikki said.

"You know where it started?"

"No."

"That same day I gave you your mother's picture; that night, everything I saw in that picture, everything you expressed on seeing, it started to flow through me to the tips of my fingers," Marisol said earnestly. "At first, it was a little tickle. But it wouldn't let me be. I kept coming back to it."

Marisol closed the piano, turned fully to face Nikki. "I didn't know if to play it for you," she said. "Quite apart from the fact that it's not the kind of thing I usually do, and I didn't know if it was any good."

The irony of that caused Nikki to smile. "Play it for me forever," one of her voices, several of them in fact, wanted to shout. "Never ever play anything else ever again."

She giggled and Marisol echoed it, delighted, and it was okay to laugh together, even if they were laughing for different reasons. It felt good. Then Marisol clasped Nikki's hands tightly; her movement so sudden and intimate Nikki found herself drawing back instinctively.

"The other reason I wasn't sure if to play it, honestly, was I didn't want to pick any scabby cuts, you know," Marisol said.

Nikki's brow furrowed.

"Your mother death bring you here, but like everything else doing it best to shove you back out into the cold," the older woman continued. "Sometimes I say to myself, why they don't give the girl an easy time—them people out Blackman Valley, Hensen J. Stephens and the square pegs in round holes at that ministry that didn't know what a good thing they had—is run they want run her?"

Nikki made a sound somewhere between a chuckle and a sigh. "Marisol, you don't know," she said.

"You think I don't know," the older woman said. Then, as suddenly as she'd reached for Nikki's hands, she pulled her into a rough hug, and Nikki fought her instincts, allowed herself to be embraced and to embrace the feeling of comfort that came with it. "You home, see, see," Marisol crooned. "Na mek nobody run you from your own home 'less you really and truly ready fu go." At that, she sang a bit of the King Short Shirt calypso classic, with all the defiance the song inspired, "Nobody Go Run Me."

Nikki drew back a little, startled that Marisol knew any calypso songs, perhaps just as startled that she recognized the old song.

"I get used to having you around," Marisol said before releasing her fully and getting up altogether, returning to the piano where she began playing her latest composition again.

Warmed and confused at the same time, Nikki curled back into the chair.

She stopped in at the family house before heading home.

"I see they start sharing licks for you, too, on the radio," Audrey said casually. "Not just Cameron and the politicians and dem."

This was news to Nikki. Sure, she knew she was in the enemy camp as some saw it, but the attacks had not turned personal.

Cam was the threat, not her. She wondered if this was part of what had unsettled Marisol. Had she heard the radio, too?

"Mmhm," Audrey said, seeing her surprise and consternation. "Some people can't keep things at a certain level. I warn you 'bout lying down with dogs."

Nikki bit her tongue.

"Don't bother wid dem, though," Audrey continued. "You can tell me an' all to go to hell. Long as you know to your heart you not doing nothing wrong."

Nikki stared at her older sister in amazement.

"What?" Audrey demanded. "You think I wish you evil?"

Nikki's lips moved, but nothing came out.

Audrey continued, "I call in to the radio, tell dem watch how they talkin', 'cause you have smadee."

Nikki laughed, a rough cough of a laugh. "I have smadee," she repeated.

"You have people, yes," Audrey said. "Wha dem think? You drop from tree. I don' mind they talk, you know, so long as they keep it at a certain level."

"I have smadee," Nikki mumbled to herself, thrown for the second—no, the third—time that day. It was a day of surprises.

CHAPTER THIRTY

Nikki came home from her morning run to the sound of laughter. She found Carlene and Aeden out back feasting on a bag of guavas and chatting.

They looked up as she stepped out.

"Hey," Aeden said, jumping up. "You back. I came by to drop off these guavas Tanty sent for you. Is the sweetest thing."

He chucked one of the guavas wholesale into his mouth, smiling around it, too smugly for her taste, as though picking up the way her eyes tracked him, Carlene and the crocus bag at his feet. "Nuh worry, man, plenty more there," he said, with that amused air.

The silence stretched, and Carlene got up. Nikki stepped aside to let her pass, but the younger woman leaned in closer. "Heng on pon him," she whispered. "Him day-wid-able."

Nikki's mouth quirked a smile at this in spite of herself and the tension eased slightly.

"What you doing here, Aeden?" she asked when they were alone.

"I just told you," he said, his brow crinkling now in confusion. If there was one thing that spoiled his too-pretty face, it was those lumberjack eyebrows.

"No, showing up like this," Nikki clarified. "I don't like that. I don't want a little kiss making you feel like you can take certain liberties."

"That's all it was," he wondered, "a little kiss?"

Nikki's eyes danced away. "I don't know all that it is, but I don't want you making assumptions," she said.

"Wouldn't dream of it," he said, that teasing, flirtatious lilt in his voice.

"Aeden, I'm serious."

"I hear you, and I know," he said easily. "You have the handle."

She said nothing, and he reached into the bag.

"So, you goin' try one of these guavas or what?" he asked. "I promise you, is the sweetest thing ever."

And Nikki smiled, in spite of herself, for the second time that morning.

"I was wondering what become of you," Tanty said, taking Nikki by the hand and leading her through the sprinkle of remaining protesters and the thick bushes to her family plot.

Tanty's hand was callused and firm around hers, yet gentle to the touch. It made her think of Mama Vi; she remembered when she'd first returned to Antigua as a child, stepping into that open yard to curious and hostile stares, and a mother she didn't remember, blocking her from it all and taking her hand in hers.

"I got the guavas, thank you," Nikki said, extracting her hand and pushing away the memory.

"I have some more here for you, and some ground provisions," Tanty said, heading to the crocus bag, packed and ready under the blue tarpaulin. Sadie, wielding a hoe among the vegetable beds, didn't look in their direction.

"No, Tanty, I can't accept," Nikki said.

"Nonsense," Tanty insisted. "Is you they for."

"I can't take food out of your mouth," Nikki said.

The old woman was visibly insulted by this, and Nikki hastened to accept the bounty. The last thing she wanted to do was get on Tanty's bad side. After the angry glares that had greeted her out by the dirt road, she fully expected to return to find her jeep jacked or keyed. Sadie's anger, meanwhile, rippled like visible waves of heat in the air between them, though the younger woman hadn't yet looked up. It was good to have a Tanty looking out for her in the midst of all the hostility.

"I didn't think I was welcome here anymore," Nikki confessed.

"Girl, stop you chupidness," Tanty admonished. "What all dat foolishness have to do wid you and me?"

"We wouldn't have met if it hadn't been for all this foolishness," Nikki reminded her, but the old woman waved this off.

"Besides, I thought maybe you were mad at me, too," Nikki continued.

The old woman sucked her teeth in irritation.

"I done tell you my spirit tek you," she chided. "That stronger than all this nonsense."

Nikki accepted this, finally, silently.

"How've you been?" she asked, settling in for the cataloguing of aches and pains expected of someone in their twilight years. But Tanty skipped that part. "My Tanty come to me in a dream the other night," she said instead.

"You believe in that stuff," Nikki couldn't help scoffing.

"Don't interrupt, child," Tanty chided. "That's what happen to you all young people nowadays, cause all this confusion. Same thing with that granddaughter ah mine. Headstrong. Don't know all-you ass from all-you elbow but won't take heed. You all don't know how all this nonsense hurt my spirit."

"I'm sorry," Nikki said. "This isn't how I wanted things to go. I wanted...I tried to..."

Tanty interrupted, her hand over Nikki's. "My Tanty dream me. She tell me is time for me to go to that place, the dungeon. She say I mus' take others with me. Remind them." Nikki didn't know what to say to this.

"You want to take people to the dungeon," she said slowly.

"Hm," Tanty confirmed, with a sharp nod. "And you must help me."

Tanty had this notion that the pilgrimage would help to heal the wounds caused by all the recent fighting. She believed, too, that it would help those who couldn't see or understand what all the fuss was about; it would help them understand the sacredness of the place. The way Tanty saw it, the land at Blackman's Valley and up to the Ridge was washed in the blood of her ancestors, people who had survived the worst one person could inflict on another, and deserved their temples like the great gods and ancient pharaohs. She believed that the pilgrimage would help ease the tension, settle the spirits, bring the warring factions to common understanding. Besides, she was getting old and hadn't been up there in a while. She longed to reconnect with her ancestors. Her tanty had given her permission and that was good enough for her. She held Nikki's hands and looked into her eyes, and said with more intensity than Nikki had ever seen from her, "People must know who dem be, must remember what important."

Nikki nodded, hearing somehow the many things unspoken. She still didn't know why Tanty was saying all this to her and not Sadie, but she accepted. It would take a little while, and more than a little effort, to pull together, but she would do it. Nikki nodded a second time as if to confirm this.

When Tanty smiled at her in response, she felt herself swell up inside and had to look away, lest she embarrass herself with tears she couldn't really explain.

CHAPTER THIRTY-ONE

Nikki was sitting in Mama Vi's restaurant, after hours, with Fanso and Tones.

"You remember Ms. Cameron?" Tones asked. Nikki, of course, shook her head, as she never remembered anyone from childhood days in Antigua; it was reflex now.

"Ms. Cameron, yes," Fanso said. He was relaxed and smiling, that weary smile that had become familiar during and after his long days at Mama Vi's. He was discovering that having his own business—especially one that was attracting good business—was a taxing enterprise, in more ways than one.

Tones—one half of his hair plaited, the other half sticking up in an unruly Afro, a purple pick sticking out of it—wore a greasy-looking pair of jeans and a T-shirt like he'd been working on cars all day and hadn't had time to bathe. He smelled of oil and sweat. Fanso smelled vinegary and salty, of fried things and seasonings, johnny cakes and snapper escovitch. Nikki was hungry thinking about it.

And happy sitting and inhaling their sounds and smells, happy to sit there listening to them forever in this little bubble of time where everything was fine, and childhood was viewed through the hazy lens of nostalgia. Both men's eyes danced happily to the melody of their childhood memories, and even Nikki could hear the music.

"Nikki, you don' remember?" Fanso asked, still on the subject of the corner shop owner, Ms. Cameron. "She was up near the entrance to the village; wouldn' pay you no mind when you come in, especially if you were little. An' if she was busy bagging sugar or something, forget it; you had to wait. An' don' forget the care of your brain an' ask her the price ah nutten."

By this time, Tones was practically falling out of his chair laughing. And Nikki giggled, but a part of her reached out with a stray arm to tell him, "Be careful."

But when she spoke, it was like he didn't hear her.

And the boys laughed and laughed and laughed.

And then Tones fell.

Nikki woke with a start.

"Nikki."

Fresh from the unsettling dream, the call, though whispered, startled her. Carlene's voice called out again, louder, accompanied by a soft knock this time.

Nikki pulled herself against the wooden headboard. She dry-washed her face with her hand, tried to answer, swallowed, tried again.

"Yes."

The door creaked open, and Carlene, wearing a white cotton nightie that glimmered like a beacon in the dark, eased through the doorway.

"You awake?"

Nikki would have made a crack at this stating of the obvious, but Carlene's voice and body language were uncharacteristically tentative.

"Yes," she answered simply instead.

"'Memba how you say, when me first come out de hospital, if me wan' see wan doctor you'd pay fi it? You mean it?" Carlene asked.

Nikki beckoned her closer, scooted along the bed, making space. Carlene accepted the invitation.

"Yes, I meant it," Nikki said.

"You can afford it?" Carlene asked.

"Yes."

She actually wasn't sure that she could; figured psychiatrists or psychologists or whatever were as expensive here as anywhere, and didn't know if there were any private ones in Antigua, but she wasn't about to get in the way of Carlene finally admitting that she needed help. Carlene sighed, the admission not coming up easy; she picked at a loose thread on the spread. "I can't sleep," she said. "I not no good to meself like this."

This was not news to Nikki. She'd heard Carlene's footsteps and the din of the TV at all hours, no matter the hour. Plus, though Carlene was back out to work, Fanso complained to Nikki that she was dragging. Nikki knew, if she wasn't family, she'd probably have been fired a while ago. But after their Audrey-laced argument, Nikki had held her tongue, though all of it pointed to the unavoidable truth that Carlene was not taking her medication. The nurse at the mental hospital had warned them that many outpatients tended to slack off once they felt better; it was about feeling in control; nobody wanted something else, something chemical, in charge of their moods and thoughts. "You have to keep at her," the nurse had warned. But they hadn't and it was showing.

"Nikki, me frighten bad," Carlene said in a hushed, hurried voice, as though afraid of being overheard and anxious to have it done with. "True say, me rather dead than crazy, Nikki."

When Nikki would have interrupted, she steamrolled on. "...an' sometimes me feel like crazy deh tek me, you know. Just de same thing ah run roun' an' roun' me head 'til it feel like de only way fi get any relief ah fi cut off de head. Jus' chop it off, mek it shut up. An' like me feeling dem not me own, you know. Is like a struggle fi keep de trembling under control, fi hol' the tears dem in, fi keep de anger under manners, you know. Me body nah feel like fi me own, nor me thoughts dem, an' like me can't see roun' corner to when tings go change, you know. It defeating me."

Nikki didn't know what to say to any of this, but could identify with more of it than she felt comfortable admitting, even to herself.

Carlene sighed. "Me miss him, Nikki. Me miss him bad. An' him bein' gone jus' don' make no kinda sense to me. Is like every time me think 'bout it, me ha fi remind meself what real and what nah real, you know. It give me a jolt every blasted time. That nah normal, right?"

Nikki hugged her then, silently, as Jazz had done for her more than once. She felt Carlene melt into the comfort, felt the trembling give way to tears. Not quiet tears either, but tears like a child might cry, unrestrained; the sound she made had the same plaintive quality. Nikki held her tighter; but as abruptly as a child's tears, Carlene's crying was over and she was by the window, solid and resolved, while Nikki wondered if time had skipped. "Me wan' be a mother to me children dem again," Carlene said firmly.

"Can you afford that?" Fanso asked. They were wrapping up their weekly meeting about the state of his restaurant's affairs, and Nikki had told him about Carlene's decision to seek professional help.

"Well," she replied. "I checked around. It's not cheap, but I'm going to do it. Carlene finally realizes she needs to talk to someone and that's a big step for her. She wants to be able to look after her kids again, and this is the first step in that direction."

Fanso sighed heavily, scratching his head, a movement Nikki connected with worry. As a boy, she'd seen him do it often enough; he would scratch his head and shuffle his feet under the weight of one of Audrey's verbal assaults.

"Yeah, that situation," he said. "It getting kinda difficult. With the kinda long hours I workin' now, Twenett dealing with twice, three times the load at home. Add to that, Carlene's kids. The way it dragging on. She not happy 'bout it. She not happy 'bout it at all."

Nikki offered to take all the children—Carlene's and Fanso's— that Sunday. She took them, and Carlene, with her to Deep Bay. They were on the way back—the children singing some song in French taught to them by Fanso's wife, Antoinette, at the top of their lungs, Carlene giggling and singing along, getting the words wrong—when Cam called.

"You hear what dem crazy people do to my property?" he barked at her.

"Is rape, that's what it is," Sadie's voice pealed out like a big old cathedral bell—tuneless but commanding. "They wan' violate all the virgin land in this country. Nothing mus' lef' that don't have a piece of rock or wall or metal on it. Nothen mus' lef' for poor people just interested in working the ground. Some politician or money man must mix up in it. Them disrespectful and God go do for them."

The newscaster's silky voice, with its pseudo-American radio accent, cut in then: "That was Sadie Humphreys, one of the leaders in the Blackman's Ridge protest action against local investor Kendrick Cameron's planned spa to the stars. Humphreys and five other protestors are currently in police custody in connection with alleged acts of vandalism and larceny at the Blackman's Ridge site. Police sources indicate there is enough evidence for charges to be laid as early as Monday morning. Several items were reportedly stolen from one of the construction trailers placed on site before government called a halt amidst increasing community resistance. Painted on the side of one of the trailers was 'King Court is Alive,' apparently a reference to the enslaved African leader, and national hero, who, in 1736, planned a slave revolt to coincide with the governor's ball, only to be betrayed and later executed at Ottos pasture with other rebel leaders. Court was recently immortalized in a song by calypso queen Ivena, the quote apparently a reference to the song's passionate cry that the spirit of the country's revolutionaries lives on in the defiant will of its people…"

As the song cut in, Nikki switched off the radio. She was en route to Aeden's helipad where she would meet Cam and Aeden to fly up to the Ridge.

She'd dropped Carlene and the kids off at Fanso's place, promising to swing by later to collect Carlene. All were curious about developments at the Ridge.

Cam was red and fuming, his likeness to Santa Claus increasing in a weird way.

"You see what I get for playing nice," he steamed, lighting into Nikki as she alighted from her car. "In the Antiguan vernacular, nice is soft. Don't know what I listening to you for. What the hell you know 'bout Antigua people!?"

The sleepy demeanour Aeden often affected around his father lifted. "Daddy, ease up nuh," he said.

His father looked at him like he'd grown a second head. "Since when you get involved in my business," Cam said. "What, she givin' you wife or something? Never have nothing to say 'bout nothing, like all the weed you smoke fogging up your brain. Now this."

Aeden lapsed into silence and Cam's eyes narrowed as he studied his son. Nikki turned back to her car.

"Where the hell you goin'?" Cam demanded.

"I'm not getting paid to take your abuse," she threw back, her heart hammering, her voice calm.

"But you getting paid though!" Cam shouted at her.

"Well, do what you have to do, but I didn't come here for this," Nikki said, slamming her car door and taking off.

"Good for you, gyal," Carlene said later. "Na tek no shit from dem."

"It was stupid," Nikki responded. "He's my biggest client. My most reliable paycheck. Who am I kidding? He's not a client, he's my employer, only sans employee benefits because I want to tell myself I'm an independent contractor. Where are the other paychecks? Except for Fanso, it's Cam, even when nothing is happening on the project, which is most of the damn time."

"So what? Dat mean you suppose to mek him chat to you anyhow?"

They were on the All Saints highway, cars whizzing by as they often did on this accident-prone road. Nikki had picked Carlene up from Fanso's without going in, barely able to keep her foot off the accelerator for the time it took to toot her horn and for Carlene to settle into the seat next to her, eyes curious. She felt the urge to drive and keep driving right off the edge of this confounding and claustrophobic island, if necessary. She was calmer now, the cool evening air coming at her, doing its job. But as Carlene pressed for details, it all came tumbling out.

"Maybe now you can take on some of them other jobs you does have to turn down," Carlene speculated.

Nikki looked across at her, surprised. Since helping Fanso launch Mama Vi and gaining some prominence on the admittedly ill-fated Blackman's Ridge project, she'd had offers. But time hadn't allowed her to contemplate them and she certainly hadn't discussed them with anyone, least of all Carlene.

"What? You forget say me live wid you?" Carlene asked.

She figured then that Carlene had heard her one-sided conversations with this prospective client or that. Made sense. They were up in each other's armpits, another situation that had to be resolved soon. Nikki turned her eyes back to the road.

CHAPTER THIRTY-TWO

"You really mash Daddy corn; he didn't stop cussing for 'bout an hour," Aeden chortled. And Nikki wasn't in the mood for it.

He'd come by, late, without calling again. They were on Nikki's front veranda this time; Nikki having stepped out rather than invite him in.

Typically, her troubles amused him, as it seemed, did the world in general. Nikki's frown deepened.

"Look, Aeden…"

"I bet you hear from him by tomorrow," he cut in.

"What?"

"Yeah," he said. "See, now you have his respect."

"Huh?"

"If you'd stood there and taken it, he wouldn't treat you with no regard again," Aeden said. "He don't respect people that take his shit; just give them more shit. An' don't get me wrong, he like to win, so he'll throw more at you, call it higher-quality shit, but he'll respect you, too."

Nikki stared at him, and he smirked. "See, is to know how the cock think," he said. "He like to strut, but he like his fowl and dem to have fight in them."

She tilted her head at him, brow furrowed but a slight smile on her lips. "Hens and roosters, Aeden?"

"Hey, whatever works."

She sat heavily on the veranda wall. "So," she said, "how bad is it?"

"Up at the Ridge? It bad, but not bad bad. Is more a nuisance thing than anything."

"And you think Sadie have anything to do with this?"

He shrugged.

"They were speculating on the radio," Nikki continued. "More than speculating, really...say an anonymous source says our recently departed government would be fronting bail money when the matter comes up in magistrate's court tomorrow."

Aeden shrugged, seeming decidedly disinterested now that they weren't talking about Nikki and his father anymore.

"Some of the radio callers say the new opposition is pulling their strings," Nikki continued. She wouldn't put it past Hensen and his cronies; everything was about politics with them.

But Aeden shook his head. "Maybe some of the others, I don't know, but not all like Sadie so," he replied.

"I know," Nikki agreed, calling to mind a picture of the slim but sturdy young woman.

"You know," she mused, "in a funny kind of way, I respect her a little. She stands for what she believes, and she's fearless about it."

Aeden made a sound that could've been agreement, or not.

"You know..." Nikki began.

"What?" Aeden asked when she didn't continue.

"I have an idea that could save this situation, broker a kind of peace but..."

"But what?"

"But I walked away from your father today, or did you forget?"

Aeden turned to her fully. "You na hear wha me say," he demanded, clearly exasperated with her. "Tell him. If it's a good idea, he'll listen. If not, he'll try to rub your face in it. So, you better come good."

Nikki quirked her lips at this. "Thanks for coming to my defense, by the way," she said.

Aeden smiled, eyes still locked with hers.

"This has taught me a lesson though," Nikki said, turning away. "I *need need need* to diversify, even if it means working more hours than actually exist in the day. I can't deal with being under someone's thumb again."

"Hmm..." Aeden mumbled, angled sideways again.

"...you know," Nikki mused, "believe it or not, I have a reputation back home, in New York, as a serial worker. Unable to stick with anything for too long. For once, I'd like to finish what I start."

"So, finish it," Aeden said.

So, she called up Cam who did listen, after a little huffing and puffing, and the following morning, he was able to beat the new opposition, with a little pull string from his allies in the new government, in posting bail for Sadie and company. And Nikki announced, on radio, their plans to support a pilgrimage to the old slave dungeon, describing it as an act of friendship meant to illustrate they were all really on the same side.

"I still watching all-you, you know," Sadie said. "Don't think you can buy me."

"Perish the thought," Nikki said, with mild sarcasm. One of Sadie's eyes began to twitch in a way that reminded Nikki of the tension in Mama Vi's body before she sprang when something in the yard upset her.

They—Nikki, Sadie, and Tanty—were sitting in the Valley, under the narrow strip of blue tarpaulin where the pair of farmers routinely took their breaks from the heat of the sun.

"Nobody's trying to buy you, Sadie," Nikki said. "We are hoping that you'll listen and see that nobody's planning to cut your livelihood. In fact, you stand to benefit quite a bit."

"How you figure?"

"I knew you hadn't been listening," Nikki said.

Sadie's face turned mutinous again at this affront.

Nikki pushed on quickly. "I foresee…"

"Oh, you ah obeah woman now."

"No, but this is what I sold to Cam who, before I did so, was convinced he could simply absorb this land. I convinced him that not only didn't he need to, there was no way on earth, in heaven or hell, he could succeed. I was convinced of this, after Aeden brought me here to meet you."

"So, you're a saint now," Sadie said with a "chuups."

And Tanty, sitting nearby, barked a harsh, "Sadie, listen!"

Sadie quieted, though her body and face transmitted her need to be upset, still, about something. Too much anger had been building for too many weeks for it simply to give now without a struggle.

"I just try to be a realist, Sadie, that's all," Nikki said matter-of-factly. "To represent the interests of my client. It's not in my client's interest to have the whole Valley and, by extension, the whole country, up in arms about this development. I either find a way to make it work, or tell him to walk away."

"So, why not tell him to walk away?"

"Because he's a pig-headed mule who won't budge, if he thinks there's a chance in hell of getting his way."

That stumped Sadie, who, though her lips twitched, didn't quite smile. Nikki did smile. "Look, there'll be jobs for people in the area…"

"Jobs," Sadie spat disdainfully. "That's the problem with your clueless politicians and you long-belly businessman and dem. Dem tink 'jobs, jobs, jobs' ah compensation enough for giving 'way yuh birthright."

"Let me finish, nuh," Nikki said, a distinctly Antiguan sing to her phrasing.

"Who stopping you?" Sadie shot back.

"The farmers in the Valley stand to benefit from the sale of goods to the property on the Ridge."

"We've heard that one before."

"And we'd be willing to sign an agreement to that effect."

"Piece of paper don't mean nothin'."

"Come on, Sadie, what are we talking about here? Some underground pipes and one road as opposed to losing your land?"

"Ent you all done cut all you road," Sadie said. "Without us having any say-so."

"That path we beat for construction purposes is hardly ideal for taxiing tourists. You know that."

"How much more you all want so?"

"It's not a matter of size; it's a matter of building a proper road. And, as I've said, the farmers will be compensated for any land upon which it encroaches..."

She held up her hand as Sadie's mouth opened to cut in.

"...and that," Nikki said, "will be minimal. And there'll be more money flowing in the valley."

"Everything not about money."

"What is this about?"

"Who tell you-all we want smadee tramping through here, especially a bunch of tourists?"

"The people this spa is catering to value their privacy as much as you value yours," Nikki assured her. "You'll barely have to see each other."

"Where one business pop up, others nuh far behind; soon after that, nothing there left to farm," Sadie said.

Nikki couldn't argue with her there. Sadie wasn't a stupid woman. What she said could happen, probably would in the long run. That understanding passed between them.

"Look, Sadie, sometimes you have to take the best you can out of a situation," she said. It was weak and she knew it; she knew Sadie knew it, too. But the younger woman seemed to have run out of steam, still resistant but deflated somehow.

"Think about it," Nikki said. "Think about it and talk to your people."

And Sadie gave a little half-shrug that reminded Nikki of Aeden and how yes, no, maybe, I'll think about it, were all conveyed with the same slight shoulder movement.

Tanty spoke up. "So, we done with all this nonsense? We can talk about the dungeon now?"

Both women laughed, and then all three turned to planning the pilgrimage to the old slave dungeon.

CHAPTER THIRTY-THREE

"So, when you all going up to this dungeon? Ah wan' see it," Audrey said.

She said this without looking at Nikki, as she shaped a huge vase in her little shed.

Nikki sat nearby on a bench chatting with Belle. Audrey's question brought both sisters to a stunned halt.

"What?" Nikki asked.

"You deaf or something?" Audrey said, still without looking up. "I say when you all doing that walk-up to the old slave dungeon in Blackman Valley?"

"Uhm…this Sunday night," Nikki answered hesitantly.

"Pick me up," Audrey commanded, and Nikki's eyebrows shot up.

"You want to come to Blackman's Ridge to visit the slave dungeon," she said incredulously.

"Mhm," Audrey said with a sharp nod.

Nikki didn't know what to make of it.

"Urh…what about Belle and Christopher?" she ventured finally. "There's likely to be a decent crowd there. Plus, it's overnight, you know. Tanty wants it to go into the following morning, Emancipation Day; August Monday, she calls it. So…"

"So, I'll bring them with me," Audrey said casually, as if she wasn't in the habit of making a production out of them leaving the village. In fact, neither of the twins had been outside the boundaries of Sea View Farm in years.

"Oh, okay," Nikki said. "Urhm…it's a bit of a climb. The dungeon is about halfway up the Ridge face."

"So, le' me understan' you good; you think this ole woman you call Tanty, like she's your own, can mek it, but not me—a relatively young, strong woman?"

Nikki wisely held her tongue at that.

As it turned out, several members of the family decided to attend the Watch Night, including Carlene and the kids, and Fanso and his family. It was baffling to Nikki, to say the least. She'd never seen Carlene, a Jamaican, express any interest in Antiguan history or culture. And Fanso, well, for him to miss any bit of Carnival, especially the stretch between Sunday night's calypso competition and Tuesday's Last Lap, was nothing short of a miracle. Nikki found it all a bit unsettling, not least because it was bringing her different worlds together in a major way.

They arrived in something of a caravan: Belle and Christopher, Carlene, Imani, and Audrey riding with Nikki, Fanso with his family, and Carlene's older son.

Aeden came with two of his sisters: Isobel, who claimed a professional interest in her daddy's Blackman's Ridge development; and Bridget, the jewelry designer, who claimed no such interest. Nikki had met Isobel, in Cam's office, and felt an undefined sort of resentment coming from her. Bridget was new, but, much like Aeden, had an eccentric streak of Kool-Aid-red hair, weathered Mexican wolf-motif poncho, and Shih Tzu-looking Ugg boots were any indication.

"I like your earrings," Nikki told her. The sisters seemed to have more Pilgrim than Cameron in them. Both were darker and taller than Aeden; Bridget, taller even than Nikki. She wore an eye-catching, hanging earring made of what looked like iridescent fish scales, yellow bird feathers, and red and black jumbie beads. On her finger was a pink diamond set in white gold. "Congratulations," Nikki told her. "Aeden mentioned that you'd recently become engaged."

She grinned toothily. "If seven months can be called recently. We haven't even set a date yet."

"And whose fault is that?" Isobel piped up. "You're the one dragging your feet."

She seemed almost washed out next to the twin peacocks that were her—clearly exasperated if the eye rolls were any indication—younger siblings. Aeden wore an ice gold-green, tie-dyed T-shirt with Peter Tosh smoking a spliff and the words "Legalize It" hand-inked into the fabric. As Isobel continued her chastisement of her younger sibling, he crossed his eyes, almost making Nikki giggle. But Isobel was on a roll: "…you can't expect him to just abandon a very promising career. If you'd move up there as he asked…"

"What about my career?" Bridget demanded, her expression hardening.

"Yes, let's compare representing some of Europe's top corporate clients with matching beads and feathers for a living," Isobel shot back.

"Well, Sis, why don't you marry him; you're up there often enough," Bridget fired back.

"I'm a travel rep with an office in London, Bridge. Don't make it sound sordid."

Nikki's head was swivelling back and forth like a tennis fan at the Arthur Ashe Stadium during a particularly heated rally.

"Well, welcome to the family," Aeden interjected, with a smirk. That elicited a cough of laughter from Bridget and that big toothy grin again.

"Yeah, welcome," she said. Isobel scowled at all three of them, then wandered off without further word.

Bridget laughed some more. "Didn't think we were perfect, did you?" she asked Nikki.

Nikki was saved having to muster up a response by Belle, who had somehow escaped Audrey. Belle slipped her hand in Nikki's; her other hand held a sprig of white flowers set against green leaves which she proceeded to thrust at Bridget. "Plumbago," she said, without preamble, smiling brightly. "Good for fever."

Nikki decided she liked Aeden's younger sister when, without missing a beat, Bridget grinned wider, accepted the gift, sniffed, and tucked the whole thing into her hair, just behind her ear, where it sat conspicuously and precariously. "Cool, thanks, this'll come in handy," she said. Belle smiled, pleased.

With Cam's money, Nikki had hired someone to clear a path to the dungeon. Still, they had to step carefully around acacia needles and branches of random shrubs whipping at bare arms and legs. Nikki was happy she'd elected to wear jeans, though she knew she'd be picking prickles from them the next day. Those who'd donned their best African garb were in a worse way, forced to hold the pretty, flowing robes close.

Nikki, Belle's arm still linked with hers, walked close to the front of the slow-moving group, behind Tanty. Sadie led the sizeable procession. The flambeaus, lanterns, and flashlights could not drive away all the shadows; the sun having dipped rather quickly for a summer day, even as the moon hid shyly behind the wispy clouds. Sadie was sure-footed, however.

Nikki heard grumblings down the line as this or that person tripped on rocks or had their shoe pierced by an especially determined cassie needle. But, her hand at Tanty's back, Nikki felt like she could almost close her eyes and feel her way there. So she did, mostly, letting her feet step lightly, following the old woman's path.

The inner voice she had given her mother's name breathed a "yes," releasing months and months of tension on a sigh. Even Belle, not used to crowds, was a relaxed and steady presence beside her. The whispers, coming down the line, blew past her like a breeze.

"This is it," Sadie announced, calling a halt. The group spread out as they moved up into the space around the dungeon.

Tanty and Sadie had agreed that Nikki should emcee the proceedings. So she did, pitching her voice to carry over the bodies to those still further down the hill.

"I want to thank you all for coming," she began haltingly. "For Tanty, and many others from the area, what you are standing on is holy ground."

She looked across at Tanty, who nodded encouragingly.

Before Nikki was a motley crew—curious expats mixed in with home-grown Rastafarians, academics mixed in with area farmers, grey heads and chinee bumps, and the odd politician: It was not only a larger, but a more diverse, crowd than she had anticipated.

A part of her dared hope, as she glimpsed some of the Blackman's Ridge project's staunchest opponents in the crowd, that this could be the bridge between the warring factions. That was the goal, anyway. She'd tried to get Cam to come, but he'd scoffed at the very idea. "Make mosquito nyam me up all night." He'd laughed. "For what? I don't hold to all that ancestors crap. Black people hang on to slavery too much, if you ask me. Is that keeping them down. I'm a practical man. I live in today. Anybody who know me, know that. For me to go up there would be a boldfaced lie; and I never lie."

The night's programme consisted of a drum call and dub

poetry. At midnight, the dawning of Emancipation Day, August Monday, when Antigua's enslaved Africans got their first taste of freedom back in 1834, plastic cups were passed around, and libations sipped and poured out ritualistically in honour of these survivors and the many more non-survivors. Tanty had insisted on that and mixed up the *"bebbridge"* herself. Everyone got a chance to enter the dungeon, in pairs and threes; some emerged quickly and unscathed, others were visibly moved by the experience of being stooped and confined in the small space.

As Sadie began her oral history of the dungeon, of slaves imprisoned for infractions, imagined or real, a reporter from one of the local stations, ignoring the mean look she shot him, stuck a recorder in her face.

"...many died here sick with their own fear as it come through their skin and full up the air 'round them 'til they were breathing their own stink," Sadie said. "Not a lot of new air could get in 'round the heavy door they had barring the entrance. Only tiny cracks leave back for insects to crawl through and torment them to the last. As for them that survive, there was madness or relief, relief that sucked at their fight and spirit..."

Nikki found herself seduced by Sadie's words and her voice, as she spoke with previously unheard serenity and authority.

A noise cut through the night: a bone-deep, belly-full moan. It was Tanty, swaying, eyes tightly shut. Nikki reached an arm toward her, then hesitated.

Tanty's moan cut through her. Not like a knife. Like waves, curling beautifully in and into her, relentlessly. Nikki sighed and even cried a little; the moment, the long moments, overwhelming her, filling her with both sadness and joy. She felt like she was being filled and emptied at the same time, like she'd eaten too much and yet not enough.

The scent of roasting cashews, which Tanty had insisted on,

perfumed the night air. Nikki had been concerned about fire spreading, but then Audrey had, unexpectedly, donated a couple of coal pots which allowed them to contain the fire. And as the scent now wafted out, the moaning swelled, continuing to fill the gaps; a chorus for Sadie's chronicle which ended with a roll call of Antiguan martyrs and heroes from King Court to V.C. Bird. Here and there, there were tears. As Sadie's voice, hoarse now, faded, the drums once again took over, taking on the timbre of Tanty's unabashed moaning. The drum talk took them into foreday morning, as the Antiguans called those hours just before daybreak. It was then, in that in-between time, that Nikki came back to herself as if from a blissful dream. She caught snatches of it, of being inside the dungeon, of not being afraid, though shadows and light, ancestral spirits, danced across the jewel-like stones along the cave wall, Tanty's voice reminding her that she was from their blood and they *wouldn't do her no harm*. As even memory faded, Nikki opened her eyes to the sight of pale light now spreading across the sky, and discovered that she was leaning against Belle's shoulder as her sister sat still as a rock.

"It was beautiful," Nikki said when next she visited her mother.

"Mind people don' start say you crazy," a voice said, startling her. It was Audrey.

Nikki, who'd come to think of this place as her own, felt encroached upon.

"What're you doin' here?" she asked, looking up from where she sat on the straw mat she kept in the trunk of her car.

"But eh-eh, I need permission to visit my mother?" Audrey shot back, though without bite. "I came to tend Mama grave. I do that from time to time. Is not you one come up here, you know."

"I didn't say I was," Nikki replied.

"Of course, me never once siddung up ya ah talk to meself," Audrey said, going down to her knees, careless of her jeans on the grassy, muddy ground.

"I'm not talking to myself," Nikki replied, defensive.

"Who you ah talk to then?" Audrey wondered, with a bark of laughter. "Mama? Mama not here."

Nikki did her own version of the Antiguan could-mean-any-damn-thing shrug. Her sister smiled at this, almost approvingly.

"Oh, you tap jump at everything, nar tell me to go to hell?" Audrey wondered, clearly amused.

"What's the point," Nikki said. "You're gonna think what you want to anyway."

Audrey pulled at the weeds silently for a bit, then said, in a low voice, "I have to admit, you heng on longer than me expec'."

Nikki's eyes swung back to her. "What, you expected me to turn tail and run?" And she thought of that fight in the kitchen and how hard Audrey worked to push her away. Then found herself wondering suddenly what Audrey was afraid of losing. But she didn't expect to get any answers.

Audrey surprised her.

"I remember," Audrey said, "when yuh father run go 'bout his business."

Nikki stilled, eyes fixed on Audrey, who kneeled in the grass like someone praying. She pulled at the weeds, Nikki realized, with more concentration than was necessary, as though to distract herself from the words she was speaking.

"Mama felt it, too, I could tell," Audrey said. "Stupid fool. Like he was ever goin' stay here with her in some shack."

Nikki studied her older sister. "Why didn't you tell anyone about Belle's pregnancy?" she asked finally, causing Audrey to look at her with a frown.

"Wasn't nutten to tell. Wasn't nutten to do but wait for the picknee fu come," Audrey said quietly, long after Nikki had decided she wasn't going to answer.

"He should've paid for what he did," Nikki said. "For raping Belle."

Audrey didn't ask her how she knew all this, why she cared after all this time. The very topic though was clearly digging at her; she glared, sat back angrily on her heels, then unexpectedly clapped her hands sharply, directly in front of Nikki's face, causing Nikki to pull back for fear of getting clipped. "Wake up, this not dream-time, Princess," Audrey snapped.

Something surged through Nikki, lifting her to her feet. Princess. Dreamtime. Like she didn't know anything about the real world; she who had lived in it while Audrey settled for the narrow boundaries of the world she'd been born into. She paced away, then back.

"Sometimes, Audrey, sometimes…"

Her older sister met her anger with a fearless dead-on stare, powerful even on her knees.

Nikki sputtered, "Sometimes, I hate…sometimes, I can't take you. You won't meet anybody halfway. I'm trying, I'm trying to understand you, but you…"

"Understand me? Girl, what you talking 'bout?"

Nikki sighed, sank back to the ground. "I've felt, my whole life, like I was seeing things from behind a pane of glass. I didn't feel connected to here, to Mama Vi, to my father. All I'm trying to do is get inside, get inside of something. But you, you, you're determined to…"

Audrey cut her off. "Look, gyal, please na mix me up in yuh complicatedness. I not determined with nutten. I don't have time…"

"…to think about me, I know."

She remembered with fresh pain the cut and burn of Audrey's words during the kitchen face-off the day she announced her intention to return to Antigua to live and to buy their mother a headstone. It was too raw to disguise.

"I do think about you," Audrey said softly. "Truth is, I don' really know what to make o' you half the time. More truth? Part o' me fight trying."

Nikki easily related to this mirror of her own feelings, and the fight went out of her.

Audrey resumed pulling the weeds, and soon Nikki rejoined her.

"That was a good thing you help that old woman do the other day," Audrey said after a while. "I still think you sitting plum in the middle of a red ants nest, but…"

The but, whatever it was, was left unsaid. And Nikki didn't ask.

After a while, she got up, mat in hand, left Audrey pulling at weeds, and walked back up the hill to the church, where she could see Marisol silhouetted in the doorway watching and waiting.

CHAPTER THIRTY-FOUR

"Come 'way with me," Aeden pestered, and Nikki swatted his hand, the one teasing her arm.

"Aeden, please," she said. They were on her back porch, sitting side by side, one of his arms slung over her shoulders. He'd been pressing the issue, increasingly, drawing closer as though no longer trusting to time.

"Why not?" he said, a distinct whine in his voice.

"Well, for one thing, I don't want to encourage you," Nikki only half-joked. "For another, we're just now starting construction on the Blackman's Ridge project. I can't take off just like that." The pilgrimage had succeeded in cooling tempers and as the bulk of the protestors backed off, the government had loosened the reins. Cam hadn't lost any time fast-tracking the project. It was impractical for her to think of going anywhere now.

"You're not a building contractor, are you?" Aeden quizzed, somehow managing to make it sound more curious than sarcastic, though it was close. Much as he'd advised her on getting back into his father's good graces, much as Cam was his father, Nikki had little doubt about Aeden's loyalties with respect to the development project. She couldn't blame him; she'd been plagued by mixed feelings almost from the get-go.

"No, but I am responsible for overseeing the project," she reminded him. "Plus, I have meetings this week."

"...so we'll go next week."

"Aeden, stop." She pulled away fully at this, got up, wandered to the edge of the porch, looked to the full moon for inspiration, found none.

"I not asking you to do nothing," he said. "I not askin' you to sleep with me, nothing. Just…"

"Just what," she wondered seriously, turning back to where he sat, sprawled, arms still spread across the back of the bench, an unconsciously inviting sight. Or maybe it was the full moon. People on the island believed the full moon and crazy called to each other. Surrendering to an unrealistic fantasy was crazy. And when had Aeden become her fantasy? It confused her.

"Just come," he coaxed.

"Come where?" And Nikki found herself stepping toward him like he had her in his thrall.

He smiled in that goofy way he had, as he sing-songed, "Come bathe in a river, come stand under a waterfall, water so cold it make you come alive." He shook himself like a senseh fowl with its feathers cocked as though remembering the invigorating chill. He was practically crooning now, "Dominica, Guyana, Suriname; we'll canoe up to one of the maroon village and sleep drowsy and happy in a hammock all day. Did that once, is the best. Or we can fly out to Jamaica, drive out to Port Royal, lick the salt from fish and bammi off each other's fingers; or we can bike up to the lighthouse in Negril and watch the sun explode and melt into the water. You cyarn picture it? The two ah we making one silhouette in the orange light."

Nikki saw it all like a film, like Lancaster and Kerr on the beach in *From Here to Eternity*, a fantasy, not real. She smiled and couldn't help teasing back, as she rejoined him on the bench, some distance between them, "So, it's to be Jamaica-Suriname-Guyana-Dominica then?"

He inclined his head towards her, then with a little smile. "Anywhere, anything. 'Cross to Barbuda, if you like, go down to the caves go look for the blind shrimp."

"You paint a seductive picture," Nikki admitted.

"So…" And there was hope in that single word.

"But it's not real," she continued.

"It's as real as we want it to be," Aeden insisted. "This don't have to be complicated."

And it was the wrong, wrong thing to say—echoes of Hensen. Nikki got up again, and Aeden looked up at her, startled by the abruptness of it.

"Maybe I'm ready for complicated," she said, not even really knowing if that was true; she wasn't prepared to be easy anymore. Not after Hensen J. Stephens. She turned and walked into the house, heard his heavy sigh and sardonic "guess that's my cue" behind her.

"It's funny how when you hit the other side of thirty, so many of your past choices just seem stupid," Nikki said to her mother on her next evening visit. She thought of the ones she'd let get away, like Terry. On this particular lonely night, she found the reasons and the rationales eclipsed by the loneliness and reawakened yearning. She craved so much more, all of a sudden, and damned Aeden for reawakening that need in her, or perhaps reminding her it existed. With little else to distract her—thanks to the fact that Carlene was in therapy and the Blackman's Ridge situation had settled down—Nikki couldn't hide from what she was feeling. She hated that feeling.

She couldn't, though, find the words to describe this; just as well, as her mother had no answers anyway.

"I have something to ask you," Fanso said.

It was Sunday. Nikki had stopped by to drop the kids off after their semi-regular Sunday romp at Deep Bay. She'd even managed to coax the kids to scale Goat Hill with her, though not into long abandoned, eerie Fort Barrington. Carlene, happy and small in the water below, had waved up at them. Now, she and Fanso were in the kitchen, washing and wiping the last of the dishes after a simple dinner of chicken vegetable stir fry with Chinese cabbage. Carlene was in the den saying her goodbyes to her boys. Fanso's boys' voices floated from the open door of their room where they were engaged in a lively boxing match, courtesy of Wii. Antoinette, quiet even for her, had disappeared into her room after dinner.

"How are things?" Nikki asked, inclining her head in the general direction of the shut bedroom door.

Fanso shrugged. "Could be better. Thanks for taking the kids. It helps. Give us a little time. The little ones are exhausting, especially the older one; he kinda wild and not much manners, you know, and his energy like it rubbing off on ours. Imani quiet, so he not a problem. But between between the kids and Twenett's teaching and tutoring, she have children coming out her ears. But the little downtime help, even if it just give us enough time to argue 'bout me not being home enough and her having to do everything." There was unfamiliar weariness in Fanso's voice.

"Give it time," Nikki said. "Carlene seems to be doing better. It's a matter of time."

"Actually, that's what I wanted to talk to you about," Fanso said.

Nikki wiped her hands on a towel, sat at the table, as he wiped around the sink. He didn't speak further until he was done, and then not until he'd checked to make sure they were still truly alone. He joined her at the table. The sound of the TV and laughter and chatter floated in, faintly, as he considered his words.

"I don't think the new girl we trying out as hostess goin' work out," Fanso said finally. Nikki was puzzled at the apparent change in topic, but held her tongue. "She not annoying like the previous one with the freshwater Yankee accent and extraness, but she still not right for Mama Vi's. Not so much too much, as too little. She look good on paper, but, well, I not happy and I don't think I can keep her beyond the probation."

Nikki shrugged. "Well, it's your call."

"But I want your advice."

"I'll help interview a replacement; you know that," Nikki said.

"Well, the thing is, Carlene approach me 'bout the job."

Nikki was surprised at this. "Really? She didn't express any interest to me," she said.

"Well, she did to me," he said. "Couple days ago. Said she want a chance to make more money, so she can take care of her own children."

"That's a nice dream, but I don't know, Fanso," Nikki said honestly.

"Well, see, I felt the same way, but I guess a big part of me want things to get back to some kind of normal between me and my wife. That's selfish, I know, but between us, I can tell you that's the God's truth."

"I understand that, but…"

"The other thing is, more I think about it, more it don't seem such a bad idea. I mean she have this outgoing but still down-to-earth personality that suit the place fine. She funny, don't have no airs 'bout her."

"Well, see that's the thing; there's no airs and then there's no airs. Know what I mean?"

"You talking 'bout her speech?"

"Well, that and…"

"You think she too rough 'round the edges."

"Well…"

"Yeah, but that can iron out, see. She have the raw talent for us to work with; is just the etiquette and thing she need to pull up on, and that's something you can teach. The other thing you can't teach."

Nikki regarded him carefully. "Sounds like you've already made up your mind."

She could see that he had.

"So, why ask me?" she asked.

Fanso's lips twisted in a half-smile. "Guess I want the back-up."

Nikki pursed her lips. "I don't know if I can give you that."

"Well, you can iron though, right?" Fanso asked, familiar smile now firmly in place as he prodded.

Nikki studied him, then, picking up his meaning, started shaking her head. "Uh-uh, Fanso, this is definitely not my thing."

"'Course it is," he teased. "Airs come natural to you; ask Audrey."

"Tickle me, tickle me, mek me laugh," Nikki intoned dryly.

It caught Fanso by surprise, but when it hit, he laughed until tears blurred his vision and streamed down his face. "Oh, Nikki, Nikki, Nikki, we goin' make you one of us yet," he said finally, still chuckling.

"Seriously, Nikki," Fanso began, once he'd got the giggles under control.

"Seriously, Fanso, I know jack about being a hostess," Nikki protested. "Besides, I don't have time for this."

"It not goin' take no time. Just one week; work with her a few nights."

"Fanso…"

"And she live right dey wid you, so you don't even have to go nowhere."

"Fanso…"

"Nikki, please."

The pleading in his voice did her in. Things must be even worse between him and Antoinette than he was saying. Nikki gave in.

CHAPTER THIRTY-FIVE

The mischief began like mosquitoes buzzing around, an annoyance really. No bite. No blood. No lingering sting.

Items were pilfered from the Blackman's Valley work site, then some more items. Cam ordered Nikki to fire the security team, get another in place, and give the contractors a warning. More items stolen, another changing of the guard.

It was baby things really. A stray tool carelessly left lying around. A couple of cans. Metal. Wire. Wood. Blocks.

"It doesn't make any sense," Nikki complained to Fanso, Aeden, Carlene—whoever would listen. "I mean, it's a helluva hike for next to nothing."

Then the workmen showed up early one morning to find feces smeared all along the walls of the cavernous cistern they'd been building. They refused to clean it. The health authorities had to be called in. After that, it was impossible to keep it quiet. The police were notified. The media, smelling trouble, started buzzing around the Valley again like flies.

"I am confident," Nikki told them, in an impromptu and reluctant press conference, "that the previous protestors have nothing to do with this. We have had no signal of any breakdown in the peace forged. This is troublemaking, pure and simple, and some other hand is in this."

"Are you suggesting," one eager, young reporter, a now familiar face on this beat pressed, "that this is some kind of politically motivated interference?"

"I didn't say that," Nikki demurred. "And on that note, I'll let the police do their work."

"It's no secret that there's been strong political opposition to this project," the kid persisted, recorder still firmly in her face, "and you've had relationships with both of the parties concerned in more than one capacity. Do you think your former allies have the potential to do this kind of thing? Do you think they have a hand in this?"

"I have no allies in either party," Nikki said, annoyed. "I've been in Antigua long enough to know it's six o' one, half a dozen o' the other. This is a job. My time with the Tourism Department was a job. Period."

That was the comment that ran and ran on each news report, and in the *Saturday Night Live*-esque spoof of the news that had debuted during the run-up to the last election when *faux pas* on the campaign trail practically demanded it. The comment also inspired newspaper headlines for several days running: *Cameron Enterprises No Friend of Government, Says Spokeswoman. Cameron Bites the Hand that Feeds Him. This Government No Different from the Last, says Cam Aide.*

Cam was on the warpath again, and Nikki had no defense, as she stared at the newspapers spread across his desk.

"This is strategy," he berated, his voice becoming mocking as he quoted. "'I have no allies in either party. Six o' one, half a dozen o' the other'?!"

Nikki's eyes flitted to windows that opened to the gas station below, then across to the open doorway. She knew there was nothing she could say; there was nothing that would stop this performance Cameron had obviously worked up to.

"I thought you were the one who knew how to play this game," he scoffed. "I would know better than to say any stupidness so. I bet even that little thing off the street that takin' up space in my front office—the one ole bwoy ask me to hire 'cause she from his constituency and he lookin' to screw her, the one with the skirt up under her ass, her timble heel scratching up my good floor, head full of false hair and nothing else—even she wouldn't be so blasted stupid. This is amateur bullshit."

His reference to Hensen's latest bedroom target was clearly intended to hurt. It maybe hurt the girl in the front office to hear herself so categorized, since Cam wasn't exactly whispering his discontent, but it didn't hit Nikki as hard as her self-disgust.

"I made a mistake," she said. "I'm sorry."

Like a wakened lion, however, Cam would not be denied the fat and bone. "You have them boys all over my case, asking if I can't keep a leash on your reckless tongue," Cam continued.

Nikki knew he was getting back at her for all the times he'd had to concede that she might know what she was doing, even if it was in his best interest. After all, he didn't like to lose; she'd been told that from the beginning.

"Some a dem want me fire you," Cam said, twirling one of those cigars his wife didn't allow him to smoke, as though considering it. "Imagine you tarring dem with the same brush as the ones they fight 'gainst all this time before they come to power. When they the same ones giving us concessions to bring in stuff for construction, and lease us the land for peanuts, and sign work permit for that Canadian architect and engineer, instead of insisting that we use all local people. The same ones, mind you, that allowing us a tax holiday that saving me millions. They want know if that don't make them allies. Fire her, they say. She not no use to you anyway, if she don't know that media twist story."

"Not all media," Nikki defended, and she really didn't know why, of everything he'd said, she was choosing to defend this. Maybe because she was the one with foot-in-mouth, the media hadn't had to do any twisting. "That's like saying all lawyers are liars, or all politicians are crooks."

"...or all businessman after a dollar? What fairy world you living in, Princess? Is just so; don't fool yourself thinking otherwise."

Nikki sighed, feeling weighted and unable to shrug it off, unable to beat his cynicism when she'd been so successfully twisted up by her own words.

Cam leaned back, his black leather chair squeaking under his weight. "I don't want you saying or sending anything to the media without consulting me again," he said.

Nikki's spirit fought these new bindings, but all she managed was a meek "so, I'm a child now, not being trusted to cross the street on her own."

"Well, I tell you," he said, a smirk on his lips, voice deceptively mild. "My kids damn near get theyself killed plenty times, and it was mostly that Aeden, contrary from the day he born. Anyway, just as they about to step off into traffic without looking or put their hand in pit bull mouth or siddown in ants nest, my wife would pull them back, shake them rough and say, 'Me cyarn speak English, you know.' Only time you ever hear any dialect come outta her mouth. Sound funny bad, too; mouth twisting up 'round the rusty words. It used to make me laugh, I tell you. But I understand the trueness of it. You cross the street, get knock down, is me have to answer for it, so best check with me first before crossing the street."

He made a smug picture and for the first time, in a long time, Nikki thought about saying to hell with it, Antigua, all of it. She didn't, though. She exited the office without saying anything further, didn't spare even a glance for the receptionist. She kept her head up, sharp nails biting into her hand, as she marched through the gas station to the parking lot across the street, to a chorus of snickers.

When Aeden dropped by to deliver the news, she was on her back porch watering the pale-blue strain of plumbago that she'd found near the slave dungeon and planted—to Carlene's amusement—in the coal pots used on Watch Night. Nikki didn't have a green thumb and Carlene assured her the wild growing shrub would outgrow the narrow confines of the pots built for cooking, not planting, sooner rather than later. But when Nikki sat out back, the *coming-to-come* blooms helped her remember that night. Besides, they didn't seem to mind that she often forgot to water them, thriving nonetheless. She liked that about them. And following Cam's blowout, tending them after cleaning the house top to bottom, and tackling all the dirty laundry in her hamper, to the bounce and bellow of her Whitney Houston greatest hits dance remixes CD, was almost distraction enough. Her mood was decidedly improved as she sang along with Whitney on "So Emotional," as she only did when alone, or in the shower, or that time during their college days, when she and Jazz had scrimped and sacrificed to buy tickets to the nosebleed section of Madison Square Garden to hear the Voice in person.

Then Aeden appeared at the side of the porch, startling Nikki nearly out of her skin, and before she could slow her heart enough to get a rebuke out, he told her.

Sadie and other ringleaders from the earlier demonstrations had been pulled in by the police for questioning. Tanty had sent Aeden, via a phone call from Little John, to get Nikki.

The old woman was visibly upset when they showed up in the Valley; tears that wouldn't spill over standing out in her eyes. Nikki was ashamed of any part she'd played in bringing this fresh pain.

"She didn't have nothing to do with this," Tanty greeted fiercely.

"I know," Nikki said. And she did.

"They drag her outta here like some criminal," Tanty fumed. "Again!"

"I'm sorry," Nikki said.

"What yuh sorry have to do with me, eh?" Tanty said, too agitated, it seemed, to keep still. "What yuh sorry have to do with me?!" She was practically jumping out of her skin. Nikki stepped back; Aeden wisely hovered at the edge of the clearing, both intimidated by the shorter-than-them-both old woman.

Tanty huffed and paced as she talked, one minute hugging herself, the next minute swinging her arms as though tugging away; then hitting out at some invisible enemy, then beating at her thighs as though punishing herself.

"I tell you, she not mix up in this," she said through these patterns of movement. "Ent ar-you done mek ar-you peace? Right ya ar-you siddung and do um. Right up so, by the dungeon, we come to understandin' an' get the ancestors blessing. Now this! This ah na no kind a way fuh treat people, good law-abiding people. She not no criminal."

She spoke the dialect more deeply and speedily than Nikki was accustomed to, even now, and she had trouble keeping up with each word, but she got the idea. Tanty was a mother, betrayed and worried, helpless and enraged. Nikki tried to offer what little comfort she could. "They don't have anything on her. It's just for questioning," she said. "They'll have to let her go, if she's innocent."

"If?! If?! I tell you she don't have nothing to do with this," Tanty roared, for that is how she seemed to Nikki in that moment, a lioness defending her cub from a pack of hyenas. It saddened Nikki that she was now seen by the mother lion as being part of that pack.

"Sadie would never mix up in stealing nothing. When she was 'bout nine, smadee with fork tongue come bring word. *'But, Tanty, you flush! You win coupon or something? Sadie spending up at the school like it goin' outta style—sugar cake, tamarind ball, ashum, suckabubby for everybody. Me can lean pon you man, Tanty, since you have it so good.'* Me tell the memelippey smadee that is a little extra change from what her mother send from St. Croix. The same mother who na look back yet pon she picknee. When Sadie come home that day, me strip she bare and me beat she, me beat she, me beat she. An' unlike so many other smadee 'roun de place I wasn't a beating woman. But me beat she with piece a tamarind that me cut from de tree, that same tree over so; cut um and skin um. An' with the sweat an' tears still a dry pon she, me whole up she han' to the coal pot arch where the coal min ah burn orange. An' she bawl murder an' try pull 'way, but me hold she steady. An' she rattle off all kind a sorry, though up to that time me never tell she wha me ah beat she for. But she cry, say she sorry, an' she nar do it again. An' me tell she me nar raise no tief. Not again. Her father, my son, was already up at 1735 lockup for he fast hand, and she wasn't goin' turn out so."

Tanty was sweating heavily now, and finally the tears spilled over. "You hear me good? Me bring she up right," Tanty said, "and she's a girl true to she word."

"I know," Nikki said, with feeling, her own unshed tears burning her eyes, her arms yearning to reach out and stop the woman's frantic movements. And suddenly, they stopped, of their own volition. Tanty slumped, like sails suddenly bereft of wind. She seemed truly old then, and beaten. Nikki's heart ached for her, at the worry she'd inadvertently dumped onto those once sturdy shoulders, bowing them. She remembered their first meeting, the two women working side by side, working the land they'd worked for generations; never making enough to be truly happy, but happy nonetheless. It didn't sit well that she had had any part in visiting this kind of trouble on them, and for what? She wondered now. For her own enrichment, that of an arrogant man whose respect she didn't even have, for a few wealthy Northerners— for that was how she thought of Americans now—to have somewhere to play when they tired of Aspen and the Riviera.

She sat next to Tanty, but the old woman shrugged her off, holding herself tight.

"I'll get her a lawyer," Nikki promised, as much to herself as Tanty. "I'll do all I can."

Tanty didn't seem to hear.

Within three days, Sadie was released, as the police had no evidence to hold her and had been unable to break her, especially after the lawyer Nikki had hired showed up to make sure they controlled themselves. Soon, the others were released as well.

"Wa Bruk Cho 'Way."

—Antiguan Proverb

CHAPTER THIRTY-SIX

New York hit Nikki like a battering ram. It felt like another world—chaotic and cold. She hadn't realized until then how much she'd settled into Antigua's rhythm. But then it had been more than two years.

She was happy to escape to Jazz and Giovanni's apartment, a two-bedroom, twenty stories up, just south of Marcus Garvey Park; one of those places so popular with new Harlemites—the kind of people who moved into the area, then complained about the decades-old, summer-long drumming in the park. It wasn't the kind of place Jazz could have afforded on her salary, but Giovanni was a world history teacher, apparently a very well-paid teacher, at an extremely exclusive private school. Even so, Jazz said it was one of the relatively low-cost units he'd got the inside track on, thanks to his volunteer work with young people in the community. That's how they'd met, actually, through his "Uncle Project," which twinned Harlem youths with African-American professionals; "kind of like a big brother deal," Jazz had explained. Her sister had had no qualms about making the move; she was still in the city, more or less, and that's all that mattered to her.

Besides, the apartment—with its bright but warm colours and lush carpeting—may have been Giovanni's originally, but now it was all Jazz. Nikki had to smile at that. Would she and Jazz have even become friends, if her sister didn't have a way of draping herself across the things—and people—to which she laid claim? Jazz's stamp was on everything from the moth orchids, like snow-flakes against the room's varied colours; to the silver-framed pictures of Bernadine, and Nikki and Jazz, on the mantle; to the chicken-wire, pan-playing miniature she'd picked up from a St. Mary's Street vendor in Antigua; to the comfortable throws and pillows softening the edges of everything; to the heavy, expensive-looking red and gold drapes—the Bernadine in Jazz coming out.

Cocooned there, Nikki felt insulated from the urgency and alienness of the city she no longer knew. Thus, cocooned, the ladies of song via Giovanni's *Ultimate Divas* CD filling the spaces around them, she and Jazz caught up well into the following morning. Giovanni wisely left them to it as they chatted over glasses of skimmed milk, in deference to Jazz's pregnancy, and squares of Fanso's coconut fudge—now little more than crumbs, thanks to the zeal of airport security. Travel had become such a hassle. But, now, she could relax for the first time since leaving Antigua at the crack of dawn that day.

"We're kinda looking for a house," Jazz was saying now, lying on the rug, her head in Nikki's lap, her swollen feet carelessly elevated to the Mestizo print throw covering the pearl-white couch.

"Giovanni wants to get out of the city," she explained. "Maybe something close to his parents; take the train into the city for work. I know it's probably the best thing for the baby; lots of yard space to run around in, less pollutants, safer. Part of me is resisting, though. It feels like I just moved. Plus, big plus, I love the smell and the stink and the rhythms of this city. Even with all the craziness."

Nikki couldn't say the same, New York having quickly become a long ago acquaintance whose features had become indistinct and whose name you had to think twice to remember. But then, this city had never been inside of her the way it was Jazz.

"You can get used to change," she said now, stroking Jazz's hair.

"Yes, island girl, I know," Jazz said. "But maybe I don't want to."

Nikki kept silent, hearing something in Jazz's voice that made her stomach clench.

"Did I tell you, he also wants me to take time off work," Jazz continued. "'The parents are responsible for raising the children; there's no more important job.' It's one of his soapboxes. This from the man who teaches privileged white kids at one of the city's more exclusive schools, mind. But then it's that school that's brought out the African in him, has him volunteering in the 'hood he never knew, as if to atone for a life of good living. But, if it wasn't for his sackcloth routine, we wouldn't have met, right? So, I guess I can't complain." Jazz sounded fondly exasperated and Nikki's stomach loosened, a bit.

"But you're house hunting…" she probed.

"Half-heartedly," Jazz admitted.

"But you're thinking about it," Nikki pressed.

"Thinking about a lot of things," her sister said on a sigh. "Hard not to with Gi always harping on it. How we, the collective we, whoever that is" …this accompanied by an eye roll… "have abdicated our responsibilities to our offspring with our selfish and ultimately meaningless desires. 'The kind of human beings we create is the only thing that matters, that's all we leave behind, and that impacts the kind of world we leave.' He tells me, in my line of work, I should be even more aware than he of the way the village has abandoned the child, shirked this most important duty."

Nikki bristled at this. "He's part of the village. He's a parent. Why doesn't he stay home? For sure, your kids need you more than his silver spoons need him."

Jazz chuckled. "Problem is his silver spoons can actually afford him."

Point, Nikki thought.

"Anyway," Jazz continued, "that's where we are in the debate. I told him I would not wish me, relegated to a life of nothing but dirty diapers and throw-up, on him or anyone; but especially him, since I love him so much."

Nikki laughed.

"So, what about you? Things settled down in Wadadli?" Jazz asked.

Nikki laughed harder, milk coming through her nose, spraying Jazz who wiped at it and swatted her.

"What?" Jazz asked.

"You sound like such a tourist," Nikki teased. "It's not 'Wurhdaaaah-dli.' It's Wa-dad-li."

"That's what I said," Jazz insisted.

"No, it isn't."

"Is. And stop it. You're tryin' to make me sound uncool because I'm not from the islands; like you've forgotten you weren't from there either, to hear you tell it, not all that long ago."

Nikki laughed even harder.

"What now?" Jazz demanded.

"Well, you'll hardly find an Antiguan saying, 'the islands.' That's tourist talk. 'Yes, Paris, I went to the islands over the winter. It was simply mah-va-lous. I did the calypso with this native boy. You must try it. Kiss kiss.'"

"Oh, screw you," Jazz said. She struggled to sit up for a minute, but soon enough, the need for comfort won out over annoyance, and she settled for glaring up at Nikki.

"You know, from this angle, you look cross-eyed," Nikki said, still giggling.

"Forget you," Jazz said, closing her eyes.

"Tek win," Nikki said.

"Hmmm."

"That's how an Antiguan would concede an argument. Tek win."

"Tek win? I don't get it."

Nikki shrugged. "I'm not sure I do either. Maybe, take the win, as in victory is yours."

"Hmmm."

Nikki stroked Jazz's hair silently for a while longer, still smiling to herself. "Hey, don't go to sleep on me," she said. "I may be fitter than I can ever remember being with all this damn jogging I'm doing, but I still don't have upper-body strength worth a damn. And you're about as big as an elephant, so don't count on me lifting you."

Jazz sighed. "I feel more like a beached whale. I can't wait for her to pop out already, much as I dread that day and all the days thereafter, you know. If it's possible to be joyful, anticipant and petrified all at once."

"So, it's a her for sure then?"

"Yip."

"How's Giovanni? I know he wanted a boy."

"Well, he'll have to take that up with the stork, or God, or Nyame, or Asherah."

"Way over my head, sister," Nikki cut in.

"Anyway," Jazz said. "Thought of a name yet? You're down to the wire, Goddie."

Nikki knew this, but still hadn't settled on anything. The latest name to occur to her—her mother's name, Violet, she knew would be a slap in the face to Jazz's mom, so she didn't dare suggest that.

"What about Giovanni? Isn't he contributing anything to this naming?" Nikki wondered.

"For sure, some profound and profoundly unpronounceable moniker complete with African naming ceremony," Jazz joked with a bit of edge to her voice.

Nikki felt compelled to wonder, "So, is everything cool with you two?"

Jazz sighed. "I know how that sounded. Things are fine really. My moods have been all over the place lately."

The funny thing, Nikki thought, was that Jazz glowed even through her frown.

"It's...he's pushy," Jazz griped, "especially when it comes to his views on the motherland. Gets tiring sometimes. I swear he's more African than Kunta Kinte. And all this harping on the move and work isn't helping. But we're fine. I love him as much as I ever did. I have less and less patience with just about everything these days. I've been so looking forward to this visit from you. I think we both got a bit worried you'd change your mind, with the latest problems you've been having on that project of yours. You only mentioned it in passing, but it sounded serious. You said police were involved?"

It was Nikki's turn to sigh. She didn't want to talk about it, much as she used to talk to Jazz about everything, even the things she didn't want to talk about. She wanted to be now, to lie on this carpet that felt like grass, only better, to caress Jazz's hair, feel the heavy weight of her head, feel close to her again. There was a connection she hadn't felt with any of the siblings back in Antigua, not even Fanso. She'd worried, especially the past year since Jazz's marriage, that that had been breaking apart, with both of their lives so changed. But sitting, lying there with her, even with her foot going to sleep under Jazz's head, it felt right.

"Can we take a rain check on that discussion?" Nikki beseeched finally.

Jazz looked up at her, cat eyes meeting cat eyes. "That bad?"

Nikki sighed. "Well, we still don't know officially who's behind the latest crimes at the site. Work has resumed. But to be honest, Jazz, it feels like we're avoiding the inevitable. Plus, you know how I put my foot in it; got on the wrong side of my boss and his political allies of the day? Well, then I went and paid for legal representation for one of those taken into custody to 'assist with the investigation.' He hasn't said anything about it, and that's not like him. He likes playing the bully, except most of the times, he's not playing. Hmm. So much for not talking about it, eh?"

"Sounds complicated; what are you going to do?" Jazz asked.

"I don't know," Nikki replied. "Mostly, I feel like I want to jump ship. And he seemed happy to have me gone for a while, which speaks volumes in itself."

"So, why don't you? Jump ship, I mean," Jazz said.

"Before I get pushed, you mean," Nikki said.

Jazz shrugged. "In general. If you're this unhappy. This isn't what you really want to be doing anyway, is it?"

"What do you mean?" Nikki asked, hearing the defensiveness in her voice.

"To be honest, Nikki, I never felt like you chose this path," Jazz said. "I don't feel like you're suited to all this."

"I hold my own," Nikki said. Yes, definitely defensive now.

"I'm not saying you don't," Jazz said earnestly. "But it doesn't bring you joy. It never has. Nothing you've done professionally has. I've watched you all these years running from this to that, really running as far from the professor as you could. For what? Why not settle down and forget him? When does your life stop being about him, or your mother, for that matter?"

"Jazz..."

"No, I'm serious. Life can't be lived reacting to shit. It's got to be proactive. That's why my debate with Gi will always be academic. I love social work. I would not be the woman he married, if I had to give that up. Not to mention that I'd be abandoning, for a second time, the kids already abandoned by 'the village' he talks so much about."

Nikki shifted. "My leg's sleeping," she said leadingly. Jazz obliged, struggling up to lean against the couch, as Nikki got up, shook out her leg, and hobbled around on it for a bit, before wandering over to the window, shifting the curtain, to look out over the park and the rows and rows of buildings beyond.

"I'm not judging you," Jazz said softly.

"That's what you do, isn't it?" Nikki said as softly. "Especially now, now you've gone and got yourself this perfect life. I guess fucked-up Nikki makes your life look even better."

She didn't have to look at Jazz to see the hurt she'd caused. "I think we just established my life's far from perfect; where's this coming from?" her sister asked in a broken voice and Nikki wanted to cry.

She turned to Jazz, saw the hurt and the hand rubbing rhythmically at her swollen stomach. "Are you okay?" she asked instinctively.

Jazz looked at her like she'd lost her mind. "The baby's fine, Nikki," she said, annoyed.

"I'm sorry, I didn't mean that," Nikki said.

"Yeah you did," Jazz replied.

"I'm…I'm not," Nikki said, fumbling for words. She heard Jazz's voice in her head…"out with it"… and smiled.

"Something funny?" Jazz asked.

"I miss you, Jazz," Nikki said. "That's all. Well, not all. But that's a big part of it. And everything feels kind of fucked right now, and you used to be a phone call and a Whitney Houston marathon away, you know."

She sat heavily beside Jazz, up against the couch, legs stretched out; Jazz's reaching only as far as three-fourths of the way down Nikki's shins. Neither spoke for several long, long minutes.

"Do I really act like a know-it-all?" Jazz asked finally, in a small voice, as Annie Lennox in the background, piped up about learning to keep one's mouth shut. Both sisters heard it and smiled, and the music and being within touching distance again had Nikki feeling downright trippy. Jazz may have been the pregnant one, but her moods were clearly all over the place, too.

"Do I?" Jazz pressed, bumping Nikki's shoulder.

Nikki's smile widened affectionately, the tension gone from her. "Yeah, kinda, but then that's kinda one of the things I've always relied on you for. One of us has to have a fucking clue, right?"

She felt the tension float away from Jazz as well, though her hand continued to make circles on her mountain of a belly.

"Thing is, you're usually right," Nikki continued, "and you're right that I fell into working for Cam as an escape from an untenable situation. And I did, deliberately, pull against Professor Baltimore and the world he would have me buried in. I didn't have the brains for it, anyway."

Jazz chided, "Hey, that's my sister you're talking about."

"By the time I hit puberty," Nikki continued heavily, "I hated it. All of it. Everything he tried to expose me to, everything he tried to teach me, everything he adored. Well, maybe except for Lady Day, Ella and Nina Simone."

"Yeah, but that's Billie, Ella and Nina. Who could hate them?" Jazz pitched in.

"I wanted to be my own person," Nikki said. "But I guess I never decided who that was." She laughed softly. "There were times I fantasized about doing nothing, contributing nothing, just being, not any particular shape or colour or texture, something impossible to hang on to or pin down like the wind or...like sunset, the way when I'm sitting on my back porch at home, the colours bleed into one another before you can even begin to name them, the colours new every evening like they're being made up on the spot; I fantasized, fantasize still sometimes, about being like that. Of course, I was never enough of a rebel, didn't have courage enough to let go, unfulfilling as everything was, is."

"You had courage enough to let go of this life," Jazz reminded her.

"Or it let me go," Nikki replied. "Anyway, you're right. If I had any cojones, I'd chuck Cam, maybe focus on smaller clients like Fanso and Mama Vi's restaurant. Working on that project has been like raising a baby, not that I have any frame of reference, mind you; but it's felt good, like it means something."

"So, do more of that," Jazz said.

"Doesn't pay," Nikki reminded her.

"Well, how much money do you need?" Jazz wondered. "And maybe you're not looking at it from the right angle. What about training, professional development seminars, that sort of thing?"

"Oh, you mean the kind of thing that people in Antigua are reluctant to pay for?" Nikki asked rhetorically. "Especially in this economy. I'd be foolish to let go of a sure thing."

"Except it's not sounding like so much of a sure thing anymore," Jazz reminded her.

"True," Nikki said. "Maybe New York beckons, eh."

"Maybe," Jazz said. "Except, I just heard you call Antigua home without blinking or thinking about it. Never heard you call anywhere home before and mean it."

Nikki was silent, contemplative. "I've always thought I needed a big client like Cameron to pay for the smaller ones like Fanso..."

"Well, maybe it's time to think again," Jazz suggested.

"Yes, Oh Wise One," Nikki teased.

"Stop it," Jazz said, her hand pausing long enough to slap at Nikki. Then, "Sorry, for being an insufferable know-it-all."

Nikki threw an arm across her shoulders, leaned into her. "Hey, that's my sister you're talking about," the younger sister chided, and like that, they were back to giggling.

CHAPTER THIRTY-SEVEN

*N*ikki had just fallen asleep, on the sofa bed in the living room—the other bedroom having been freshly painted in anticipation of the baby's birth—when the commotion started; Giovanni, rushing around like a chicken with its head cut off, was looking more dishevelled than she'd ever seen him.

"She's in labour," he shrieked at her. And Nikki flew into action, something of an old hand at this by this time. However, Jazz's baby, like Jazz, was easy. By eleven that morning, she came quietly into the world, having to be prompted into crying, and soon settled peacefully against her mother, who as peacefully fell asleep.

"She looks like your mother," Nikki said. "She doesn't have any of the signature Baltimore features at all."

"She has Giovanni's eyebrows," Jazz said, the child at her breast.

"Yeah, that's too bad," Nikki said.

"Hey, I'm in the room," the proud father protested, only then coming in, bearing more flowers to add to the greenhouse that Jazz's room had become. *If her sister had glowed before, she was like sunshine now,* Nikki thought, the baby in her arms, a little pink rose basking in its glow—and not a regular rose, but one of those hardy Antigua roses, gentle but strong-willed, defying the harsh noonday sun, blooming gaily, in spite of.

"So, any name yet?" Jazz wondered.

"Tapanga," Giovanni declared.

"Ta what?"

"Tapanga, it's African for unpredictable," he explained, taking the child into his arms. "That's what you are, aren't you?" he crooned to her. "You make your own rules, Baby. Frightening Daddy with your early arrival. But you're as sweet as can be, right, Tapanga? Sweet and unpredictable."

"Oh, God, please, Nikki save me," Jazz implored.

"Rose," Nikki said firmly

"Rose? That's so blaaah," Giovanni said with a frown.

"I like it," Jazz piped up. "Rose Tapanga Levy." And Nikki hid a smile, her mind picking for the umpteenth time at the riddle of how an Afrocentric African American wound up with a part-Italian, part-Jewish name, and more than that, why he'd never bothered to change it, given his Afrocentrism. Another unsolved mystery.

"Tapanga Rose," Giovanni said. "It has a nice ring to it."

"It's Rose Tapanga," Jazz insisted.

"Hey, potayto-potahto," he crooned as he swung his daughter around the room. "Isn't that right, Tapanga-Rose?" He then plunged fully into the old tune.

The sisters smiled at each other, rolling their eyes indulgently.

"She's smiling at me," Giovanni said, that note of wonder still in his voice. It was the day of the baby's naming ceremony, to be held right there in Giovanni and Jazz's apartment. Tapanga-Rose was in her bassinet—a white frilly number, gifted by her maternal grandmother—eyes locked with her father, pink lips spread, face scrunched up in an approximation of laughter.

"You always have a smile for Daddy, don't you?" Giovanni said, in that baby voice Jazz and Nikki had gotten used to since before Christmas, before the baby came home from the hospital.

"It's gas," Jazz's mother said dryly.

And Nikki laughed as Giovanni frowned, then made a face at the baby who smiled some more. "Grandma's jealous, isn't she?"

"Wanna see a man act the fool? Put a baby into the picture, especially his first-born," Bernadine said, catching Nikki's eye. "Winston was the same way when we brought Jasmine home from the hospital."

Nikki grew uncomfortable at this reference, but then she was uncomfortable around Bernadine at the best of times. She remembered the one time, back in college, she'd taken Jazz up on her invitation to Sunday lunch at her mother's roomy townhouse in the Ozone Park area of Queens; how she'd spilled grape juice on the hand-embroidered linen tablecloth in her nervousness, how she'd hardly spoken at all, how she'd felt like she shouldn't have been there in the first place. She remembered cracking the door to the downstairs bathroom in time to hear Bernadine's voice float up from the dining room. "That girl has no etiquette," the older woman had declared. Nikki had shrunk in on herself and disappeared back into the patchouli-scented, mint-coloured bathroom, not wanting to hear the rest of it. In fact, she'd never let on, not even to Jazz, not even after all this time, that she'd overheard that much. She'd never been back, although, of course, circumstance had thrown her together with Jazz's mom often enough since.

Nikki supposed Bernadine was all the things her mother hadn't been—middle-class, educated, classy even. An English and pre-Law major when she'd met Winston Baltimore, Bernadine's law school ambitions had gotten sidetracked by marriage and motherhood. "The Professor was a professional student back then. Mom started clerking to pay the bills. I don't know if she minds that he cheated so much, as she feels he didn't hold up his end of the deal," Jazz had explained once, a sort of apology for her mother's aggressive coldness. Post-divorce, Bernadine landed a surprisingly well-paying job as managing clerk at Burrell and Ford, then a relatively new firm. She worked there to this day, though routinely rubbing shoulders with now-quite-successful lawyers had only made her progressively bitter over the years as far as Nikki could tell. To Nikki, Bernadine seemed the antithesis of Jazz. But mother and daughter were really quite close. Nikki was always careful not to let a critical word pass her lips, even on the days when Jazz bitched about her mother dipping into her life.

It was weird to be drawn into the joke now, at Giovanni's expense—Giovanni, for whom Nikki felt genuine affection. Nikki issued a tight smile, but did not comment, praying for Jazz to return. There was always more balance in the room when she was there.

"Of course," Bernadine continued, to herself it seemed. "For all their early passion, soon enough, it's out of sight, out of mind. Just ask Jasmine."

"Ask me what?" Jazz asked, re-entering the room, changed into a majestic-looking white robe with yellow trim, twin to Giovanni's attire.

Nikki exhaled. "Nothing."

Giovanni spoke up, a teasing tone in his voice, a kind of steel in eyes directed at Bernadine. "Your mom's jealous because my Tapanga-Rose loves me best."

Jazz sat next to her mother, after dropping a kiss on the baby's lips and sparing one for her husband. "Yeah, I don't get it," she said. "I'm the one who suffered through labour with her; now she only has eyes for him."

"Well, let's hope he continues to earn that affection," her mother said, as a buzz sounded from the direction of the front doorway. A little frown marred Jazz's face for a heartbeat, then she rubbed soothingly at her mother's back, giving her a little hug as she got up to answer the door.

Nikki escaped to the kitchen.

Likely it was their father, though it could as easily have been Giovanni's clan, or one of the few invited friends on either side arriving for the naming ceremony.

"Can you believe all this foolishness," Bernadine said, coming up behind her. "In my time, you took the child to a church and that was that."

"Well, they're doing both," Nikki said, amazed to hear herself defending a ritual she didn't truly understand, and which was likely to be a hodgepodge of different African rituals at best. But, as Jazz said, it was important to Giovanni, and for Nikki, it meant she could officially get to stand up with her godchild, since she couldn't be present for the christening.

Jazz came to the doorway. "Stop hiding in here, you two. Daddy's asking for you, Nikki, and Mom; Giovanni's parents are asking for you. Go ahead. I'll bring some drinks in."

"I can get that," both Nikki and Bernadine offered at the same time.

"No, I can get them. You two go on." And with that they were shooed out of the kitchen.

"You've lost weight," Nikki said to her father by way of greeting, as they stood uncomfortably facing each other. Nikki couldn't help wondering if he regretted giving her the journals. She couldn't deny he felt different to her, more real, on account of what she'd read.

Her father smiled, somewhat chagrined, his eyes seeking out Lorene. "I'm on a strict diet. It's either that or suffer incessant nattering about cholesterol and diabetes."

Nikki smiled to herself, thinking that Professor Winston Baltimore had finally met his match, and that the wispy-looking Lorene may have more mettle to her than was obvious. She'd need it, Nikki decided.

"Marcus, come, meet your niece," Giovanni said. Nikki and Jazz still couldn't get used to the idea of the rugrat as a sibling, but Giovanni was easy with him, taking his hand and leading him over to where Tapanga-Rose lay contentedly in her bassinet.

"What's a niece?" Marcus wondered.

"Well," Giovanni patiently explained, "a niece is the girl child of your sister, Jazz. Like you're your mom and daddy's child."

"My daddy's old," Marcus announced loudly, as Jazz was emerging from the kitchen with the drinks. The rattling of the glasses was the only sound, as all chatter ceased. Bernadine's cackle was the next thing to intrude on the quiet.

"Out of the mouths of babes," she mused, her voice carrying across the room.

By the time the ritual began, everyone was still present and accounted for, if ill at ease. Nikki avoided Jazz's eyes at all costs, for fear she'd break into laughter. The sisters had conspicuously disappeared into the bathroom earlier, as soon as it proved fairly safe to do so. No words had been exchanged, only muffled laughter—the kind that made their eyes water so much that reapplication of makeup had been required.

Giovanni had done his research online. He'd opted for the Yoruba ritual, simply because he was able to find more detailed information on it, and found a Yoruba priestess in the Yellow Pages. A table was laden with the requisite ceremonial food, some of which Nikki had never heard of and would not have known where to find. Alligator pepper, cola nut, and bitter cola were on the table alongside other life essentials—water, salt, palm oil, honey, and wine. Added to that were a pen, a book, and a dollar bill. The finishing touch was a knife, representing iron, which

Giovanni said symbolized Ogun, the god of iron. "Reeks of devil worship to me," Nikki heard Bernadine stage whisper as they gathered around Jazz, sitting with Tapanga-Rose and Giovanni standing beside her.

Nikki hadn't been raised in any particular religion, the nature of God being the only area of life in which her father admitted agnosticism. Mostly, she thought that particular line of study held no real interest for him. Some of his girlfriends had had religious leanings, however, and the more zealous of these would occasionally take little Nikki along to church with them. On the island, she sometimes went to Sunday school with Belle, who liked the singing, but Mama Vi didn't push it, unlike most of the villagers, who sent their offspring off in their Sunday best, even if they couldn't be bothered to go themselves. These fleeting encounters, and her occasional acceptance of Marisol's invitations of late, and she supposed her visits to her mother's gravesite were the sum total of Nikki's contact with the church. She supposed she did believe in a greater power. However, defining it had eluded her, and organized religion—Christianity or whatever—with their "don'ts" and built-in prejudices didn't particularly appeal to her. Maybe she was more like her parents than she realized, and certainly in this, they were more alike than she'd thought.

Jazz had been raised in the church by her mother, who'd re-embraced religion with a passion after her divorce. Jazz led things off with a hymn, one even Nikki recognized, a regular Christian hymn. The priestess then picked up each of the items on the table in turn, coaxed the baby into touching or tasting each. Tapanga-Rose, already a lover of the limelight, basked in the attention, smiling as the wine wetted her lips, her pink tongue flicking out for more.

The priestess intoned the value of each item as she went through this process, "...water, vital to life, as the child is important to the

family…bringing joy to her family as salt makes food palatable…
wine bringing happiness…"

Nikki couldn't help smiling at this; the child's glee at the tasting
seeming to underscore the truth of the statement.

The last was the money, which the priestess said must not be
made or used in any way that harms others. Nikki felt the stab of
this.

There were tears in more than a few eyes as the baby's names,
and their significance were announced. The baby's godparents,
Nikki and a close friend of Giovanni's, were also named and their
responsibility to care for the child as if it were their own spelled
out, a departure from the usual script, Nikki was made to understand, but one Jazz had insisted on.

Nikki had had to write something on her name selection and
heard it said back to her now, as the child was named and so
welcomed into life: "Rose, because just like the flower, you have
an undeniable beauty and a quiet but fierce strength. May your
spirit, too, be marked by both beauty and strength."

The priestess explained that in Nigeria, the ceremony would
have taken place outdoors, and the child's foot made to touch the
ground. "But I think we can all agree it's good to be inside and
warm on a day like today," she said, earning a little chuckle from
the group. The priestess, regally attired in scarlet robes with yellow trim, reminded Nikki a little bit of Florida Evans from the old
TV series *Good Times*. She emanated the same warmth, humour
and underlying no-nonsense demeanour.

Candle lit, she led the way with Jazz and Giovanni to Tapanga-
Rose's room, painted in the same primary colours as the rest of
the apartment. A prayer and another hymn, and soon the real food
and other presents appeared as if from nowhere, and a party
atmosphere quickly built as Tapanga-Rose slept quietly in her
sunrise-yellow crib.

CHAPTER THIRTY-EIGHT

*N*ikki heard the baby snuffling quietly and got up to check on her before she woke her mother and father from much needed rest. Between Christmas, a new baby with feeding, changing and general cuddling demands, they'd been running on empty, though with few complaints. Nikki suspected it hadn't hit them yet. She wished she could stay longer, but her flight left in only a few days, after the start of the New Year.

Nikki was pacing the room, crooning softly to Tapanga-Rose, a part of her still amazed at the reality of the baby in her arms, when Jazz came in. "Don't tell me my off-key singing woke you," Nikki said. "I was hoping you could get some more sleep. She's a little diva, hungry for attention, not food, not yet." She felt comfortable with the baby in her arms; it was a new feeling for her, and probably an extension of her relationship with Jazz and a reflection of Tapanga-Rose's sweet spirit. Either way, it was no bother for her to hold her niece and godchild longer while her sister rested.

But Jazz was already relieving her of her light burden. "Please," Jazz remarked, "I think there's some wiring connecting us. The minute she's awake, my eyes pop open and I start leaking."

Nikki pulled a face. But Jazz only smirked in response. "I've actually been up since the phone rang, what, an hour ago?"

"I'm sorry," Nikki said automatically.

"Don't be."

Jazz settled into the handmade wooden rocker Nikki had struggled with from Antigua, and unleashed her breast, settling Tapanga-Rose against it. The child began to suckle hungrily, belying Nikki's earlier assertion.

"So, was it that same guy?" Jazz asked.

"Not much gets past you," Nikki replied.

"Well, he's been calling here practically every night since you've been here," Jazz said. "I was bound to notice. I do answer my phone on occasion."

Nikki sat on the floor; leaned against the crib watching her sister.

"Does that hurt?" she asked.

"No, and stop changing the subject."

"I'm not."

"So, how come you never told me about him?"

"There's nothing to tell."

Jazz arched a brow, hard to miss even in the dim light. "Nothing to tell and he calls here every night? The only person who's called from Antigua, I might add, since you've been here."

"He's persistent; what can I say?"

"And mysteriously, he has my number," Jazz lobbed back, chuckling.

Nikki was silent.

"So..."

When Nikki didn't bite, Jazz sing-songed again, "So-oh..."

"So what?" Nikki wondered, delaying the inevitable now.

"That's what I want to know, what is he?" Jazz quizzed.

"What, like mammalian or amphibian?" Nikki joked. "He's one hundred percent Homo sapiens, I assure you."

"Ah, so it's a sexual thing, at least," Jazz teased.

They were both giggling like schoolgirls now.

"I don't know what he is," Nikki finally confessed, and like that, the laughter died. The only sound in the room was the baby's loud meal-taking.

"What? I don't!" Nikki defended or asserted; she wasn't sure which. "He's my boss's son. So don't wanna go there. He's younger than me. He's weird. Directionless. Has no internal filter. And he's a pothead."

Jazz nodded, a tiny smile teasing her lips again. "Ah, a fixer-upper."

"Oh, bite me, you!" Nikki shot back.

"Oh, is there biting involved?" Jazz teased. "Kinky."

Nikki sucked her teeth. "Look, Jazz, he's wrong wrong wrong," she said soberly. "Not that I've lucked out with Mr. Right, right? Look at Terry, perfection. Hensen, perfection."

"Perfection is an illusion," Jazz said.

"Tell me about it; means you have to look that much harder for the knocking under the hood," Nikki replied. "Still, Aeden, Aeden is so far from perfection I don't know what I could possibly see in him."

"And yet you see something," Jazz guessed.

Nikki hesitated to answer, shy about it almost. But Jazz's cat eyes held hers, until she gave it up. "Yeah, I guess I do."

Jazz smiled, holding her eyes some more, looking to Nikki like the fucking Madonna with child.

"Wipe that look off your face," Nikki admonished. "He's seriously weird. Stalker weird. No manners, at all; all impulse and irreverence."

"But?" Jazz prompted.

Nikki sighed; it was a happy girlish sigh, the kind she'd only allow herself with Jazz. "But...hmm...exciting and seductive in a way that has me wishing for..."

"For?" Jazz prompted again.

Nikki shook her head vigorously, as if clearing her ears of sea-water or something. "Whatever it is, it scares me," she admitted.

"Because of Hensen."

"A bit."

"It's been a while, though. Might be time to get back on that horse," Jazz suggested.

Instantly irritated, Nikki tossed back, "I'm not a jockey."

"I know," Jazz quickly appeased. "It isn't easy. Didn't mean to suggest it was. Nikki, I know you, better than anyone probably, and you have so much to give. Why keep it to yourself? Or maybe you want to disappear back into that shell you had when we first met, or wake up at the end of your life and realize that you never lived your life. Terry was the wrong guy for you; I see that now. And Hensen J. Stephens was an asshole who let a good thing slip through his fingers. Neither of them deserves the rest of your life."

Nikki got up. "I'm tired. I'm turning in," she said, relieved when Jazz let her get away with cutting the conversation short.

Proving that New York was as much a small town as anywhere, Nikki ran into Terry at a New Year's Eve party, a posh fund-raiser event at the Upper East Side apartment of an "Uncle Project" executive member. None of the "nephews" were in attendance, but some of New York's most successful black men were. Nikki should have anticipated running into Terry, not because he was into community service, which he wasn't, but because he rarely missed an opportunity to network.

She was Giovanni's date for the night, filling in for Jazz, who was at home with the baby. Jazz had begged off but insisted they go, claiming to need the mother-daughter time.

Terry was with a Tyra Banks type: Amazonian and striking. Her hair was an elegant hybrid of bangs and a French roll; her black dress was shimmery and clingy in all the right places. Nikki was uncharacteristically glad for her own considerable height and her many months of manic jogging; glad, too, that she'd agreed to wear an elegant number, not usually her style. It was green and certainly felt expensive—a Christmas gift which Jazz had assured her, "brings out your eyes." She held her arms stiffly, willing them not to wander to check on stray strands of hair in her own complicated up-do. Good as Jazz and Giovanni and the mirror had told her she looked; standing before "the Amazon," it was hard not to feel like a morning glory wilting in the mid-morning sun as she and Terry exchanged polite pleasantries amidst the clinking glasses, gay chatter, and live and lively Latin jazz combo.

"Old boyfriend?" Giovanni whispered once Terry and "the Amazon" had moved on. He was, no doubt, picking up on her tension—tension which irritated her because after all, she was long over Terry and had been the one to call things off.

"Yeah, before your time," Nikki confirmed.

"Drinks?" he suggested.

"Drinks," she agreed. And they headed for the bar.

She wasn't much of a drinker, though, and the Bailey's she sipped did little to give her a buzz or ease her headache.

It wasn't hard to convince Giovanni to leave early, anxious as he was to welcome the New Year with his wife and baby girl.

Nikki met up with Terry again when she went to collect their coats from the bedroom doubling as a coatroom.

"How are you doing?" Terry's voice asked, startling her in the dimly lit room.

She swung around. "Good," she said, echoing what she'd said earlier.

"Antigua still everything you wanted?" he asked blandly.

Nikki wished she could see his face properly.

"It has its moments," she replied pleasantly enough, deciding to take the question at face value.

"So," Nikki asked. "Monique, huh?"

"Veronique," he corrected.

Nikki was unsure why she'd brought up the woman, clearly not the associate who'd wedged between them in the first place.

"A model?" she asked.

Terry laughed softly. "She'd be flattered but no, she's a literary publicist. I was doing some legal work for one of her clients. Not my usual type of work, but we were old college friends; he insisted he wouldn't be comfortable with anyone else vetting his contracts. We met at his book launch party."

His voice petered off as though the weirdness of it all suddenly hit him, as it had Nikki. "Weird, huh," she said. "Me and you, semi-dark bedroom, bed full of coats..."

"Me chatting up my girl," he finished. "Yeah, weird."

"So, she's your girl, huh," Nikki said, surprised at the way the idea of that caused her stomach to dip, like when a plane fell into an air pocket.

Though shadowed, she saw the way his chin cocked when he said, "Yeah, she's my girl."

And Nikki felt frozen. This always seemed to be the case with Terry; there was no protocol for this either.

"*I'm happy for you,*" she started to say, even as he ventured, "So, are you seeing anyone?" In the end, they both settled for a "take care," and the awkward conversation was over and Nikki was out on the curb, still nursing a headache, toes already freezing in the cold, as Giovanni flagged a cab. Somewhere "Auld Lang Syne" played prematurely.

CHAPTER THIRTY-NINE

On the flight back to Antigua, the screening of *I Now Pronounce You Chuck and Larry* proving neither amusing nor a distraction, Nikki's thoughts sprinted backwards. Tapanga-Rose's face came up often. It was difficult to explain, even to herself, how Tapanga-Rose filled her with joy. Maybe because she was Jazz's child. Maybe because that's what children did, take up residence like they'd always been there.

For Nikki, cobwebs had grown around and dust settled over any yearnings she might have had for a child of her own. Hell, she couldn't even get the relationship part right; notions of surrender and forever seeming sometimes like so much insanity. But she couldn't deny that this baby made her happy.

And Aeden made her…well, she wasn't sure what he made her yet. But she had given him Jazz's number. Why was that? And when and how had he wormed his way under her skin? For Nikki, who'd felt connected to very little in her life, it itched. But it was a good itch, she realized, as she soared above the clouds, musing on Tapanga-Rose and Jazz's glow and Giovanni's new-daddy-delight, and Aeden. She allowed herself to dream a little bit about being connected in the way Gi and Jazz were, the way her parents had never been, with her or each other. The way she'd never been with anyone; not even the ones she mourned a little bit, still.

She'd visited her father before leaving New York, crossing

paths at the bottom landing briefly with Lorene and Marcus who were on their way out as she came in, the outer screen door banging behind them. She closed the door and ventured up the dark stairway and into the second-level doorway, following the call of the music.

Billie Holliday, wistful and wearily defiant, segued to a gay-sounding Ella as Nikki came up behind her dad, where he sat in that brown, creaky, sagging leather chair, finger tapping against his legs, bushy hair haloed by the light coming in through the closed balcony door, a glass partition that overlooked the street below. She remembered as a kid the odd feeling of peeking from behind the drapes at that white-sheeted street in winter from the warmth of the apartment. Her father always kept it a little too warm, never having really got used to the cold.

"I have to admit," she said, by way of greeting, "I'm confused."

Her father, in his standard home attire of vest, pants, and leather slippers, startled. He'd been in another world.

"Confused?" he queried.

"Well, yes," Nikki said, wandering over to take up the CD case, a collection of female jazz and blues greats. "You always listened to Billie when you were feeling melancholy or just plain moody. You listened to Ella when you felt good, sitting in this same chair, tapping your finger against your leg, a little smile on your lips, your head thrown back, in another world, kind of like you were just then."

She didn't mention that he always played Dinah or Sarah when he was squiring a new lady, or that she knew he'd had a bad day at the university and was contemplating the meaning of his very existence when Nina's "Sinnerman" boomed powerfully. She'd curl in on herself behind the chair, inexplicably afraid. Climbing into his lap was not an option.

"With you playing both Ella and Billie at once, I'm not sure whether I should enter the lion's den or steer clear," Nikki continued brightly. "That used to be my cue, you know. Then, of course, there's the shock of seeing you park your record player and vintage records for a, what, a multi-disc CD changer, top of the line, at that."

She was kneeling now in front of the obnoxious silver-and-black set, out of place in this space of old, familiar things.

Her father gave a little shrug. "It was a gift from Lorene. The mix CD is one of those hotchpotches that no real jazz aficionado would admit to putting together; there being no consistency of mood, period, or even artifice. It's the kind of thing a novice would buy."

If he found the conversation odd, he didn't say so. He gamely played along, and Nikki was relieved at that, letting Ella's playful singing—like sunshine—seduce her.

"Oh," her father said suddenly, "I almost forgot. We have a present for you."

Nikki was surprised, and she didn't miss the "we," still getting used to the idea of her father being part of a "we."

He reached under the tree, a small one for sure, but still, the presence of a Christmas tree in her father's place was truly bizarre. Holidays had always gone unmarked in his home, and religious holidays, in particular, were scoffed at. She'd never received a present, Christmas or birthday, graduation or otherwise from him—apart from those damned journals.

The gift was a photo album, soft and velvety to the touch, cursive silver framing. "It's beautiful," she said, opening it, and pulling up short. There was a picture, a staged studio shot, of a woman and a boy of about ten. The boy was skinny and rangy, and wore knee socks and short pants, the face recognizable as her father's, even through the yellowing of the image.

"Is this your mother?" Nikki asked, wonder in her voice.

Her father had rarely spoken of his family, had claimed not to remember much of Antigua, said he had no people left there.

"Yes," he said now. "Lorena...Mama." Nikki opened her mouth and closed it. It hardly seemed likely that her father had been drawn to a girl one-third his age because her name sounded like that of his long dead mother. Though she had to admit she and Jazz had been looking for a reason, and this was the closest she'd come to one. If Nikki's father noticed her reaction, he didn't acknowledge it; he merely continued, "This is the same day we were leaving the island, I believe. People always wore their Sunday best to travel in those days."

Nikki took in the woman's tall build, her long thick rope of hair. Though she'd assumed her hair was from her father's side, she'd always thought she'd gotten her build from her mother's side. Seems that was only half the story, she mused. A hat decorated with flowers sat atop the woman's head, and she wore a flowered dress, gloves and heels.

The woman seemed to be in her late twenties and she was smiling, but her eyes were wary.

"We went to the Virgin Islands first," her father said, startling her a bit. His voice was rusty and his eyes distant. He didn't look at her, and she found she couldn't look away from him. "After a couple of years, we headed to mainland America," he said. "She grew sickly in the cold. Died after a few years. I worked hard. Jobs and school, that was my life in a place where my skin colour and the accent I still struggled to lose back then, not to mention our abject poverty, marked me sure, as the theologians say God marked Cain. No, America, even up North, wasn't exactly welcoming to the likes of me, and I worked really hard to wash the island off of me, scrub it from my tongue. That, at least, I could do something about. And it was all for her, because she wanted more for me. I was a mama's boy, I suppose, even before I came here." A little smile teased his lips, his eyes remained far away, and Nikki remained transfixed. "Back in Antigua," he said, "we lived in a city slum, Garling, where I wasn't allowed to wander from the yard or play with the other boys. She became even more possessive after we moved. Raising a bookish mama's boy, whose one dream was to make her happy. And then, she was gone."

He quieted, looked lost. Nikki was afraid to breathe.

"She was raised by an old aunt in Antigua," her father continued, eyes even more distant as though smelling the sea salt, or, more likely the sourness of stale memories. "It was after the aunt died that she cashed in the insurance money, paltry as it was, and we left. There was no one left. Besides, she hated Antigua. She was educated, stressed the importance of education, sent me to TOR Memorial, the first school on the island to give illegitimate children, which I was, access to primary and secondary education back then. The aunt that raised her, Tia Maria-Augusta, Titi, was a half-Portuguese woman, particularly proud of her Portuguese lineage, if only because it was non-African. The family had come over from Madeira a generation or so earlier to work the plantations, but soon moved on to other things. Titi's only son, in fact, was among the wave of Antiguans who'd left Antigua in the early part of the century for work in Cuba, Panama, and other places. He was lost to her, not even letters, by the time I came along. Titi was a laundress, married to and living apart from a local stevedore, a condition she eternally lamented but did nothing to remedy, like it was inoperable cancer. She was very big on marrying up, hammered that into my mother, in spite of her own failing in this area, perhaps because of it."

Nikki struggled to keep up as her father rushed on, his eyes losing some of that vagueness. "My mother never spoke of my father, but my own deduction says he couldn't have been a local boy. He was white, maybe Irish or Scottish, mixed at least by my thinking. Mama did speak of a summer spent working on a farm in the country, as a laundress and all-around house maid, with a family, relations to the ones her aunt worked for in the city. She never named my father, nor claimed anything of his. Not even his name. I could've investigated while I was there, I suppose, but by then, it didn't seem to matter; I was the only one left and I'd long outgrown the need for a father. The name I carry was that of my mother's father. Edward John Baltimore. He migrated near the end of the Great War to fight, Mama said. She still believed in him after all that time, though he'd never looked back, had maybe died or maybe got himself a new life. Either way, her mother died of heartbreak. Or that's what her aunt said. Often. She always claimed, even by the time I came along, you can't expect anything from 'them local Antiguan boys.' Her estranged husband included.

"What a self-abnegating condition we lived in. Of course, coming to the States didn't alter that reality. My mother hated her life, hated herself, maybe hated me a little bit, hated Antigua, hated the man she never spoke of and whom I always believed had paid, at least in part, for our exodus from the island. My mother, I believe, is what ignited my quest for learning, and my desire to unravel the mysteries of the ways we are, or in the hip lexicon, the ways we be."

Nikki's father laughed dryly, then continued, "As I get older, no closer to the answer, I'm beginning to think that maybe the answer doesn't exist, not in books anyway. I'm beginning to discover that I have no appetite for grand experiments, and ceaseless inquiry, anymore; only for time with my boy, Marcus, and for listening to this hotchpotch. You never know, retirement may even be on the horizon."

He leaned back in his chair, giving over, it seemed, to the music again. "…you can have that picture," he said. "I don't need it anymore. Like I didn't need the journals anymore. It's like it all belongs to someone else."

Nikki sat there with him until he started to snore softly, and then sat a while longer, listening to the looped voices of females who'd been there and lived to sing about it. This, she decided, ranked up there as one of the strangest days of her life. When her tears came, she blamed it on Billie.

CHAPTER FORTY

The sun was a balm after the chill of New York, especially in early January late afternoon when it didn't so much glare as wink at you.

Nikki smiled at the picture Aeden made, waiting for her amidst the huddle of people outside the Arrivals lounge, wearing a big grin, brown denim cut-offs and an orange tie-dyed T-shirt, orange sneakers, his usual wild reddish hair, and a white grin. He was almost coordinated. He swept her up into an enthusiastic hug, and she gave herself over to it, never mind the curious stares.

"Girl, the sight of you like sunrise at Devil's Bridge," he said near her ear, hot breath tickling skin for the first time in, it seemed, forever.

She laughed, feeling kind of silly. "I thought it was starlight from the Ridge."

"No, no, no, no," he said. "That's your smile. Na try trip me up."

"Wouldn't dream of it," she said, as he hoisted one of her bags and she tugged the other behind her, settling her carry-on more securely over her shoulder.

As they drove out of the airport in her jeep which he'd been babysitting for her, she glanced across at his profile, a beautiful profile she had to admit, and decided not to look too closely at why she'd allowed him to collect her from the airport. Why she'd given him Jazz's number. Why the sight of him, being here with him now, made her feel so buoyant. She'd think about it later, she decided. She was not about to walk into anything blind-folded again, in spite of what Jazz said. But for now, for this moment, she gave herself permission to drift.

Aeden was taking great pains to drive with considerable care past the now familiar blend of open land and buildings of all hues. Trying to impress her, she realized. Part of her pulled back from the hope in his eyes, the little smile playing on his lips; part of her leaned in to it.

"You look beautiful," he said, meeting her eyes fleetingly. She'd never really been able to believe that kind of thing, but then, no man had ever said them to her with such wonder and surprise in his voice. He was bolder now, perhaps a result of being her only link to Antigua while away. She'd wanted a clean break and had gone so far as to leave her cell phone in the desk drawer of her home office. But when after dropping her off at the airport, Aeden had asked for Jazz's number; Nikki had given it to him, a knee-jerk reaction. And he'd called and they'd talked, long rambling talk about films and family, music and memories, food and fan-tasies. Well, he'd done most of the talking; Nikki listened. He was good company. And she couldn't deny now that something had deepened between them. But she was almost afraid to look too closely at it. Later, she promised herself, as she acknowledged his endearment with a little smile and a sound deep in her throat.

"How's your dad? The Project?" she finally asked. She'd avoided asking him about this her entire time in New York.

When he looked across at her and then back at the highway, the smile was gone from his lips.

"Great," he said finally. "The big man always great. Had his big Old Year's Night look-at-me-who's-who-to-do. It's all good."

"Any more trouble at the site?" she asked. He shrugged.

She took the hint.

"How've you been?" she asked.

The grin was back, even as he shrugged again.

Nikki dug into the carry-on sitting on her lap, pulled out a vintage "Space Oddity" T-shirt, brown with pink lettering. "Got this for you," she said, holding it up with both hands. He looked over, all gums now. "You're a Bowie fan, right?" she confirmed. He'd mentioned it during one of their marathon long distance conversations. Bowie, Marley, Lennon, Short Shirt; those were pretty much his musical gods.

"You remembered," he said, the gravitas in his voice making her stomach do a little flip. She waved it off, dropping the shirt into his lap.

"Don't read too much into it," she teased. "It was like five dollars in this little vintage place in East Village. Besides, the words reminded me of you."

Aeden scoffed, taking the dig in stride, then said with a little chin point, "Check the glove compartment." Nikki did, pulled out a box, an innocuous white box. Inside were square clay earrings, painted with yellowish-green swirly patterns outlined in white and navy, and a matching pendant.

"What's this?" Nikki asked.

"Merry Christmas," Aeden said quietly, eyes on the road. "Bridget's handiwork. She used a picture from the newspaper to try to match them to your eyes."

Nikki had to admit Aeden's sister did outstanding work, but somehow, it felt like she was accepting more than earrings and that unsettled her; after all, she'd convinced herself that a T-shirt was just a T-shirt. "Christmas is gone," she reminded him. "Besides, this whole Santa Claus deal isn't exactly me, you know, growing up with Professor Baltimore and all."

He rolled his eyes. "Put in the earrings, please."

"What? Now?" she asked, but threaded the gold hooks through her lobes anyway. She left the pendant where it was, then took a breath and angled her body towards Aeden, waiting.

They were at the house before he looked at her again. He stopped the jeep and turned off the engine, turned toward her, then smiled. "Beautiful," he said. And Nikki, all nearly thirty three years of her, blushed.

The house was empty.

Nikki, still wearing her earrings, left her bags in the living room, opened the back patio door and two of the Wadadlis they'd bought on the way, and sat, putting her feet up. She was home. Home was good, she decided.

"It's nice to be back," she said.

"It is?" he asked, studying her face.

"Yes," Nikki confirmed. And they were silent, comfortably silent, together.

Sometime later, the front door opened and closed. Then there was a muffled curse as someone bumped into her luggage in the semi-dark; then the lights went on.

With a huge smile, Nikki jumped up to go greet Carlene, Aeden on her heels.

"Carlene," she said, advancing, offering a hug, as the other woman stood before her in her Mama Vi's hostess uniform. The hug was not returned; in fact, it was thrown off.

"Don't touch me," the younger woman said, enunciating exaggeratedly. "Me too vex me na make it outta ya before you come back. Anyway, me ha wan car dey wait pon me. Me find one place. Tonight self, me gone."

Nikki stood stunned, at the ugly fury on Carlene's face.

She reached out again, and Carlene's hand shot out, balled up, punching her in the chest. Nikki fell back, catching the edge of a chair, slipping to the floor, jarring her spine.

"Hey, hey, hey," Aeden said, advancing, beer bottle still in hand. Seeing the situation spinning out of control, Nikki grabbed at his leg and pulled herself up. Her chest felt tender and pained where she'd been hit.

"Carlene," she said, hating the baffled, confused, yearning sound of her own voice.

"Don't 'Carlene' me," the other woman said. "Matter of fact, don't never call mi name again. Audrey was right 'bout you. Feel say you better than everybody. Feel you ah lady, an' everybody fi up under you."

Aeden stood there looking like Nikki imagined she did— frozen. Except she wasn't; still as she was outside, the inner quaking she'd nearly forgotten made her world feel like it was rocking and rolling. She felt disoriented.

"Don't look so innocent," Carlene raged. "Fanso tell me wha yuh say."

"What I say?" Nikki said, finding her tongue. "What did I say?"

"Pretending you have any kind of regard for me, but just ah try keep me down. Grudgeful! He tell me how you try discourage him from gi me this job. But you know what, me good at it. So, tek that!"

She turned down the hall towards her room, and after a stunned second, Nikki followed. She didn't feel or hear Aeden following, and was glad for that. This was clearly a misunderstanding. She and Carlene would sort it out.

"Carlene, I'm sorry if you misunderstood, or if Fanso mis-represented…"

"Don't start throwing your words at me, no 'if' there. The kinda regard Fanso hold you in, he not about fi lie pon you. An' if you say he did, you's a liar."

"Carlene, it's not like that."

And she forgot herself, reached out to touch again. Carlene flung her hand away. "Ooman, you hear me say na touch me. You're the devil, dat self. You touch me an' is like the devil self touching me."

The younger woman was moving frantically, pulling her belongings together, and chucking them into a bag. Nikki found herself wondering if Carlene was still taking her medication, keeping up with her doctor visits. She knew better than to ask.

Carlene continued spewing her venom, seemingly unable to stop. "People see you, think them know you. But dem na know how you heart black. You possessed. You evil. Possessed by envy and keepdownness and badmindedness. You're an evil, evil woman. Wussa still 'cause you na know say you evil. Bring me here so, so you can kick me in mi ass. All the while ah pretend say you ah friend, ah pretend fi care. But just wanting to lord yourself over me. You's a proper bitch. Only 'cause people don't know."

Nikki tried again. "Please, Carlene, let's talk about this."

"Talk? Talk? Don't say nothing to me, never again. Not to me, not to any o' mi picknee. You see, Imani, yuh godchild, forget say you even know 'im."

A horn sounded outside, and Carlene grabbed up what she could, pushing past Nikki and leaving the room. It took three trips, and some man Nikki didn't know tramping through her home, but soon, all evidence of Carlene was gone. Nikki sat in a corner of the living room couch watching these goings-on. Aeden stood around looking uncertain, and she wanted desperately for him to leave, but show her a man who could take a hint, and she'd show you Jesus.

Finally, they were alone.

He sat next to her on the couch.

She cleared her throat. "Aeden, I think maybe it's time for you to go."

"No," he said.

She turned to him, arched a brow.

"That's the last thing you need now," Aeden said firmly.

She was on her feet, towering over him and like that, the inner quaking exploded outward. "Don't tell me what I need. I'm tired of everybody telling me about myself. Do I walk around spewing unsolicited advice? When Audrey was treating me like fowl shit under her shoes, did I point a finger, say, 'Audrey, you're a cold bitch'? When I first met Marisol, did I say, 'You're a busybody'? Am I calling fucking Fanso now, telling him, 'You're a deceitful excuse for a brother'? Cam? Telling him, 'You're an arrogant peacock'? Do I? Do I? Do I tell Mama Vi how fucked up I am because she gave me away? She gave me away, she gave me away, and he took me, but he never gave me what I needed. Do I call him on it? Do I? Do I tell you, Aeden, how the idea of caring about you, with the way you float around without a care in the world, scares me? Do I? Do I? Fuck you, Carlene! Do I? Do I? I? Fuck you! DoIDoIDoIDoIDoIDoI...?"

It was hot and burned as it flowed out, and she couldn't see anything but it, noxious and grey like pyroclastic clouds. The flow was continuous, neverending, until she felt hollow and still it coughed out, leaving her raw inside and out.

When Nikki came back to herself, she was on the couch, and he was holding her, his shirt wet beneath her cheek, her cheeks wet, her eyes hurting, her throat raw, and her body humming. He stroked her hair, most of which had come loose somehow.

She didn't remember the last few minutes, hours, however long she'd been there, what had happened to get her there. She only remembered feeling very hot, feverish, like she was burning up. A volcano; that was it. She was a volcano. She giggled at this, and the rhythm of Aeden's caress changed, transmitting worry. Nikki laughed harder.

When she finally got around to checking her messages, there was Fanso's voice, sounding worried, asking her to call.

She did. Aeden had stayed with her all night, was still there somewhere fiddling around, if the sounds from the kitchen were any indication. It had felt good to let go, to dance with crazy, and know that he would catch her, that he'd be there when the music stopped. She'd never done that with a man before, had only come close with her sister Jazz, and, in a way, sexually, with Hensen J. Stephens. She didn't know what to do now, felt more exposed than she ever had in her life.

One of Fanso's boys answered the phone and she suffered through the small talk, then the shouts of, "Daddy, Auntie Nikki on the phone."

"Hey, how was your trip?" Fanso asked.

"Good," Nikki replied, amazed at the calm in her voice, its hoarseness grounding her in her anger.

He sighed. "Look, I don't mean to dump this on you, but..."

And he hesitated again.

"I already know," Nikki said. "You told Carlene I didn't want her for the hostess job."

"Nikki, jack, is not so the story go," Fanso defended. "I was congratulating her on doing such a good job, especially through the Christmas season. She was marvelous. I mean, this job fit her like a skin. And I was giving her a little bonus. I know we didn't budget for it, but I thought she deserved it, so I pinched it from my money. And I told her she was exceeding expectations. Then I made a stupid joke about what you said, stupidly thinking that it was funny; you know, ironic. It was…it was a stupid thing to say, and I knew it as soon as I saw the look on her face. I knew I messed up. I called you right away. Then she told me she was moving out, was getting a place, would be taking back her kids, what I'd wanted all along. And I felt worse. I was getting what I wanted, but at your expense. You have to believe me, Nikki, it's not what I meant to happen."

The rush of words stopped and he was breathing hard.

"Okay," Nikki said.

Fanso sighed again. "You brushing me off."

"No, I'm not. I believe you."

"You do?"

"You're not a malicious person. Why should I not?"

"Why are you so calm?"

Nikki shrugged, remembered he couldn't see her, then said, "I worked up to calm."

"You haven't seen her yet, have you?" Fanso said. "She told me earlier yesterday that she got a place and would be collecting the kids soon, but she wanted to fix up the place first. Said it was cheap but it would do."

"I saw her."

"What happened?"

"She cussed me out, took her stuff, left. There might have been some battery involved."

"Oh, shit! Nikki, Nikki, I'm so sorry."

"Okay," she said.

"Nikki, please talk to me."

"I don't really want to talk about it, Fanso. We'll meet Monday as planned to go over the books, etcetera."

There was a long silence, then another sigh. "Okay," he said.

"Okay," Nikki said, and hung up.

"How are you?" Aeden said, handing her a cup. His hair hung damply and he was wearing his "Space Oddity" shirt. Yesterday seemed so far away, but there it was. Nikki's eyes burned again, but she was done crying.

"Don't want to talk," she said.

And so they sat, silently sipping tea he'd made from sour sop leaves plucked from somewhere outside. "To calm your nerves," he said. It wasn't bad, though she yearned for a cup of coffee.

CHAPTER FORTY-ONE

"Aeden."

"Trust me."

"Those are seriously scary words coming from you."

"That hurts. Come on; relax."

"I thought that was the whole point. I'm not."

"Exactly. And I've been told I'm very good at this."

"By whom? Your harem? Speaking of which, do you have a girlfriend?"

"Come on."

"What? It's a perfectly logical question. Sure, you're a bit of a space oddity, but money and looks will go a long way and you've got both."

"I've got looks?"

"Do you have a girlfriend?"

"Would I be trying so hard with you if I had a girlfriend?"

"Well, you are an Antiguan man."

"Ha ha."

"So, who told you you're good at this?"

"My sister."

"Your sister?"

"Yes, my sister."

"Okay, this is venturing into super weird territory, even for you."

"What, it's not an inherently sexual thing."

"Oookay."

"Serious."

"As a bug."

"Seriously."

"So, you're good at this, huh?"

"The best."

The air smelled of lavender and lemon and other things Nikki couldn't name. Aeden's hands on her were warm and slick, thanks to the massage oil he'd lifted from her dresser. Technically, it wasn't massage oil; it was scented hair oil, which she used to help tame her thick mane, but he assured her it would do. She wondered what she was doing listening to him anyway.

Before beginning, he'd flipped through her CD collection, slipping the *Love Jones* soundtrack, *Najee Plays Songs from the Key of Life*, Bob Marley's *Kaya*, and Aubrey "Lacu" Samuel's *Pan Rising* into the CD changer. Next he'd pulled the heavy drapes and unplugged and turned off the phones, shutting out time. Then he'd settled alongside her on his knees, the bed rocking a little at this new presence, starting at her admittedly tight shoulders as her favourite song from the first CD, Lauryn Hill's *The Sweetest Thing* worked its magic.

Soon, his hands on her were the only things she was aware of physically. They molded her, gentle and firm, circling her back with feather-light touches, before returning to deepen the pressure right there, where she needed it most. The music provided the rhythm, and Nikki had to concede that Aeden was, in fact, quite good at this, settling into the motion as though he himself was hypnotized by it. She tried to lose herself in it, too, but her mind still danced a Carnival: Carlene's rage-twisted face, Tapanga-Rose's eternally smiling one, Hensen's, Terry's, Cam's, her sisters', her father's, her mother's...

"What you thinking so hard 'bout?" Aeden's voice interrupted. "Relax." His hands tilted her head so he could reach both sides, found her temples, applied gentle pressure.

"Shh," he said. "Forget all that now. So life stay, knock down, drag down. Stop fight it, leggo. The more you fight, the quicker you drown. Find the wave and ride it."

She smiled a little at this. "What's that, surfer philosophy? Don't tell me you surf now, too?"

"Windsurf, and shhh, you killing the mood."

"You started it."

"Shhh…"

The CD was on to Marley's "Sun is Shining" and to quiet her mind, Nikki tried picturing the wave at daybreak, the sun a sliver of light, just a sliver, cutting across the water, then spreading until it bathed everything in its glow.

"Beautiful," she whispered.

Aeden's hands moved down the side of her face, back to her shoulders, taking their time, inch by baby inch. By degrees, she surrendered to it.

"What you 'fraid, eh? Wha you runnin' from?" her mother asked, looking down at her as she held her hand.

"I'm not running," Nikki said in a little girl's voice. She was the little girl, but with the sum of the woman's experiences.

"Yes." Her mother was skeptical.

"Who you share wid? Who know your dreams? And the light and darkness inside you? Who you trust fu gi yourself to? Who trust you enough fu gi demself back? Comf'table in yuh company? Make you comf'table in fu dem company? Give up deyself to you allow you fu give up yuhself to them? Make you free to feel alive? Alive with you? Love you? You love?"

The little girl with Nikki's voice offered no answer.

She gripped the mother's hand tighter, and was led to a palm tree, where she was seated in the dirt on the ground between the mother's legs. There her hands were brought, the mother's hands laid over hers, to the mound of clay, cool to the touch.

"Feel," the mother said, her voice a whisper. "Feel."

And the little girl found she was crying. And the clay, though not fully shaped, was cracking. But her mother's hands smoothed the fissure away. And Nikki felt the tears on her cheeks, and the coolness of the clay, and the cotton shirt hugging her torso, and the earth beneath her naked feet, and the wind meeting her face gentle as a mother's hands, and her mother's hands gentle despite the leathery, weathered look.

And Nikki felt alive even as she woke to the bland tones of her room, and the soft feel of her sheets and comforter.

And she felt the tears on her cheeks.

Facing Monday seemed an impossible feat, and Nikki burrowed away from the heat and the call of the day. Her running shoes sat somewhere in her closet, missing her. Her shorts and shirts, laundered since before her Christmas jaunt, were in a drawer, wondering which of them would be picked today. Beside her, the bed was empty. She'd built her resolve and imposed on Aeden to go home. She turned over, throwing off the covers and winced at the lingering pain in her chest. It set off a chain reaction, finding and igniting the heart of that pain, the memory of Carlene's rage-ugly face.

She turned back over into the bed, her face in the pillow, unwilling to face the day. She thought instead of Mama Vi, of the dream, what it was trying to tell her, of the picture she carried everywhere now but no longer needed to remember her mother's face.

Later, as she drove to Sea View Farm, she reflected on the whirlwind that had been her day. A meeting with Cam, at which she gave him notice of her intent to quit the project, having typed up the letter that very morning, after her morning run. One line:

I have decided to withdraw from the Blackman's Ridge Project and my role as consultant with Cameron Enterprises, effective February 1st.

A month's notice, give or take, seemed fair. She didn't give herself time to think about it, worry about it, pick at it, hold it up to the light for the flaws and such. She rode the wave of her decision into his office where he sat behind his big desk, huge as life. She took a little thrill in the way the prop-cigar stilled its twirling. Her muscles burned like she'd lifted that heavy table and turned it on him; and the phantom pain was welcomed.

He'd masked his surprise first with annoyance, then a kind of flippancy. "Well, the project, well on its way, likely woulda had to give you your walking papers soon."

She allowed him his little victory, leaving before he broke her bubble of joy with further talk.

Things had been stiff with Fanso. He'd apologized again. She'd accepted again.

She acknowledged the bubble of fear for the first time on the road to Sea View Farm. She might have to look for a place with a lower rent. She definitely couldn't foot psychiatrist's bills and the like anymore, but then, it seemed she didn't need to.

Sitting with her mother, she didn't speak, tried not to think. Restless, she didn't stay long. Marisol waited for her, and though she begged off, insisted on her having a slice of too-sweet fruit cake and slightly bitter sorrel drink. She didn't stay long.

Belle was delighted with her present, a new teal-coloured dress and matching shoes, an outfit she could wear to church without looking so much like a child, or rather a grown-up stuffed into a child's clothes. Audrey seemed surprised at her gift, a burnt-orange designer bag and matching hat.

"I don't much them things, you know," she said, turning the hat this way and that.

"I know," Nikki said. "But a gift ought to be a surprise, right; something you might not necessarily get yourself, but may well find you like."

"Well, I definitely wouldn't get myself this, that's for sure," her older sister said, a bemused expression on her face.

"I got you some fabric as well," Nikki said, handing over a wrapped package. "It was easy to sneak a look at Belle's size, but apart from the fact that I've rarely seen you in a dress, I couldn't think of a discreet way to sneak a look, even if I had."

Audrey actually cracked a smile at this, and Nikki found herself marveling at how far they'd come. Not "high spars" surely, but the crack had sealed somewhat, though she supposed there would always be a scar there. Just as it seemed there was always destined to be with Carlene. Nikki had bought her a gift set of Jennifer Lopez's *Still*, which it looked like she'd be using herself.

"So mi hear you an' the Jamaican fall out," Audrey said, her timing impeccable as always.

Nikki shrugged. "So it seems."

She was tense now, waiting for Audrey's indictment, verdict, whatever. Her nail cut into her palm, as she waited. But the silence stretched, and before long, she realized that Audrey had stuck the hat unto her plaited head and was peering into the bit of glass that hung on a wall; her expression bemused.

"I look like a peacock," she said. And Belle laughed.

"Blood Thicker Than Water."

—ANTIGUAN PROVERB

CHAPTER FORTY-TWO

*T*omorrow was her last day on the Blackman's Ridge project. Construction had progressed significantly; mischief still in effect here and there, despite the doubling of security at the site. Nothing significant enough, however, to slow things down.

Just the other night, Aeden, a steady part of the landscape that was Nikki's life these days, had remarked, "I don't know 'bout this thing, boy. Part of me feel like Daddy shoulda cut his losses a while back."

She'd visited Tanty and Sadie, and was saddened to discover that Sadie greeted her with more warmth than Tanty. When she let them know of her decision to leave the project, she was greeted with a kind of apathy she didn't understand.

"It don't change nothing for them," Aeden said. "You ha fu understan' they been farming that land for generations. Now they caught up in something they can't control, when all they want to do is continue farming that land and be left alone. It hit them, I guess, how much it's outta their control when Sadie got hauled in last time."

That saddened Nikki more, and she felt responsible. Responsible and helpless.

Aeden, hands playing in her hair, whispered, "You carn fix everything."

She laughed. "I don't want to fix everything; just one thing."

"Well," he said, leaning up on one elbow, in her bed where they lay, "you can help me fix up my business."

She looked sideways at him.

"No, seriously, ent you say you goin' be working with smaller businesses. All that stuff you say my business need, you know to make me a serious businessman and all, help me out with that. Add me to your client list."

Nikki sighed. "Aeden, who're you doing this for?"

"Wha you mean?"

"Are you saying what you think I want to hear because you think it'll get you into my bed?" she pressed boldly.

Cheekily, he responded, "I am in your bed."

He was right; that boundary had been breached the night of the massage. She hadn't even considered going backwards, but then they hadn't necessarily moved forward either.

"You know what I mean," Nikki said.

Aeden sighed and admitted, "Well, yes, I guess, maybe a little."

"Aeden…"

"No, I wan' be the kind of man you not scared to love."

"By changing who you are?"

"By becoming more of what I can be."

"You can't pretend to be something you're not."

"I don't want to."

"So…"

"Look, Nikki, mi nar pretend when mi say mi dream 'bout you."

"Aeden…"

"No, serious serious, no bullshit. Waking, sleeping, you me want. I dream an' wake up in the feeling, the hope that maybe you might want me even a little bit."

Nikki sighed.

"You think you might?"

She sighed again, and it was her hands this time caressing his face, his hair, his lips.

"I think I might," Nikki agreed, brow furrowed, stomach fluttering at the very idea.

On the eve of Nikki's new life, her second new life in less than three years, they went up to the Ridge, her jeep hugging the curves of the new road. With construction fully underway, the chopper was out of the question until a proper helipad could be put in. The entire set-up was far from ideal. With security on hand, questioning them as to the reason for their business there, Aeden, not Nikki, was the one to get them clearance. With the security, and the nearly finished wall structures, it was hardly the same place they'd come to two Old Year's Nights ago. They went to the mill where they sat on a blanket on the dirt floor, drank a toast with Coke in plastic cups, and nibbled on chocolate. And there they lay, Nikki's head in the soft pillow of Aeden's stomach, peering at the stars through the roof of trees that climbed the walls of the mill and arched over the top. If she remembered correctly, it was to be converted into a gazebo of sorts for private dining.

"I hate how this place come," Aeden said.

"I miss lying on the grass and losing myself in the stars," Nikki said.

"Yeah."

"I say that like I did it all the time," she said.

"Once is enough," Aeden said sadly. After a bit, he continued, "You were right 'bout me, you know. What you said that night, Old Year's Night, when we come up here. Remember?"

Nikki did, though was surprised he did, given how high he'd

been, how high they'd both been. "I do," he confirmed, "I do resent Daddy's money. So, I guess we both have daddy issues. You and 'the Professor,' as you call him, me and Daddy, me and both my parents, actually, and, of course, the late, great, indomitable 'Rabina the First.' Me na wan' come like them. Never have. People dancing up to you 'cause of yuh colour, yuh money, yuh class, even when you don't really have no class; people deciding you better than this or that smadee because of the luck of yuh birth. My grandmother revelled in it like Queen Elizabeth herself, that one. And yet, still just my grandmother, her gray hair dyed red, like she was fooling anybody, though her hair had never really been red. That come from my father-father line; Rabina had the high colour and that was that, but she was definitely one of the picky-head masses, and heaven help anybody who remind her of that." He chuckled to himself. "Donella name after her because she's the first, but Isobel is herself," he said. "You met Isobel. Don now, is the opposite, peace to the dead, always lock up in her lab; between you and me, I think she might be a social phobic and who can blame her in this family." Nikki wisely held her tongue; he felt like talking, let him talk. That too had become familiar. "Anyway," he continued, "that was Rabina the First, all about appearances. But I remember the time I burst in her bathroom, saw the red stains in the sink, and her without the mask of makeup, thought she was goin' tek een. But it was kinda sweet in a way, 'cause it meant she wasn't as perfect or secure in herself as she affected and maybe I wasn't as imperfect as I felt." Nikki thought then of what her father's diaries had revealed about both her parents, and though she hadn't yet unravelled it all, she knew what Aeden meant, sort of.

"You're right, I fought the conditioning," he continued, "rebel without a cause. Move with the people who not no worse than me, just worse off, like it was a mission. But blood is blood and much as Daddy disappointed in me, much as he and Mammy disappoint me, ah me people still, you know. Me love them an' all; me no wan' be them, you know."

"I know," Nikki responded. And she did.

"My baby sister, Bridget, is the most like me," Aeden continued. "But to be honest, I think we all a bit lost, me an' me sister an' dem. What mountains we have to climb?"

"Well, that's the trick, isn't it?" Nikki mused. "We all have to make our own way."

"I know; I know. Poor little rich kid whining about what mountains to climb."

"No." Nikki sat up, turned to him, and in the light of the three-quarter moon, didn't even have to squint to see him. "I'm thinking about how I invested so much time in not being my father's daughter, in feeling disconnected from my mother, and in trying to fix other people. And it's all bullshit. I am my father's daughter. My mother was always with me." She paused then, mind tracking back to that last conversation with her father and how the overarching presence of his mother and aunt, and the absence of his father had shaped him; of his decision, finally, to cut the navel string. Not that she thought it was possible. While his decision to not research his daddy's roots probably made sense, all things considered, his dad had imprinted on him, as surely as he had on her; there was no getting away from it. Hell, for all she knew, given her dad's obscure possibly Irish roots, even she and Aeden could be distantly related, given the way the Fates had of getting the last laugh. She shuddered at the thought. But if it was so, and she certainly wasn't going to undertake to find out, there was no escaping it.

But maybe, she was discovering, there was more to it than that.

Maybe... "People, including me, have to fix themselves," she told Aeden. "It's like you were saying the other night, you can't fix everything. It's a full-time job trying to fix yourself."

He looked up at her, reached up for her, pulled her face to his, kissed her. And she kissed him back.

When he pulled back, there was that now familiar mischievous grin on his face. "What?" Nikki asked.

"Want to give the security a thrill?" he responded.

Nikki had never taken a moon bath before; it was much like skinny dipping without the cover of water. Still, it was a full moon almost, they were on a sugar high, and both their sanities were suspect; how could she refuse? So what if they were ejected from the Ridge?

That night, in bed, Nikki felt awkward, like a virgin discovering intimacy for the first time. She was shy about her body, shy about his, uncertain about how to connect with him. But sometime between the minute the bed dipped under his weight, and the time his fingers started dancing over her skin, and his lips found her lips and nipples, and his voice sang praises to all the parts of her, she stopped thinking.

CHAPTER FORTY-THREE

Nikki was invited to appear on TV's *Sunday Chat*.

"To talk about what?" she wondered.

"Blackman's Ridge? There was some more vandalism reported this week, as I'm sure you've heard," the show's wily producer responded.

"I'm sorry, but I don't think it would be ethical for me to come on and do that," Nikki responded. "Until a month ago, Cameron Enterprises was my client."

There was a pause, then, "fair enough. Will you still come? You don't have to talk about Cameron or Blackman's Ridge."

"What would I talk about?"

"Other issues of the day. See, we're trying to mix it up a bit, with various people in the know, not the same voices every week."

"I'm a person 'in the know'?"

"Sure."

"What do I know?"

She wasn't being facetious; really, she wasn't; she'd kind of missed the moment she'd become such a part of things that this stranger saw her as insider, not outsider.

"You can comment on business issues," he said in all seriousness, as Nikki's eyes got wider and wider. "CSME; the WTO and the U.S. Gaming issue; how the government can claim the economy's grown in one breath and in another claim fiscal imbalance; what

the tenuous world economy will mean for the tourism industry...
minus Blackman's Ridge, of course."

Nikki's mouth was hanging open by this point. "I don't think
so," she said finally. "I'm hardly an authority on any of that."
Including Blackman's Ridge, she thought.

"But you know business," he said. She didn't even know if that
much was true, but she had to admit that she was, inexplicably,
tempted. She liked the way his words made her feel—competent,
a part of things, accepted. So what if he was only trying to butter
her up?

"I don't know," her voice of reason piped up. "It's kind of high-
profile, isn't it?"

"Well, you're already high-profile," he reminded her, "coming
off of Blackman's Ridge. Besides, as I understand it, you've got a
budding management and communications consultancy. Seems
to me high-profile might be just what you need."

She had to admit he was a good salesman, even if his cockiness—
like he knew he had her, even before she did—was a turn-off.

"What do you think?" she asked Aeden that night, in bed. Not
her best idea, considering where they were and what they'd only
just been up to.

"Don' matter what I think; what matter is what you think," he
responded.

"I think I'll be lucky if that security officer from the Ridge
doesn't call in and say, 'What class ah people dat you all have
there on radio? She had her backside expose de other night for
all the world to see,'" Nikki responded, with a laugh.

"And, hmm, what a pretty backside," Aeden teased, dipping his
head to offer it a kiss.

"Uh-uh, don't start," Nikki said, shifting away, "I'm being serious here. Come on, Aeden, what do you think? He's right; it'll

be good publicity, for attracting clients and paying participants to my seminars and workshops."

Distracted still, he murmured, "Well, there you go."

So Nikki went, after researching as much as she could on the various subject areas. She felt like a bit of a fraud speaking with any kind of authority on Antiguan issues. But, as it happened, her peculiar reticence proved a welcome contrast to the microphone-hogging know-it-alls the show usually attracted and that went over well with the show's audience when, in fact, they weighed in on radio the morning after. "She make some good points," they said, like a stuck record; one adding, "So she pretty!" One of her sound bites made the next day's news. She was asked back. She decided not to overdo it, becoming a resident authority on all matters, but said "yes" she'd do it again, if the topic fit.

"You handle yourself okay," Fanso said. "That's a gift I don't have, thinking and talking on my feet like that."

It was off-hours, and they were in the kitchen, where he preferred to meet so that he could keep his hands busy. Today, he was experimenting with something he wanted to add to the menu, vegetarian rice pudding; Antiguan rice pudding, without the cow intestines and blood.

"Try this," he said, thrusting a plate at her, little black circles stuffed with rice and other things. It certainly looked like rice pudding. Nikki popped one into her mouth without hesitation, having learned long ago that even Fanso's culinary accidents were tasty ones. "Kinda sweet," she mumbled around the treat, reaching for another. Rice pudding was usually well-seasoned, salty not sweet. Fanso pursed his lips, clearly not happy.

"You're much more of an extrovert than I'll ever be," Nikki said, picking up the earlier conversational thread.

"Yeah, but you can talk; I can't. You remember Mama Vi's opening," Fanso replied distractedly. "Sweet like mango, or sweet like pineapple?" he asked.

"Like pineapple," Nikki said, "kinda sour-sweet, not sweet-sweet."

He nodded. "Okay, I can work with that. I have to…"

Nikki smiled, as he took his mental detour, popping another into her mouth.

She began to shuffle together the files from their meeting, remarking as she did, "You were pitiful that night, hiding out in the kitchen, stuttering your way through my well-written, if I do say so myself, speech. I almost didn't recognize you." She laughed at the memory.

"It's good to hear that again," Fanso remarked, finally distracted from his experiment.

The laughter died. Nikki didn't look at him. The files kind of hung in her hands, as the "rice pudding" settled heavily in her belly.

"I wonder to myself sometimes when you goin' trust me again," Fanso said gently, as if speaking to a skittish animal. "This is two strikes, right?"

Nikki shrugged, the move incredibly child-like. It was hardly their first encounter since her return and the Carlene incident, but they'd always kind of danced around the issue. "You didn't mean to hurt me," Nikki said now in a small voice, wanting to be past it, but still feeling the burn of Carlene's punch; though, of course, that wasn't possible after all this time.

"But I did," Fanso said, leaning forward, taking the papers from her as she sat heavily on one of the kitchen stools. He set the files down, carelessly, sat on the facing stool, took her hand. It was awkward for them both. They may have grown up nearly two-thousand miles apart, but neither had been raised in homes where physical affection came naturally. Still, Fanso held her hand, and Nikki didn't pull away. "I'm sorry," he said.

"I know," she admitted. "And I forgive you. I know you meant no malice."

She heard how formal and distant she sounded and didn't doubt that Fanso would pick up on it, too.

"But," he prompted.

Nikki shrugged. "It's fresh, and it...it...hurts, I guess. I liked Carlene."

"She'll come around."

"Maybe," Nikki agreed. "I'm not sure I will."

"Yeah, I hear you," Fanso said, with a little sad smile. He reached for one of the veggie rice disks, bit into it. "Not rice pudding, but not bad," he decided. Nikki agreed, reaching for two more of the circular items, one in each hand, and practically inhaling them. They polished off the tray between them.

As time went on, Nikki didn't have time to dwell on Carlene, or anything else that wasn't quite working in her life. Business was booming. Much of Nikki's expanding client base were small businesses like Mama Vi's. A good portion was short-term, and she was finding it difficult getting used to the rhythm of that, the uncertainty of it. But, in a way, she found she preferred it to the longer arrangements with the medium-to-big companies, and the expectations and demands that came with those. What she was digging was the diverse projects she got to work on: scouting new personnel, event management, project management, marketing and public relations. The Antigua Development Foundation even commissioned her to teach a couple of courses targeting successful small business loan applicants, which netted her some new clients as well, much like her ongoing radio appearances. As bizarre as it seemed, not only didn't she have to move out of her house, she had more clients than she could manage at times. Aeden, one of those clients, encouraged her to pace herself.

When she advertised the first of her workshops for business owners, "The Caribbean Single Market and You," she had to turn people away, and schedule a follow-up session.

"I'm glad things are going well," Jazz said.

"I'm relieved," Nikki confessed, "and tired."

Jazz laughed. "Well, better that than broke, so don't complain."

Nikki laughed with her. "I'm already craving a vacation, though."

"You and me both," Jazz said. "What say we run away to Greece next summer?"

"I thought you and the family were coming down for Carnival."

"Okay, the next summer then."

"How are things?" Nikki asked, sensing something in Jazz's voice.

"I'm tired," Jazz admitted. "Cranky. Did I mention tired. And I can't exactly make a huge deal out of it, because then I get to hear about how I shouldn't have gone back to work. Gi's mother has even joined the campaign. Mom has been my only support. 'Don't give up everything for a man,' she keeps telling me. I guess she knows what she's talking about."

"I guess," Nikki echoed, uncomfortable as ever—when the subject or reality of Jazz's mother came up.

"I'm sorry," Jazz apologized, misinterpreting the tone in Nikki's voice. "I don't mean to complain. I have nothing to complain about. I guess I'm worn out from having this same argument over and over. And over and over."

"You don't have to apologize, Jazz," Nikki rushed to assure her. "Lord knows, I've talked your ear off enough. Where is it written that you have to be perfect and charmed all the time?"

"I'm not perfect, far from. You see me as 'charmed'?"

Nikki rolled over on her bed, regretting her words. "I guess what I mean is that things seem to work out for you," she tried to explain. "You're happy. You don't seem to make the missteps I do."

"That's bull, Nikki. You of all people should know that," Jazz shot back, even as Nikki wondered when the conversation had gone off the rails. "Starting with the minute I lost my father when I was barely two, my life has hardly been charmed."

Unfamiliar silence settled between the sisters. Nikki remembered their conversation on Jazz's wedding eve. "Do you resent me?" she asked.

"Are you jealous of me?" Jazz countered.

"Sometimes," Nikki admitted.

"Well, there you have it, ladies and gentlemen," Jazz said sarcastically.

Nikki was silent after that. Jazz, too.

In the distance, Nikki heard Tapanga-Rose begin to cry, and Jazz seemed to jump eagerly on the summons. "My mistress beckons," she said.

"Okay," Nikki said, feeling the weight of a conversation unfinished, a conversation that perhaps they could never really finish. To what end? she wondered. What possible resolution could there be?

"Rose, you wanna say hi to your Goddie Nikki," Jazz sang in that baby voice people used with infants; the reality of the baby was now in her arms, leeching the tension from her voice.

"Hi, Tapanga-Rose," Nikki sang back. There was a spark of laughter, what Nikki liked to think of as recognition, from the baby. "Yes, that's right," she continued. "It's your Auntie Nikki. Do you still love me? I still love you."

Another giggle. And Nikki smiled. "That's right, I love you. Yes, I do. Yes, I do."

The baby cried, and she heard shifting around. "Sorry," Jazz's voice said. "The call of the breast. A siren song she can't resist."

Nikki laughed.

"I better go then," she said.

"Okay," Jazz agreed.

Both sisters knew well that a baby feeding did not mean the conversation had to end, but both went along with the lie.

"Give Rose a kiss for me," Nikki said.

"Okay."

"And…arm…give her daddy and mommy my love."

"Given," Jazz said, and Nikki wished she could see her face. Maybe conversation would be easier between them then; maybe then she could really get a read on what was going on with Jazz.

She hung up the phone.

CHAPTER FORTY-FOUR

"What does this mean?" Aeden asked, his finger tracing the pattern of the design along the inner part of the bottom half of her left leg. Nikki shivered.

She sat across from him, an open file in her lap, the leg he'd pulled from under her lying across his lap.

"Aeden, concentrate, we're supposed to be working on your investment proposal," she said. "Thought of a name yet?"

They'd discussed changing the name of his one-helicopter service to underscore that the enterprise was not another part of the Kendrick Cameron empire, but a separate entity. Well, Nikki had proposed it. Aeden had resisted, not seeing how it mattered either way.

"It's like you're this kid playing with one of Daddy's toys," she'd explained. Sometimes, it was hard not to think of him like that; after all, he still lived rent-free in an apartment, an admittedly cosy apartment, in his parents' house; had probably never had to do something as mundane as buy groceries for himself, and ran his business like a hobby—an expensive hobby.

"That helicopter belong to me, not Daddy," he'd retorted. "My father made a loan, an investment."

"Well, which is it?" Nikki had challenged.

He'd pouted. It was the only way she could think to describe that little thing he did with lips—pretty, kissable lips, as she knew well from experience. She softened at that thought. Besides, as he had pointed out, if anybody should understand daddy issues, she should.

"Look," she'd said more gently, "You asked my advice, right?"

"What the name have to do with anything?" he'd wondered stubbornly. "Cameron is my name. Kendrick Cameron is my father."

Quiet as it was, she recognized that they were having their first argument, and found she liked the idea of firsts with him, even if it was a silly argument over the name of a helicopter.

She'd leaned toward him, his hand in hers, lightly pressed her lips against his lips. She found it hard to resist when they were pursed like that. So much for business being business, she'd mocked herself. "I'm not trying to get between you and your father," she'd said finally. "I think that the line needs to be clear. But it's up to you."

"I'll think about it," he'd mumbled finally. And, ultimately, he'd agreed. If they could come up with a name he liked. That, she'd told him, was his job. But weeks later, she was still finding it difficult to pin him down. And, in bed, she should have learned by now, was not the best place to try to have a serious conversation with him; he was too easily distracted.

This time was no different as he continued tracing the pattern of her tattoo.

"Come on," he said. "What is it? When you got it?"

"What is this fascination with my tattoo from a man who has, what, three, four of them?" she asked.

He laughed. "Five. I remember the night you search out all o' them, too." She smiled at the memory of feather-like touches mapping his entire body, leaving him hard and her wet, leading to the inevitable entanglement of limbs and the kind of release that had her questioning her sanity for fighting this in the first place. "As I remember it," he continued now, "I was very, very patient with you."

"Such a good boy," she mocked.

He pressed his advantage. "Should I bring out the candles, incense, Sade's *Lovers Rock*?" That had been the background to their lovemaking on the night in question; he, Nikki decided, had the memory of an elephant.

"Don't try to distract me," she said, a smile in her voice. "Why the preoccupation with my tattoo, like you've never seen one on a person before? And more importantly, any flashes of inspiration on a new name for Cameron's Charter Helicopters, which is false advertising, by the way, since you just have the one helicopter."

His fingers still teased her flesh as he smiled. "Well," he said, ignoring the latter part of her comment. "A tattoo on me and a tattoo on you is like, what, mangoes and bananas."

"What?" she asked. "I'm not cool enough, not enough of a rebel to have a tattoo?"

"Nowadays, it would be more like whether you're enough of a fad disciple since is the t'ing these days to have tattoo."

"So..."

"So?"

She sighed dramatically. "In the interest of getting you to focus, I got it when I was at university, and rebelling against everything that represented my life with my father. I remember I was really scared, not of the pain, but of marking myself for all eternity. The commitment of it. This elevated the selection of just the right symbol to such a ridiculous level of significance that I nearly drove Jazz crazy."

"What does it mean?" he pressed.

"It's Ananse Ntontan," she responded.

"No, man," he teased, "a bite you wan' man bite he tongue. So, wha that mean?"

"Wisdom. Of which I had little but craved plenty. Like the Brer Anancy character I'd read a bit about as a kid, it also represents craftiness and creativity, ideals important to the wannabe rebel I was then. It also refers to the complexities of life, which, I knew nothing about, but did not know that I did not know. You know what I mean? Think back to nineteen. Shouldn't be too much of a leap for you."

He rolled his eyes. The fact that he was younger than her was something she harped on, much too much for his liking.

She smiled. "So, that is the story of the spider's web. Now can we get back to work?"

He kissed the tattoo, sending another shiver along her skin and through her.

"Well," he commented, "that's more thought than I put into any of mine."

"Yes, I know, which makes me a big nerd, I know."

"No, it make you you. My approach to things make me me. Impulse and restraint. We complement each other, if you think 'bout it." His voice was barely above a whisper, like a smoker's rasp, and Nikki found herself wondering if he still smoked. No, that wasn't quite right. She knew he did, smelled it on him at times. She actually kind of liked the smell, a secret part of her admitted. But he'd never smoked around her, not since the occasion of her first protest that time, so long ago now, on her back porch. Nikki found herself yearning for all of him, including the parts of him he held from her, the parts of him that parts of her still hadn't quite accepted. Besides, being in Antigua had kind of cooled her attitude on burning weed; not that it wasn't illegal, and guys weren't busted for it and fields raided from time to time, but many she'd come across were pretty laid-back about it. She'd even seen it smoked in plain sight at certain types of events with no one batting an eye: dance hall concerts, the King Court monument right along Independence Drive on African Liberation Day, the Ridge during their Watch Night ceremony last August Monday. Bottom line, Nikki no longer thought less of him because of it; she had to tell him that sometime, and maybe get lost with him again. Or maybe not; she didn't really want to smoke with him, just didn't want him to feel like he had to hide himself from her. She knew from experience that that did not go well.

Nikki was distracted from her thoughts by Aeden's next man-oeuvre. He tickled the soles of her feet, causing papers to fly everywhere as Nikki struggled to get away.

She ended up on the floor, him on top of her, tickling everywhere he could reach as she laughed and squirmed, feeling alive as she always felt with him, sucking huge breaths of the carefree aura that glowed like coronal loops around him.

Soon enough, they stilled and she was reminded through firsthand experience of what a sweet gentle joy kissing him was. When his lips withdrew, she contemplated him, his face close enough for her to see each brown freckle on the lighter skin, and the nice surprise he'd become in her life. Especially now, with the fight with Carlene still weighing on her, and her worry about Jazz still nagging at her, and work threatening to consume her even as, like a life line, he refused to allow her to drown in any of it. True, she felt weird about their ages, and him being Cameron's son, and the fact that they were glaring opposites. But the memory of those soft but firm lips still fresh, those concerns seemed distant, insignificant. He made her happy, she admitted to herself in that moment, and happiness was okay, even for the teasing ten minutes it was offered in each day. It was okay.

I love him, she thought then.

"I've got it," she said, apropos of nothing. "The Frigate."

Aeden frowned. "Hmm?"

"The name of your company, the Antigua-Barbuda Frigate," Nikki said. "It's perfect. Intimately identifiable with the island and with aerial manoeuvres. A unique, dynamic, bold bird with that red puffy chest and that drumming. But even better, it fits your spirit. It's a bit of a renegade. The scourge of the sea."

"E tief," Aeden said, shifting a little so that she could get up.

"It's resourceful," Nikki countered.

"Frig It," he said.

"Yes, The Frigate."

He quirked his lips. "Sounds like a curse word. I like it."

CHAPTER FORTY-FIVE

"So how goes it?" Nikki asked.

Though rushing on foot from one meeting to another at the other end of St. John's City, on a day when the city was flooded with ambling cruise ship tourists, Nikki had answered her cell phone on realizing who the caller was.

"It goes," Jazz said. She didn't sound any better than the last time they'd spoken.

"You're still coming for Carnival, right?" Nikki asked, weaving through traffic.

"Yeah," Jazz said. "Actually, if it's okay, I was thinking maybe of coming earlier, staying through the summer, you know."

Nikki's steps slowed under one of the bank awnings along High Street, where vendors set up to ply their incense and oils, pirated CDs and DVDs, and "Antigua Nice" T-shirts.

"Is everything okay?" she asked finally.

"Yeah...yeah..." Jazz replied, not sounding very convincing at all. Again, Nikki wished she was there, with her, because something was definitely off.

"Jazz?" she prompted.

"Well, more of the same. I think maybe I need some breathing room."

"Room?"

"Yeah, and, well, don't...you can't tell anybody this, okay?

Especially the Professor. But, okay, you know how he always talked of doing this great book, but apart from journal articles and conference papers, has not really published anything?"

"Yeah."

Nikki lowered herself unto a city bench; a Jehovah's Witness sat at the other end, *Watchtowers* in her hand mutely offered.

"And you know how I always talked about doing a book of my own, once I had enough experience under my belt?"

"Okay."

Nikki remembered no such thing, but would play along in the interest of seeing where this was going.

Jazz though, uncharacteristically, struggled to explain. "Well, I look at how he's never followed through on that. And I'm at the big three-five, and there's all this pressure to conform to a role that doesn't fit my life goals or self-image."

"You aren't getting divorced, are you?" Nikki blurted and the Witness stirred, glancing across at her, and down again when their eyes met.

"No, no, no, no, no, no, no," Jazz assured her. "I love Giovanni. I love my baby. But the other night, I couldn't sleep, and I was going through journal entries, and I was kind of fascinated by the ones beginning at the start of my marriage. The adjustments, internal and external. The negotiation. The compromise. And I realize how ill-prepared I was in a lot of ways, the things I didn't even know to wonder about."

"Married people go through changes," Nikki offered softly, the city rushing by around her. "Or so I'm told." Her throat felt tight.

Jazz sounded earnest as she continued. "Exactly," Jazz said. "And I was thinking with my training and experience, I'm uniquely positioned to make sense of this terrain, the mapping of life as a new wife and mother, the changes within and without, negotiating landscape so markedly different from the paths of our mother's, you know."

"Okay."

"It would be putting my learning to use in a way that social work doesn't."

"Okay."

"If I had a project like that to fill my days, I might be willing to take an extended hiatus from work."

Nikki said nothing.

"Don't give me your silence," Jazz snapped. "I'm not giving in. This is something I've wanted to do. Remember? I even took those writing courses when we were at the university?"

"Yeah," Nikki said, though truly it was the first she was hearing of any of this.

Jazz sighed. "The more I think about it, the more it seems that now is the time."

"Okay."

"Okay, okay," Jazz mocked. "Will you stop saying that?"

Nikki swallowed, and swallowed again before answering. She was worried, no two ways about it. "Don't know what else to say," she said, "except, whatever you want to do, I got your back, you know that."

"Yeah, I know," Jazz said. Neither sister spoke for what felt to Nikki like an hour, at least, but probably was no more than a few moments. Jazz broke the silence with a sigh, one too many sighs. "Anyway, the idea is to draw on my own experiences. Families, social expectations, romance, aspirations, myth and reality, how we move from 'I' to 'We,' and how scary it all is."

"It sounds like an interesting project," Nikki said, and that, at least, wasn't a lie.

"Well, nothing's set," Jazz said. "I haven't even spoken to Gi about it. I don't want to, until I'm clear on what I want to do. I don't want to be talked into anything. I thought I'd use the summer to work up an outline and see how I feel about it."

"But what about your job, and can you be separated from Tapanga-Rose so soon?" Nikki wondered. "She's still breast-feeding, right?"

"I won't be," Jazz said. "I'll bring her with me."

Nikki's eyebrows shot up. "Will Giovanni go for that?" she asked. "It's not like he can take the entire summer off. Can he?"

"Well, he'll have to go for it, because I need to do this. And as for the job, well, I have unused time and I'll take whatever else I need in unpaid leave. I need to sort this out." And Nikki couldn't argue with that. It was another five minutes before she moved again, continuing on to her meeting, at least twenty minutes late now, but unhurried and still deep in thought.

"Have you ever thought of getting married?" Nikki asked Aeden that night.

They had made love not too long ago and were lying on her rumpled bed; Aeden was likely on the periphery of sleep, Nikki's brain racing.

He turned his head to meet her eyes.

"Married?"

His voice sounded choked.

She slapped his chest.

"Don't worry, I'm not asking you to marry me."

"No," he said, visibly swallowing. "Married? Never really t'ink 'bout that, no."

"I have," Nikki admitted. "When I was with Terry, I thought about it quite a bit. We never talked about it, and I probably only thought about it because it was what we were supposed to think about, what we were supposed to want."

"But you didn't?"

"No. I dreaded it, actually," she admitted with a dry laugh, "and though I fancied myself a feminist, it wasn't about rebelling against the death to self, the obliteration of one's identity as symbolized by the erasing, the surrender of one's 'maiden' name. It wasn't about bondage of any kind, really."

"Nikki, me swear me na know wha you just say," Aeden said drowsily.

But, she continued, "It was the notion, the impossibility, it seemed, of fitting with someone else, your rhythm with theirs. Sitting down to breakfast with them every day, turning around and finding them always there, sharing a toilet, cleaning the toilet we shared."

"What?" He laughed.

"I know, it sounds crazy, especially considering that Terry and I already shared his apartment, but these were my concerns, because you know marriage changes everything anyway," she said with another laugh, self-deprecating this time. "My idea of ideal was separate lives, separate spaces, uncomplicated but accessible companionship to fill the inevitable loneliness. It was a selfish kind of loving. It was all I thought I was capable of giving. And it was easy, too easy, to live with him and yet keep myself locked away from him."

"Meaning you didn't keep him up after blowing his mind, sharing your feelings," Aeden teased.

And Nikki smiled. "No, no mind blowing, no feelings."

And if he seemed a little pleased at that, Nikki allowed him; because he was a space oddity, didn't mean he wasn't still a man.

"What about now?" he asked.

"What about now?" she asked back.

"Do you still feel the same way, about marriage?"

"Now...I don't know," she said.

Nikki turned from the questions in his eyes, acknowledging deep down that now, maybe she yearned for more, but dreaded it still.

She continued, "I've said more on the subject than I ever thought I would, Professor Winston Baltimore's appropriately repressed spawn, flesh of his flesh. Is that progress?"

Aeden didn't answer, and Nikki looked across to see that he'd lost his battle with the sandman.

She woke him at fore day morning and they made love again before facing the day.

CHAPTER FORTY-SIX

"Hello," the voice was tentative.

"Hello." Nikki's voice was groggy. She felt for her watch on the nightstand, turned bleary eyes to it. 3:56 a.m.

"Nikki?"

"Belle?"

She sat up, alarmed. Belle never called.

"Nikki, is me…Belle. Sis sick."

"Sis" was Belle's affectionate term for Audrey.

Nikki shook off sleep, while assuring Belle that she would be there shortly. "Wait, where are you? At the house?"

"Yes, me call ambulance and dem gone wid she. Just me and Columbus here."

"Did Audrey ask you to call me?"

"She na say nutten."

Nikki interpreted this to mean Audrey had been unable to speak, since giving orders, especially to her simple wards, was knee-jerk for her. Her mind began a chant of "not again, not again, not again…" all the while picking up speed. It seemed too soon, seemed like they needed a break from tragedy. It was too soon after Tones and all the losses since—Carlene's baby, Carlene herself almost, sort of. It was too soon after Mama. "Death come in threes," she'd heard Marisol comment once, at the burial of Carlene's baby, Toni, born shortly after Tones' death and promptly following her father into the hereafter. Was she not to be counted as the third then? Did they still have a credit against their account?

The front door was open when Nikki arrived at the Sea View Farm house; Belle stood in the doorway. Silhouetted against the light within, she seemed so similar in stature to their mother. Similar enough that Nikki's heart flipped a little, imagining for a moment that it was Mama Vi standing there waiting for her, to take her hand and make everything okay as she had done at their first meeting. That fantasy quickly faded as Belle grabbed her, and Nikki buried her face in the cottony material of Belle's night-gown, rubbing soothing circles along her sister's back, taking the very comfort she gave, then giving it back. She did not know how long they stood there. Over Belle's shoulder, she saw Columbus sitting on the old couch, in a vest and boxer shorts, staring into space.

She wanted to call the hospital, or Fanso, even Lars or Ben Up; not Deacon, though, for he would have been more burden than help. She wanted to go to the hospital, find out what was wrong with Audrey, what needed to be done, but she focused instead on getting Columbus and Belle settled. She knew how much any disturbance at all to the familiar order of things, much less seeing Audrey taken off in a screaming ambulance with lights flashing, would have upset them.

By the time morning light began to fade in, she'd fed them a breakfast of slightly burnt porridge, which was barely eaten. Columbus went out to his garden afterwards, as usual, but Belle remained restless. Nikki tried to get her to lie down.

"Pray wid me," her sister beseeched.

Nikki stared at her and hesitated. But filled with sudden certainty, Belle took her hand firmly and led her into the bedroom she shared with Audrey. There, she took up the well-used Bible from a shelf along the partition. Sitting on the bed, Nikki beside her, however, she didn't open it, merely held it.

"God can fix anything," Belle said calmly. "He go fix Sis. Bet you."

"I hope so," Nikki said, feeling her throat close up.

"Pray wid me," Belle repeated. And so they prayed, or rather Belle prayed: a repetitive, winding sort of prayer, with a lot of "Jesuses," "Oh Gods," and "Sises" thrown in. As time slipped by, Nikki found herself relaxing into the rhythm of it. She may even have fallen asleep, because the next thing she was aware of was an "*Inside!*" and a knocking at the front door, and herself curled up against Belle who was likewise curled around her as they lay on the bed.

She opened the door to find Marisol wearing a worried expression.

"I heard what happened," her friend said. "What can I do?"

"Well, I want to call Fanso, go to the hospital, but I don't want to leave Belle alone and I don't think it's a good idea to take her with me. Plus, Columbus is out in his garden."

"Go," Marisol said. "I'll take care of everything."

Leaving proved difficult, however, as Belle started rocking and crying. Nikki called Fanso.

"He's at work," Antoinette told her, the sound of her boys clattering breakfast dishes and chattering in the background.

When she got him on his cell in the car, he reported that he was outside Carlene's place, collecting her and her kids; Nikki hadn't known that he did that. She filled him in. "I'll drop the kids off and bring Carlene with me," he said. "She can stay with Belle, so she won't be frightened."

"What about the restaurant?" Nikki asked absently, as she digested this.

"The restaurant can wait," he shot back, sounding a bit annoyed.

Nikki hung up, relieved that the weight of decision-making had been lifted from her. Fanso was on his way. They were going to see about Audrey. Everything would be okay.

In the end, it was anti-climactic, her brief crossing of paths with Carlene. A head nod from Carlene, a reflex nod from her, and before she knew what was what, Nikki was seated beside Fanso in the white van with the Mama Vi's Restaurant lettering on the side as he sped towards Holberton Hospital.

"Your sister had a mild sort of stroke, a mini stroke or Transient Ischemic Attack," explained the young bright-faced doctor, who introduced herself to them as Dr. Lorrianne Henry.

"So, it's not serious," Fanso cut in as Audrey lay silent on the bed, a mild twist to her familiar features and weariness in her eyes.

"Well, it is and it isn't," Dr. Henry said with a little smile. "As with a full-on stroke, it means that a part of the brain has been denied oxygen. This results in the death of nerve cells, in the case of full-on stroke activity. A TIA is a warning and can signal an impending stroke, which is why we'd like to keep your sister for observation."

"For how long?" Nikki asked, though Audrey was already shaking her head.

"At least a couple of days; we have to run some tests, in any case, and prescribe medication," the doctor said.

"So, it can be treated," Fanso said hopefully.

"What kind of tests?" Nikki asked at the same time.

"Well, the main thing is to identify what caused the episode," the doctor said. "If we can confirm that there's no impending danger, your sister can leave here with blood-thinning medication to prevent her blood from clotting, as well as strict instructions related to diet and fitness, and to pay better attention to the signs—loss of vision, clumsiness or weakness, speech problems. But let's not jump ahead of ourselves."

Before leaving, she asked, "You don't have any history of diabetes, hypertension, anything like that in your family, do you?"

"No," Fanso answered.

"Our mother died of cancer a couple of years ago," Nikki added, feeling the pain of that even now, not sure why she'd picked at that pain when it hardly seemed relevant.

"Your father?" the doctor asked.

"Unnatural causes," Fanso said.

"Not staying here," Audrey slurred as soon as the doctor was gone.

"Yes, you are," Fanso said.

"Not staying," she slurred, with a firmness perhaps only she could muster in such a situation.

"Audrey," Nikki chimed in, "you're staying in that bed even if I have to sit on you. If you can't think about yourself, think about Belle and Columbus. You want them to see you like this? They're frightened enough as it is."

Audrey subsided, and Nikki slumped into one of the chairs alongside the bed, sending up thanks to the God, who'd so far answered Belle's prayer, for small blessings and victories.

She called Aeden from the hospital, and he'd offered to come by, get her key, go to her house, check her planner for her appointments and call to postpone. Later, as she walked him off the ward, having given him her key, she tried not to think too much of him being in her home alone, going through her stuff.

"So, you all serious?" Fanso asked.

She bit back many things, including a retort marveling at his sudden interest in her love life, the bitter memory of the Hensen J. Stephens episode surging up unexpectedly within her. Of course, that was probably misguided annoyance, at the reality that she didn't know the answer to that question. She knew how she and Aeden both felt, but as to what that meant, she didn't know.

Eventually, she shrugged, and Fanso seemed to accept that. "Cameron must love that," he murmured before wandering off, phone already pressed to his ear. Actually, Nikki had no idea how Cameron felt about her ongoing relationship with his son. She barely glimpsed him these days and preferred it that way. Aeden's mother, Raisa, had been cold the times their paths crossed—Nikki dropping Aeden off, or picking him up, or leaving his apartment one or two mornings after—but she got the sense that that's how Raisa Pilgrim-cum-Cameron was, period.

Fanso closed his phone, reported that he'd asked Antoinette to pick Carlene's boys up from pre-school later in the day and issue a radio notice that the restaurant was closed due to a family emergency and would remain closed the following day. Carlene would call the staff, he said.

At some point during the day, Lars and Ben Up stopped by, but both were on their way to a building site and didn't linger long. Nikki had to admit that a part of her wanted to run after her brothers as they left. There seemed little point to her being there. Audrey mostly slept, in between being taken in and out for tests. Fanso read a paper he'd borrowed from one of the nurses, walked the ward and the lanes around the ward, and finally sat in his chair staring into space.

Aeden came by around two, bringing sandwiches from Philton's for both of them. He was wearing a red tie-dye T-shirt, faded blue jeans and scuffed combat boots, a lavender scarf tied around his head.

"Must be love," Fanso teased.

Nikki smiled at this, in spite of herself.

"He funny looking bad," Audrey slurred from her bed.

"What did your father die of?" Nikki asked on the drive back to Sea View Farm that night.

"All I have is rumour, really," Fanso replied. "If I saw the man two time in my life, I saw him plenty."

He was silent for so long after that, as the car ate up the miles along the dark stretch of road, Nikki thought he wasn't going to say anything further. But then, suddenly, he did.

"From what I understand, he hit the wrong woman one time too many, and she do for him."

This, of course, cleared up none of the mystery for Nikki, but it was the way people spoke in Antigua, she acknowledged. It was, in fact, one of the things that still kept her outside the community; the way people said without really saying, knowing that the meaning was clear, if you were truly a part of things. If you weren't, then it wasn't yours to know anyway. There was a saying on the island popularized by a one-time calypsonian, Boldface, "When you na know, you just na know," and the truth of it slapped Nikki cold in moments like these. She felt as much in the dark as she'd been at the start of their strange stop-and-start conversation, felt sharply this lingering sense of outsiderness. It seemed her destiny—following her from childhood into adulthood, following her to wherever she tried to put down roots and into the relationships she tried to forge.

"Mama never spoke of him," Fanso said, startling her—his long comma had seemed like a full stop. They were turning into the village now. "Audrey said it was no less than he deserved, said Obeah was involved. He was a healthy-healthy man, she said, up to the morning he didn't wake up. But who knows? He died. Belle was the only person to cry for him, but I doubt she knew what she was crying for."

Nikki doubted that; Belle was smarter than most gave her credit for. Columbus, on the other hand, was like a closed book to her. And while he'd gone catatonic that morning, Belle had had the presence of mind to call for help, so, clearly, she wasn't so senseless after all. They pulled up at the house, and Belle stood, again, in the doorway, silhouetted again against the light, waiting for them. Nikki wondered how long she'd been standing there.

That night, as she lay in bed with Belle after everyone had gone home, the light on, because Belle needed it that way, Nikki studied her sister's hand clasped in hers. The once smooth flesh had started to wrinkle, not dramatically, but enough so that the texture resembled something like a laundered shirt in need of starch and a hot iron. It called to mind her mother's hands.

It saddened her that even Belle, with her happy smile and girlish ways, should deteriorate, diminish, disappear, that everything must change always. Death. New Life. Comings. Goings. Love. Love's fading. Sickness. Death. It was like that night, under the stars, at the Ridge, with Aeden. Everything had seemed so big. In that moment, she was a little girl missing her mother, leaning into a comfort that assured her everything would be as she remembered it when she woke in the morning. She was that little girl leaning towards something that had never been.

"What you thinking 'bout?" And it was such an un-Belle question, the voice calm, reasoned, adult.

"Nothing," Nikki lied.

"You just laka Sis," Belle complained. "'*Nothing*.' Never wan' talk."

Nikki smiled at being likened to Audrey and at the pout so evident in Belle's voice. "What do you want to talk about?" she asked.

"Sis ask for me?"

Before Nikki could answer, she asked again, "She goin' be okay?"

"Yes, I told you, she'll be home soon," Nikki replied gently.

"Me miss Mama," Belle said.

"Me, too," Nikki replied, but then she'd been missing her mother most of her life. Still, she couldn't deny that there was a fresh ripple of surprise and sadness every time she thought of Mama Vi, dead, goodbye, gone. Even after all this time.

"But she dey in heaven, right?" Belle asked, "And Tones wid she. Right?"

I don't know, Nikki thought. Still, it was a comfort, to them both to say to Belle, "Yes, yes, she is. Tones, too."

"Na Audrey time yet," Belle said firmly.

"No, no it's not," Nikki agreed.

She felt Belle nod against her, and was pleased that she could offer this, at least.

"You go sleep wid me 'til she come back, right?" her sister said, a child again.

"Yes," Nikki assured her quietly.

"Good. Me na like sleep by meself. Audrey keep me safe."

Nikki frowned. "Safe from what?"

But Belle didn't answer. Her hand slackening in Nikki's, she started to drift and Nikki let her.

CHAPTER FORTY-SEVEN

*S*eeing Jazz alight from the Caribbean Airlines plane with the iridescent hummingbird logo on its tail was like feeling the sun come out after weeks of haziness. It was like the infectious rhythms of the island's hottest soca band, Burning Flames, at Carnival. It was a little bubble of laughter, sneaking out and changing everything with its unexpected arrival.

Nikki felt happy.

Tired, sure, given these past weeks of negotiating time between Sea View Farm and Elizabeth Estate. It was wearying: the effort to hold on to whatever she and Aeden were forging, while staying on top of her client list, being at the beck and call of the family that needed her, worrying about Audrey's diet and the fact that her sister had spent very little time off her feet since leaving the hospital. Then there was the tenuous truce with Carlene. Circumstances had necessitated an uneasy peace, but, to Nikki, it felt false and superficial, and her with it. She felt small and petty at the vestiges of anger and hurt. Still, she couldn't shake them.

But Jazz was here, here for the entire summer, and they would laugh and talk and lean on each other as they had done for years.

Nikki hugged baby and sister, as if she hadn't seen them in years, ignoring the Red Cap waiting impatiently for his tip after packing the luggage into Nikki's vehicle, ignoring the fact that Tapanga-Rose slept through her boisterous greeting, ignoring the fact that Jazz looked tired and harassed. Nikki doubted she looked much better.

When they got to her house, there was a message from Audrey on her voicemail. "Nikki, we need to talk 'bout CARICOM Day next time you come out here," her sister said, getting straight to the point, as always. "You coming out tomorrow, right? Mek time."

"Shit," Nikki said to herself.

"What?" Jazz asked.

"Audrey," Nikki said. "She doesn't know how not to give orders, I think."

"Big sisters," Jazz said tiredly.

"You're a big sister," Nikki reminded her.

"Just barely," Jazz said soberly and Nikki longed for the Jazz who might have teased, once upon a time, "and don't you forget it," or "yeah, but I'm special," or some other such thing.

Nikki showed her to her room, where she had a crib set up for the baby. It was borrowed from Audrey. "It used to belong to Tones," her older sister had said as she took the parts, still in pretty good condition, from the shed out back—the one used to store pots before they were fired or baked on the trash bed. "One of the boys made it; I think it was Ben Up."

"You kept it all these years," Nikki had marveled, though understanding things as she now did, she was more surprised that Audrey was prepared to let it go.

"Well, I wasn't about to give it to the Jamaican," Audrey'd shot back, and Nikki wisely held her tongue, realizing that Audrey was at least equal parts bark and bite when it came to Carlene.

Jazz oohed and aahed over the old thing. "I didn't know you were going to all this trouble," she said.

"It's no trouble," Nikki said. "It's actually on loan from Audrey, so don't get too attached."

Jazz laughed and laid down her precious burden on the clean sheets in the freshly aired-out crib. It was yellow like the one in Tapanga-Rose's New York nursery.

"So, Terry's getting married; did you hear? There was an announcement in the *Times*," Jazz said, as she unpacked her clothes, handing them to Nikki who put them on hangers in the closet. Best to get it out of the way, Jazz said, while the baby slept.

Nikki was stunned at this bit of news, but, for some reason, tried to keep this to herself.

"To Monique?" she asked casually.

"Veronique," Jazz corrected, then, as if quoting the *Times*, "successful literary publicist Veronique St. Juste, Haitian ancestry, a descendent of Dessalines himself, New Orleans-bred: old money, gumbo blood." Had she not been so distracted, Nikki might have taken comfort in seeing something of this familiar playful Jazz, but she was distracted. Jazz's laughter faltered when Nikki didn't join in.

"I didn't realize it was that serious," Nikki said. "Frankly, she didn't seem the marrying type."

Then, she stopped, hearing the malice in her own voice. Jazz was studying her now.

"Don't worry," Nikki said. "I'm not about to fall apart. The book on Terry and me is long since closed, closed, sitting on the shelf gathering cobwebs. You surprised me, is all."

"That's all," Jazz echoed.

"Well, yeah, what do you want me to do, cry, mourn what might have been?" Nikki asked, hearing the defensiveness in her voice.

Jazz shrugged.

"Well, it's not going to happen. Everyone isn't yearning for wedded bliss," Nikki continued flippantly. "I hear it's overrated anyway."

If the words had been a solid thing, Nikki would have reached out to grab them, stuff them back down her throat. Jazz looked like she'd been slapped, and Nikki knew her hand wore the sting.

"Jazz, I'm sorry. I didn't mean anything by that; I didn't mean it the way it sounded," Nikki said desperately.

Jazz said nothing.

"I was deflecting, you know," Nikki tried desperately to explain a feeling she didn't understand herself. "Terry was my possibility thrown away, and I felt the finality of that, truly, I guess, when you told me he was getting married. It's not that I want him back; it's that now I could never have him back, even if I did want him. I'm sorry."

Jazz sat on the bed, tears beginning to fall, and Nikki felt like her heart was breaking. She rushed to her sister, and shushed and hugged and soothed her, feeling the guilt caused by her own careless tongue and the helplessness of trying to offer comfort when there was none to be given.

"Is he still coming for Carnival?" she asked later, as they lay on the bed, from which they had not moved since Jazz's tears. Partially unpacked luggage littered the floor, and in the crib, Tapanga-Rose slept on.

"Of course," Jazz said, her voice hoarse. "Everything's fine. I don't know what those tears were about. Stupid."

"You're worried," Nikki said. "I knew that. I should have been more thoughtful."

"It's all good, or it will be." Jazz sighed. "I need to get my head together. Remember what's important."

"Hey," Nikki said, nudging Jazz with her shoulder. "You're

important, too. Marriage and motherhood doesn't mean you don't exist anymore, that you disappear. If you do, then you know there'll be no hope for me. And I can't accept that."

Jazz laughed. "Tell you what. Don't ever become a motivational speaker," she said. "What are you talking about?"

Nikki laughed. "I don't know. This is your job."

"Idiot," Jazz said, faced turned towards Nikki with a smile. Nikki smiled back, a little relieved at the life, still in her sister's eyes.

"Me," she protested, the following day, facing down Audrey in her workshop. "I can't cook."

"You na ha fu can cook," her sister shot back. "You ha fu can tek direction."

But Nikki was shaking her head, eager to escape this conversation, to join Belle and Jazz elsewhere in the house; Belle cooing and giggling over the baby, who cooed and giggled back.

"Look, it have to be done, and that's that," Audrey said.

"Excuse me?"

Audrey stared her down. Even after her illness, she was a formidable woman—more so in some ways.

Nikki sighed. "But what about Fanso? Doesn't he always do this stuff?"

"He does do some, but his han' can't turn to certain things like me," Audrey replied. "Anyway, he goin' do some, but with the restaurant so busy an' everything, he can't do everything. And I suppose to be taking it easy, remember? Ent is you say you wan' be a part of this family? Well, you goin' have to put han' and do your part."

"I cannot cook."

"Well, that's a blasted shame, big woman like you, and is high time you learn. Now, this is the shopping list. And I don't want none of them supermarket vegetables. I want spinach, sweet potato, antroba and so from the market…"

Nikki sighed heavily, resigned to her fate.

"It should be fun," Jazz said, as they drove home. "Besides, like she said, she'll be there, guiding you. And I'll be there to help."

"Look, that's not even the point," Nikki fumed. "I don't know where she gets off thinking she can boss everyone around. I think I preferred it when she wasn't talking to me. Imagine, throwing her illness in my face!"

"Calm down, would you, before you run us off the road," Jazz cautioned. Nikki eased up on the accelerator, though still fuming. "Nikki, it's not the end of the world. In fact, it's a positive sign, if you think about it."

Nikki took her eyes off the road and looked at her sister like she was crazy.

"Hello, eyes on the road," Jazz instructed. "Besides, you know, I'm right. It means she's accepted you, in her way. I mean, she's hardly the type to walk up and hug you, is she? Start treating you like she treats everyone else."

Nikki's eyes turned back to the road. "Whatever," she replied.

Nikki hadn't been into the Valley since announcing her departure from the Blackman's Ridge project, and she was uncertain of her welcome. Looking up onto the hill, she saw, what she'd come to think of as "Cam's folly," construction well-advanced.

"So, this is the infamous Blackman's Valley," Jazz said, looking around. Tapanga-Rose was swaddled in a sea-blue wrap slung around her mother's torso and seemed to be taking in the scenery as well.

"Yep! We're standing in the ominous shadow of Blackman's Ridge," Nikki agreed.

They began the trek through the Valley and, shortly, crossed paths with a group of women and children. Heads wrapped, locs peeking out, babies secured much like Tapanga-Rose against their mothers' warmth, as toddlers toddled along, they made an impressive and colourful site. To Nikki, they seemed almost to glide. She and Jazz stood aside as they passed with shy smiles and courteous nods, and then stood still, watching them walk away.

"Whoo," Jazz whispered. "That was surreal. I feel like I just stepped back to the motherland. They live through here?"

Nikki shrugged. "I know there's a community of Rastas who live in the valley, not farming, but actually living here. Aeden says they've got their own school, tabernacle, everything they need; not much need to come out except to take goods to market." She checked her watch. "It's about lunchtime; maybe school just let out or something. I've never seen so many of them through here at once. They keep pretty much to themselves."

"Huh," Jazz said.

"What?" Nikki asked, eyes still on the last of the retreating line of women moving gracefully away from them.

"I don't know," she replied. "You've talked about this project and the protests so much…and I guess it hit me that there are real people involved, people who wouldn't be themselves anywhere else, doing anything else; it's a cause worth fighting for, holding on to who you are."

Nikki's eyes wandered to her sister, but Jazz's eyes remained on the women.

The sisters walked on. The path was much clearer due to the

traffic into and out of the valley these past months. Nikki almost wished it was less accessible. Then she would've been able to talk herself out of it, go to the infinitely safer terrain of the public market where she'd be expected to haggle with vendors over prices, which her lingering American accent would likely place at a premium.

Here, she wasn't at all sure of her reception.

"Hi," Nikki offered, by way of greeting, when she entered the clearing where Sadie and Tanty worked as they always did, as though nothing had changed, although, so much had changed and much more would still.

They stopped working and looked at her.

"This is my sister, Jazz," Nikki ventured. "She's visiting me from the States."

The silence stretched, and she kept expecting them to return to their hoeing, pretend she wasn't there.

Finally, "you scarce," Tanty said.

Nikki's heart started beating again, and Sadie did turn back to her hoeing at that point.

"Well, I wasn't sure, you know, with the way we left things..."

Tanty sighed. "When you vex an' you hurt, you say anything. I tell you long time me spirit take you. You did what you could for Sadie."

Sadie's head came up at the sound of her name, and she leaned on the hoe. "And since you gone, not one jack sprat come say 'hm' to us," she added. "I waitin' for them to see what they up to next, 'cause if dem think dem out mi fire, dem lie."

"Sadie," Tanty said, but it was tired and sad.

To Nikki, even Sadie's words felt like more bravado than real fire; it was like a fighter who couldn't stop fighting, though she knew in her heart that the battle was lost.

"Anyway, point is, you know the devil you have; you don't know the devil you goin' get," Sadie said, turning back to her work.

Nikki smiled, saying *sotto voce* to Jazz, "I don't think anyone has ever complemented me by calling me a devil before."

When they left the Valley, they were laden with most of what they needed, and Tanty had even allowed Nikki to pay this time. Her heart was heavy, though, as she worried anew about them, and at the sense of defeat she sensed, especially in Tanty. Watching them drag Sadie away in handcuffs all those months ago had clearly taken its toll. Her resolve, so clearly voiced at their first meeting, that the fact they'd been farming the same plot of land for generations somehow protected them, was clearly shaken.

"Had a time, right after slavery," she'd said to Nikki, as they sat under the blue tarpaulin sipping lime water while Sadie helped Jazz fill their shopping list. "Neaga people hotfoot it off the plantation an' dem, so me Tanty say. Was a whole ton ah free village 'round de place then. But bakkra bu'n dem out, make sure neaga people know dem place. Now, dem village nuh exist. Not even in memory." There were tears in her eyes as she continued, and she seemed old, older even than she was. "When money ah change hand," she said with quiet force, "and big people ah flex dem muscle, laka smadee na exist. Smadee come laka masquita, dem clap dem han' together so, and out you lights, and you na even see de blow ah come. Me jus' ah wait and see."

Nikki had jumped at Tanty's sharp clap, and remained chilled by the intense quietness of her voice, long after leaving the Valley.

CHAPTER FORTY-EIGHT

"Thanks for offering to take us out, Aeden," Jazz said, adding with a teasing wink in Nikki's direction, "We have a fridge full of food and nothing to eat."

Aeden chuckled. "Well, it was a pleasure to finally meet you, after hearing so much 'bout you. Had to give you a real Antigua welcome."

They pulled up at Mama Vi's restaurant, Aeden at the wheel of one of his dad's cars. Nikki wasn't sure if it was because it was more sedate, or because his own newly purchased fixer-upper was in the shop again, but she was thankful. Best to introduce Jazz to Aeden in stages. Still, sleek, plush BMW or not, she couldn't quite relax. It was Jazz and Aeden's first meeting, and Nikki had fussed at him to "dress normal." Normal for Aeden turned out to be a blindingly orange button-down shirt with yellow and blue flowers, which went surprisingly well with jacket and pants the colour of Antiguan sand, and matching ankle-length suede boots. With his hair pulled back into a ponytail, he wasn't looking half bad. They were almost coordinated, thanks to Nikki's Bridget Cameron earrings, which he was visibly pleased to see her wearing, and the knee-length green Athena dress Jazz had brought from New York.

"Brings out your eyes," her sister had said.

"Hmm," Aeden had commented appreciatively.

So far, it was the most embarrassing thing he'd done, which was to say not embarrassing at all, so really she could relax, she told herself. Still. She was strung tight.

Plus, there was the Carlene factor; her in-law was on duty tonight, and Nikki was still uncertain how to act around her.

Carlene, Nikki had to admit, as they approached her station, looked hostess chic in her madras blazer, white shirt, black slacks and heels, blonde braids done up in a French twist. Plus, she had lost some of her perennial post-pregnancy plumpness. And when she smiled, as she did on seeing them, the shroud of sadness and other things that she'd worn since Tones' and Toni's death wasn't visible to the naked eye, not to Nikki, at least. Carlene even had an enthusiastic hug and a "long time, no see" for Jazz. Jazz, though she'd been taken aback by news of Carlene and Nikki's tussle, hugged back. Aeden hung back, and Nikki looked on, bemused.

"I'll tell Fanso you here," Carlene said brightly after giving them a prime seat in the two-thirds full restaurant.

Fanso came from the kitchen to greet them all with more hugs, lifting Jazz off her feet in his enthusiasm, and proceeding to fuss over Tapanga-Rose. He insisted that dinner was on the house, despite Nikki's raised brow. "One dinner nar bruk the bank," he said in response.

They chatted about this and that over a dinner of red bean soup, conch water, and saltfish fricassee, followed by snapper, the catch of the day, steamed, escovitch, and pan-fried, respectively. They talked of Aeden's plans for his helicopter business, Jazz's book, Nikki's consultancy. Aeden cooed at Tapanga-Rose who reclined in the high infant carrier Carlene had pulled up to their table. The baby took to him, too, squeezing his finger and cooing back. All in all, Nikki mused over her banana yogurt parfait dessert, it went better than anticipated. Dinner almost done, she finally allowed the tension to unknot.

Later, after Aeden dropped them off and Jazz and Tapanga-Rose had gone inside, she asked Aeden about his meeting with his dad. He'd finally spoken up about his plans for the business. "It went all right," he replied. "He accept what I have to say. Say you ha' wan good head pon your shoulders, and me wise fu listen to you."

Nikki looked askance at him. "He did not say that."

He laughed. "No, not quite. But I know him, and under all he grumping and warnings for me to be careful, I could feel a kinda grudging respect for you."

"I think that's wishful thinking," Nikki said. "Wait, he warned you to be careful? Like, like I'm a black magic woman working some kind of spell on you?"

Aeden wrapped his arm around her. "You can work your magic pon me anytime, 'cause me ha fu tell you you look good enough to eat."

Nikki squirmed. "Let's not start what we can't finish."

"Why we cyarn finish it?"

"My sister…"

"Please, we not all big people? Your sister know we together, right?"

"Yeah, but…"

"But nothing," Aeden pushed, pulling her closer. "I only been catching glimpses of my black magic woman these past weeks between this and that. I feeling neglected."

He'd said it as a tease but Nikki stiffened nonetheless, pulled away. "Don't get possessive, Aeden."

He frowned, blinked. "What?"

She stared at him, and he huffed a frustrated breath, turned away, turned back. "So, let me understan' you good," he finally said, "while yuh sister here, me nar see you 'tall?"

"I'm not saying that," Nikki replied.

"What then? Look we out pon veranda when wan nice warm bed inside," Aeden argued. He leaned in again, teased her neck just behind the ear, where she was especially sensitive. Hot air blew against her ear as he whispered, "Really warm, if memory serve." Nikki shivered involuntarily. She put some distance between them, again.

"I'm tired and I have an early meeting," she mumbled.

And he blew out another angry puff of air. "Nikki, na start do this," he said.

"Start what? What am I doing?" her voice communicating well enough that she knew what she was doing, if not why. Aeden called her on it.

"You know," he said, voice tight. "Me bend over backwards fu become wha' yuh need, fu 'grow up' as you say, but I comin' to think maybe you the one need fu grow up."

Nikki's brain misfired in a hundred different directions and every time she opened her mouth to speak, nothing came out. Finally, Aeden turned to go. "Okay, I guess I'll see you then."

"Aeden," she called as he started down the steps.

"Yeah," he said without looking back.

Nikki opened her mouth, and, again, nothing came out. "Thanks for dinner," she said finally. She knew it was lame, but didn't know how to give more than that then.

And then he was gone.

"Why didn't he come in?" Jazz asked. "Don't let me keep you from getting your groove on." Tapanga-Rose was down for the night and Jazz, toting a glass of water, was making her way back to her room when Nikki came in and leaned against the door.

"He had to leave," Nikki lied.

"He's cute," Jazz said. "Colourful, but cute."

Nikki smiled. "He scares me," she admitted quietly, moving to the couch.

"Why?"

"I don't know...I feel like we could go on this wild adventure together. He excites me...but I'm afraid..."

Jazz nodded, perhaps understanding this better than she might have a time ago. "Yeah, lovin' is scary," she agreed. And Nikki wanted to interrupt, to ask her who'd said anything about loving. But she didn't. "But maybe it's supposed to be," Jazz offered, sitting next to her and putting the glass down. "Maybe it's supposed to, I don't know, prickle the skin, get the senses on alert."

"Like getting mugged," Nikki quipped, prompting Jazz to jostle her slightly. "No," Jazz said. "Like, like, like bungee jumping."

"There's incentive for you," Nikki said dryly. "I think I'd rather be mugged."

"All I'm saying is maybe that's why they call it falling into love—because you're free falling and you don't know how you're going to land," Jazz said. "Maybe that's the point sometimes, that we can't control everything; that sometimes with some things, with this thing, we've got to let go and feel. Maybe. Sure, in my line of work, I see a lot of women who could've stood to do a lot less feelin' and a little more thinkin'. I'm saying, though, that sometimes we overthink when we need to be..."

"Overfeelin'," Nikki quipped again.

Jazz smiled, a little wistfully, at that. "Well, yeah."

Nikki considered this. "You know," she said, "that's exactly what my mother said."

Jazz looked at her funny.

Nikki laughed. "Don't worry, I'm not hearing voices."

"What then?"

Nikki considered her answer. "I guess you could say she dream me."

Jazz looked confused.

Nikki smiled. "Yeah, I know. It's the kind of thing I would've dismissed as nonsense before I came to live here. Hell, after I came. But maybe it's because of all those months reading my father's journal, sitting at Mama Vi's gravesite, talking to her, connecting. I was open; and there she was in my dream, so vivid I could touch and feel, even hear."

"And this isn't just a dream?"

"Well, it is and it isn't, you know. It doesn't really matter, I guess; just that I believe what I got from it."

"And that was?"

"That I need to have the courage to take a certain leap of faith, to open myself up to life, to feel."

"Well, that's good advice."

"Yeah, except sometimes I think about what happened the last time I allowed myself to go with the feeling."

"I thought you'd gotten past that."

"I had." Nikki sighed. "I have."

Jazz quirked an eyebrow.

"Sometimes, I backslide," Nikki quipped, then sighed, fingering the clay pendant which had rested all night against her breast bone. "We're so different."

"So?" Jazz countered. "Different isn't necessarily bad. From what I know of Daddy, and the little I know of your mother, strikes me they were very different."

"Look how long that lasted," Nikki said dryly.

"Well, maybe it isn't about how long it lasted," Jazz insisted. "They must have known going in that it couldn't last. Maybe it's about how much it is while it lasts."

Nikki looked at her, unaware that her thoughts were transparent.

Jazz said, "I know, I know, said the woman who signed on the dotted line forever and ever. What I'm saying, though, doesn't change that. I love Giovanni, our present 'growing pains' notwithstanding. I do want him for as long as life allows. But if I could only have him for a minute, if it isn't destined to be forever and ever Amen, I'd still want to embrace everything we've been able to have so far together. Because it's made me richer."

"Yeah…"

"But don't worry, I haven't given up on us yet," Jazz said with an impish smile. "Neither should you. Every time your mind starts racing ahead of the here and now, think of…"

When Jazz didn't say anything more, Nikki pressed, "Think of what?"

"Well, Hon, you have to fill in the blanks. That's what I do every time I start to think of Giovanni trying to bully me into certain choices. I think of the first time I saw him, and his broad smile and bushy eyebrows. I think of how sexy I thought his mind was. No, seriously, he was so smart and so knowledgeable about so much and so concerned about things, not only dollars and the bling-bling; it turned me on. I think of what a nice surprise it was when I discovered his silly nature beneath that seriousness. I think how much I loved that he was a man who knew what he wanted. Call it positive reinforcement. I remember that I love him, and that means that I have to find a way to keep myself from conking him over the head. I know, very Pollyana of me, but it's kept me sane, especially these last few weeks. That's why I want to write. I want to work through the mixed feelings and the changes in myself and the compromises I'm fighting not to make. I fight the feelings pulling me under, thinking about all the ways in which he makes my world richer."

That night, when Nikki put her head on her pillow, her mind was busy pulling at threads.

"Like bungee jumping," Jazz had said. And Aeden did make her feel like she had bungee cords strapped to her and was preparing to leap into the wind. It was exciting and daunting all at once; and she felt like a coward for even thinking of turning from it, yet the notion of leaning into it caused her stomach to clench.

"Fill in the blanks," Jazz had said. If Nikki did that, scrawled across the page in bold messy lettering would be how comfortable Aeden was in his own skin, how much of himself he was, that he lived free and added colour to her world. All the things that should have turned her off drew her in, including what a mess he was; after all, she was a different kind of mess. *Who'd have thought it*, Nikki thought, smiling a little to herself. Terry, polished as he was, hadn't tingled her senses the way this rainbow-coloured misfit had from day one; curiousity giving way to tolerance to grudging affection to, at some point, she couldn't pinpoint, passion. Is this what her parents had felt in the moments when Mama Vi opened up to Professor Baltimore? They'd held on to it for a moment. In truth, Nikki didn't believe this thing with Aeden could roll over into years; and while she wasn't sure she wanted years, she didn't know if a moment would be enough. Sometimes, she knew she was her own worst enemy—wanting and not wanting at the same time. She envied Aeden that, how certain he was about this. She wished she could hold on to his certainty; let it be enough for both of them.

Nikki sighed.

There was no closure to be found tonight, only more loose threads, and Jazz singing to Tapanga-Rose at odd hours throughout the night.

CHAPTER FORTY-NINE

The kitchen was a hive of activity. Audrey sat in the centre of it all, dispensing orders while her hands busily rolled flour for the fried and boiled dumplings. Nikki was chopping the eggplant, eddoe top, spinach, okras, cucumber, pumpkin, green pawpaw, peppers, carrots, onion, chive, thyme, garlic, potatoes—the whole range of vegetables, herbs, and greens procured from Tanty. Belle was shelling the pigeon peas. Jazz was peeling and grating ginger. Carlene was cleaning and seasoning chicken. The salt beef, pig foot, pig mouth, and pig tail had already been set to boil in water sweetened with brown sugar, "to cut the salt," Audrey had explained. The kitchen was sweltering, even with the back door flung open, thanks to the clouds of steam from the giant pot. Nobody but Nikki, dripping sweat, and Jazz, wiping her brow compulsively, seemed bothered by it, though. The kids—Carlene's and Jazz's—were elsewhere in the house, the kitchen entirely too hot for comfort. A part of Nikki wanted to join them, but there was work to be done, lots of work if the bloated CARICOM Day picnic menu of pepperpot, barbequed chicken, bakes, fried plantain, banana and pumpkin fritters was to be completed. To Nikki, with the ginger beer and various sodas, drinks and snacks piled in a corner of the kitchen, it sounded like several separate and complete meals in one sitting.

"This is ridiculous," she'd grumped earlier. "Who's gonna eat all of this?"

"But eh-eh," Audrey'd responded. "Ah all day arwe go at the beach nuh! An' Lars, Ben Up, Deacon, Fanso, tout monde sam and bagai ah come wid dem 'tring bang and posse. You laka you nah understan' how t'ings go."

Belle and Carlene, even Jazz, had laughed; and Nikki had kept her mouth shut after that. She still didn't see how they were in any danger of running short with enough food to fill the entire Antigua Recreation Grounds on Calypso Show night. And that wasn't all. Fanso was going to kick in a pot of goat water, while his wife, Antoinette, would bake up some bread and crepes with fruit filling, which Audrey dismissed as "fru-fru white people food." Not surprisingly, she'd sent out for some rock, tart, bun, and bread from the village baker shop. She had no problem trusting the fungi to Fanso, however. That, she explained, would be turned over a coal pot on the beach; hot from the pot and rolled into an appetizing ball was the only way to eat fungi. "Can't stomach the two together meself, but plenty Antiguan lub dem fungi wid dem pepperpot," Audrey said. Nikki knew that; it was the national dish, after all. "Fanso hand good when it come to fungi," Audrey had continued, the compliment directed at the much abused younger brother silencing Nikki for a second time that night.

Audrey had said neither yes, no, nor thank you, meanwhile, when Carlene had shown up with breadfruit and saltfish saying that she would make roast bread fruit, Jamaican style, and saltfish cakes. Nikki remembered Carlene's peppery saltfish cakes from when they'd lived together. They were good.

Marisol, invited by Nikki, was expected to add to the table with her signature fruit drinks, some actual fruit, and homemade fudge, tamarind balls, and sugar cake. The kids would be on a sugar high all day.

It made Nikki feel bloated, thinking about it.

When she was done chopping the vegetables, about midnight, Audrey told her to set them to boil in one of the huge pots under the cupboard, twin to the one already on the stove with the "meatkin'."

"No, no, no," Audrey called out as she moved to dump the mountains of vegetables into the pot.

"What?"

"The 'troba and pawpaw can't go in the cold water so," Audrey said, coming over. "Dem will boil hard."

Nikki raised her eyebrows at that.

Audrey took over the task, explaining as she went. "You ha fu mek the water boil up first. Plenty people that call themself cook always mek that mistake, an' you eat them 'troba, e tough tough. You wait til e boil up, then put um in. You put any salt?"

"No, I didn't know how much…"

"Is to your taste," Audrey said. "Pass it here." And Nikki did.

Jazz laughed. "That reminds me so much of my mother. 'Mom, how much of this, how much of that?' To give it some flavour, she'd say. And I'd be no clearer."

"Is so my mammy did stay, too," Carlene said. "'You wan' learn, come watch,' she'd say. 'Don' ask me nutten.'"

Laughter filled the crowded kitchen. "Hey, Nikki," Jazz said, "You should get Fanso to publish a cookbook. Put down some particulars."

"Please, cookbook!" Audrey scoffed. "The knowing in the doing."

And there was another eruption of laughter at that, Nikki, Carlene, Jazz, Audrey, and Belle joining in.

"The knowing in the doing, that was Mama philosophy," Audrey continued when they settled again. "Every t'ing Mama Vi ever teach me is tek I had to tek it een on my own, watching her. Ah so me learn fuh mek coal pot. Wasn't no classroom and she wasn't one to say t'ings once, much less twice. Fact, if she had to talk twice, min' yuh head."

This stirred laughter as well, even as this teaser of Audrey talking about Mama Vi had Nikki salivating for more. But Carlene was the next to throw in her two cents. "So, Tones say," she said, dimples winking in and out as she chuckled. Nikki smiled at the sight of them, noting, for the first time, how Carlene's eyes lost none of their sparkle, nor her voice, none of its steadiness at the mention of her love's name. "He used to live up under you and Belle, so him say," she continued, through her laughter, "'cause like 'im wan' shit himself every time Mama Vi bark pon 'im."

"More bark than bite, though," Audrey mused, and her eyes on Carlene were surprisingly warm. "She wasn't a beating woman. Not for purpose. Mek sure you know early on what is what, and long as you toe the line, you and she can live in peace. Of course, you know wha dem say 'bout two woman dog living in the same yard. So, soon as me start smell meself, me and she had our tugga tugga over every t'ing from me finishing school and staying outta de muddy to..." And, at this, her eyes flicked in Nikki's direction, and Nikki felt her stomach flip in reaction. Audrey shut down then, abruptly, her natural stoicism returning; everyone accepting it because she was Audrey and more like Mama Vi than maybe even she cared to admit.

Sometime later, as Nikki mashed the boiled greens and vegetables, Aeden stuck his head in the open doorway, startling her, as had become his habit. "Something smell good," he declared approvingly. "Me come just in time."

Nobody said anything for the longest while. Then Jazz, long done with the peeling and grating of the ginger, took the masher from Nikki's hand, and said, "Go on."

And she did.

They didn't talk until they were in his car, a quirky little green Volkswagen Bug he'd bought secondhand not too long ago. "Because you can't have woman in Antigua and nuh have no car," he'd teased, self-mockingly declaring his days of footing it, or bumming cars from his dad behind him. Could moving out of his folks' place be far behind? Nikki wasn't holding her breath for miracles. Besides, after their recent fight and what he'd said about bending himself to fit her world, she worried that this wasn't exactly the healthiest relationship. Of course, looking at the lime-and-orange-coloured Bug, no one could accuse Aeden of not being himself. It fit his colourful personality as comfortably as the now well-worn Bowie shirt. Nikki was reminded, though, that he came from money whenever she sank into Rogue's sleek leather seats, or took in her stereo system. He'd spent thousands on the upgrade. The car was named Rogue for Aeden's favourite *X-Men* character and, in fact, the character's likeness—as seen in the comic books, not on film—decorated the car's backside. This was the only attempt he'd made to dress up the car's exterior, no spinning rims or under lights for Rogue, and only the most per-functory overhaul. Still, her body might have been well-traveled, but Aeden hadn't skimped on the interior. In fact, he had this whole theory that people who spent time and money sprucing up the exterior of their cars were showboats, doing it for others rather than personal comfort. Doing up the insides, meanwhile, he insisted, was all about personal satisfaction. "And I'm all for personal satisfaction," he'd drawled as Nikki rolled her eyes. The times she'd driven in the car, the stereo surrounding her with the strains of, say, Irma Thomas singing, "I've Been Loving You

Too Long," or of Rufus featuring Chaka Khan funking it up on "Tell Me Something Good" from Aeden's extensive CD collection, Nikki had to agree, however.

Tonight, the air-conditioned cool was welcomed after the heat of the kitchen. Still, the seats didn't feel comfortable and the car felt entirely too small; and, when Aeden turned on the radio, The Wailers sang "Chances Are," a beautifully moody melancholy song if ever there was one. Coincidence, probably, but Nikki was surprised that Marley was on the night's playlist. Aeden usually said he couldn't drive while listening to Bob, John Lennon, or any of those guys. "Total attention," he'd said. "Me, the music, some weed...ha fu be in the right head space, you know."

He'd introduced her to the experience, minus the weed, of lying in his room in the dark, eyes closed, listening over and over to Marley's *Rebel Music*, humming along and going completely quiet when his favourite tracks "War" and "Rat Race" came on, even as Nikki opened her eyes and angled her head in the no-light to take in his shadowy profile, and the way he mouthed the words silently and emphatically. So, no, this wasn't car music, and the fact that it was playing had her wondering what was up. He seemed okay, though, and frankly, she was too put out by him popping up as he had, and too busy still sorting him and her out in her head to be overly concerned with his mood.

"What're you doing here?" she demanded, and she hadn't meant to sound quite so abrasive, but every unsettled thing between them was filling up the car.

"Couldn't sleep," he said. "Wanted to see you. What, I crowding you again?" He sounded testy.

Nikki pushed her knee-jerk defense mechanism down and

coached herself to speak what she really felt. It took some doing and the silence stretched, Aeden looking about as miserable as she'd ever seen him.

She reached across, laid her hand gently on his, where it cupped the gear stick as though poised for flight. "You not crowding me, Aeden," she said. "I'm happy to see you."

His hand slackened, turned over, his fingers curling around hers.

"Whey Laugh Dey, Cry Dey."

—ANTIGUAN PROVERB

*I*t took about every car they had at their disposal—Nikki's, Fanso's, Aeden's—to transport everything and everyone to Long Bay, and a trip or two extra, at that. Nikki was wiped, but Audrey promptly set her and everyone else to work. The table had to be set up, the food set out, and the coal pot and grill had to be lit. Nikki almost wondered out loud at the point of having the day off, only to tire oneself out. Of course, looking around the beach at the many families who were similarly engaged, everyone thought it was worth it, clearly. It turned out Audrey was right, too. Every bit of food would find its way to someone's stomach. There were faces Nikki had never seen before, presumably connected to her family in some way. She had a fleeting sense of that old feeling of not belonging. But then, she had Jazz with her, Jazz who was smiling and taking Tapanga-Rose into the quiet shallow end of the water for a dip. She had Belle, who splashed nearby, looking silly in a red bath suit with a little skirt, but oblivious and happy. She had Aeden, who tickled her legs, trying to get her to go in with him, now that she'd finally escaped Audrey's constant orders and slumped onto the nearest beach towel.

Nikki closed her eyes on Fanso turning the cornmeal for the fungi over the coal pot, Lars at the barbecue grill, Audrey pouring a drink for Imani, the crowds and crowds of people filling the beach. The tiredness of a sleepless night caught up with her, and she drifted.

Her dreams were pleasant, a mix of fantasy and reality, leaning forward and kissing Aeden in his car along the quiet Sea View Farm main road, their hands exploring, lips begging...

"Too long," he groaned.

"I thought you said you'd gone much longer without before we hooked up," she teased.

"Yeah, you spoil me," he responded, with that little smile she liked to see. And as she looked at his freckled face up close, she prayed she didn't allow her fears and need to be in control to screw up something that felt so right, in spite of all the reasons it should be wrong. She prayed to hold this moment of reaching for each other in a parked car like teenagers forever, to hold the memory of his smile. She liked his smile, too. Had she ever told him that?

"I like your smile," she said in this dream.

"Is that a yes?" he replied.

"Unfortunately, if I ran off now, Audrey would get a cutlass, find me, and chop off my head," she replied. "But tomorrow night, after the picnic, okay?"

"You not goin' claim you tired?"

"I'll probably be dead on my feet, but no, I won't flake out on you. Okay?"

"Okay," he said solemnly as though sealing some deep and binding promise.

The sun had started to dip; some people had left, and others were packing to leave when the scream cut across the beach. It jarred Nikki from her slumber. She opened her eyes to see Carlene running up from the sea, Imani in her arms, and Belle on her heels. A crowd quickly gathered as Carlene laid her youngest, Imani, still as death, on the sand.

"Oh, Gad, ah drown he drown," someone exclaimed.

"Anybody ha wan cell phone? Call emergency," somebody else said.

"But dem nar reach clean out ya now," another said.

"Ah dead he dead," still another declared.

Through it all, Carlene cried; Belle kind of danced around; Jazz looked on in horror, her baby held to her chest. Nikki sat frozen. Aeden crouched down, lifted a small hand, checked for a pulse, put his ear to the boy's face, checking for any sign of breathing. Then Audrey pushed through the melée and grabbed the little boy, even as Carlene grabbed for him, trying to fend her off.

"Leggo me son. What you doing?"

But Audrey determinedly sat in the sand and drew the boy to her, his back against her chest, a determined look on her face. She formed a fist and started compressing his chest.

People started fussing.

"You na supposed to move him."

"She know wha she a do?"

"De boy dead."

Carlene's wails rose. Fanso held her back as she made a grab for Audrey's hair. Still seated on her beach towel, eyes riveted to the scene playing out right in front of her, body frozen, Nikki heard a low steady murmur.

"Not this one, you hear me good. Not this one. Na time yet. You nar get he yet. Enough. Enough."

And she saw something she'd never seen before—tears filling Audrey's eyes, tears which stubbornly resisted falling, and a mouth twisted in determination, as it murmured, as the hands flexed and pumped, the fleshy parts jiggling with the effort. Soon, she couldn't hear the chorus of voices at all. Only Audrey's determined murmurs, as she battled for the life of the son of the only son she'd ever known.

"Not this one, not this one here. You hear me good. Not one more. Na time yet. You nar get he yet. Mercy. Mercy. Mercy."

And, it was on this last word, that the tears' stubborn will gave up the ghost, and they wet Audrey's still rigid face. "Please," she said, as Nikki sat entranced, reminded of her mother's picture, the one she still kept within easy reach. "Please," she whispered.

And then Imani coughed, water gushing from his lips, and all murmuring stopped.

By the time the ambulance arrived, the family was packed and ready to go, all without a single order issued by their big sister and task master. Audrey had withdrawn into herself, only Belle daring to approach and hug her. They sat on a log, two sisters leaning on each other, giving Nikki a sense of what they might have been like as girls, until the day when the one sister outgrew the other.

The Emergency Medical Services fussed. He shouldn't have been moved. His chest was tender like someone had been pounding on it. People really shouldn't mess with things they didn't know about, as they could do more harm than good.

"Ent he alive?" Fanso snapped finally.

Carlene reached for Imani convulsively, again at this, though the EMS technician easily fended her off. "We still have to take him in," the man said.

When they pulled out of the beach, lights flashing, sirens blazing, Carlene and Imani were with them, leaving the sombre party behind.

Nikki called back to the homestead as soon as she and Jazz got home. She'd so wanted to say something to Audrey, but even with the walls that had come down between them, she'd been at a loss for words.

"Have you heard anything?" Nikki asked.

"Yes," Audrey said, her voice uncharacteristically soft. "They sending him home. He goin' be fine."

"Thanks to you," Nikki said, and the sentiment fell easily from her lips.

Audrey said nothing, and Nikki started to say goodbye. Then her sister said in that same whisper she'd heard on the beach, "I wasn't ready to lose another one."

Nikki couldn't help thinking that there were layers and layers to that statement. The loss of Tones was still too fresh, true, on the heels of Mama Vi. And then the baby Audrey had refused to mourn. But she couldn't help but wonder at what other secrets those words veiled. She couldn't shake the feeling that there was some unspoken something—something else. However, maybe she was seeing shadows. And, even if the something tickling at her had substance, everyone had a right to keep what was theirs, and give what they could.

The understanding that passed between them now was more than she'd ever dared hope. Nikki understood this; Audrey had her own pain, and a resolve that compelled her to battle even God and Fate for a little boy's life, and a tenderness she kept encased behind that resolve. She had, too, Nikki acknowledged, a fragility that one more loss would certainly have shattered, and yes, a kind of wisdom.

Nikki remembered how, when she'd returned from Aeden's car, the still dark foreday morning of CARICOM day, Audrey had been sitting on the back step, the door only half open, the voices beyond faint.

"Everything finished?" Nikki had asked.

"Everything cooking up," Audrey had responded. "Watching it not going make it cook no faster."

Nikki had joined her on the step, reluctant to step back into the hot box that was the kitchen.

"So, you serious 'bout this boy? Cameron son?" Audrey'd asked.

And Nikki'd shrugged. "I might be." Then, with more confidence, "I am." And then the confidence slipped. "I care for him, feel good with him. I know we're very different, but…"

Audrey's look had stopped her. "What?" she'd asked. What would Audrey say now, she'd wondered; Audrey, who as far as anyone knew, was a fiftysomething-year-old virgin. Perhaps Audrey had read her mind, because she'd hesitated, seemed uncertain, which she rarely was. "You think too much," Nikki's big sister said finally. "But then is so you stay ever since you born." Then, as though a door had been opened, the door that had maybe been *garped* earlier in the kitchen, over cooking and conversation, Audrey continued, "Since you born 'til letter come from he, letter I had to read to her like all the other letter an' dem. Letter that convince her it was best, what he was asking, to sen' you to him. Best for you."

Nikki had been startled. No one had ever spoken to her of Before. She didn't remember Before. Audrey did. "You used to stare at people," her sister continued. "Stare, like you trying to figure dem out. An' you didn't laugh easy wid any and anybody either. I liked that."

She said all of this with a little affectionate smile that left Nikki open-mouthed.

Audrey had looked at her then, at her baffled expression. "Not much change. You still pick pick pick," she said, her smile teasing now. And you could've knocked Nikki over with a feather. Audrey sobered a bit, added, "Although it wouldn'ta hurt for you to pick

pick pick more with that Hensen. Hm. But you pick pick pick kick kick kick an' de bwoy 'til ah come back. Maybe de time come fu gi he wan easy time. Not that me would know too much 'bout dem kinda t'ing, mind you, but Sis, I hear tell it don't have to be all that complicated." Nikki hadn't heard anything after "Sis," barely registering Audrey's dry joke about her and Aeden making "pussy-eye, red-shenky, albino-looking babies together."

Sis.

It's what Belle and Audrey called each other, and here she was not only being invited into the circle of her big sister's arms, but finding that she wanted in.

Sis.

Nikki heard its echo in her brain now.

"I know," she said now. And she did.

CHAPTER FIFTY-ONE

"He's lost weight," Jazz observed, as they stood on the observation deck, watching as Giovanni crossed the tarmac to the V.C. Bird International terminal. There was worry and relief in her voice.

The echoing concern in Giovanni's eyes, as he hungrily drank in the sight of his wife and child for the first time in weeks, before pulling them into a long embrace, was also telling.

That night, in bed, Whitney Houston lullabying through her iPod headphones, Nikki held Tapanga-Rose against her side, giving the reunited couple a little privacy. The baby had taken a while to settle, but finally, they both drifted to sleep with a reassuring sense of the world righting itself.

It was on Fanso's balcony that the whole idea of them playing Mas was raised. Nikki was there, and Aeden. Jazz, Giovanni, and Tapanga-Rose. Carlene and her boys. Fanso's family.

It was Antoinette who brought up the topic of Carnival, relating that her boys were supposed to be playing with their school troupe that year.

That set Fanso off, reminiscing about watching the troupes as a boy, and fantasizing about playing Mas. "Is back then they had Mas, not them swimsuit they wearing nowadays," he said. "The

King and Queen of the band costume used to take up the whole street. And the troupes, the back pieces, the head pieces! It was fantasy, man, fantasy! I remember this one called Fire and Ice, a back piece of red and silver. Dynamics. Oh, and don't talk bout the year of 'Satan coming down'; that was a sight."

"Carnival wasn't no big thing back ah yard," reported Carlene. "Is just now it kinda coming up."

"Well, Carnival was the adventure in my day, from Marcus Christopher's skellihoppers to the jam bull—scared me more than any movie as a child," Fanso said, shaking his head fondly. "Yeah, Carnival was it for me. Don't play Mas no more, but calypso still deep in me. When you hear Carnival come, I don't want hear nothing, can't feel nothing but calypso."

"We know," Antoinette intoned uncharacteristically, even as Nikki cut in with a sarcastic, "Naaaaw!"

Fanso ignored them, caught up in the excitement of the Carnival talk. "When Carnival Monday and Tuesday come, and I see the troupes coming up Scot's Row, I does feel a longing to be with them, a pull like you wouldn't believe," he said.

"So, why do you not do it?" Antoinette wanted to know.

Fanso was silent, apparently unable to think of a good reason.

"Actually, I've always wanted to, as well," Giovanni suddenly piped up. "But all I ever heard of was Trinidad and Rio Carnival, and of course the Brooklyn West Indian Carnival on the Eastern Parkway. Can we still get in?"

His eyebrows twitched excitedly, and in spite of her desire to sit this one out, Nikki smiled, catching Jazz's eyes for a moment. Her sister smiled back indulgently, wiggling her own eyebrows and causing Nikki to laugh outright.

"Share the joke," Carlene interjected even as Fanso mused, "it kinda late, but maybe we can squeeze in somewhere."

"Let's do it," Aeden said, and Nikki wanted to clamp her hand over his mouth, not keen on donning one of the bathing suits that passed as Carnival costumes.

"Come on, Nikks, live a little," Jazz wheedled, sensing her sister's reservation.

"Well, we can't all go," Nikki said. "Who'll look after the kids?"

"I cannot," Antoinette piped up, before anyone could even look in her direction. "I will be with the school troupe. I have already volunteered to assist."

"Audrey," Carlene said. "I'll ask her."

She winked at Nikki, and, somehow, the vestiges of Nikki's resentment toward her slunk away. She did feel like celebrating, she realized.

"I'll need lots of liquor," Nikki quipped.

The liquor helped, and the music from the speakers echoing in her chest, and the spirit of Carnival moving through the crowd. And the rain. Lots and lots of rain, licking them like flames. At its burn, their spirit caught fever, a cheer going up from the crowd as they jumped higher, danced harder.

"Jump and le we, mash it up…"

The singer, feathered and beaded, danced alongside the hulking, speaker-laden Burning Flames truck, microphone in hand. And they did just that.

"…mash it up…"

"…mash it up…"

"…mash it up…"

"…mash it up…"

The buzz was unlike anything Nikki had ever felt, even during sex; even during sex with Aeden. She kissed him then, amidst the sweltering, gyrating bodies and the rain. Always game; if he was surprised by this show of exhibitionism, he hid it well as he responded eagerly, in kind, his slick body grinding against hers. She turned her face to his neck and buried her lips and nose there, breathing him in, tasting him. His dreads tickled and she shivered a little. Oh, she felt alive! She laughed, and unexpected tears joined the rain, wetting her cheeks. She laughed more before pulling away and rejoining the frenetic jumping. Aeden let her go for a time, but was soon tugging her back to where it felt good, in his arms, her back to his chest as their hips moved in unison. Nikki, crushed against him, found she didn't mind one bit.

During the last leg of the marathon parade, they spotted Audrey, who'd opted to leave Columbus and Belle at home. She stood on the sidelines, sheltered by a huge umbrella Nikki could only imagine her owning, with Tapanga-Rose in her arms while Imani and Judah held on to her shirttail. When the boys spotted their mother—a jubilant Carlene, uncaring of the folds and ripples of skin forced into a too-small costume—they made a break for it; and soon they, too, were a part of the bacchanal.

They were singing—Jazz and Giovanni, Aeden and Nikki—as they walked to where Nikki's vehicle was parked. Aeden's sister, Bridget, who'd danced with them for a while, red hair now icy white, was still back in the thick of it. "She going be going 'til the last pan knock," Aeden joked. The rest of them had called it quits, feet burning, after the onstage jump-up. Fanso and Carlene had peeled off from the group in search of Antoinette, Audrey and their kids. Tapanga-Rose would spend the night in Sea View Farm. Jazz and Giovanni, arms slung around each other, were a bit drunk on life, the music, being in rhythm with each other. So, too, were Aeden and Nikki. To Nikki, it was perhaps her most perfect moment since coming to the island. Behind them, Last Lap still raged in the city, speakers piled precariously high on huge trucks navigating the narrow streets. And they sang Claudette Peters' popular "All I Know."

The chirping at first didn't penetrate the din. Then Aeden reached for the cell phone which hung like jewelry around his neck. It struck Nikki as odd, this most casual of guys bothering to bring along what she'd heard him describe as a "shackle."

"Yeah," he said into the phone, trailing behind a little.

"What?" he asked, sounding alarmed, and at that, Nikki stopped and turned as Jazz and Giovanni, oblivious, continued on.

"Okay, I coming straight there," he said. "I 'cross by Country Pond heading outta town now. No, no, I only had a couple of drinks; I'm good. Yeah, meet you there."

He closed the phone, and stood there with his mouth open. "What's the matter?" Nikki asked.

"Somebody set fire out at Blackman's Ridge," Aeden responded. "Daddy wan' me take him out there in the helicopter."

They were at the helipad in no time.

When Cam saw them, his face reddened. "Who all them people?" he demanded of his son.

"You know Nikki; this is her sister."

"Boy, you retarded or something? What they doing here? I tell you one thing, they not coming in that helicopter."

"They will, if I say they will," Aeden shot back, raising his voice to his father, startling the other man and Nikki both. "It's my helicopter," he finished, more quietly.

His father said nothing, and Nikki was about to offer to drive out, or go home, though she badly wanted to go along with them. She chalked this feeling up to her having invested so much of her time into the Blackman's Ridge project.

But then, Aeden spoke again, turning towards the red-and-black helicopter with "Frigate" emblazoned in white on the side. "I thought you were in a hurry."

No one spoke the entire flight there; Nikki wanted to ask Cam what he knew, how the fire had started, how bad it was. Was it more nuisance, or was it serious? Was anyone hurt? It seemed unbelievable. Just that morning, the news on the radio had been about the grand opening planned after Carnival. Was that what had set the arsonist off?

It took no more than ten minutes to get there by helicopter. Since news traveled like fire in Antigua, there was already a crowd there. Landing on the Ridge was out of the question; they were forced onto the road that had been cut through the valley, leveling the already low-cut foliage and sending nearby bodies scampering. Fire trucks and firemen were ahead of them, scratching their heads as they tried to figure out how to get water up the hill. Police, none of whom reprimanded Cameron's son for his reckless landing, were busy trying to keep back the crowd.

The fire was huge; Nikki could feel its heat, even from so far below. She heard, too, the murmurs moving through the less-than-sympathetic crowd.

"God nuh like ugly," one woman said distinctly.

Nikki almost felt sorry for Cam, watching his multi-million-dollar investment burn right in front of his eyes, the fire blazing as if driven by the will of the people.

Jazz and Giovanni got pushed back, but Aeden held on to Nikki, kept her at his side, as he stood at his father's side. She twisted, trying to see her sister and brother-in-law, and almost let go of Aeden's hand, not wanting to abandon them. But she couldn't make out distinct faces in the swarming crowd.

Then that reporter, the one who'd popularized her infamous quote, was there, tossing questions off; "Did anybody see anything?"

Then a new murmur started; one of the security guys claiming he had seen something, someone just before he'd high-tailed it down the hill. He couldn't say for sure that they'd started the fire, but he definitely had seen someone.

Soon, there was a murmur of another kind. "Tanty." It was Sadie's voice. "Anybody see Tanty? Tanty." And the police held her back as she moved beyond the crowd toward the hill, and she began fighting them. A feeling of dread began to creep along Nikki's skin like goose bumps. She shivered, even in the heat, and Aeden pulled her close instinctively.

"No," she whispered, leaning into him. "No."

"Of course not," Aeden assured, hands rubbing her arms, a move at once brisk and gentle. "What would she be doing up there?"

"Burning me out," Cam said, in a tired voice.

"No," Nikki whispered, as Sadie's frantic shouts filled the night.

"Ar-you le me go! You hear me say lemme go! Tanty! Tanty! Tanty!"

Nikki gazed up into the blaze, willing herself to see something. And in her head, Tanty's voice, her words from their last meeting, were as real as if the old woman stood next to her now, whispering them in her ear. "Had a time, right after slavery... Neaga people hot foot it off the plantation an' dem, so me Tanty say. Was a whole ton ah free village 'round de place then. But bakkra bu'n dem out, make sure neaga people know dem place. Now, dem village nuh exist. Not even in memory." Nikki remembered the tears that made her eyes seem glossy; remembered the broken spirit, the quiet but venomous way she said, "When money ah change hand and big people ah flex dem muscle, laka smadee na exist. Smadee come laka masquita, dem clap dem han' together so, and out you lights, and you na even see de blow ah come. Me jus' ah wait and see."

Sadie was moaning, clutching now at the young policeman who'd held her back, as though seeking comfort from him. The mood of the crowd swayed under the weight of this unbearable new pain, thinly disguised glee at Cam's folly replaced by worry and grief and a weary acceptance. A part of Nikki still prayed for a miracle, that Tanty would emerge from the crowd wondering what all the fuss was about. Maybe she was somewhere else— at Carnival, at home sopping her bread in warm cocoa before turning in for the night.

But Nikki's heart knew the truth. She felt it all in her bones; that news of the planned opening broadcast that day had been too much, enough. She felt it all on the soles of her feet that what she'd seen in Tanty's eyes at her last visit wasn't defeat but defiance. Sadie got it from somewhere, after all. The people knew it, too. Police and Fire Police alike had their hands full, trying to keep people from scrambling up the hill for an ill-fated rescue.

Nikki pictured Tanty waking up that day, turning on the radio in the small house she shared with Sadie in the village. She pictured the pursing of her lips. She pictured her going still as Sadie raged; moving quietly through the day as though accepting of it all, stealing her moment to wander off and take what she must have known would be her last trudge up that hill. It wouldn't have been easy on her, even with the new road. Did she stop at the dungeon? Sit a while? Seek the ancestors' blessing? Was the guard maybe listening to the parade broadcast on his own radio? Had he nodded off as they tended to do? Did she look up, stop to take in the new structure that sat on the hill like a crown of alabaster? They sometimes used diesel on the ants nests down in the valley. Did she lay a trail of it around this particular pest? What did she do then? Nikki couldn't bear the thought of her waiting for the flames to claim her, too, but then neither could she bear the thought of her being trapped inadvertently. Her stomach turned over and then bottomed out, and when Aeden's grip tightened around her, she realized she'd been sinking. When his hand brushed at the wetness on her face, she realized that she was crying. Then she started crying for real, and she wasn't alone.

ABOUT THE AUTHOR

Antiguan Joanne C. Hillhouse is the author of two books of fiction: *The Boy from Willow Bend* and *Dancing Nude in the Moonlight*. *Oh Gad!* is her third book of fiction and first full-length novel. A 2008 Breadloaf fellow and announced recipient of the 2011 David Hough Literary Prize from the Caribbean Writer, her fiction and poetry have, also, appeared in *Tongues of the Ocean*, *Mythium*, *Ma Comère*, *The Caribbean Writer*, *Calabash*, *Sea Breeze*, and more. She was awarded a 2004 UNESCO Honour Award for her contribution to literacy and the literary arts in Antigua and Barbuda. Among her projects is the Wadadli Youth Pen Prize (http://wadadlipen.wordpress.com). She's a freelance writer, journalist, editorial consultant, and producer (having worked in print, film, and TV in Antigua). For more information, visit http://www.jhohadli.com

AUTHOR Q & A

Why is the novel called *Oh Gad!*?

Oh Gad! is a colloquialism I grew up hearing from time to time for the coal pot—and various other utensils made from clay. I'm actually not sure how common it is—I can't say I've heard any actual coal pot makers use it—but I had heard it time and again growing up; and after a while, it didn't matter to me if it was a real expression or not, but this idea of things falling and cracking open, just worked. The pots' beauty and fragility, as demonstrated in the novel by Mama Vi, proved an ideal metaphor for Nikki's life.

Is the novel based on a true story?

No. But the tradition of coal pot making in the Sea View Farm community in Antigua as captured in the novel is very much culturally true, with my family on my father's side having a generations-old involvement in the craft.

Are any of the characters or their stories based on real people?

No, and this is truer of this than anything I've written in the past. If I used anything of anyone, it often had to do with stature, their physicality—ah, that's what he looks like, that's how she stands, that kind of thing—and often in an instinctive, non-deliberate way. I remember my paternal grandmother, from my child's perspective, though I didn't know her very well, often seemed an imposing presence. I used that; not her as she really was, just that childlike sense of her ownership of space, what a formidable presence she seemed. Stuff like that.

Did you have a personal reason to write the novel?

Family and identity are recurring themes with me; I suppose the things that concern you in life spill over into your art. The preoccupation of an island country trying to balance its development needs and the politics of convenience with cultural traditions and conservation issues are certainly among those concerns. The desire to connect in a real way with someone else and to know ourselves, well, that's a concern we all have, isn't it?

Is it your intention to make a political statement about environment/development in the Caribbean?

In some ways, that aspect of the story snuck up on me as Nikki settled into life in Antigua; because the reality of the tensions between the fantasy and the reality of life in "paradise" is something that can't escape anyone who lives here for a while, Nikki included. In our Caribbean archipelago, we have beautiful countries, wonderful people, yet all the flaws and contradictions, and sometimes shortsightedness and cynicism, that you'll find anywhere. And, in part because of our sizes, that struggle between conservation and development, between who we are and who we're told we have to become, between tradition and modernity, between our past and our future, can be so all-consuming. Besides, it echoed the "smaller" journey of Nikki's life, and that more than anything, made it work for the story; and that was my primary concern, what worked for this story. That said, while the climaxing act is extreme and not something I'd recommend, environmental balance and respect for the traditions and values of the people is something I definitely advocate. But this is intended as an engaging, and hopefully thought-provoking story, not a position paper on the subject.

How did writing *Oh Gad!* differ from your writing experience with your previous works?

Striking the right note with the characters—especially Aeden and Nikki—took more effort than it had with Vere in *The Boy from Willow Bend* and Selena and Michael from *Dancing Nude in the Moonlight*. I liked them both from the get-go, but Nikki isn't an easy woman to identify with, and Aeden isn't as uncomplicated as he seems; plus, there's the unlikelihood of these two people connecting in any way. By contrast, I had fun with characters like Cam and Jazz, and Audrey was a force of nature from the beginning—and yet I had the challenge of making Cam more than just the villain of the piece, making Jazz more than just the sounding board for Nikki's angst, making Audrey more than just the antagonist; the challenge of making them fully drawn characters in their own right albeit that this is primarily Nikki's story. But, with so many more characters than normal and the concurrent plots, the knitting of it all together took a lot more skill, determination, and endurance than anything I'd done before. I loved the challenge, and I relished the discovery.

Do you expect readers to like Nikki?

I hope they find her interesting, complicated, sometimes infuriating and contradictory, and someone they ultimately come to care about. I know from early readers and from my own experience of writing her, that she's not always an easy person to like—maybe I identify with her in that regard.

Why did you choose to tell the story of Nikki's parents in flashback?

It was about me (and the reader) discovering it as she did, figuring out, firsthand, the mystery of them. I wanted to see their story as intimately as possible. Plus, it was all part of Nikki coming to terms with whom her parents were beyond the limited view she'd previously had of them both.

Did you have to do a lot of research for the book?

A fair amount: from African naming ceremonies to coal pot making and the coal pot making tradition to place names and meanings to geographic locations to my mom's pepperpot recipe. But as it's fiction and not documentary, I also allowed myself a fair amount of license as well; for instance, so much of the book happens in physical spaces I didn't know so well, so there was a balance of research and inventiveness in rendering some of those spaces. It kept me off-balance in an interesting way and helped me to understand that same feeling in Nikki.

You thank your mom for her pepperpot recipe? Is your mom a great cook?

She makes the best pepperpot I've ever tasted.

Does Nikki get what she wants in the end?

Well, she figures out where she wants to be. But this isn't a fairytale. Life goes on and paradise has its flaws.

How would you define yourself as a writer?

Journeying.